BOOK SALE

THE
NATURE
OF A MAN

THROUGH THE EYES OF A WOMAN...

Dear Reader:

Too often people feel like their lives are defined by others. We are the architects of our own future. That includes our happiness—and our despair. Sylvester Stephens is an excellent storyteller who brings the main character, Alicia Forrester, to life in *The Nature of a Man*. Alicia, like many women, feels that she has to have a man in order to lead a fulfilled life. Love can be a beautiful thing. It can be uplifting, spiritual, and satisfying. But unless a woman loves herself first, love is inconsequential. Bringing damaged emotions, distrust, and low self-esteem into a budding relationship never works. That is one of the messages that I hope readers will walk away from in this book.

If you get a chance, please check out the other two books in Mr. Stephens' series, evolving around many of the same characters: *The Office Girls*, and *The Nature of a Woman*. Relationships can be a complicated thing; in fact, that is almost guaranteed. But if you can sustain the bad times, the good times will come. Mr. Stephens has a talented way of expressing those views and it is always nice to read a male perspective on love and relationships.

Thanks for giving this book a chance and as always, thanks for the support of all of my Strebor authors. You can visit me online at www.eroticanoir.com or join my online social network at www.planetzane.org.

Blessings,

Zane

Zane
Publisher
Strebor Books International
www.simonandschuster.com/streborbooks

ZANE PRESENTS

THE NATURE OF A MAN

OF A MAN

THROUGH THE EYES OF A WOMAN...

SYLVESTER STEPHENS

SBI

STREBOR BOOKS

NEW YORK LONDON TORONTO SYDNEY

Strebor Books
P.O. Box 6505
Largo, MD 20792
http://www.streborbooks.com

ISBN 978-1-59309-289-4
LCCN 2010920966

First Strebor Books trade paperback edition May 2010

Cover design: www.mariondesigns.com
Cover photograph: © Keith Saunders/Marion Designs

10 9 8 7 6 5 4 3 2 1

Manufactured in the United States of America

For information regarding special discounts for bulk purchases,
please contact Simon & Schuster Special Sales at 1-866-506-1949
or business@simonandschuster.com

The Simon & Schuster Speakers Bureau can bring authors to your live event.
For more information or to book an event, contact the Simon & Schuster Speakers
Bureau at 1-866-248-3049 or visit our website at www.simonspeakers.com.

DEDICATION
To JoAnna Rhambo

ACKNOWLEDGMENTS

To my entire Stephens Family; to my fraternity brothers of Wiley Spence Lodge #704 of Jackson, Mississippi; to my entire Free & Accepted Masonic Order family; to my alums of the Jackson State University Tigers, Jackson, MS; and to my fellow alums of the Saginaw High School Trojans, Central Junior High and Emerson Elementary of Saginaw, Michigan. Thanks.

RETRO

I walked around the party nervous as hell and trying to steer clear of Kimberly. Pam was drunk, mad, and didn't give a damn. I pulled Pam to the side to douse her overzealous spirit of vindication.

"Pam, you might want to stop making a spectacle of yourself," I whispered.

"I'm just having fun."

"But what if Kimberly sees you?"

"I'm tired of running and hiding, Alicia."

"What are you saying?"

"I'm saying that I'm tired of running; that's all."

"You're drunk, Pam."

"You're right! I am drunk!" Pam said as she slurred her words. "But I'm not so drunk that I can't make the decision of ending all of this tonight."

"Ending what?"

"The lies, the deceit, the hiding." Pam took a drink out of the glass she was holding.

"You need to lie down, Pam."

"Where Johnny at?" Pam held her glass in the air and started to walk through the crowded room. "I'm going to talk to Johnny."

"No!" I said.

"Hi!" Shante was standing in front of me with two suitcases in her hands. "I made it."

"Yes, you did, dear!"

It had totally slipped my mind that Shante was coming to live with us that night.

"How did you get here?"

"I took a taxi."

"Oh, okay. Let's put your stuff in your room."

I had to forfeit my interception of Pam's confession to Johnny. Hopefully she was only talking nonsense.

Shante followed me upstairs and we put her in the guestroom next to Brittany's room. We didn't talk long because I had to get back to the party and stop that crazy-ass Pam from running her big mouth. When Shante and I got to the bottom of the steps, Wanda and Kimberly were standing right there.

"Hey, girl!" Wanda shouted.

I couldn't speak. I stared Kimberly straight in the eyes with my mouth wide open and couldn't speak. I was hoping and praying that she did not recognize me from the hotel. I wanted to run back upstairs, but it was too late. The moment of truth had come.

"I know you." Kimberly pointed at me.

"No," I said nervously. "I don't think you know me."

"Yes, I do." Kimberly pulled her hair. "Gizelle!"

Although Kimberly suffered from schizophrenia, it didn't mean that she wouldn't recognize me from the hotel, the night Gizelle was murdered.

"Don't pay no attention to her, Alicia, she needs to have her medicine." Wanda laughed. "Right now, she probably thinks you're a Martian."

"Are you my friend?" Kimberly asked.

"Uh." I looked at Wanda for an answer.

"It will probably go a lot quicker if you just say yes," Wanda said.

"Yes, I'm your friend."

"You're pretty."

"Thank you." I smiled. "You're pretty, too."

"Some people say I'm not so pretty on the outside, but I'm very pretty on the inside and that's what counts."

"They're right, Kimberly."

"I just got through talking to your husband and girl, he just dropped a bomb on me!" Wanda said.

"What did he say?" I asked curiously.

"I can't tell you right now but can you say," Wanda moved her hands as if she was playing a slot machine. "CHA-CHING!"

"Good for you," I said nervously. "Have you seen Pam?"

"Yeah, she's in y'all basement."

"Oh shit!" I shouted.

"What's the matter?"

"Nothing! I just have to go!"

I RAN TO THE BASEMENT AS PAM WAS OPENING THE DOOR. I stood behind her as she walked in first. My objective was to start talking before Pam to keep the subject off of Gizelle. But before I could speak, our little secret was revealed.

"I'm sorry," Pam said.

"Oh my God!" Johnny said. "It was *you*? You were the one who texted me?"

"Yeah, it was me."

I walked in and stood beside Pam.

"Alicia?" Johnny quickly stood up looking bewildered. "Will somebody please tell me what's going on?"

"We're responsible for Gizelle's death," I said.

"What is this all about?" Johnny looked back and forth at Pam and then me.

"You wouldn't hurt a fly, Alicia."

"Not intentionally."

"She didn't kill her." Pam clutched my hand in hers. "I did."

"I want to tell you everything, Johnny, for once and for all."

Pam and I sat down and explained what happened on the day we killed Gizelle.

"Pam and I followed you and Gizelle to Tybee Island the night before she was killed. We saw you two making love on the beach."

"You were there?" Johnny was stunned. "Where were you?"

"That's not important. The next day when you returned to Atlanta, Pam and I went to her hotel to discuss her reneging on our contract. She was belligerent and things got out of control."

"The truth is," Pam explained, "Gizelle and I started fighting and as we were tussling on the bed, I pushed her against the headboard. She stopped fighting and grabbed her head. She sat on the bed and then keeled over. There was no blood. I didn't see a bruise on her head or anything. I knew she was hurt but I didn't think she was hurt that bad. But Alicia wasn't even there. She had run out of the room for help."

Johnny didn't say a word. He had his hands folded on his desk and looked at Pam and me as we talked back and forth.

"And then there's the matter of Big Walt." I fumbled nervously with my hands.

"Who?" Johnny asked. "Who the hell is Big Walt?"

"The bodyguard who was killed. We knew him as Big Walt."

"Okay, what about the bodyguard?"

"I shot him!" I was very demonstrative in my explanation. "I tried to stop him from taking the gun out of my hand and it went off! I saw him fall to the ground!"

"Okay, let me think." Johnny rubbed his chin over and over. "Look, the police don't know anything about you two, and they're not going to. We're going to have to keep this to ourselves and never mention it again. And I mean never!"

"I don't even know what you're talking about," Pam said quickly.

"Sweetheart?" Johnny asked. "How do you feel?"

"I don't know how to feel right now," I said.

"So…" Pam sighed heavily. "What happens next?"

"You walk out of that door and forget about everything that happened that day."

Pam hesitated and then stood up. She walked up the steps to the door and put her hand on the doorknob. She turned around and looked down at us.

"Thank you, Johnny."

"For what?" Johnny asked.

"For giving me back my life."

Pam walked out and Johnny reached across the desk and held my hand. He pulled me around the table and I sat on his lap.

"Do you love me?" Johnny asked.

"Absolutely!"

"Do you trust me?"

"Of course."

"Then forget this ever happened and let's move forward with our lives."

"I want to, but before I do, there's something else I think you should know…"

CHAPTER ONE

When I was five years old, my father looked me in the eye and disclaimed me as his child. "You're not my child! I don't know who your father is, but it sure as hell isn't me!"

From that day forward, I repudiated my birth, my life and myself. No matter what success I achieved, my father's rejection superseded the accomplishment. I loved that man with all of my heart and spent my entire life searching for acceptance that I would never receive. Do you hear me? My whole damn life! Not a word of confidence! Not an ounce of encouragement!

When I was ten, he and my mother divorced. He packed his bag and moved to St. Louis, Missouri. What the hell he found interesting in St. Louis, I'd never know. On his way out of the door, the man handed me a Bible and said, "Here, read this!"

I was like, "Niggah, please!" Even at that young age, I knew he was feeding me bullshit. He was walking out on his family but asking me to read the Bible. What a hypocrite! If he wanted to impress me he would have stayed his ass at home with his family.

I don't know where, but somewhere in the Bible it has to say, "Thou shalt not walk out on thy family." I threw that Bible down somewhere and I haven't seen it since.

As I grew older, I replaced his absence with resentment. I held on to that contempt to the point where it manifested inside of me and I started to rot from the inside out.

Now here we are, twenty-five years later, and he's on his dying bed. Twenty-five years later, he sends for me to say good-bye to his old ass! Do you hear me? How dare he ask for my love now, when he has ignored my total existence? He may get my time, my good-bye, maybe even my sympathy, but the one thing he will never get from me is my love.

As I PARKED MY CAR IN THE GARAGE OF THE HOSPITAL, I remained seated to compose myself. Memories of my childhood flooded my mind as I stepped out of the car and approached the entrance. I walked through the hospital doors and the smell of medicine and death consumed me.

I approached his room, and prepared myself one last time before I opened the door. I took a deep breath and pushed the door as gently as I could. As the door opened, I could see the images in the room revolving in a circle from left to right.

My two sisters, Rita and Bobbie, and brother, Glenn, were already there, along with my two other half-sisters from his second marriage. The youngest of our siblings, from yet another one of our father's relationships, was en route. None of us had met her and had just recently found out she even existed.

When the door opened wide enough for me to capture the first glimpse of my father, my eyes instantly filled with tears. He had wires running from his body to several machines. He looked weak and vulnerable. His eyes were closed and his arms were resting peacefully at his side. I confessed to myself that deep down I really did want to see him again, but definitely not in that condition.

I hugged my siblings and then walked to my father's bedside. They informed me that he had been floating in and out of consciousness and that he may not remember or recognize me.

As I stood over him, I stared and wondered what my life would have been like if he would have only been there, if he would have only taken the time to love me. Slowly, he opened his eyes and looked up at me as I looked down on him.

"Alicia?"

"Yes," I said, trying desperately to hold back tears. "I'm here."

It took him a while, but he slowly raised his hand so that I could hold it. I looked at his hand and then I looked over my shoulder at my siblings, seeking guidance. Glenn nodded and smiled. I held his hand and placed it in mine.

"Alicia?" my father repeated.

"Yes, yes, I'm here."

His eyes were barely opened and they were yellowish. He was small and frail; nothing like the big strong man that I had last seen as a child. I almost felt sorry for him.

"Where you been?"

"Where have *I* been?" I asked sarcastically.

I realized the man was sick but the mere fact that he would ask me where I'd been, after abandoning me twenty-five years earlier, nearly pissed me off.

"Alicia?"

"Yes, I'm here."

"You know who I am?"

"Yes, you're my father."

"Alicia?" my father asked faintly.

"Yes?"

"Alicia?"

"Yes!" I said firmly.

"Alicia…"

WATCHING MY FATHER TAKE HIS LAST BREATH put the meaning of life into its true perspective. We can have an entire lifetime of experiences but our legacy can be determined by the very last moments of our lives. Looking down on my father's dead body,

I pitied and resented him at the same time. My emotions were running rampant and I didn't know how I wanted to feel. However, I knew for certain, I did not want to die the way he died, with my children standing around with conflicting emotions of love and hatred toward me.

I also knew for certain that, like my father, I didn't know who the hell I was, or who I wanted to be. All of my adult life I believed that my womanhood was determined by sexuality and self-sufficiency. It has taken me a while to arrive at who I am. And along the way, I had to reinvent myself multiple times.

For example, I went from being impulsively promiscuous to compulsively celibate. Both were extremes and both resulted in disappointments that made me confront the insecurities of my sexuality. Insecurities brought on by being the victim of disappointing heartbreak after heartbreak.

Despite the daily confirmation by males, and females I may add, of being a beautiful woman, I lacked confidence. Imagine being high school homecoming queen, college homecoming queen, Ms. Ohio, placing in the top five in the Miss America pageant, but not being able to keep a man. That was embarrassing and left me doubting who I was as a woman. My self-esteem was all but destroyed.

I tried to differentiate the men in my present from the men in my past, but the behavior of men never changed, and neither did the results of my relationships. Men pursued me like vultures until I succumbed to their persistence. Once they felt like they had me, they neglected me. Cheating, lying, deceiving; I was a magnet to any fool who meant no good. After so many of those types of relationships, I couldn't help but think that maybe I was the problem. My friends were attracting good men. Why the hell couldn't I?

Eventually, I stopped looking for relationships and simply started to have sex with those I found attractive. That way, I got my needs met without risking my heart being broken. It was a *"get them before they get me"* type of deal. I can't say that I felt good about myself after having sex with all of those men, but I'll tell you what, it felt a helluva lot better than having my heart broken. I should know, I'm an expert on the subject of having a broken heart; that shit hurts!

Once I realized I got more out of a man when I didn't give a shit, my role reversed and I became an expert on being the heart breaker and not the broken-hearted. I took their money, their minds, and their manhood. It didn't matter if they were married, single, or whatever. If I saw them, and I wanted them, I got them. It was as simple as that, until I met who I thought was the man of my dreams.

I was eating with a friend at a restaurant in Atlanta; that's where I live. Oh my God, the most beautiful man in the world walked in and I couldn't keep my eyes off of him. I wasn't the only one; my friend couldn't take her eyes off of him either.

I practically stared at him, and nothing else, from the moment he walked through the door. We finally made eye contact and I gestured for him to come to our table. He told me his name was Julian and we exchanged telephone numbers. He was Italian and Nigerian, born and raised in Milan. He was six feet tall, light-skinned with green eyes. His face was symmetrically perfect with two square jaws. He had jet-black curly hair, and a very toned and tanned body that revealed a thin muscular frame through his clothing.

As gorgeous as he was, his use, or should I say misuse, of pronouns was abysmal. Every time he opened his mouth to speak was an act of atrocity to anyone associated with the English language. Call me shallow but I wasn't about to let a minor communication issue prevent me from falling in love with that incredibly sexy man.

Julian and I dated for a while and then, like a fool, I fell head over heels in love. I became consumed with love. I ate, drank, and slept that man. The more attention I showed him, the less attention he showed me.

Julian was a model who traveled all around the world. That beautiful face and his flirtatious personality should have been a red flag that he couldn't be trusted, but I convinced myself otherwise. Time would prove me wrong. It was nothing for me to find telephone numbers, women's panties, condoms and other miscellaneous infidelity items. Whenever I would question him on it, he would turn it back on me for snooping through his personal things.

I would cry; literally cry like a little baby. He would console me, we would make love, and everything would be fine. He couldn't seem to control his desire to have other women, yet every time I tried to leave, he would go berserk. And like a fool, I stayed every time. But despite how much I loved Julian, I could only take so much neglect. If infidelity was a game he wanted to play, I could play it, too.

When Julian was away, I started to see other men. Initially, I didn't sleep with them, but I went out to dinner or to the movies. I was lonely and I needed attention. Even though the men I dated were well aware that I had a man, they thought they could win over my affection. It wasn't going to happen. I was using them to occupy my time and that was all I wanted. They kept my mind off of Julian and his other women. I didn't feel guilty for what I was doing to them, or Julian. Hey, it was a part of the game. I didn't make the rules; I merely enjoyed them.

I WAS WORKING AT A PLACE CALLED UPSKON AT THE TIME. I worked in the claims department. It was an office composed of all women, no men. Boring! Don't get me wrong, they were like my sisters, but it would have been nice to have an attractive male figure to look at from time to time.

One day, I got my wish. This fine chocolate black man was hired. His name was Michael Forrester. We were immediately attracted to each other but didn't act on it. I think he was a little nervous about approaching me at first, but I broke him down.

He was a really nice guy. Definitely different from the types of men I was used to dating. He was fascinating; an intellectual and very respectful. I started to develop strong feelings for him but I couldn't get too involved because I was still involved with Julian. Now that didn't mean that I didn't sleep with him. I will never forget the first time we made love.

We were at his house, his big beautiful house. I knew once we walked in, there was going to be sexual activity. It was only the matter of which of those big-ass rooms we would target.

"Hey, do you eat pizza?" Michael asked.

"Of course I eat pizza," I responded.

"One hot pizza coming up!"

Michael ordered the pizza and then went upstairs to take a shower. I sat in his den and waited impatiently. When he came downstairs he was wearing a tight T-shirt and a pair of big shorts. Oh my God, I could see his penis shift from side to side as he walked toward me. I wanted to reach out and grab it, but I was still torn between being a lady or being a freak!

I sat in a recliner; I guess it was his favorite chair because he made me get up and then he sat down in it. But he wasn't totally selfish; he let me sit on his lap.

"This is nice," I whispered in Michael's ear.

"Yes, it is, isn't it?"

I made sure that when I sat down, I sat on top of that penis. As soon as I made contact, I felt it rise. It felt like a big thick cucumber. Please don't ask how I knew that. Anyway, I didn't want to act too aggressively, so I tried to take my time and be passionate. After all, Michael wasn't nervous at all.

He put his big strong hands around my waist and I began to move my hips back and forth. I wanted to kiss him so badly, but I didn't want to rush. When I couldn't wait any longer, I slowly opened my mouth and slipped my tongue into his. He kissed me back and that was about all I could take. I reached into his shorts and pulled his penis out. It was enormous. It was almost intimidating; almost, but not quite.

He ripped open my shirt and started to suck my breasts. I leaned my head backward and raised my breasts closer to his mouth, giving him complete access. The harder he sucked, the harder I squeezed his penis. I was close to having an orgasm when he stood up and told me he'd be right back. I didn't know where he was going but I knew he'd better hurry his ass back.

Once he left the room, I stripped completely naked. I was so excited that I started to tease myself while he was gone. When he returned, he was ready to go. He had the condom on and his penis was bursting through his shorts. It was standing like a flagpole at full attention.

He pulled his shorts down and sat in the chair. I faced him and put my legs on either side of him. I grabbed his penis and slowly lowered myself. It had been so long since I had sex, that when I first felt his head go inside, it felt like he was splitting me in half. The pleasurable pain was unbelievable.

I sighed. "Please, go slow, baby."

"Okay, baby, I'll go slow."

Once the head was in, it went from pleasurable pain to unimaginable pleasure.

I slid more of him inside of me. "Oh shit, baby, it feels so good."

"You like that, baby?" Michael asked seductively. The sound of his voice only intensified the passion.

"Yeah, baby! Yeah, baby! Give it to me like that, baby!" I moaned incoherently.

I grabbed Michael's face and shoved my tongue so deep into his mouth that I could feel his larynx. The more passionately we kissed, the harder he shoved his big stick inside of me. I was trying to keep my moans to a minimum but it felt so good that I couldn't stop screaming.

Just when I thought Michael was about to have his orgasm, he picked me up, with his stick inside of me, and carried me over to the couch. He laid me down and pushed my knees all the way back to my shoulders. I braced myself for his entry. If I had a hard time riding him, this was going to kill me.

He grabbed his stick and slid it inside of me all at once. I grimaced and yelled as loud as I could. It felt as if he was all the way into my stomach. My legs started to shake uncontrollably as he pounded me with long, deep strokes. It felt like he was stretching my insides. I wasn't trying to scratch his back the way I did, but I couldn't help it. He kept hitting the same spot every single time he stroked me. I could feel a full-fledged orgasm approaching. You know, one of those toe-curling experiences and not the subtle sensations of blah! And I was right.

"Oh shit, Michael! I'm coming, baby!" I shouted. My hips bucked up and down like they had a mind of their own.

As I was finishing my orgasm, Michael picked me up and tossed me on my stomach. He lifted my ass and grabbed me by my hips. I backed up until I felt the head of his stick touching my vagina. Inch by inch he pushed until he was completely inside of me.

He moaned and then pushed his stick forward and pulled my hips backward. He kept me in that position, grinding as deep as he could go. He turned my head to the side and kissed me wildly. He reached beneath me and squeezed my breasts, sliding his stick in and out.

I could feel his muscular body on top of mine, covering me from head to toe. I was so moist by then I was sucking him in and out like a vacuum. I could feel another orgasm approaching as he stroked me over and over. I stood on all fours to try to get every single inch of him.

I dropped my head, and gripped the arm of the couch, digging my nails into its soft cushion. I started to push back as fast I could, feeling his hard stick rip my insides apart. Before I could explode, Michael let out the weirdest, loudest sound I had ever heard during sex. Although weird, it was also sexy as hell.

Michael stroked me so hard that he lost his balance and fell on top of me. He kept moaning and kept sliding in and out of me until I felt his juice running down my leg. I wanted to have another orgasm, but he had done me so well, how could I be mad at him?

"It's taking that pizza a long time, isn't it?" I joked.

"It sure is. It's been well over an hour."

"Have we been going at it that long?"

"Yup," Michael said.

"We should get that one for free then."

"Yeah, we should. I'll call them to see what's taking so long."

The pizza delivery guy made it perfectly clear that he had knocked on the door several times but nobody answered. Needless to say, we had been incapacitated!

We stayed up all night talking. It was very refreshing and exactly what I needed. The next morning we woke up, the same way we went to sleep, talking.

"If you would have asked me on Friday if this weekend had a chance of turning out this way, I would have told you never in a million years," I said.

"A million years? The odds were that far off?" Michael asked.

"For me, they were."

"Were you attracted to me before yesterday, Alicia?"

"Yeah, silly."

"You did a pretty good job of hiding it."

"I wasn't trying to hide it. I didn't think it was necessary to act on it."

"So, I guess the question now is, where do we go from here?"

"I don't know, Michael. Right now, my heart is going in several different directions."

"Is one of those directions coming toward me?"

"I'm here with you, aren't I?"

"Yeah, but where will you be tomorrow?"

"I don't know."

Although I enjoyed my night of pleasure and passion with Michael, that's all it was to me, a night of unbridled passion. I was still in love with Julian. We talked for a little while longer and then Michael fixed breakfast. After breakfast, I showered and got ready to go.

"See you tomorrow, Michael."

"Yup, nine to five."

"Bye-bye!"

"Bye."

Michael and I continued to date outside of the office, but it was our little secret. We really enjoyed ourselves, perhaps a little too much. My experiences with Michael made me realize my relationship with Julian was over. I wasn't afraid of ending my relationship with Julian because Michael provided a comforting transition as my road to recovery.

Michael wanted to keep our relationship a secret; I couldn't do it. I didn't tell everybody; just a few coworkers. After all of the jerks I had told them about, it felt good to tell them that I had found a good man. If the shoe was on the other foot I'm quite sure he would have boasted to some of his friends, so I didn't feel guilty at all.

Darsha, Lisa and Val, three of the office girls, were sitting in the break room pressuring me for information on my relationship with Michael. I have to admit, it didn't take much pressure and I popped!

"So what's the deally, yo?" Darsha asked.

"What do you mean?" I asked.

"You know what she means," Val said. "What's up with you and Mike?"

Val was our resident out-of-the-closet lesbian who was the closest thing to a man that we had in the office. We flirted from time to time, but I have absolutely no interest in women.

"I don't kiss and tell."

"Then don't tell," Val said. "Nod."

"Come on, Alicia, was it good?" Darsha asked.

Darsha was the youngest in the office and she kept us updated on hip-hop and modern technology.

"Was what good?" I asked back.

"Mike, fool!" Val shouted.

"Can he put it down?" Darsha asked.

After resisting as much as I could, I anxiously shouted out, "Oh my God! It was amazing!"

"Damn, Mike put it down like that?" Darsha asked.

"Girl, let me tell you, Julian don't even need to try to go back up in there."

"Whaaaaaat?" Val shouted, covering her mouth. "That niggah packin' all like that?"

"Val, let me tell you something; packing is not even the word for it."

"I want to see the videotape," Darsha said.

Lisa laughed. "Me too."

"Hey, you better keep that on the low-low. I think your girl, Cynthia, has a crush on your boy." Val held a finger in front of her lips.

"I know, right?" I said. "I keep telling Michael, but he keeps saying that she's just his friend."

"She may only be a friend to him, but he's more than a friend to her," Lisa said. "This will destroy her if she finds out."

"Well, let's make sure we keep this between us," I said.

Ms. VIRGINIA, THE MATRIARCH OF THE OFFICE, was having a Thanksgiving Day dinner. She invited all of the office girls. Michael and I decided that we would go as a date. That would be our subtle way of informing the office of our relationship.

On Thanksgiving morning, I spoke with Michael and we confirmed the time he was going to pick me up. As soon as I hung up the telephone, Julian walked through my front door.

He told me that he wanted to surprise me for the holidays, but that's not why he came home. When I had my birthday, he wasn't here. He wasn't there for Valentine's Day, or even on his birthday. So why should he come home for Thanksgiving? Let me tell you why, that niggah brought his sorry ass home because I told him that I didn't want him anymore.

I tried to hurry and get dressed and get the hell out of there but he was following my every move. I couldn't even break away to call Michael to tell him Julian had come home. When I went into the bathroom to take a shower, he followed me. I laid my cell phone on the sink and, when I stepped into the shower, he went through my calls and saw Michael's number. He went ballistic!

Julian snatched the shower curtain back and held my cell phone in front of my face. "So, this is what you do when I'm not here, Alicia?"

I wrapped a towel around me and stepped out of the shower. "I don't know what you're talking about, Julian."

"You know exactly what I'm talking about!" Julian shouted. "Who is this man?"

I rushed past him trying to get dressed. "He's a friend!"

"A friend, huh?" Julian asked. "Why do you put a star by this guy's name? Who is this Michael?"

"He's a guy that I work with; calm down!"

"Where are you going?"

"I have a Thanksgiving dinner to attend."

"What Thanksgiving dinner?"

"Ms. Virginia is giving a Thanksgiving dinner for the office and I'm going."

"Why did you not tell me about this Thanksgiving dinner?"

"You weren't here, Julian!" I snapped. "Get off of my ass! I'm going to a Thanksgiving dinner. I'm not going to have sex with anyone, okay?"

"I am going with you to this Thanksgiving dinner!"

"Please, you don't have to go, Julian!"

"Why not?"

"Because I'm used to going places all by myself anyway. And I'm tired of you never being at home, never spending time with me. The many, many affairs! I'm tired of it, Julian!"

"Okay! Okay, my darling." Julian pulled me into his arms. "I will stay home and spend time with you, sweetheart. I know I was wrong about the other girls but they are behind me. I realize what I have with you, my dear; and those other girls are not worth it."

"I don't want to be hurt anymore, Julian."

"Listen to me!" Julian held my face gently in his hands. "Listen to me, Alicia. I came home to tell you that I love you. Forget about the other girls. Forget about being lonely; I'm home. You understand this?"

I sighed. "Yes."

"So, are you ready to go have fun at this Thanksgiving dinner?" Julian flashed his bright smile. I smiled back. "Yes."

"Then hurry, my love, let's go."

Julian and I hurried to get dressed and went to Ms. Virginia's house. When we pulled up I recognized all of the parked cars. I wanted to make an inconspicuous entrance, but that wasn't going to happen. Mostly everybody was already there. My heart started to beat faster and faster as we entered the house. I didn't know what Michael's reaction would be to seeing Julian and me together. I was praying there wouldn't be a scene.

When we walked into the dining room, everybody stopped talking and stared at us. I'm sure the girls were staring because of Julian, but they were also curious to see how Michael would react. At that time, I didn't know how many people in the office knew about our affair.

Julian and I walked around the table, shaking everybody's hands, which meant eventually, he would have to talk to Michael. I tried to make the introduction swift and cordial. I don't care which part of the world they're from, men will be men. Territorial!

"Julian, this is Michael. He works with us at the office."

"Good to meet you, Michael," Julian said. "How do you do it, my friend?"

"Do what?" Michael asked.

"How do you keep your hands off of all the women?" Julian asked sarcastically.

If looks could kill, Julian would have been a dead man. Michael is usually very easygoing, but I could see smoke coming out of his ears.

"You must either be a gay, or you have the strongest resistance to temptation I have ever seen." Julian laughed.

"No, I'm not *a gay*." Michael pointed at me. "Ask Alicia."

Julian looked at me. "What do you mean by that?"

Oooh-kay! I had to get out of that situation quick. The testosterone was way too high and the boys looked like they were about to do battle. I grabbed Julian's hand and led him to our seats.

We ate dinner and then Ms. Virginia put in a movie. Michael and Pam left early; neither one of them wanted to be there anyway. Michael was pissed off and was probably going to tell Pam all of our business out of spite. I couldn't be mad at him; I had told a couple of people myself.

WHEN JULIAN AND I GOT HOME THAT NIGHT, I slept in my bedroom and he slept on the couch. I told him that I needed time before I could become intimate with him again. He told me that he understood and would give me all the time that I needed. Bullshit!

During the middle of the night, I felt him crawl underneath the comforter with me. He wrapped his arm around my waist and kissed me gently on the back of my neck. He knew that was my hot spot. I was ready for him to try to make a move so I could knock his ass out but he didn't; he went to sleep.

Later on that night, I must have really gotten horny because I dreamed an incubus seduced me. I felt my legs being raised in the air. Next, I felt my clit being teased by a million fingers. That really got my fire burning. It was so stimulating I was about to have an orgasm in my sleep.

I felt a second hand grip my breast, squeezing my nipples with his fingers. I wanted to see the face of the man in my dreams, but I wasn't allowed. I was only allowed to feel his fingers, his magical, wonderful fingers.

In my dream, I could feel my hips move and it felt so real, especially when I felt the stiffness of a stick sliding inside of me. My hips responded with each of his strokes, sliding back and forth, but the motions of my thrusts were not matching the way I wanted to move. I woke up and realized Julian was inside of me, making love to me in my sleep.

"What the hell are you doing?" I shouted.

"What am I doing? I am making love to my woman!"

"I told you not to touch me until I'm ready!"

"It looks like you are ready to me." Julian reached between my thighs and rubbed the moisture of my vagina on his fingers and then held his finger in the air.

I pushed Julian off of me and jumped out of the bed. "Get off of me!"

"Come back here!" Julian grabbed me by the arm.

"Let me go!" I tried to pull away.

Julian pulled me on the bed and held my hands above my head. I was tossing from side to side, trying to keep my legs closed. He forced his way between my thighs and slid his stick back inside of me. That shit felt so good I couldn't even pretend not to enjoy it.

"Damn, baby!" I said.

"You want me to stop?" Julian pulled his stick almost all of the way out and slid it in again. "Huh?"

"No," I said. "Don't stop."

"What did you say?" Julian gave one long, deep stroke.

"I said, don't stop."

"Tell me you want it!"

"I want it!" I moaned.

"What?"

"I want it!" I shouted, grabbing his ass and forcing him inside of me. "Ram me, baby! Ram me hard!"

Julian stroked me as hard and deep as he could, but he wasn't touching the same spot Michael had touched. I don't only mean physically; I mean emotionally and mentally. Although I was calling his name, I was seeing Michael's face.

The next morning, Julian told me he wanted to work things out and we made love again. While I was in the shower, he received a call saying he had a shoot in London and he had to leave immediately. I had been lied to again, but that time it didn't matter. I didn't feel used or manipulated by having sex with him. He received "*get the hell out sex*," not "*I love you sex*." As far as I was concerned, it was a small price to pay to get rid of his punk ass.

CHAPTER TWO

We had Friday off for the Thanksgiving holiday so I wouldn't have to deal with Michael until Monday. I wanted to distract his frustration so I threw on this hot mini-skirt that showed off my legs and my ass. I wore open-toed shoes because I knew Michael was attracted to every single inch of a woman. I normally had my hair pinned up, but I let it down that day.

I purposely arrived to work late, to give him time to cool down. I expected him to rip into my ass as soon as he saw me. I walked in as if nothing had happened. I didn't want to make a big deal out of it, but I didn't want to make it seem like I didn't care either.

"Good morning, Michael," I spoke softly.

"Good morning, Alicia."

"Can I please talk to you about Thanksgiving?"

"No explanation needed."

"I didn't know he was coming to town until he showed up at my house, Michael."

"Whatever, Alicia."

I was about to say something else when Michael stood up and started to walk away. I reached for his arm but he kept walking.

"Michael," I whispered, trying not to cause a scene. "Michael, listen to me, please."

He ignored me and went to the break room. I waited for him

to come out but it was taking too long. I was impatient and I couldn't wait any longer. I went into the break room to talk to him right then. When I walked in, he and Pam stopped talking. It was obvious that they were talking about me.

"Can I talk to you please, Michael?"

"Is it urgent?" Michael asked.

"Yes, it's very urgent."

"Well, I need to get back to my desk anyway. Talk to you later, Mike," Pam said.

"See ya later, Pam," I said.

Pam stared at me as she walked out of the door.

"What was that all about?"

"What?"

"When did you and Pam become so buddy-buddy?"

"We were in the break room at the same time; that's all."

I didn't appreciate Michael talking about me behind my back, but that was the least of my concern.

"Michael, look, I'm sorry about Thanksgiving. I didn't know he was coming to town."

"You could have told me you were bringing him, Alicia!"

"How? How could I have told he was coming?"

"With your mouth!" Michael snapped.

"Stop raising your voice at me!" I snapped back.

"I'm not raising my voice."

"Listen, Michael, how can I make it up to you?"

"You wanna know how you can make it up to me?"

"Yeah, I'll do anything."

"Kiss my ass!" Michael said.

He stormed out of the break room, pushing chairs to the side along the way. When I went back to my desk, he wasn't there, and neither was Pam. They were probably somewhere talking about me behind my back again. I went back to the break room to see if they were in there, but they weren't. I took a break for about fifteen minutes and then went back to my desk. When I got back, Michael had returned. But before I could talk to him, Cynthia showed up.

Cynthia and Michael were close. They did everything together; watched football, basketball. She even babysat his kids. Everybody knew Cynthia had a thing for Michael, but Michael. His desk was right in front of mine so I could hear every word they were saying.

"What's up, man?" Cynthia asked.

"What's up, Cynt?" Michael said.

"I had a ball this weekend."

Cynthia was kind of an introvert and didn't date. She had met some guy over the weekend and she was going around like a silly high school girl telling everyone in the office. While she was talking, I looked at Michael to see his reaction.

"I can't wait for you to meet Stewart, Mike," Cynthia said. "You two are going to get along so well."

"Why do you say that?"

"Because you're just alike."

"I don't think so, Cynt."

"How do you know? You haven't even met him."

"Believe me, I know."

"He's coming to visit me this weekend."

"Is he staying with you?"

"Of course. Where else is he going to stay?"

"I don't think that's a good idea, Cynt."

"Why not? He's a nice guy."

"But you just met the guy."'

"So what?"

"So you should be more careful."

"What's wrong with him staying with me?"

"Nothing."

"No. Tell me, Michael. What's wrong with him staying with me?"

Michael? I was like, since when does she call him Michael? I'm the only one who calls him Michael. He was just Mike to everyone else.

"I didn't think you were like that."

"Like what?"

"Forget it, Cynt."

"No, let's not forget it," Cynthia said. "Like what?"

"Okay." Michael chuckled. "Like meeting a guy one week and sleeping with him the next."

"Okay, so now I'm a whore?"

"I didn't call you a whore, Cynt."

"That's okay, Michael! Thanks for nothing!"

Cynthia walked away in a huff and left Michael looking like a damn fool, begging her to come back.

"Cynt! Cynt!"

Their conversation didn't sound like friendship; it sounded like lovers. I had no right to question Michael; especially after what I had put him through, but if he had feelings for Cynthia, I wanted to know.

"Are you in love with her, Michael?"

"In love with who, Alicia?"

"Are you in love with Cynthia?"

"Aw, damn! Now what are you talking about?"

"I heard you, Michael. Why were you so against her having a man visit? It's none of your business who she sees and what she does."

"See, that's where you're wrong. It is my business. It's my business because she's my friend and I care about her."

"I believe you're in love with her."

"A woman like you can never understand a man and a woman just being friends."

"What do you mean by that?" I asked the question but I really didn't want to hear the answer.

"You think you're so beautiful that a man can never love you just for being you. You're never going to be happy and you're never going to be satisfied because you can't see past your own beauty to see your own soul."

Even though Michael was telling the truth, I responded with anger; it was a diversion from facing the truth.

"You black bastard!"

"Black, I am. Bastard, I am not. Unlike that mutt of a boyfriend you had on your arm Thursday night."

"At least he loves me!" I said, knowing I was lying.

"Woman, please! He only sees you every six months; the other six months he's sleeping with real models."

"So are you calling me a fool, Michael?"

"You said it; I didn't."

I didn't want to face what Michael was saying, but it was the truth. But truth or not, I needed sympathy, not reality. I pretended to cry to get comfort from him, instead of the coldhearted-in-your-face sermon he was throwing at me. And it worked like a charm.

"Alicia, I'm sorry. I didn't mean it like that."

"You know what, Michael? I barely slept this weekend, think-ing about how you may have been hurting. Julian tried to touch me but I wouldn't let him; all I could think about was you. I should have let Julian have his way. That's all that matters anyway, huh?"

I was lying, but all that Michael needed to know was that I was hurting and I needed him to make me feel better.

"You need to calm down so that we can talk about this rationally, Alicia."

"Too late for that, Michael! Don't say anything to me unless it's dealing with Upskon!"

"I'm afraid I can't do that, Alicia."

"Just leave me alone!"

I had flipped the script and I wasn't going to let up. Who cared if he hadn't done anything? It was his turn to feel guilty.

"No, I care about you and I want to apologize for hurting your feelings, okay?"

"Your apology is accepted." I smiled. My purpose had been served. He wasn't mad and I wasn't feeling guilty anymore. Everybody won.

MICHAEL AND I CONTINUED OUR LITTLE OFFICE ROMANCE, but we weren't having sex. Not having sex wasn't discussed; we just didn't bring it up. Meanwhile, Julian came back on one of his mini-visits.

He walked in the house with the same old "*I love you*" crap. I put his ass on the couch again, but I made sure that I locked my bedroom door when I went to sleep. He was nice that time and stayed there.

When I woke up, I stayed in the bed for a while and then I got dressed to make breakfast. I was surprised beyond belief to find a cart sitting outside of my bedroom door with breakfast already made. It was very romantic. There was a note telling me to get back in the bed and wait for my servant to arrive. I ran as fast as I could and dove on top of my bed, bouncing up and down several times. Minutes later, Julian was knocking on the door.

"Come in!" I yelled.

Julian walked in wearing black silk pajama pants with no shirt. The pants were baggy and clingy at the same time. The muscles in his stomach rippled as he pushed the cart closer to the bed. Wow! He looked delicious.

"Are you ready for your breakfast, madam?"

"Yes, sir."

"Please do not call me sir, madam. I am here to serve you; you are not here to serve me."

I laughed. "I heard that!"

"What would you like to eat first, madam?"

"May I have a piece of fruit?"

"Which fruit do you desire, madam?"

"Can I have some of that pineapple?"

"It is my pleasure."

Julian picked up a piece of pineapple and slowly placed it to my lips. He held it in his hands until it was completely devoured. I licked the pineapple juice from his well-manicured fingers as he stuck the last morsel in my mouth.

"What would you like next, madam?" Julian's submissive role-playing was turning me on and he knew it.

"I, uh, I would like a croissant, please."

"Buttered, madam?"

"Please."

Julian picked up a croissant and buttered both sides. He placed the croissant to my mouth and held it patiently as I took my time with each bite. He continued to feed me a piece of every item on the tray. By the time we were finished I wanted to snatch him in the bed with me. But I resisted the temptation.

"Would you like something to drink, madam?"

"Yes, I'd like some grapefruit juice, please."

Julian poured a glass of juice and held it to my mouth and watched me drink swallow after swallow. When I told him I had had enough to drink, he wiped the sides of my mouth with a napkin. Once my mouth was thoroughly dry, he put the napkin away and then reached beneath the cart and pulled out a small basket. He sat the basket on the bed and rolled the cart to the side.

"Are you ready for your morning massage, madam?"

"Massage?" I asked. "Oh, yes, yes, yes, I'm ready."

"Please remove all of your clothing and lay face down, madam."

Julian didn't move a muscle as I stripped naked in front of him. I rolled onto my stomach and prepared for his touch.

"This technique is called fire and ice, madam. Do not be alarmed by the contrast in sensations."

"Okay," I said and then braced myself.

Julian rubbed oil on my body. At first it felt like regular lotion, then all of a sudden it started to heat up. My entire body was on fire. But then I felt the sensation of Julian's tongue licking the oil from my body. The feeling was unbelievable. The moisture from his tongue cooled the burning sensation of the oil. My body started to shake in certain areas, and then other parts of my body would shake. I couldn't even speak to tell him how good it felt.

Julian turned me on my back and opened my legs. He paused momentarily and then placed more oil on me. Again, the oil felt like regular lotion but then the sensation changed. It became cool, and then cold. Before it became unbearable Julian began to lick it off but this time his tongue felt warm, almost hot.

As he licked closer to my inner thighs, my body went into involuntary convulsions again. When he sucked my left vaginal lip, I spiraled out of control into a powerful orgasm. He held me down and licked my clit vigorously. I covered my face with my pillow and punched it over and over. He removed his tongue from my clit and watched me writhe from side to side.

"Oh shit!" I shouted. "What are you doing to me, baby?"

"Fire and ice, baby!" Julian whispered, snatching me by my ankles and pulling me to him. "You want some more fire and ice, baby?"

"Please, Julian, please stop it, baby!" I pleaded. "I can't take it! It feels too good! I can't take it!"

Julian reached in his basket and pulled out a vibrator with a rotating head. He opened my legs and cut the gadget on. Let me tell you, all that I remember after that is the melodic sound of buzzing.

I felt the vibrator pass my vagina lips and then I could feel that head turning inside of me. It felt like it was touching every nook and cranny of my vagina. My toes were curled so tightly I caught a cramp in my foot. As Julian twisted it inside of me, he licked my clit, sending me to another explosive orgasm.

"Julian, please!" I screamed. "I can't take it! I can't take it, baby!"

I raised my hips off of the bed, shaking in midair. I turned on my side and eventually ended up sitting on his face. I continued to grind because I felt that I had one more orgasm ready to pop.

"Stay right there, baby," I said, grinding on Julian's face. "Stay just like that!"

I raised one leg in the air, so he could have licking room and moved back and forth. I didn't mean to be rude but I snatched the vibrator out of his hand and placed it on my clit. The reversal of his tongue in my vagina and the dildo on my clit felt just as good. When I felt another orgasm coming, I held the toy directly on top of my clit. MY GOD! I bucked my hips so fast and so hard that Julian and I fell off of the bed and onto the floor.

I ended up with a pillow between my legs. I trapped the pillow with my thighs and slid my clit up and down on top of it until I came for the third and final time. That orgasm was so strong that I dug my toes into the wooden base of my bed frame. I screamed so loudly that Julian covered his ears.

"Damn, woman!" Julian shouted. "Calm your voice!"

"Oh my God!" I shouted over and over. "Damn!"

"Now do you believe I love you?" Julian asked.

"Oh, hell yeah." I pulled Julian to me and kissed him passionately. "Yes, baby."

"I have to get cleaned up and go pick up your next surprise, Alicia."

"Next surprise? Are you serious?" I sounded like a child receiving additional toys the day after Christmas.

"You just relax. I will take care of you today. I will clean your house from the bottom all the way to the top. Relax and allow me to take care of you."

"This is unbelievable, Julian."

"No, you are unbelievable, my love."

Julian took a shower while I watched television in bed. After he was dressed, he left to get my next surprise. I was on top of the world. My man had finally come to his senses and realized he had a good thing in me.

Although he told me to relax, I decided to help him out and wash the dishes on the breakfast cart. As I was putting the basket away, a DVD accidentally fell out of a shiny black bag. Normally, I would have placed the DVD back in the bag, but it had *XXX* written on it. That could only mean one thing: nasty! Not only that, it was lying on the floor at my feet like it was telling me to watch it.

I resisted the temptation and put the DVD back in the bag. I tried to get it out of my mind and clean up, but I couldn't. I was torn between trusting Julian and facing the truth. What if I looked and there were only scenes from his fashion shows? I would have violated his privacy for no reason. On the other hand, what if there was undeniable proof that he was sleeping with other women on that tape? Come on now; you know what I did.

I put the disc in the DVD player and pushed "play." I sat on the bed and put my hand over my heart, preparing for the heart attack. I saw all that I needed to see on the very first scene; Julian strutting down the runway, with me sitting in the front row. Damn! That's what I get for being so nosy.

I heard him coming through the door downstairs so I hurried to take the DVD out. He was practically running up the stairs and I was so nervous, I kept pushing the wrong buttons. He opened up the door and caught me red-handed.

Julian pointed at the television. "What is this?"

"I'm sorry!" I tried to sincerely apologize. "The disc fell out of the basket and I was curious to know what was on it."

Julian walked toward the DVD player. "You mean you were spying on me?"

"No, not spying. I was just curious."

"I do not believe you! Are you satisfied with your investigation?"

"I'm sorry, Julian, I will never do it again. I apolo..." I paused in mid-sentence. "What the hell?"

Julian turned around and saw that the disc had switched scenes.

"Is that you, Julian?"

Julian tried to cut the DVD player off. "I demand that you cut that machine off right now!"

"Get your goddam' hands off that DVD!" I screamed. "Is that you?"

The camera was a closeup shot of Julian lying down and a woman obviously giving him head.

"Oh my God! Oh my God! Oh my God!"

"I said, cut that machine off right this minute!" Julian shouted.

I caught Julian off guard and pushed him on the bed. At the same time, the woman's face came in to view on the screen. I fell on my knees and screamed as loud as I could. There it was right in front of my face; Julian moaning while a man's mouth was wrapped around his stick. I bent over and vomited up all of the breakfast I had eaten.

"It's not what you think, Alicia!"

"I'll kill you, niggah!"

I ran downstairs to my kitchen. I grabbed a knife and ran back upstairs. I met Julian running down the stairs. When he saw the knife in my hand, he ran back upstairs to my bedroom and locked the door.

"Open up this door, niggah!" I kicked and pounded on the door.

"Let me explain!" Julian shouted from the other side of the door.

"Niggah, you screwin' niggahs?" I shouted. "I'm going to kill your faggot ass!"

"I'm calling the police!"

"Call the police, bitch!" I screamed. "Tell them to come pick up your corpse, niggah!"

"You're crazy, bitch!"

I plunged the knife into the door. "Oh yeah, bitch! I'm going to show you just how crazy I am!"

Looking back, I understand why Julian was so afraid of me. He probably thought I had snapped. I guess I did snap. I couldn't believe what I was seeing, my man having sex with another man. That's the ultimate humiliation. You hear about that down-low shit here in Atlanta, and when it's somebody else's man you think of it as a joke. But that shit is like death; no matter how much you prepare for it, when the reality hits your ass, it's devastating!

"I have called the police! They're on their way!" Julian shouted.

"I don't give a shit about the police! I'm going to shove this knife up your faggoty ass!"

"I am not a faggot!"

A few minutes later the police banged on my door, but I ignored them. I stayed in front of my bedroom, waiting for Julian to come out. My landlord had a tendency of letting anybody into my house upon request so she could stay in my business. Every time she let someone in, she brought her nosy ass in with them.

When the police arrived, they burst through my doors like we were on *Cops*. They grabbed me and threw me on the floor. They told Julian to come out but he was so afraid that I was still waiting on him with that knife; he wouldn't come out, nor would he let them in.

They handcuffed me and sat me on the couch as they finally convinced Julian to open the door. When he came downstairs he wouldn't even look my way. The police questioned us separately. I explained to the police that I wasn't usually that angry. As a matter of fact, I had never reacted like that before in my life. I pleaded my defense but Julian's statement would decide my fate. I don't know what Julian told them, but whatever it was, they didn't arrest me.

After everybody was gone, I went back to my bedroom and the freaking DVD was still playing. I watched it and cried every second until it finished. Before the disc was complete, I had watched Julian have sex with four men and five women. I should have been just as angry over the women, as much as I was over the men, but I wasn't.

I was embarrassed and humiliated. Seeing my man with other men's mouths on his stick, kissing and caressing, emasculated him to nothing. And if he was nothing, what did that make me for loving him?

I needed a man to make love to me. I needed to be held, kissed, and caressed. I needed to be validated as a woman. I needed it to come from a big strong, masculine man who would rip my body to pieces. And I knew exactly where to find that man.

CHAPTER THREE

"Hello," Michael said.

"Can I come over?"

"Now is not a good time."

"Too late. I'll be there in five minutes."

"Alicia, don't do that. My daughters are with me this weekend."

"So what? You don't have a problem with Cynthia coming over while they're there!" I snapped. "I think now is a fine time for me to meet them."

"No. Not today."

I wanted to continue talking with confidence, but I couldn't. I needed a man to treat me like a woman or else I was going to lose my mind. I started to beg him to see me.

"Please, Michael, I really need to see you. Julian and I broke up."

"All right, Alicia. My daughters are about to go shopping with Cynthia; give me a few minutes and I'll call you back."

"Okay, baby, I'll wait for you to call back."

"Okay, bye."

"Bye-bye."

I hung up the telephone and waited for Michael to call. I took a shower, got dressed, ran a few errands, and he still hadn't called. He was the one man who truly claimed to love me but even he wasn't there when I needed him. Impatience took over and I thought that if Mohammed wouldn't come to the mountain, then the mountain would have to go to Mohammed. I drove over to Michael's house.

There were no other cars in his driveway except his Navigator so I assumed that the coast was clear. I quick stepped up his sidewalk and rang his doorbell. I was hoping he would be naked and snatch me inside and have his way with me. I waited a moment and then started to pound on his door.

"I'm coming! I'm coming!"

There was a pause and then he opened the door.

"What's up? Come in." Michael stepped to the side.

"Thanks for the return call, Michael," I said sarcastically.

"I was trying to get my girls out of here and it slipped my mind."

"What are you doing?"

"I'm taking a shower."

"Looks like I came at the right time."

I squeezed Michael's stick in my hand. I didn't have time for small talk. I wanted sex, right then and there.

"Not quite." He moved my hand and then secured the towel around his waist. "Well, I need to get back in the shower."

"Don't let me stop you."

Michael told me to wait for him in the den and went back upstairs to finish his shower. Hearing the shower made me eager to take advantage of the moment so I stripped one article of clothing at a time all the way to his shower door.

"Scoot over," I said, stepping into the shower.

"Alicia, this is not a good idea right now."

"There's nobody here but us."

"Yeah, but we don't know when they're coming back."

"They're not here now, so let's enjoy ourselves."

"I can't, Alicia. My kids might come back here!"

"Come on, Michael, you don't want me anymore?" I asked, thinking he was playing hard to get because I had hurt him with Julian.

"Right now, no!"

I grabbed Michael's stick and it was as hard as a rock. I massaged it, rubbing soap up and down the shaft, and then squeezed it tightly.

"Well, I think you better tell your little head, 'cause he's saying something different."

"Alicia, please get out and put your clothes on! Please!"

"Come on, Michael!" I kissed him all over his chest. My frustration was rapidly turning to desperation.

"Look! Don't you understand? My kids could come back at any time, Alicia!" Michael shouted.

I realized Michael was serious. He wasn't playing hard to get; he really didn't want me. I wanted to fall on the floor of that shower and cry until I ran out of tears. Instead, I stood a strong front and redirected that pain to anger.

"Is it your kids, or Cynthia, you're worried about?"

"Let me tell you something! I don't give a damn about you, or any other woman when it comes to the welfare of my kids! Now go put your damn clothes on! NOW!" Michael screamed very loudly.

Embarrassed and dejected, I slowly picked up my clothes on the way downstairs. I started to cry as I put them on one at a time. I don't know how I ever ended up where I was emotionally, but I was going to have to get myself out of it. I simply didn't know how.

On my way out of the door, Michael ran down the stairs and stopped me.

"Look, I didn't mean to be rude, but I can't jeopardize my children finding me in an inappropriate situation like this."

I could feel Michael's sincerity and I understood where we he was coming from. It didn't make me feel better, but I understood.

"I understand, Michael, you don't have to explain."

"Maybe we should go get a bite to eat or something."

"That's fine; I just need to be with you."

Michael started upstairs and then turned around and said, "It's ironic that you only seem to need me when Julian is not around."

"That's not true, Michael."

It was true and I knew it. I just wasn't woman enough to admit it.

"Yes, it is. But it's okay. At least now I know where we stand."

Michael and I ate lunch and then we went to the park to talk about our relationship. Sitting on that bench talking, I realized that he was in love. It just wasn't with me.

"What kind of woman would make you remarry, Michael?"

"She has to be level-headed, emotionally controlled, and logical, you know, everybody has problems, but I need a woman who's willing to listen first and react second."

"You don't think I'm that type of woman?" I asked sarcastically, hoping his answer would be a sincere yes.

"Well, right now, Alicia, I couldn't tell you what type of woman you are. I think once you figure yourself out, you'll be all that and more."

"Is Cynthia that type of woman?" I asked, hoping to get the same answer for her that he had given to me.

"Cynt is unbelievable. She loves unconditionally. She doesn't love for a reward. She loves for love. That's something you don't find every day."

"Wow!" I tried to pretend that Michael's words were not tearing me apart. He may have even believed me. "Well, if you feel that strongly about Cynthia, why don't you go after her?"

"She's my friend, first of all, and I don't want to mess that up. Secondly, I'm not even good enough for a woman like her."

Damn! Smack dab in my face! There I was practically throwing myself at the man while he confessed his unworthiness for the love of another woman. A man that I thought I had in the palm of my hand. A man that I thought would jump at the snap of my fingers. Perhaps my decision to ignore his advances influenced his current lack of affection toward me, or, perhaps not. Either way, I had to deal with the consequences of my actions. I chose a low-down snake in the grass and it cost me the elusive mythical good black man. As I sat quietly listening to Michael's *"it's not you, it's me"* speech, I kept asking myself the same question, *what the hell was wrong with me?*

THE FOLLOWING MONDAY I WAS ONE OF THE FIRST TO ARRIVE for work. My girls, Lisa and Val, were pulling up at the same time. We walked to the door together, talking about our weekend.

"Hey, what y'all do this weekend?" Val asked.

"I had a date but nothing major," Lisa said.

"I almost had to kill me a niggah this weekend, girl," I said.

"Who you almost kill, Alicia?" Val held the door open, while Lisa and I entered first. Val was one of the office girls, but she was also one helluva gentleman. We cut on our computers and then went into the break room.

"Julian."

"Julian?" Val asked. "I thought you were through with that fool."

"I was, but he keeps popping in and out of my life."

"He can't do shit if you don't let him," Val said.

"Hey! I don't want to hear all that! I want to know how you almost killed him." Lisa laughed. "What happened?"

Before I could respond, Wanda walked in. We were startled and stopped talking. Not because we didn't want Wanda to join in; we just didn't know who was coming through the door.

"Why y'all stop talking when I walk in?" Wanda asked. "Y'all talking about me?"

"I know you think the universe revolves around your big-ass head, but it don't. Ain't nobody talkin' to you."

"See, there you go talkin' 'bout my head, Val," Wanda said. "Don't say nothin' when I report your steroid-takin' ass to the damn Feds."

"You stupid, Wanda." Lisa laughed.

"That shit ain't funny," Val snapped.

"I still wanna know what y'all was talking about when I walked in!" Wanda said.

"None of your dam' business!" Val said.

"A'ight! Y'all be like that." Wanda walked out of the break room, fussing under her breath.

"Okay, long story short," I said. "I found a DVD with Julian…"

Wanda burst back through the door, yelling, "Y'all done hurt my damn feelings. We supposed to be cool and y'all talkin' 'bout me behind my back."

"Ain't nobody talkin' about you, man!" Val shouted.

"Then what y'all talkin' 'bout?"

"If you shut up, I'll tell you," I said.

"Okie-dokie, Smokey!" Wanda grabbed a chair and sat next to me.

"Anyway, I found this DVD with Julian having sex."

"It was with a man, huh?" Wanda shouted.

"Wanda, shut up!" Val shouted. "Was it a man, Alicia?"

"It was with men and women."

"Oh hell, nawl!" Wanda shouted. "That niggah would be dead if that was me and no jury in the country would convict me!"

"Don't think I didn't want to kill that niggah, too!" I said emphatically. "I chased his ass all around my house with a knife trying to get at him, but he locked himself in my bedroom."

Wanda slammed her fist on the table. "I woulda broke that damn door down."

"Don't think I didn't try."

"So are you breaking up for good this time?" Lisa asked.

"Girl, please, I better not ever see that fool again in my life."

"You been saying that ever since I met you," Val said.

"Okay, watch and see."

"I'm gon' watch alright."

"At least now you can see what's up with your boy, Mike," Lisa added.

"Mike Forrester?" Wanda asked.

"Oh Lord," Val said. "The mouth of the south done found out your business."

"What about Mike?" Wanda asked. "You messin' around with Mike, Alicia?"

"We're not messing around, some stuff just went down," I joked.

"Uh-huhn, now you know that if you don't tell me what went down," Wanda said sarcastically, "I'm gon' have to make up some shit that's probably even worse."

"You make me sick, Wanda!"

"You got benefits; take yo' ass to the doctor!"

"See, I was going to tell you, but I'm not telling you nothing now!"

"I was just joking, Alicia." Wanda laughed. "Girl, I'm gon' bust wide open if you don't tell me."

"I mean, it's nothing major; we just hooked up a couple of times."

"Hooked up like sex?" Wanda asked.

"I'm not saying anything else."

"You boned Mike?" Wanda shouted.

"Wanda, be quiet!" Val said.

I covered Wanda's mouth. "Would you lower your voice?"

"Set me free! Set me free!" Wanda shouted as she removed my hand from her mouth.

"I knew I shouldn't have told your big-mouth ass!"

"Answer my question! Can he get down?" Wanda asked.

"Can he get down?" Val repeated. "Who are you, Florida Evans with that seventies shit?"

"Why I got to be Florida Evans?" Wanda shouted. "Why I can't be Thelma?"

While Val and Wanda were doing their daily morning comedy routine, Pam walked in. Since we had switched subjects, it slipped my mind to swear secrecy from the office girls about my confidential information about Michael.

"Come on now, Wanda, even if you got the world's best make-over, cosmetic surgery, plastic surgery, everything they got out there, you still ain't gon' look nothin' like Thelma Evans." Val laughed.

Pam often worked the room as the instigator, keeping things going between Val and Wanda.

"Hey, Val, what about if they put her on that *How to Look Good Naked* show?" Pam chuckled.

"You see, y'all gon' try to gang up on me." Wanda laughed. "I told y'all before, if you gang up on me, I'm takin' everybody the hell out! I'm tellin' everythang!"

"Tell it! I ain't got nothin' to hide," Val shouted.

"Okay then, Alicia ain't the only one Mike hittin' up in here, Alicia!" Wanda said. "Ain't that right, Pam?"

"That's some fake-ass shit, Wanda." Pam laughed.

"Nah!" Wanda said. "I ain't through! Val was the one who left the used tampon in the bathroom! Lisa and Alicia on probation and they might get fired! Yeah, y'all bonin' the same dude! Now what?"

I looked at Pam, and Pam looked at me. We laughed and gave each other a high-five.

Pam leaned on me as she laughed out loud. "That's some good shit, ain't it, girl?"

"Oh my God!" I said. "Big, black and juicy!"

"Damn!" Wanda said. "I thought you hoes would be embarrassed!"

"For what?" Pam sat down and crossed her legs, twirling her foot round and round.

"Y'all gon' make me try that niggah," Val said.

"Sir," Wanda said, "Stick to your own team."

"Shut up, niggah."

"You two are the most ghetto women I have ever met," I said.

"I ain't ghetto, I'm real," Wanda said back.

"Me, too," Val repeated. "I'm from the streets!"

"You ain't from no damn streets, Val!" Wanda said. "They don't have no streets in St. Lucia; they got land! Dirt! Sand! Shit like that!"

Our supervisor, Tazzy, and our coworker, Ms. Virginia, walked into the break room and everybody lowered their voices.

"Why did you all stop talking when we walked in?" Ms. Virginia asked.

"No reason," Wanda said.

Tazzy laughed. "Are y'all talking about us?"

"Did I sound suspicious like that when I came in here?" Wanda asked.

"Hell yeah!" Val shouted.

"Watch that mouth, Valerie," Ms. Virginia insisted.

"I'm sorry, Ms. Virginia," Val said.

Ms. Virginia and Tazzy got their cups of coffee and started to walk back to the floor.

"You all can continue your little private conversation," Tazzy said sarcastically.

"Y'all ain't out the door yet." Wanda held the door open for Ms. Virginia and Tazzy to exit.

Lisa followed them out of the door. "Tazzy, I need to ask you a question."

Wanda playfully pushed Lisa as she passed by. "Brown-noser."

"Whateva!" Lisa smiled while she was going out of the door.

"We got the uh, the diet contest today, don't we?" I asked.

"Man, I don't wanna talk about no freakin' weight contest." Wanda stood up to leave. "I'll see y'all on the grind."

Val laughed. "Don't nobody care about that diet contest but you, Alicia."

"I know I don't," Pam said.

Pam and Val walked out with Wanda, leaving me alone in the break room. I was about to get up when Cynthia walked in.

"Hey, Alicia," Cynthia said, getting a cup from the cabinet. "What did you do this weekend?"

"Nothing much. I pretty much stayed in and watched television. What about you?"

"Girl, I hung out with Mike and his kids." Cynthia smiled. Her face was glowing like the sun was shining from inside of her. I had seen the same look in Michael's eyes on Saturday. "We had a ball."

"Good. You and Mike must be really close."

"Yeah, we're cool," Cynthia replied like it was no big deal. "That's my boy."

"I think it's a little more than that."

"Nah, that's it."

"Okay, if you say so."

Cynthia asked, "Did you get caught up with your claims?"

"Not yet. Those things are kicking my behind."

"Don't worry about it. I'll knock 'em out for you."

"That's okay. You have your own work to do."

"Girl, please, I got it. Don't let this job stress you out."

"Thanks!"

"I'll see you on the floor," Cynthia said as she walked out.

I looked at that simple woman and wondered if she knew how special she was in this world. All that she cared about was making other people happy. Michael was right; she wasn't anything you ran across every day.

Since Cynthia was helping me out with my claims, that gave me time to pressure the office girls the rest of the morning to have the diet contest and guess who won? You damn right; yours truly.

ONE DAY, WE WERE GOING TO LUNCH and Tina, another one of my coworkers, got into it with her husband. Tina and Cynthia were walking together ahead of us. I don't know where Curtis, Tina's husband, came from. I saw him standing in front of Tina and pointing his finger in her face. At first he was calm, but then, when she wouldn't go with him, he went nuts.

Tina shouted, "I don't want to go with you, Curtis!"

"Get your ass outside!" Curtis pulled Tina by her arm.

"Let me go, Curtis!" Tina shouted, snatching away from him.

"Get yo' hands off her, you sorry-ass bastard!" Val shouted.

Val and Wanda, the bodyguards, stood in between Curtis and Tina, trying to stop him from hurting her. I wanted to do something, but I was scared. I had heard about Curtis and his violent temper, but seeing it up close and personal was sheer frightening.

Wanda and Val grabbed Curtis and tried to get him off of Tina. There was nothing they could do. The more they tried to stop him, the angrier he became. Wherever I found the courage to attack Julian, it was totally nonexistent on that day. I was scared stiff. There was a big difference in challenging a sensitive pretty boy like Julian, and a crazed maniac like Curtis. Curtis looked like he would kick ass first and take names later. To be honest, I didn't feel like getting my ass kicked that day.

While they were shouting and screaming hysterically, Michael came to the rescue like Superman. It was so dramatic. He burst through the doors like he was trying to knock them off the hinges.

Michael pushed Curtis away from Tina. "What are you doing, man?"

"Get outta my face, man!" Curtis shouted, still reaching for Tina. "I'm gon' kill this bitch!"

"Hey! Let go of that woman, man!"

Michael stood between Tina and Curtis, shoving Curtis against the wall. By that time, Jaline, our manager, and Tazzy, were in the hallway with us.

"You ain't got nothin' to do with this, man! Step off!" Curtis shouted.

"Get him off her, Mike!" Pam yelled.

Curtis pulled out a gun, but before he could do anything, Michael pounced on top of him.

"Mike, look out! He got a gun!" Cynthia shouted.

Michael and Curtis fell against the wall and then down to the floor. Michael was on top and Curtis was yelling and screaming like a madman. During their struggle, Curtis dropped the gun. I don't know if Michael realized it or not, because he never went for it.

I was standing the closest to it, but I was afraid to pick it up. I was hoping Michael would get the gun before Curtis. We surrounded Michael and Curtis tussling on the floor. Michael shouted for us to back up. We took one step backward, and then two steps forward.

"Get back! Back up!" Michael shouted.

"Michael, look out!" I screamed. "Get the gun!"

I saw Michael looking around, as he kept Curtis at bay, but he obviously didn't see the gun next to his feet. Cynthia was bold enough to kick the gun away. Calmly, Ms. Virginia stood over Michael and Curtis and pulled a gun out of her purse.

She aimed the gun at Curtis and said, "Michael, get off of him. And Curtis, you better not move a muscle."

Michael let go of Curtis, and Curtis released Michael. Curtis was no longer yelling and screaming, threatening to kill Tina. His punk ass was lying on the ground with his hand in the air, begging for his life.

Michael seemed confused as he stood up, wiping his clothes. Ms. Virginia walked right above Curtis and pointed her gun at his penis. Curtis grabbed his crotch and closed his legs tightly, backing against the wall.

"How dare you put your hands on her?" Ms. Virginia yelled. "I'll kill you, you son of a bitch!"

That was the first time I had ever seen Ms. Virginia angry. Oh, and the language! Never thought I would have heard profanity come out of her mouth in a million years.

Ms. Virginia aimed the gun at Curtis and then cocked the trigger as if she was about to pull it. The situation was way past crazy and we went into total chaos mode. Michael shouted for Ms. Virginia to put the gun down but she was gone. I mean completely out of her mind.

"Ms. Virginia! Ms. Virginia!" Michael shouted.

"Please, don't shoot me, Ms. Virginia!" Curtis pleaded.

"I told you to leave her alone! I will kill you dead!" Ms. Virginia screamed.

Michael carefully walked behind Ms. Virginia and then slowly reached over her shoulder and grabbed her wrists. "Ms. Virginia, let the gun go!"

"Get that gun from her, man!" Curtis pleaded.

Michael slid his hand on top of hers. "Ms. Virginia, it's okay."

"Don't let her shoot me, man!"

"Ms. Virginia! Please! Give me the gun! Please!" Michael slowly took the gun out of her hands.

When the police finally arrived, late as usual, they had the nerve to pull their guns on Michael.

"Put the weapon down! And get down on the ground!" one cop shouted.

"Wait a minute; he's the one who attacked us!" Michael explained with Ms. Virginia's gun in his hand.

"Put your weapon down! And get down on the ground! NOW!" another cop shouted.

Cynthia screamed, "Mike, drop the gun!"

Michael put the gun on the ground, and then he lay face down. They yelled at him to spread his legs and arms. They told him to make sure his palms were turned upward so that could see the inside of his hands. We yelled at the police, telling them that they had the wrong man. They cuffed Michael and Curtis until they finished questioning us. Once we told them what happened, they let Michael go, and took Curtis to jail.

Later that day, we met over Michael's house to console Tina. I don't know whose idea that was, but it worked out well for Tina. Michael was concerned about her and felt it was dangerous for her to return home. He invited her to live with him until she was back on her feet. I knew they were cool, but I didn't know they were that cool. At first she said no, but who's going to turn down free rent in a big beautiful house like Michael's? I didn't say anything, but I was thinking to myself, either Michael was the nicest guy in the world, or he was trying to get a piece of ass. What do you think?

CHAPTER FOUR

Between Thanksgiving and Christmas, we picked up a new office girl, a preacher's wife named Cherie. I think she came to work there just to recruit more women to their church and pick up a little extra cash for Christmas. She was only there for a few weeks because after Christmas, she was out.

Speaking of Christmas, it went very well that year without Julian. I visited several friends in the morning and ended up at Michael's for a late dinner with a few other office girls. We had a ball. It was like being around family.

On New Year's Eve, Michael invited some of his Masonic brothers and the office girls to his house to bring in the New Year. There were more office girls than Masonic brothers, but we managed to make a party out of it.

The day of the party, Tina, Cynthia and I went shopping. We dropped Tina's girls off at her mother-in-law's house and we hit the stores. Tina was kind of nervous about dropping them off because even though her mother-in-law promised she didn't know where Curtis was, he could have jumped out of the bushes and attacked all three of us.

Cynthia walked Tina to the door to alleviate the possibility of a confrontation, like she could have stopped Curtis from harming Tina if that's what he wanted to do. I stayed my yellow ass in the car with the windows rolled up and the doors locked.

Everything went okay with dropping off the girls, and then it was grown-up time. When we got to the mall, Cynthia acted like she was afraid to wear anything that revealed her shape. She kept grabbing long skirts and I kept putting that shit right back on the rack.

"I'm not going to be walking with my butt all out for everybody to see, Alicia." Cynthia laughed, as I handed her a fitted dress.

"You got to show a little ass, to get a little ass."

"I don't want any ass. I want a good man."

"You got a good man."

"Please don't start."

Tina sighed. "I'm so tired of Cynthia and Mike, I don't even want to hear it."

Cynthia laughed. "What?"

"You know what," Tina said. "Y'all done played that friendship game too long, man. Either go after that niggah, or let that niggah go."

"He needs to come after me."

"Take my word for it, Cynt," I said. "If he thought you wanted him, he'd definitely come after you."

"Girl, please."

"Girl, please, nothing. That man is in love with you."

"Like I said," Tina repeated. "Either go after the niggah, or let the niggah go."

"I'm going to make him come after me!" Cynthia posed in a dress.

"Not wearing that Laura Ingalls dress, you won't." I laughed.

"What's wrong with this dress?"

"You couldn't catch a cold in Alaska wearing that dress," Tina said.

"Then what do I need to wear?"

"This." I held up a tight-fitting dress.

"Shoot! Give it here." Cynthia snatched the dress out of my hand. "This better work, Alicia."

"Trust me."

Tina, Cynthia and I arrived back at the house around seven o' clock. We ran upstairs to dress Cynthia. About an hour or so later, some of our girls started to show up, but Michael's boys were nowhere to be found.

Cynthia was nervous about wearing the tight dress and the high-heeled shoes, but we talked her through it. Tina and I walked behind Cynthia as she cautiously took one step at a time walking down the stairs.

She had on a tight red mini-dress that showed off her cute little shape. I had known the girl for years and didn't even know she had a figure like that. I mean, once we got her out of those Wal-Mart rags, she was gorgeous. But we could only do so much. When she started to walk in those high-heels, she looked like Sandra Bullock in *Miss Congeniality*.

"Look," Tina said, "when we get downstairs, sit your ass down so you won't be falling all over the place."

"Okay," Cynthia replied. "How do y'all walk in these shoes like this?"

"It's all in the calves, baby," I said as I strutted past her.

"That heffa always gotta show off, don't she?" Tina laughed.

"Wait for me, Alicia," Cynthia whispered as she stumbled behind me.

When Cynthia, Tina and I walked into the room, Michael's Masonic brothers had arrived and let me tell you, all eyes were on me. It was Cynthia's moment and I didn't want to upstage her so I stepped to the side to let the men see what else the party had on the menu.

I think Michael was happy with what Cynthia was wearing because he couldn't take his eyes off of her. I stood beside him as he was trying to hold a conversation with one of his brothers.

"Mike," Reggie said, "you work with all these women, man?"

"Yeah, bro," Michael answered.

"Damn! How do you do any work?"

"It's not easy, believe me."

Reggie pointed at Cynthia. "Hey, who is that right there?"

"Oh, that's my girl, Cynthia."

"You hittin' it?"

"No, man, we're just friends."

"I'm gon' ask you again, niggah, which one of these sisters you hittin'?"

"None of 'em, bro! Strictly business!"

"Sheee-iit! It ain't no way in the world I could work around all these fine-ass chicks and not hit one of 'em. And you neither, niggah! Somethin''s up!"

"I know you couldn't handle it, Reg," Michael said, "that's your M.O."

"It's a dirty job, but somebody got to do it." Reggie laughed as he took a drink.

"Enjoy yourself, Reg."

"I see Mel over there trying to get on ol' girl, so let me put a halt to that shit right now." Reggie pointed his glass toward Cynthia.

"She's not going to give either one of you the time of day."

"She won't give who the time of day?"

"You and Melvin. You're not her type, Reg."

"Who's not her type?"

"Cynthia is a laid-back type of sister, bro; she don't fall for those lines you throw at women."

"Care to make a little wager, Mike?"

"Not on her."

"Hey, you sure you don't have some kind of feelings for that chick, bro?"

"Naw, bro."

"All right then, Square." Reggie patted Michael on the back. "Now when I tap that ass, I don't want to hear no shit from you."

"If you get the ass, you get the ass, Reg," Michael said. I could tell he was becoming jealous, but he was doing a good job trying to play it off.

"Dam'!" Reggie peeked around Michael and looked at me as if I couldn't hear him. "What the hell is that?"

If Reggie wanted me to pretend I didn't hear him, I was going to play along. I was thinking though, damn niggah, I'm only two feet away.

"That's Alicia."

"That's the most beautiful creature I have ever laid eyes on. I'm going to marry that chick, Square."

"Calm down, man," Michael said. "You can't have them all."

While Reggie was drooling over me, Michael's doorbell rang. He left the room to answer the door. When he came back, he had this tall, dark and handsome man at his side. Masonic brother or not, I was going to get to know that man.

He had a neat, close haircut. He was clean-shaven, with smooth dark skin. Oh my God; he looked like he was seven feet tall. He had a V-shaped build from his waist to his shoulders. I couldn't take my eyes off of him. None of the office girls could. No moustache. No beard. No signs of hair anywhere on his face, with the exception of eyelashes and eyebrows.

I realized the guy must have been important to Michael because he stopped the party to introduce him. He cut the music off, and wrapped his arms around the man's shoulder.

"Hey, everybody, I want you all to meet my little brother, Johnny."

"Good to meet you all," Johnny said as he waved at everyone.

I made sure I made direct eye contact; I wanted him to know that by the time the night was over, he was going to have a new woman in his life. He smiled at me but before he could make his way over to me, Michael snatched him off and they disappeared.

While they were gone, I sat down and watched everybody do his or her thing. I wanted to position myself so that when Michael and his brother came back, I could make myself available for conversation.

When they came back in, they stood together and chatted. Johnny couldn't have been paying much attention, because he had his eyes on me and I definitely had my eyes on him. It wasn't long before he cut off his conversation with Michael and walked his fine ass over to my chair.

"Excuse me, Alicia, do you mind if I sit here?"

"Help yourself," I said.

"It's kinda noisy in here. Can we go somewhere else and talk?"

"That's fine."

Johnny took me by the hand and we went into the den to talk privately. I smiled as I passed Michael and he smiled back. I assumed he was fine with it.

I sat next to Johnny on the same couch where I had once had sex with his brother. I decided to be more responsive than informative. I didn't want to give up any more information than necessary.

"I didn't mean to pull you away from the party, Alicia," Johnny said.

"That's okay; I was pretty much watching everybody else anyway."

"If I appear nervous, it's because I am."

"Why are you nervous?"

"Come on, look at you. You must have guys hitting on you all the time."

"Not all the time," I joked. "And I'm sure you have women coming on to you all the time, too."

"No more than any other man."

"Hmm," I said sarcastically.

"Hmm?" Johnny said. "What does '*hmm*' mean?"

"A good-looking man like you, come on." I looked Johnny up and down. "Don't lie to me. You have plenty of women."

"Not anymore," Johnny said. "I have '*had*' a lot of women, with an accent on *had*. But as I've matured; the gratification of an orgasm is no longer about shooting sperm from my penis. It's about encompassing the nature of a woman. Her joy! Her pain! Her fear! Her pleasure! Everything that makes a woman, a woman! Like when I make love to you, it's not going to be about your body, or my body, it's going to be about our souls. The passion, the pleasure, I just can't find that compatibility with any woman anymore. But I think I'm going to find it in you."

"So you think you're going to make love to me?"

"Don't you?" Johnny asked very confidently.

My panties were soaking wet. I wanted to throw him on his back, pull his stick out, and ride him right there. I didn't give a damn who saw, or who heard. His confidence, or arrogance, whichever it was, was turning me on. I actually felt juices filling the front of my panties.

"So what do you do, Mr. Johnny?"

"I am a psychologist."

"A psychologist, huh?" I asked. "You know better than to try that psychological bullshit on me, right?"

Johnny smiled. "Absolutely."

When midnight struck, Johnny and I went into the living room with the rest of the party to bring in the New Year. I noticed Cynthia, and Michael's friend, Reggie, were not in the room. Judging by Michael's lack of enthusiasm, he did, too. I could tell he was distracted because he kept to himself, sitting alone in the corner.

He disappeared for a while, but when he emerged, Cynthia and Reggie surfaced as well. Cynthia whispered to us that she and Reggie were about to leave together. I was surprised. I didn't think my girl had it in her. Once she told the other office girls, they started to act like a bunch of drunken frat boys.

"My girl is about to get that monkey off her back!" Val shouted.

"It's about time!" Pam added.

"It ain't no way in the hell I could go that long wit'out gettin' some!" Darsha said.

"You keep talkin', you gon' get somethin' tonight!" Melvin joked.

"That's okay, too." Darsha sat on Melvin's lap and danced. "I hope you can handle it!"

"If I can't, this can!" Melvin went into his pocket and pulled out a pill.

"What the hell is that?"

"This makes us the same age!" Melvin laughed.

"Let's go, baby," Reggie said.

Reggie grabbed Cynthia by the hand and she followed him out of the door, looking back over her shoulder at us to smile.

"Excuse me, I'll be right back," I said to Johnny. "Mike, can I talk to you for a second?"

"Sure," Mike said. The guy was paying no attention to me. But still, I felt I should let him know that I was very interested in his brother.

"How do you feel about me dating your brother?"

"I really haven't thought about it, but I guess it wouldn't bother me."

"Good, because he seems interesting and I would like to get to know him."

"What about your boyfriend, Alicia?"

"What about my boyfriend? I'm willing to see where this can go with Johnny. He is a very nice guy."

"But he doesn't live here in Atlanta. You're putting yourself right back in the same situation you were with Julian."

"I thought about that, Mike. We're not talking marriage. We're talking dating. If we're meant to be, we'll get together. Right now, I just want to get to know him."

"I don't have a problem, as long as you don't do to him what you did to me."

"I will never do that again. Not to you, not to any man."

"Then I don't have a problem."

"Thanks, I wouldn't feel right unless it was all right with you."

"To be honest, I think you two make a much better couple than you and I ever could have made."

"You think?"

"Without a doubt."

"Now..." I punched Michael on the arm. "How could you let Cynthia leave with that piranha?"

"She's a grown woman; she can do what she wants."

"Come on, Michael, it's me! Be honest. How do you feel?"

Michael tried to pretend it didn't bother him, but I wasn't buying it.

"I really don't know how I feel, Alicia. I know that I don't like it, and I wish that I had stopped them but what can I do now? They're probably somewhere having wild sex by now."

"Hold on," I said.

I pulled out my cell phone and dialed Cynthia's number. She answered the phone, talking about Michael.

"Hey, Cynthia, where did you take your butt to, girl?" I asked.

"I know you're calling for Mike, girl. I saw how he was looking at me when I left, and that's what he gets! I want that niggah to suffer. Don't tell him this, but Reggie's gone. He dropped me off and kept pushing. Just answer yes, or no; does he look like he's suffering?"

"Yes."

"Is he next to you?"

"Yes."

"Did he ask you to call me?"

"Not exactly."

"Okay."

"Hold on, Cynthia, Mike wants to say something to you." I handed Michael my cell phone. "Here, handle your damn business!"

I walked out of the kitchen and gave Michael his privacy to talk to Cynthia. Johnny was sitting alone, waiting for me to come back. I sat beside him, and he gave me a drink.

"Here you go," Johnny said.

"Thank you," I said, taking the glass.

Michael walked up and handed my cell phone to me.

I asked, "So what happened?"

Michael looked like a man who had just had the beating of his life. He was rubbing his hands together, and for an articulate man, he sounded like Porky Pig.

"I uh," Michael said, "I asked Cynthia to come back, but she wouldn't, Alicia."

"What was your response?"

"I hung up the phone in her ear."

"Bad move, big brother," Johnny said.

"I don't know what to do, you guys."

"Go get her," Johnny said.

"I've already made a fool out of myself with them once."

I asked, "What do you mean?"

"I went to the basement to check up on them and caught them kissing."

"Oh, in that case, Mike, you better run over there," Johnny said.

"I want to, but I can't."

"Michael, listen to me. Go over there and tell her how you feel," I said.

Michael kneeled in front of us as if he was about to propose. I didn't know what he was going to say.

"All right, I'm going over there, but if I humiliate myself, I'm coming back here and kicking your ass, Johnny. And Alicia, you and I are going to have some sex! Rough sex!"

"Get!" I said. I planned on having rough sex, but only with the other Forrester brother.

Michael rushed out of his house like a knight going to save his fair maiden. I could have told him not to worry, but Cynthia had asked me to stay out of it. So I did. I had other business to tend to anyway.

Johnny asked, "What time is your curfew?"

"I'm grown. Why?"

"It's late, but I don't want this date to end, Alicia."

"So this is a date?"

"Oh, you didn't know?"

"This is a cheap date," I joked.

"In all fairness, I can only do so much in this house."

"Well, you're going to have to do more than this if you want to impress me."

"No problem." Johnny stood up. "Let's go."

"Go where?" I looked at Johnny like he was crazy.

"This is your city; you tell me."

"I don't want to empty your wallet, so let's go have breakfast."

"Sounds good to me."

"I have to tell my friends good-bye, and I'll be right back."

"I'll be outside waiting for you in my car."

"Okay, I'll be right there."

I told the office girls that I was leaving, but I didn't tell them I was going with Johnny. He followed me to an IHOP restaurant and we talked and talked and talked. We talked so much that we didn't want to finish the conversation. He asked me to his room and I initially said, no. I was playing the hard-to-get role. He told me he wanted my company for conversation and nothing more. I agreed to go but I was kind of hoping he was lying.

We went back to his hotel room and he took a shower. I sat in a chair, contemplating in my mind if I should let him make love to me, or if I should wait. When the shower cut off, I realized it would be only a matter of minutes before he walked out, showing off that incredible body.

I was prepared not to react to his nakedness. I had to be strong and not show signs of lust. I had just met the man; I had already had sex with his brother, so how much more of a whore did I want to present myself to be?

Any question that I had was answered when he walked out of the bathroom. He had on a huge T-shirt with pajama pants. He went to his suitcase and pulled out another T-shirt. He threw it at me and laughed.

"I know that may not be your normal sleeping attire, but that's all we got," Johnny joked.

"I can't fit this." I held up the shirt. "This is way too big."

"You're going to sleep in it; not dance in it."

"Ha! Ha! Very funny!"

I took a shower and when I came out, Johnny was working a crossword puzzle. Needless to say, I was very disappointed.

"Hey…" Johnny put his crossword puzzle on his lap. "What's your favorite flower?"

"My favorite flower? I guess the rose is my favorite flower."

"Good." Johnny picked up his crossword puzzle and continued to play.

"No!" I said. "I want to change that to tulip. No! Make that a rose! I can't decide. I love them both."

Johnny laughed. "Okay."

"Why?"

"Just curious."

I slid into the bed and rubbed against Johnny, deliberately making noises, trying to distract him from his all-too-important crossword puzzle.

"Is this your idea of a date?"

"Huh?" Johnny chuckled. "This is a perfect date. We partied. We ate. And now we're ending up in bed together. What else is there?"

"This!" I crawled on top of him and kissed his chest.

Johnny tossed his crossword puzzle to the side. "Are you sure you want to do this?"

"What do you think?"

Johnny pulled me closer to him and kissed me. I couldn't get over the size of his massive chest. As we kissed, I continued to rub it over and over. Squeezing it; kissing it; caressing it. It was so defined and toned.

"Oh my God, I love your chest."

"You do?"

"It feels so good; I could sleep here all night."

Johnny gently rolled me off of him. "Good, that's a good idea."

"What's the matter? Aren't you attracted to me?"

"I am very attracted to you, but I'd rather wait and see what's going to happen between us before we do this."

"Are you serious?"

"Yeah." Johnny chuckled. "Hasn't a man ever told you no before?"

"And meant it?" I asked shockingly.

"Yes."

"No. No, not and meant it."

"It's not that I don't want to," Johnny said. "It's just that I think I want more from you than sex."

"Wow!" I said, turning on my back. "I don't believe this."

"Hey, come here." Johnny pulled me to him. "I've done that my whole life and it's gotten me nothing but immediate gratification."

"I understand what you're saying, but it's still kind of embarrassing for a woman to be rejected by a man."

"Would it make you feel better if I asked you to make love to me and you told me no?"

"Yes. Much better." I stuck out my bottom lip.

"Okay, here we go," Johnny said. "Would you please make love to me, Alicia?"

"HELL no!"

CHAPTER FIVE

The next morning we woke up to constant pounding on the door. Johnny got up and peeked through the peephole.

"Who is it?"

"Room service!"

"Oh," Johnny whispered, slightly opening the door. "I didn't order room service."

"Get up, boy!" Michael said, walking past Johnny and shocking the hell out of me.

"Mike!" Johnny exclaimed. I guess he was surprised, too.

I don't know why I reached for the blanket; it's not like I was naked or anything.

"What are you doing that for?" Michael snapped. "It's not like I haven't seen you naked before."

"It's timeout for those type of jokes, Mike," Johnny said.

"I'm serious. Why are you covering yourself, Alicia? Have you told my brother how you and I had sex? You seem to tell everything else."

I didn't know what was going on, but Michael was upset and going the hell off on me.

"Mike, are you joking or what?" Johnny asked.

"Hell no, I'm not joking! Did you tell my brother about how we had sex, Alicia?"

I wanted to let Johnny and Michael talk it out themselves but he had gone too damn far!

"Why are you acting like an asshole, Michael?"

"Asshole? I know all about your asshole, don't I?"

"Mike, I think you need to leave, man," Johnny said.

"I'll leave, but answer one question first, Alicia!"

I could only assume that Michael had snapped because he was pissed, thinking that Johnny and I'd had sex.

"Michael, what's the matter with you? I asked you, and you said you were all right with this!"

"I don't give a damn about you and Johnny, Alicia! You were supposed to be my friend!"

"I am your friend, Michael! What are you talking about?"

"If you're my friend, Alicia." Michael sat on the bed and shook his head. I jumped off the bed; I didn't know what that fool was going to do. "Why would you play your little office girl games? Huh?"

"What games? What are you talking about?"

"You told everyone in the office about us! All the time I was thinking you and I were such good friends and all the time you were making a fool out of me behind my back!"

"Michael, it's not like that!" I said, trying to make him understand that I didn't purposely try to hurt him.

"Cynthia knows, Alicia! You told Cynthia!"

"Michael, I didn't tell Cynthia anything!"

"Then how does she know?"

"I don't know, but I didn't tell her!"

"You had to tell someone, because she knows!"

"I'm sorry that Cynthia knows but I didn't tell her anything! I swear to God!"

"That's bullshit, Alicia! From now on, don't you say anything to me! You don't know me, as far as I'm concerned."

Michael threw the blanket at me and started to walk out of the door. On his way out, Johnny tried to talk to him, "Mike, what's this all about, man?"

"Johnny, you're my brother and I love you, but please take your hands off of me before I forget who you are!"

Johnny released Michael's arm, and he watched him walk out. He turned to me and then apologized.

"Hey, I'm sorry about that."

"I have never seen Michael act that way."

"I know." Johnny sighed. "I'm sorry; I have to go check on my brother."

"Go ahead! I understand."

Johnny washed up quickly, threw on some clothes, and headed out of the door. I was putting on my clothes as he was leaving.

"Can I call you later?" Johnny asked, standing in the doorway.

I forced a smile. "You better."

Later on that day, I received a call from Lisa asking me to meet her and the office girls at Michael's. I told her that I didn't think that he wanted us around. She told me that Tina needed us. That was all I needed to hear.

When we got there, Tina was on the verge of a breakdown. When she went to go pick up her kids, her mother-in-law refused to give them back. I can't begin to imagine how she felt.

Michael called his friend, Robert, who was his ex-wife's current husband, and who also worked with the Atlanta Police Department, to help. Robert, Michael and Johnny went to Tina's mother-in-law's house and the next thing we know, Robert was calling Tina to pick up her kids. The office girls piled in our cars and went over with Tina to show our support.

It was wild! I thought Wanda and that old lady were going to square off right there on her front lawn. The police had to restrain that crazy-ass Wanda. That heffa drives us nuts with that mouth of hers, but she doesn't take any shit off of anybody when it comes to one of her office girls.

That incident allowed everybody the opportunity to let out a little steam and realize our problems could be much worse. Michael and I made up. Michael and Cynthia really made up. They made up to the point of where he asked her to marry him. And guess what? She accepted. Good for them.

JOHNNY SPENT A FEW MORE DAYS IN ATLANTA, and we really made the most of that time. I spent every night in his hotel room. Nothing happened those first few nights; we talked and then we slept. His last night, we went dancing and then, afterward, we went back to his hotel and I put on one of his huge T-shirts. We lit a few candles and he held me in his arms.

"I can't believe I've gotten this close to you so soon," Johnny said.

"This does seem unreal, doesn't it? It's like a fantasy come true."

"This may seem clichéd but I never thought I'd ever feel this way about a woman. I've always thought that making love was about having sex and then saying the words, '*I love you*,' during, or after an orgasm. But with you, Alicia, I feel like sex is inconsequential. It feels like I'm having an orgasm every single time I touch you."

"Is that right?" I rubbed my body against Johnny's trying to get him to put his words to action. "I want to make love to you."

"The next woman I make love to is going to be my wife."

"Hmm! Is that right?"

"Oh, yeah," Johnny said. "I'm putting all of this on lock, until I say I do."

"What is that?" I asked, laughing out loud.

"What is what?" Johnny asked back.

"What is all that, '*I'm putting all of this on lock, until I say I do*'?" I laughed, mimicking Johnny. "Please don't try to speak Negro."

"Ah, here we go with the urban vernacular jokes." Johnny chuckled. "Go ahead, get them all out. Criticize me for speaking the English language as it should be spoken."

"Go 'head," I joked, sticking my tongue in Johnny's mouth, and catching him off guard. "Say something articulate!"

"Pulchritude," Johnny said. I didn't know what the hell it meant, but it sounded intelligent.

"Oh God." I reached into Johnny's shorts and grabbed his penis. Wowee! I thought Michael was well-endowed. "What does that word mean?"

"Beautiful," Johnny moaned. He rested his head against the headboard as I massaged his enormous stick up and down with my hand.

"Say something else intelligent, schoolboy." I kissed his neck, his chest, and then his stomach.

"Ah…" Johnny sighed as his body tensed. "Acquiesce."

"Mmm." I licked the head of Johnny's stick with my tongue. His legs trembled and he slid all the way down the bed until he was lying flat on his back. "What does that mean, schoolboy?"

I engulfed the entire head of his penis in my mouth and then went down as far as I could. I held my mouth in that position, until my eyes were about to pop out of my head and then I came back up, gagging and gasping for air.

"Oh shit!" Johnny grabbed a handful of my hair, and twisted it in his fingers. "It means, ah, it means to consent without protest."

I started to pump his penis faster and faster with my hand, as I sucked him ferociously. "Talk to me, schoolboy!"

"Copulation!" Johnny yelled out.

"What does that mean, schoolboy?"

"It means to have sex, baby!" Johnny mumbled. "Ah, that feels so good!"

"You wanna have sex with me, schoolboy?" I removed my mouth from his penis and waved it from side to side. "Huh? You wanna put this inside of me?"

"Yeah, baby."

Men are such simple creatures. All that it took was a little seduction and a stroke to Johnny's intellectual ego and I had made the man change his stance on marriage and morality. A few more requests for intellectual words and I would have made him switch from Republican to Democrat.

I climbed on top of him, placing my legs on either side, and then put his head at the entrance of my vagina. I lowered myself down, feeling the initial sensation of penetration. I never got the chance to put it all inside of me, because I swear, it felt so good, I didn't know whether to have an orgasm or piss all over myself. My legs shook, chill bumps covered my body and I came, and came and came.

I was embarrassed by my premature orgasm. Yes, women have them, too. The terminology may differ, but the upside for us is that the result from a woman's premature orgasm encourages more sex in lieu of a man's, which shuts down the entire party.

"Whoa," Johnny said. "What was that?"

"Damn, schoolboy," I said, still breathing heavily. "That was incredible."

"I haven't even gotten started yet."

"That's fine. Neither have I."

I rolled on my back, pulling Johnny on top of me. I opened my thighs as wide as they could go, and prepared for him to enter. He positioned himself between my legs and waited for me to guide his stick inside of me. I held his thick head in my hand and closed my eyes as I felt him force my vagina lips out of the way. I plunged my fingernails in his arms, lifted my head from the bed and bit into his chest.

"SHIT!" I screamed. "Oh my, God!"

"Ah, shit!" Johnny yelled. He moved his chest from my mouth and rammed me hard with his stick.

"OH GOD!" I screamed. "Oh, baby!"

Johnny grabbed my legs and placed them over his shoulders. He pushed my legs backward to where my feet were touching the headboard. I wasn't as young as I used to be but I still had the skills to maneuver my body where it needed to go in order to get the job done.

"Baby, you're all up in my stomach!" I moaned.

"Is it deep, baby?" Johnny asked.

"Oh hell yeah!" I screamed. I planted my toes against the headboard and pushed off, giving me leverage to bounce my hips up and down. "You better not stop pounding me, schoolboy!"

"You like that?" Johnny pounded me harder and harder.

"Yeah." I looked him straight in the eyes. "You know you wanted this all the time! Didn't you?"

"Yeah, baby!" Johnny moaned as his body stiffened. "Oh, I'm about to come, baby!"

"You better wait for me!" I increased the speed of my hips. "You better wait for me, niggah!"

"Oh, I'm getting ready to come, baby!" Johnny slowed down his thrusts and gave one long incredible stroke that must have touched my G-spot because I exploded immediately.

"SHIT!" I shouted. "SHIT! SHIT! SHIT! SHIT! SHIT! SHIT!"

I wanted to say more, but that was the only word that would come out of my mouth. My gosh! I knew Johnny was meant to be my man at that moment, because, for the first time in my life, I felt love, while making love. He didn't need all the gimmicks that Julian used, or the counterfeit romance that other men had tried. He gave me his love and he received my love. It was a wonderful feeling. The only other time I had come close to feeling that way was with Michael.

"I'm coming too, baby!" Johnny shouted.

I dropped my legs from the headboard and wrapped them around Johnny. I slid them up and down the back of his legs as Johnny continued to release his juice inside of me.

"I love you, baby!" Johnny shouted.

I thought to myself, did this niggah just say he loved me? He knows that he doesn't love me. Shit, he just met me. Even though I think he spoiled the moment by overdramatizing the climax, I went along with it.

"I love you, too, baby!" I screamed back.

What was I supposed to do? Ignore the fact of that fool screaming that he loved me in my ear? Scream back that I didn't love him? That was a difficult situation.

"Oh my, God," Johnny said as he continued to move inside of me. "Oh, that felt good."

"Oh yeah, baby." I rubbed Johnny's sweaty back. "Damn, I needed that." He rolled over.

"I meant what I said, Alicia."

"Meant what?"

"I meant what I said about the next woman I made love to, was going to be my wife."

"Boy, I'm not one of those naïve women that you have to create some big fantasy for, in order to have a good time."

"So, is that all this was to you?" Johnny asked. "A good time?"

"No, I'm not saying that."

"Then what are you saying?"

"I'm saying you've only known me three days and you tell me that you love me the first time we make love. That's impossible!"

"Anything is possible when it comes to being in love. It depends upon the individual."

"Aren't you a psychologist? You should know better than that."

"Know better than what?"

"Than to believe in love at first sight."

"Love is an imperfect science because it's associated with human feelings," Johnny said. "I met you three days ago, but I feel like I've known you my entire life. I feel like when I leave Atlanta, I'm going to be leaving behind a piece of me. Time can't dictate that."

"So what are you saying, Johnny?"

"I'm saying I want you to be my wife."

"Don't play with me." I laughed.

"Does it look like I'm playing?"

"Listen, this is crazy; we just met. We need time to get to know one another."

"We just did." Johnny kissed me on my forehead. "So what's your answer?"

"Answer to what?"

"Are you going to be my wife or not?"

"Can I get back to you on that one?"

"Of course. So long as you get back to me before we leave this hotel room."

"Uh, okay?" I replied and asked simultaneously.

Johnny and I fell asleep. The next morning, Johnny didn't mention his marriage proposal and I sure as hell wasn't going to mention it. I drove him to the airport and dropped him off. We kissed good-bye and I thought to myself, I really had a strong connection with him, but on the other hand, experience had me emotionally prepared to never see him again.

WHEN WE WENT BACK TO WORK AFTER THE NEW YEAR'S HOLIDAY, we had an awful lot to talk about. Everybody was congratulating Michael and Cynthia on their engagement. Jaline, our manager, called Michael and Cynthia into her office and congratulated them personally. Something much more than congratulations went on in that office because when Michael came out, he was highly pissed off.

As a woman, I can appreciate working under other women, but Jaline was a complete asshole who loved being in charge. She used her authority to micromanage the office. She also felt that she was above us because she was white and the majority of us were black. All I can say is thank God that bitch was gone most of the time.

Michael quit and stormed out of the office. It was cute watching Cynthia running after him. I was like, *"aw, look at Cynt-Cynt, supporting her man."* Of course we started to gossip. Everybody had a different rumor for what may have happened.

Ms. Virginia left work early, too. For a minute, we thought she had quit, along with Cynthia and Michael. But she came back the next morning, ready for work as usual.

I arrived at work very early. I needed to catch up with some of my neglected workload from the holidays. When I got to my desk, there was a note telling me that I had a meeting with Jaline. I think that was my first one-on-one meeting that wasn't associated with my annual review. I was on probation but it couldn't have been about that because I was performing much better. Tazzy or Susan usually handled those types of situations, anyway.

After I logged on to my computer, I went to Jaline's office.

"Good morning, Jaline," I said as I stepped into her office. "You wanted to see me?"

"Yes, Alicia, please have a seat."

I sat down nervously, waiting for Jaline to drop a bomb on me. I was not disappointed. She was short and straight to the point.

"I'm sure you're curious about why I called you into my office."

"Very much so."

"Well, you've been on probation the past three months and I've reviewed your progress thus far and, regrettably, I have to say that I'm not happy with the results."

"Okay." I was still uncertain of which way she was going. "So that means what?"

"It means that I'm going to have to let you go."

"Let me go?" I was totally surprised. I was expecting perhaps a verbal reprimand, but definitely not termination.

"Yes, I'm afraid so," Jaline said, with her hands folded on top of her desk. "Normally, this would call for immediate termination, but Susan and Tazzy suggested we give you two weeks to try to find something else. That being said, we wish you luck in your future endeavors."

I looked at Jaline, and she looked at me. Neither one of us said a word. I couldn't believe that woman was actually firing me.

"Is there anything else I can help you with?" Jaline asked, as if to say to me, "Why are you still here, bitch?"

"I, I, guess not."

"Then have a good day."

Luckily, I had come to work early to try to catch up on some of my work so there were no other office girls there, sparing me unwanted embarrassment. Tazzy and Susan came to my desk to say good-bye.

"Hey, we didn't have anything to do with this," Susan said. "We told Jaline that your work performance is back to exceeding job expectations. She's just trying to be a hard-ass."

"Girl, I am so sorry," Tazzy said, wiping her eyes. "I wish that I could do something."

"Tazzy, girl, you better not be crying. This is just a job; I came in looking for a job, and I'll go out looking for a job. No biggie!"

"Come here." Tazzy hugged me. "But you were one of the ones who never terrorized me."

"Me, too." Susan hugged me as well. "Keep in touch."

"Keep in touch for what?" Ms. Virginia asked.

"I just got fired, Ms. Virginia." I smiled as I was putting my personal items in a box.

"By who?" Ms. Virginia placed her coffee cup on my desk.

"That old witch in there." I pointed toward Jaline's office.

"Why is she firing you?"

"Because she said I haven't raised my level of performance since I've been on probation."

"Has she?" Ms. Virginia asked Tazzy and Susan.

"Yes, ma'am," Tazzy said.

"Girl, put your stuff back on that desk; you're not going any-where."

"But Jaline said…" I was saying before Ms. Virginia interrupted.

"What did I say?" Ms. Virginia pointed to my desk. "Put that stuff back!"

"Yes, ma'am."

"I'll be right back."

Ms. Virginia turned around and walked into Jaline's office.

"I'll wait for the outcome before I put all of my stuff back on this desk," I said as I sat in my chair.

"If Ms. Virginia says hitch a plow to a mosquito, don't ask any questions; hitch that plow and ride." Tazzy laughed.

"What in '*THEE*' hell does that mean, Tazzy?" I chuckled.

"That means unpack your shit."

I started to unpack my box and place my things back on my desk. A few minutes later, Ms. Virginia and Jaline walked out of Jaline's office and came to my desk. Tazzy and Susan conveniently walked away when they saw them coming.

"Alicia," Jaline said. "We're going to extend your probation another three months to give you time to show us what you can do. We have faith that you won't disappoint us."

"Thank you, Jaline."

"You're welcome." Jaline walked away with her hands behind her back.

"Thank you, too, Ms. Virginia," I said, kissing her on the cheek.

"Oh, you're welcome, sweetheart."

You're probably wondering how Ms. Virginia had so much clout that she could get my job back without being one of the supervisors. It's because she used to be the supervisor before Tazzy. They created the manager's position for Jaline after Ms. Virginia stepped down as supervisor.

Jaline, Tazzy and Susan respected Ms. Virginia. The whole office respected Ms. Virginia. She was older than all of us by many years and served as the surrogate mother. If anybody wanted trouble, you tried disrespecting Ms. Virginia.

Pam was the only one of us who had ever dared. She had issues with Ms. Virginia for helping Tazzy get the supervisor position. She thought she was next in line, and if not her, at least someone else internally. She used to trip with Tazzy and Ms. Virginia until Ms. Virginia got tired of that shit and Pam got her ass told off. Believe me, she left Ms. Virginia alone after that.

Not long after almost being fired, I suffered one of the hardest trials of my life. I had always thought that I was only a strait-jacket away from being clinically insane, but when I found out that I was pregnant, I became suicidal.

I took three pregnancy tests, and all three were positive. I refused to accept that I was pregnant so I went to my gynecologist for a professional examination. Positive! I went behind my gynecologist's back and had a clinic examine me. Positive! My last resort was prayer. I went to see a priest; hell, I'm not even Catholic, but I went anyway to try to pray my way out of it. Positive! God wasn't having it. I was forced to accept the inevitable. I was about to become a single mother. For me to accept the inevitable was one thing, but I had no idea how the father would feel. Which brought forth the next stressful ordeal. Who the hell was the father?

When Johnny and I had sex, we didn't use a condom. When Michael and I had sex, we used a condom, but not every time. Julian was my boyfriend and I didn't use a condom with him. Well, with all of that free love and no protection I had to figure out which one of these men was my child's father.

The notion of having to explain to three men that one of them was the father of my child weighed heavily on my conscience. Think about it, the poor bastards would have to wait the remainder of my pregnancy to find out which one would receive the prize. Perhaps I should say, sur-prize, of an unexpected lifelong commitment.

Keeping my little secret bottled up brought on tremendous stress. I slipped into a deep state of depression, hoping the situation would cure itself. My depression started to affect both my personal and professional life. I withdrew from the office girls and my work performance suffered severely.

One morning, I got up to go to work. When I was about to step into the shower, I looked into the mirror and I noticed my stomach protruding from my body. My pregnancy was beginning to show. I was proud to be a thirty-something woman with the flat stomach of an eighteen-year-old, but motherhood was changing all of that.

I dropped the lid of my toilet and sat on the stool. I looked down at my jagged, half-polished toenails and decided that was the last straw. I had been through so much in my life and looking at my pitiful feet was the last straw! I put my hand over my stomach and I sat in my bathroom and cried and cried and cried. When I finished crying, I stood up and looked in the mirror.

My eyes were puffy and baggy. My skin was loose and saggy. My hair was long and nappy. And my spirit was broken and unhappy. Never said that I was a poet.

I opened my medicine cabinet and I pulled out a bottle of pills that my doctor had prescribed for me years earlier. The bottle was still almost full; apparently, I thought it best to ignore the doctor's advice. Well, they would come in handy for my mission on that day.

I grabbed the bottle of pills and ran water into an empty glass. I went into my bedroom and sat in the middle of my bed. I fluffed the pillows behind me and swallowed all of the pills in the bottle, one handful at a time. They didn't have an immediate effect, so I put on some music to die to.

As I reached for my favorite artist, Phyllis Hyman, I could feel my eyes fill with tears. I didn't feel sadness. I didn't feel pain. So I don't know why I was beginning to cry. I guess it was because I knew relief was in sight. Relief from sadness! Relief from pain! Relief from disappointment, struggling and shame! Again, I never said I was a poet. I turned the volume up as loud as it would go, and closed my eyes momentarily.

I pushed repeat, and went back to my bed. As the words, *"Somewhere in my lifetime,"* began to reverberate across the room, I smiled and enjoyed the moment. I recall hearing the entire song, although I could have just heard bits and pieces as it played over and over.

I tried to pray and ask God for forgiveness. If indeed suicide was the unforgivable sin, I was still going to take a chance that God was a forgivable God. I took deep breaths, waiting for the great moment of death to arrive. However, it didn't come with a bang; it came peacefully. Just as I did every single night, I closed my eyes, but instead of welcoming sleep, I welcomed death...

CHAPTER SIX

When I woke from death, Ms. Virginia, Cynthia and Pam were standing above me. I could barely understand what they were saying. They were smiling and talking, but I just couldn't understand what they were saying. I was experiencing my worst nightmare. Sleep paralysis! I wanted to scream and tell them, look, I'm not dead! But I couldn't speak.

They were looking me straight in my face but were not responding to me. I tried to kick! I tried to sit up! I tried to scream! But I couldn't do anything! I moved my eyes from side to side, trying to recognize my surroundings. Wherever I was, it wasn't the familiar environment of my bedroom.

I started to feel drowsy but, as much as I tried to stay awake, I couldn't resist falling asleep. I felt that if I fell asleep I would surely die. At that point, I didn't want to die anymore. I wanted to live, and I wanted to live to redeem myself. I did not want to die like a coward who couldn't face the trials and tribulations of life. I wanted my life to have meaning. I wanted my child to live and respect me as a mother and a fighter. I decided to fight to stay awake. I decided to fight to stay alive. I batted my eyes frantically to remain conscious, but try as I may, slowly but surely, I drifted back to sleep.

The next time I opened my eyes, Ms. Virginia and Cynthia were standing at my bedside. I didn't try getting their attention;

they wouldn't respond anyway. I turned my eyes toward Cynthia and focused on her eyes. I stared intensely, I mean, I didn't blink one time. Finally, she smiled and then spoke to me.

"Oh my God!" Cynthia said. "Welcome back!"

"Hey, sweetheart, I am so glad to see you open your eyes!" Ms. Virginia said.

I wanted to speak, but I couldn't. It was as if I had no control over my body. I started to move my eyes around the room and realized that I was in a hospital. I was connected to an oxygen machine and had intravenous cords running in and out of my body. I remember thinking, *what have I done to myself?*

I was a pitiful excuse for a woman. All the pain that had happened to me in my life had been self-inflicted. Men! My job! Myself! Everything that had happened to me, I had allowed it to happen. I had a choice to make. A choice to die in that hospital room, or get my ass out of that bed and stop feeling sorry for myself.

"Hey, sweetheart, can you talk?" Ms. Virginia asked.

I felt like I had the ability to speak; I just didn't have the energy. I responded by nodding my head very slowly.

"Good! Good! That's my girl!"

"It's about time you woke your butt up." Pam peeked over Cynthia's shoulder. "Get up!"

You can't imagine how good it felt to know that people actually cared about me. I looked at Ms. Virginia on one side of my bed, and the two least likely of people for obvious reasons, Pam and Cynthia, on the other side.

"You have to hurry up and get out of here because we have to go shopping," Cynthia joked.

"You better put some makeup on that heffa first." Pam laughed. "This is my first time seeing you without your war paint, Alicia. All I can say is you must clean up very well."

"Yeah, she's not as pretty as people think, is she?" Cynthia added.

"And everybody's going to be coming in here looking at her without her makeup because I'm not putting on nothing!" Pam said.

"You're right," Ms. Virginia said. "I think I do see a pimple right there on the tip of her nose."

They were instigating to get me to react and when Ms. Virginia joined in, their plan worked. Enough was enough.

"Pass my makeup bag, please," I whispered.

"There you go, girl!" Cynthia said.

"Boy, you light-skinned, pretty heffas!" Pam said. "Can't do nothing without your makeup kit!"

"You know you're still the prettiest of the prettiest," Ms. Virginia said.

It didn't take long before my mind began to clear and my speech became much more understandable. Ms. Virginia, Pam and Cynthia didn't leave my side. They had to know what happened and I wanted to explain so that I wouldn't appear insane.

"What happened?" I asked the question because I wanted to know how much they knew before I admitted to a suicide attempt.

"I don't know, you tell us, sweetheart," Ms. Virginia said as she rubbed my head.

"I mean, how did I get here?"

"We'll tell you, after you tell us," Pam said.

"Things have been so hard for me lately. It seemed like life was getting worse and worse. Normally, if I wasn't feeling up, I could, you know, find a man to regain that confidence."

"Hold on," Pam said. "Why do you need a man for confidence? You're beautiful! You got a good job! You're intelligent! You don't need a man for confidence. You can use what the rest of us women use when we need a pick-me-up. Look at the woman next to you and say, *'I know I look better than her.'*"

The four of us laughed. Pam had a good point, because I would use that pick-me-up line in a minute.

"Well, it's not just that. I'm about to get fired from that so-called good job you're talking about. I don't know; I guess I got tired of struggling. Death seemed so peaceful."

"Stop talking like that!" Ms. Virginia said. "You don't rush death! You deal with life as it comes. Good or bad. You don't disappoint God by showing Him you don't believe He'll pull you through."

I never really thought of suicide as disappointing God. I kind of figured He wouldn't be too happy about it. But I never considered it from that perspective.

"I'm sorry," I said apologetically. "I didn't mean to put you all through this."

"You don't plan on trying anything like this again, do you?" Cynthia asked. "Because when we went shopping that day, I really thought that you wanted to be my friend. I thought you wanted to get to know me."

"I did," I said. "I mean, I do."

Cynthia looked at me and I could feel the sincerity of her words when she spoke.

"If you're my friend, Alicia," Cynthia said, "don't you ever, I mean *e-ver* try anything like this again. Do you understand me?"

"Yes." I was so overwhelmed with emotions I was barely able to speak.

"Now that Sleeping Beauty has awakened, I think I'll be going home to get a nap," Ms. Virginia said.

After Ms. Virginia left, we decided to have a girl talk and get everything out in the open. We were all aware that Michael had been the object of all our romantic interests and we needed to know where everybody stood.

"So, I guess it's up to me to kick this party off, huh?" Pam said.

"What party?" Cynthia said.

"Y'all know what party! The Michael Forrester party."

"I don't know nothing about a Michael Forrester party," I said.

"I wanna know," Cynthia said.

"Okay! I was with Mike a few times, but it was strictly sex," Pam said.

"Okay," Cynthia said. "And you?"

"Well, Michael and I had sex a couple of times, too," I said. I wanted to tell the truth and say our relationship was much more than sex, but I didn't think that was what Cynthia needed, or wanted to hear at that time. "Our relationship was purely sex, too. We were both lonely, and working together made it convenient for us to get together."

"Are you two sure?" Cynthia asked. "Mike and I are going to be getting married soon and I don't want any residual relationships lingering."

"Mike is like my brother now," Pam said. "Ain't nothing going on with us."

"I'm not going to say we're like sisters and brothers, but there's absolutely nothing going on between us. Believe me, he loves you, Cynthia," I said. "And I'm not thinking about anybody but Johnny."

"Speaking of which, how did that happen?" Pam asked.

"I don't know, girl." I laughed. "But I'm glad it did."

Cynthia giggled. "I was about to ask the same thing!"

I looked at her. "So are we cool with everything?"

"I'm good," Cynthia said.

"Are you sure, Cynt?"

Cynthia smiled. "I am now."

"Good," I said.

Pam poked out her lip. "Everybody got a man but me."

"If you fix that attitude, you'll get a man, too," Cynthia said.

"I'm kind of going a little off base here, but I want to ask a favor of you two," I said.

"What's up?" Pam asked.

"How many people know what happened today?"

"Nobody knows the specifics, Alicia," Cynthia said.

"When you didn't come into the office, and didn't call, we were worried about you because that's just not you. If you're going to be late, or not show, you call every time. The three of us decided to find out what was up, so we went to your house. We got your landlord to let us in and we found you knocked out on your bed," Pam said.

"My nosy-ass landlord!"

"You better be glad you got a nosy-ass landlord," Pam joked.

"Wow," I said. "Thank God, y'all got to me in time."

Pam asked, "So what's your favor?"

"I don't want anyone else to ever know what happened today."

"It's nobody's business," Pam said.

"Pam's right; it's nobody's business," Cynthia said.

"But what about when you and Michael are exchanging deep secrets?" I asked. "I don't want him to know, because he may tell Johnny. I don't want anybody to know. Not Michael! Not Johnny! Not any of the girls from the office. Nobody! Okay?"

"Okay, girl," Cynthia said. "That's your business; we told you."

"I have something else to say that's been stressing me out," I said. "I don't really know how to say this; it's so unbelievable. At first, I was completely stressed out, but now, I'm happy. I'm glad I've been blessed and no matter what happens, I'll love my child with all of my heart. I guess you all have figured out that I'm pregnant!"

I looked at Cynthia and Pam, but neither one of them reacted the way that I expected.

"I expected a little more enthusiasm than that, ladies."

"This is not easy for me to say, Alicia," Cynthia said softly.

"What?" I looked back and forth at Pam and Cynthia. "What's wrong?"

"I'm sorry, Alicia," Cynthia said. "You lost the baby."

My heart was shattered into a million pieces. I couldn't breathe and started to hyperventilate. Pam ran to the door and screamed for the nurse. Cynthia wiped my head and then I blacked out.

When I woke up, Pam and Cynthia were gone. But lying next to me on my pillow were roses and tulips. Sitting across from me, bundled in a small chair, was Johnny. I moved around to face him and the sound of the bed woke him up.

"Hey, sleepyhead," Johnny said.

"What are you doing here?" I mumbled.

"I came here to relieve your friends."

"Isn't it past visiting hours?"

"Yeah, but your nurse felt like she could bend the rules a little for a man who had flown all the way from the frontlines of Iraq to see his sick fiancée."

"You liar." I laughed. "What happened to me? I remember talking to Cynthia and Pam and then I blacked out. Did they tell you what happened?"

My heart felt like it was beating a million times a minute as I waited for Johnny's response.

"Yeah, sweetheart," Johnny said. "They said you're completely stressed out."

"Stressed?" I asked.

"Yeah, baby, you have to relax."

"Oh my God." I picked up the flowers on my pillow. "You remembered."

"How could I forget?"

"Thanks, schoolboy."

"Look," Johnny said, "You need somebody to take care of you, young lady."

"And I suppose you're the somebody for the job?"

"Who else?" Johnny said as he was going into his pocket. "Alicia, I want to offer you this ring, with a promise that I will never, ever take my love away. If you believe in me, baby, our forever will start today."

I blushed. "What are you trying to say to me?"

"Will you marry me, Alicia?"

"Is this a joke?"

Johnny looked at me very sincerely. "Am I laughing?"

"Oh my God! Yes! Yes, I'll marry you!"

"Good," Johnny said. "As soon as you get out of here, we can get started on making us some little Johnnies and Alicias."

As Johnny spoke, I realized what really caused me to have that stress. It was the devastating news of the loss of my child. I prayed to God to spare me from the embarrassment of having to tell those three men that one of them was the father of my child. Sometimes you get what you pray for.

MICHAEL AND CYNTHIA WERE MARRIED A FEW WEEKS LATER and honeymooned on some Caribbean island. We were slightly pissed because they screwed up their flight arrangements and weren't present for the wedding reception we had for them in Atlanta.

After their wedding, they didn't visit the office as much. Pam, Tina and I became very close and we started to hang out more outside of the office girls' group.

Cynthia began to talk about starting a marketing firm and she asked us to become partners. Come on now, can you imagine me in public relations? I don't think so.

But let me tell you something, the more Cynthia talked, the more excited I became. The more excited I became about becoming an entrepreneur, the more disinterested I became with Upskon. My decision to leave Upskon was a tragic one that almost drained the very life out of me.

The day started out as any other day. We came to work and had our little morning meeting and that was that. We worked, joked, ate; we did everything business as usual.

We were excited because we were going to be celebrating Cynthia and Michael's wedding later that evening. We had complained so much about them bailing out on their wedding reception, they felt obligated to redeem themselves.

They were expecting a small get-together with just the office girls. What they didn't know was that we had gone behind their backs and invited everybody in Atlanta.

Everybody had different responsibilities. My duty was so insignificant I don't even remember what it was, which goes to tell how much they respected my organizational skills. I didn't care, though. It didn't hurt my feelings. Workflow was slow so Tazzy gave us a few extra minutes for lunch to prepare for Cynthia and Michael's party.

"Listen, ladies, you all can extend your thirty-minute lunch breaks this afternoon. Just don't leave at the same time. We are almost out of claims so we all may be getting out of here early today, anyway," Tazzy said.

"Tina, are we still meeting the Forresters for lunch? They said they had some big news for us," Ms. Virginia said.

"Uh-huh, oh, that reminds me! Don't forget, everybody, Mike and Cynthia's belated wedding party is tonight at my house," Tina said.

"We know! We know! Party at your house, Tina," Darsha said.

"Boy, you know when niggahs get new shit, they got to show it off."

When Michael and Cynthia were married, Tina moved into her own house, so the party was just as much a house warming as it was a wedding reception.

"You damn skippy!" Tina said.

"They been married for damn near a year now, Tina," Wanda said.

"It's only been a couple of months, girl, so stop tripping!"

"I'm about to leave, Tina, so give me your debit card and I'll deposit the money for the party into your account." Ms. Virginia held out her hand.

"Okay, everything is already ordered; I just have to go pick it up."

"Damn, Tina, Ms. Virginia is like your husband," Wanda stated.

"I don't even want to hear this." Ms. Virginia laughed. "Bye, ladies!"

"Me neither," Tina said. "Oh, Ms. Virginia, don't be late for our lunch date with Cynt and Mike."

"I'll probably get there before you."

"I don't think so because I'm leaving now."

Tina and Ms. Virginia left for lunch together. The rest of us left in different groups. When I got back, there were police everywhere. They had Upskon on lockdown. We were standing in the parking lot like it was a fire drill.

They started to let us in one by one. By the time I got into our office, some of the office girls were already there. It was chaotic. People were asking questions and Tazzy didn't have the answers. God bless her, she was trying her best to maintain control.

"What in the world is going on out there?" I said, hurrying to clock back in.

"We're still trying to find out," Susan said.

Tazzy walked out of her office and said, "At this point, ladies, we still don't know exactly what has happened. But we do know that we are not allowed to leave our office until security notifies us."

Wanda rushed into the office, breathing heavily and very excited.

"Guess what? Two people got shot up here at Upskon and they dead!"

"How do you know, Wanda?" Darsha asked.

"The police told me!"

"Wanda, why would the police tell you anything, and not security?"

"'Cause I'm inquisitive, that's why!"

"Wanda is just runnin' her mouth, Tazzy; don't pay no attention to her," Val said.

"I'm just runnin' my mouth, huh?" Wanda said to Val, taking a deep breath to talk as fast as she possibly could. "Two women were speed-walking at approximately twelve forty-five this afternoon. They noticed a conspicuous vehicle parked in the middle of the street at the rear entrance of the Upskon building. They investigated the aforementioned vehicle and noticed two bodies lying in the car. The first body was discovered on the first seat, while the second body was discovered moments later in the rear of the vehicle, perched on the floor."

Tazzy's telephone rang again and she ran into her office to pick it up. Wanda continued to run her mouth.

"The medics arrived at the scene at approximately twelve fifty-three, while the police arrived at twelve fifty-eight. The medics tried gallantly to save their lives but both victims were pronounced dead at the scene. The police are withholding the names of the victims until the family first has been notified." Wanda took a deep sigh, then asked, "What else you wanna know?"

"I hope it wasn't anybody who worked at Upskon," I said.

"Well, at least everybody in our department is here except for Ms. Virginia and Tina," Pam said.

"Tina!" Susan covered her mouth. "Oh my God! Oh, no!"

"What's the matter, Susan?" Pam asked.

"On my way to lunch, I saw a strange man at the door and he wanted to get in. He had flowers and said he was looking for the claims department. At the time, I thought he looked familiar but I was in a hurry so I let him in...I...I...I didn't know!"

"Didn't know what, Susan?" Pam said, quickly interrupting.

"That it was him, Pam!"

"Him who Susan? What are you talking about?"

"It was Curtis! I'm sorry, I didn't realize at the time! I didn't know it was..."

"Somebody call Tina and see if she's all right! Now!" Pam shouted.

Susan covered her mouth and sat in a chair.

"Oh naw, Pam!" Wanda said.

I picked up the telephone and tried to dial.

"I can't think!" I shouted. I was so nervous I couldn't remember Tina's telephone number.

"I got it!" Pam snatched the telephone out of my hand. "She's not answering!"

"Something's wrong! That girl always answers that phone," Wanda said.

"Let's try to remain calm until security lets us know what happened," Pam said.

"I can't stay calm," Wanda said.

"I'm going to talk to Tazzy," Pam said, but before she reached Tazzy's office, Tazzy was on her way out.

"I need everybody to come over here for a second, please." Tazzy was visibly disturbed. "I, uh, I just received some bad news. The police have identified one of the bodies found in the car by a credit card, located on the floor of the car...and it was Tina's."

"Oh no, Tazzy!" I shouted.

"Lord, have mercy!" Wanda screamed.

"What happened, Tazzy?" I asked.

"The security officer said they believe it was a murder-suicide. They believe the man's body is Curtis'. He didn't have any identification on him so they have to wait for positive identification."

"So he killed Tina, and then killed himself?" I asked.

"I'm afraid so," Tazzy said.

"Death ain't good enough for that no-good bastard! They need to cut his di...," Wanda said.

"Wanda, that's not going to help anything," Tazzy interrupted.

"I'll feel better! They need to cut his shit off and burn it up," Darsha said.

"We need to compose ourselves. No other department knows of Tina's death, so upper management wants us to keep this within our department until they send out a memo. So please, as hard as it may be, let's try to get through this day, and get home to our families safely."

"Don't you want to cry, Tazzy? Don't you wanna stop being management for once and be an office girl?" Wanda asked.

"Right now, my job is to be the manager," Tazzy said. "And whether you all like it or not, I will always be an office girl!"

"Look at us," Pam said. "We come to work every day, fussing and complaining about the same ol' bullshit! And with all that Tina had to deal with, she came with a smile on her face. Now it's time for us to stop this and grow the hell up, and start acting like we care about each other! If Tazzy doesn't want to cry, leave her the hell alone, and let her deal with it her way! And if y'all want to cry, cry your eyes out! Tina is dead! Don't you understand? She's dead! Just stop this bickering before I lose it for real!"

Pam lost it! She collapsed in a chair and burst into tears. With everything going on, I was surprised that I was able to maintain my composure as well as I did.

"I'm sorry, Pam!" Wanda hugged Pam tightly. "I'm sorry, baby."

"I'm tired of this shit, Wanda!" Pam shouted hysterically. "I'm tired of it!"

"Come here, Pam." Tazzy pulled her away from Wanda, and then looked her in the eyes. "No more arguing, Pam. It's okay! It's okay!"

"No more." Wanda wrapped her arms around Pam and Tazzy. "No more."

"Oh my God," Lisa said, wiping her eyes. "Ms. Virginia is going to be devastated."

"Tina was her heart," I said.

"Hold on," Darsha said. "Tazzy, didn't you say they identified the body by a credit card?"

"Yeah, why?" Tazzy asked.

"You sure it wasn't a debit card?"

"What difference does it make?"

"Didn't Ms. Virginia have Tina's debit card?" Pam asked.

"Come to think of it, she sure did," Wanda said.

At that moment, Tina burst into the office, running to her desk.

"Tazzy, I'm sorry I'm late but the police wouldn't let me in. I think someone may have been robbed or something 'cause the police are all over the place. Did Ms. Virginia call? I was supposed to meet her at the bank, but I got behind. Then I was supposed to meet her, Cynthia and Mike for lunch, but I was too busy getting ready for tonight."

The entire office stood in silence and stared at Tina.

"What's going on? Why y'all staring at me, like that?"

"Sit down, Tina," Tazzy said. "I have something to tell you."

"What?" Tina jumped out the chair and grabbed Tazzy's arms. "Is something wrong with my kids?"

"No, your kids are fine," Tazzy said.

"Thank God," Tina said relieved. "Then what's wrong?"

"Did you give Ms. Virginia your debit card for lunch?"

"Yeah, she was supposed to be depositing some money in my account for the party tonight. What's up?"

"They found a body outside in a car and we think it's Ms. Virginia."

"What? Are you crazy? I saw Ms. Virginia right before lunch."

"Tina, the woman's body they found outside was identified by your debit card. So that means that it is either you, or Ms. Virginia…" Tazzy paused momentarily. "…and you're here."

"I'm sorry, baby, but you know Tazzy wouldn't lie to you," Wanda said.

"No." Tina shook her head.

"Tina, baby, she's telling the truth," I said.

"No."

"Tina," Tazzy said, "it was Ms. Virginia."

"NOOOOOOOOOOOOOOOOOOOO!" Tina screamed, then fell to her knees. "NO! NO! NO! NO!"

"Tina! Tina!" I shouted, kneeling beside her. I tried to get her to stand but her body was completely limp. "It's going to be all right!"

"NOOOOOOOOOOOOOOOO! NO! Please, God, no!"

Wanda and Tazzy kneeled down beside Tina as well, and tried to help me get Tina to her feet.

"Tina! Tina, she's gone!" Wanda shouted. "She's gone!"

"Let her cry," Pam said. "If she wants to cry, let her cry!"

"Pam's right," Val said. "Just leave her alone!"

We laid her down and watched her as she cried. We consoled her and ourselves, trying to rationalize why anyone would want to kill Ms. Virginia. Once she finished crying, she stayed on the floor in the fetal position, motionless.

Tazzy thought it would be best for everybody to go home and try to deal with the situation away from the office. She had the task of staying behind to explain to the police that they had identified the wrong body. She bought us time with the police to go to Michael and Cynthia's to tell them what happened in person, before they found out about it on the news.

Cynthia did not handle the news very well. The experience, as a whole, took its toll on all of us. But Cynthia was crushed. Like Tina, she refused to accept Ms. Virginia's death. It took her a while, but she finally allowed herself to deal with reality. The joy of finding out she was pregnant earlier in the day started her healing process.

I dealt with Ms. Virginia's death a little differently. I never stepped foot back into that office, its parking lot, or the neighborhood! If I have to go on Peachtree Industrial today, I'll take a side street instead of going past that building.

We took over Ms. Virginia's funeral, making all of the arrangements. We dismissed the pallbearers and decided that we would carry her to her grave. It took all of us, but we did it. It was Wanda's idea. She said that the men chosen didn't know anything about Ms. Virginia and had no business carrying her to her final resting place. We manned up, lifted our matriarch, and walked like proud women. We met at the funeral home and we had planned to ride to the church in a limousine.

"Hey, who picked out the pallbearers for Ms. Virginia?" Wanda asked.

"We left that up to her family," Cynthia said.

"My husband and some of their family members are the pall-bearers," Susan said.

A lot of secrets came out after Ms. Virginia's death. Although we knew that Susan, our white supervisor, was married to a black man, we didn't know he was Ms. Virginia's nephew. As it turned out, Ms. Virginia had anonymously helped Susan get her job at Upskon when they were struggling financially. Another secret was a whopper: When Pam picked up Ms. Virginia's death certificate, she found out Ms. Virginia was her biological mother. Neither one of them knew.

Also, the man who killed Ms. Virginia was her estranged husband who had hunted her for nearly fifty years. He had tried to kill her before on several occasions. Now here's the kicker: the man ended up being Pam's biological father.

When it came time for the funeral, we were so fired up to make sure Ms. Virginia got a respectful sendoff that we were willing to do anything.

"Susan, no disrespect, baby, but Ms. Virginia don't need no welfare pallbearers. She didn't need them to carry her in life and she don't need them to carry her through in death," Wanda said. "Tell them that won't be necessary."

"And what is our back-up plan?" Susan asked.

"Us! We need to be carrying Ms. Virginia, not them," Wanda said.

"Wanda, we can't carry Ms. Virginia's body," Cynthia said. "She's too heavy."

"The hell we can't! She's been carrying all of us ever since we met her. Now are you trying to tell me that she's too heavy for us to carry her now?"

"You know that's not what I'm saying, Wanda," Cynthia said.

"You don't need to be in this anyway, mama." Wanda smiled.

"Just make sure we don't trip on anything and make ourselves look like some fools."

"I got that covered," Cynthia said, giving her the two thumbs-up sign.

"Well…" Wanda grabbed the first handle on the right side of the coffin. "Is anybody going to help me get Ms. Virginia to the church on time, or what?"

"Let's go!" Pam grabbed the other first handle on the left side. "So what y'all gon' do?"

"Let's go," I said, standing behind Wanda.

"Now if this little prissy thang can grab a hold, the rest of y'all need to be shamed."

"Let's go!" Tina grabbed a handle and stood behind Pam.

"Let's go!" Lisa said, standing behind Tina.

"Let's go!" Valerie said, standing behind me.

We struggled momentarily, then we lifted the casket in the air.

"Wait a minute. Where do I lift?" Michael asked. "I'm one of the office girls, too, right?"

"For life!" Wanda said. "Mike, you get the rear to keep us steady. The rest of y'all can get in where you fit in."

We didn't talk very much on the way to the church. The little conversation we did muster was not about Ms. Virginia. We wanted to keep our spirits up because we felt that if one of us cracked, the whole damn group was going to fall to pieces.

When we walked into the church, people were staring at us. I would have stared, too, if I had seen a coffin carried by a group of women pallbearers. We convinced ourselves they were looking because they wanted to give Ms. Virginia her last respects, but we knew some of those looks were straight, *'what the hell?'*

We were silent and walking in order until that damn Wanda opened her mouth and started whispering. Wanda's whisper is like most people's normal volume. The woman never understood the difference between outside and inside voices.

"What the hell they starin' at?" Wanda whispered.

"We're carrying a coffin, Wanda," I answered. "What do you think they're going to do?"

"Naw, they lookin' at us 'cause we women," Wanda said a little louder.

"Wanda, would you shut your big-ass mouth before somebody hears you," Val said.

"I ain't shuttin' shit," Wanda said.

"Do y'all realize that you're in a church?" Lisa asked.

"I know where we at," Wanda said.

"I know where we at, too," Val said.

"Show Ms. Virginia some respect," Tina said. "And shut the hell up."

"Ms. Virginia know how we are," Wanda said. "Ain't no use in actin' funny now."

"Will y'all shut up before we mess up?" Pam said.

"We ain't gon' mess up nothin'! Stop actin' so dam' nervous," Val said.

"Tell 'em, Val," Wanda said.

"SHUT UP!" Tina whispered sternly.

"Tazzy, would you tell them to shut up? People lookin' at us like we crazy," Darsha said.

"We ain't at work; Tazzy can't give no orders up in here. This God's office up in here," Wanda responded.

"I don't care where we are, y'all need to be quiet," Tazzy said.

"Okay, Tazzy," Wanda said, laughing under her breath.

"But I guess Ms. Virginia would appreciate one last laugh from you heffas!" Tazzy smiled and winked at Wanda.

CHAPTER SEVEN

We managed to get through the funeral and eventually moved on with our lives. Johnny and I were married a couple of months later, with only a small group of people. I sold my house and moved into Johnny's home. It was nice and spacious. Much more room than we needed. But definitely the type of house I had always dreamed of living in.

The week of the wedding, I met his daughter, Brittany, for the first time. He was just as anxious to see her as I was to meet her. Her mother, Deirdra, brought her to Atlanta for the wedding a couple of days early. I thought it was very considerate of her. We invited her over for dinner so that she and I could get to know one another prior to the ceremony. It would have been awkward for her to drop Brittany off on the day of the wedding and say, *'By the way, I'm the ex-wife.'*

I was running around, wiping and cleaning everything, making sure the house was spic and span. You know how the ex-wives are always so competitive with the new wives, or is it vice-versa?

We also invited Cynthia, Michael, Brimone and Alexiah to meet the little lady, Brittany. I'm sure she wasn't aware of the reception she was about to receive. On the other hand, neither was I.

"DING-DONG!"

The doorbell rang, and I rushed to the door to open it. As soon as I laid eyes on Brittany, I instantly fell in love with her. She was dressed in a gorgeous bright yellow dress with a matching hat. Her long curly ponytails hung down past her shoulders. She had a cute yellow purse that she hung on her right arm. She was gorgeous. Absolutely gorgeous!

When I looked at Deirdra, based on looks alone, I could certainly see why Johnny had married her. She had beautiful exotic features. Her eyes were light brown, a total contrast to her dark complexion. Her skin was immaculate. I envied her slender shapely hips, still firm breasts, real or paid for, and her ridiculously slim waistline. Despite all of her obvious physical attributes, I would find out later that they were not comparable to the woman's character.

"Hello, Alicia?" Deirdra asked.

"Yes, it's a pleasure to meet you," I said. "Come in."

"Oh my, Alicia," Deirdra said as she looked around. "You have a beautiful home."

"Thank you," I said.

"Hi!" Brittany said as she waved her hand back and forth.

"And who might you be?" I asked, bending over to her face.

"I'm Brittany."

"Is that my little angel?" Johnny said as he walked into the foyer.

"Daddy!" Brittany yelled and then jumped into Johnny's arms.

"How's my angel?"

Johnny was so excited to see Brittany, he forgot that Deirdra and I were standing there.

"Ahem!" Deirdra cleared her throat.

"Oh," Johnny said, "Forgive my manners, Dee, how are you?"

"I'm fine and you?"

"Great! Just great! Glad you could make it," Johnny said.

"No problem."

"Come in the living room and meet your welcoming committee," I said.

Johnny picked up Brittany and the four of us walked into the living room.

"Hey, Dee," Michael said, "It's been a while."

"I know, right?" Deirdra laughed.

Michael and Deirdra hugged each other like old friends.

"Who is that?" Michael pointed at Brittany. "Johnny Junior?"

"Oh…" Johnny laughed. "I forgot all about that. Johnny Junior is actually named Brittany."

"So you don't have a son?" Michael asked.

"No, man," Johnny said. "I just wanted to win the bet."

"What bet?" I asked.

"Mike and I made a bet a long time ago that whoever had the first male child in the family gets a ten thousand dollar check from the other one."

"What?" Cynthia said. "That's sexist."

"Don't even get started, Cynt." Michael reached for Brittany. "Give me my niece, and I want my money back, man."

"If you would have been in contact with the family, you would have known that you had a niece instead of a nephew. That check is cashed and the money is in Brittany's college fund."

"If she wasn't pretty, I'd get my money back." Michael kissed Brittany on the cheek. "But how can I take anything from you? Huh?"

"Deirdra," I said, "Forgive our rudeness; this is my sister-in-law, Cynthia."

"Hi!" Deirdra shook Cynthia's hand. "I've heard so much about you."

"Yes, wife number three," Cynthia joked.

"Number three?" Deirdra asked. "I must have missed wife number two."

"And these are my nieces and Michael's daughters, Brimone and Alexiah," I said.

"Hi, girls." Deirdra waved at them.

"Hi." Brimone waved back.

"Hi," Alexiah said shyly.

"That's your cousin, Brittany." Deirdra pointed to Brittany in Michael's arms.

"Can we play together?" Alexiah asked.

"I'm sure Brittany would love to play with you," Deirdra said, "But on one condition. You have to give me a hug first."

"Okay!" Alexiah ran to Deirdra and gave her a huge hug.

Michael put Brittany on the floor and Alexiah grabbed her by the hand and they disappeared upstairs. My first impression of Deirdra was either she was the greatest actress in the world, or the nicest person in the world. You would have thought she was Mary Poppins, the way she was asking for hugs, smiling and acting all nice to everybody. I mean, just a house full of sunshine. As if she didn't have a care in the world.

Brimone joined Alexiah and Brittany upstairs and the rest of us sat around the living room talking.

"I can't thank you enough for bringing Brittany, Dee," Johnny said.

"Stop that!" Deirdra said. "It's nothing. You're my daughter's father."

"Trust me," Cynthia said. "Not all mothers are as kind as you."

"That's an understatement." Michael laughed.

"Thank you," Deirdra said.

"Can I offer you a drink, Dee?" I asked. "Can I call you Dee?"

"Girl, please, of course," Deirdra said.

"What do you drink?"

"Purified water, if you have it."

"Okay. I'll be right back."

"Do you mind if I come with you?" Deirdra asked.

"Sure, come on," I said.

I knew she wanted to have a private discussion but I was not prepared for the bomb she was about to drop on me.

"I guess it's pretty obvious I wanted to speak with you alone, huh?"

"I kind of figured as much."

"Well..." Deirdra stumbled slightly and then caught herself. "Do you mind if I sit down?"

"Sure, is everything, okay?"

"That's why I wanted to talk to you."

"What's going on?" I asked, sitting down and handing Deirdra a bottle of water.

"Thanks," Deirdra said. "I don't know if Johnny told you, but I've been battling cancer for a long time."

"No," I said with sincere concern. "He hasn't told me a thing."

"Well, I've been fighting and winning my battle with cancer ever since I was first diagnosed. Every time I think I have it defeated, it comes back stronger. And every time it comes back, I find a reason to keep on fighting. This time, I'm tired of fighting."

Listening to Deirdra reminded me of my days of hopeless despair, the times when I didn't have the mental strength to go further. I wanted to provide inspiration for her to keep fighting, if not for herself, then for Brittany.

"I can't say that I know what you're going through, Dee. But there was a time in my life when I couldn't go any further and I tried to commit suicide. I couldn't face another day of disappointment and sadness."

"I'm not disappointed, Alicia. Nor am I sad. The Lord has added so many years onto my life that scientifically couldn't be explained. If it were left up to the doctors, I would have been buried a long time ago. I am very grateful for every second that

I have lived, in good health and bad health. It's not that I'm giving up the fight. I just realize that it's time for me to give up the ghost."

"Oh my God," I said, holding back tears.

"Girl, please, it's alright."

"I don't know what to say. I just met you, Dee, but I feel like my heart is being torn out."

"No, no, no, Alicia," Deirdra said. "That's not why I'm telling you all of this. I don't want your sympathy, dear. I want you to help Johnny raise my child."

My tears stopped instantaneously and I said, "Excuse me?"

"I'm here because of my baby. I don't have much longer on this earth. And when I'm gone, I want to go with a peaceful mind. I want my daughter to have a mother. She needs a mother! And as they say, first impressions are lasting impressions. I think you would make a wonderful mother for Brittany."

"Are you serious?"

"Dead serious."

"Of course I will! I'll do everything in my power for Brittany. I'm so flattered that you would ask me something as important as that."

"And I'm grateful that you'll accept."

"Looking at you, I would never suspect that you're sick. You're beautiful."

"Thank you, Alicia," Deirdra said, "You're a beautiful woman yourself."

"Johnny is a lucky bastard, isn't he?" I joked.

"Uh-huhn, he doesn't deserve either one of us." Deirdra smiled wryly and laughed.

"He never told me why you two divorced. Curious minds would like to know."

"I'll just say that we grew apart. I couldn't handle his playing in the National Football League. Everything was about the league. The league! The league! The league!"

"I can imagine," I said.

"You know, as far as this conversation is concerned, I would like to keep it between us."

"Sure," I said, "but may I ask why you don't want Johnny to know about it?"

"Because this is a woman-to-woman conversation. It's strictly about me asking you to be the mother of my child. To let you know that I have no problem with you filling the role as Brittany's mother. Not just as her stepmother, but as her mother. My daughter has a lot of love to give. And she's going to need to receive a lot of love. So, from woman to woman, I needed to know what type of situation my daughter is going to be raised in. Do you understand?"

"I understand perfectly," I said. "You don't have to worry at all, because I promise to raise that little girl as if she came out of my own womb."

"Thank you, so much." Deirdra grabbed my hands and held them tightly. "Thank you! Thank you!"

"So where are you staying?"

"I'll get a hotel downtown somewhere. But if you don't mind, Brittany wants to stay with her dad. I know you guys are going to be extremely busy so she can come with me during the day."

"Yeah, she can stay here with us. And if you don't stay, I'm going to be insulted."

"I appreciate your offer, but I can't impose on you like that."

"It's not an imposition; I would be honored."

"How do you think Johnny would feel about that?"

"He would be honored as well. I have never heard that man say anything but good things about you. If you don't mind sleeping under the same roof with the new wife, I sure don't mind sharing with the ex-wife."

"You're incredible," Deirdra said.

"No, sweetheart," I said. "You're the one who's incredible. You have inspired me in so many ways."

"I don't know how." Deirdra smiled. "But I'm glad that I finally got the opportunity to meet you."

"Well, I guess we better be getting back in there with everyone else. After all, you're the guest of honor."

"I know, right?" Deirdra laughed, struggling to get out of the chair.

"Are you okay?" I asked, helping her stand up.

"I'm fine. Sometimes I move a little too fast for my body; that's all."

"I'll get Johnny to get your luggage out of the car."

"Thank you, Alicia."

"You're more than welcome."

WE HAD A BEAUTIFUL WEDDING. Johnny denied it later, but I could have sworn that I saw tears coming out of his eyes during the ceremony. We honeymooned in Hawaii on the island of Maui. Oh my God, it was like a dream come true. Each day was more exciting than the day before, but none more memorable than our first night.

Once we arrived at our hotel, we showered and then went downstairs for dinner. The restaurant was unbelievable. It had a romantic ambience catered for newlyweds. The service was incomparable; we didn't have to make one solitary request. Everything we desired was brought to us before we could ask.

After dinner, we went back to our suite. When I walked through the door, I stopped in my tracks. While we were at dinner, our suite had been transformed into a paradise of roses and tulips. They were scattered from the doorway to the bed, to the bathroom, everywhere.

"Oh my God, this is beautiful!" I was consumed by the moment and kissed Johnny passionately.

"Come here." Johnny took my hand and led me to the bathroom.

I was hoping to make love in a room a tad bit more romantic than the bathroom. It was our honeymoon night and I was expecting more than a "wham, bam, and thank you ma'am" type of performance. I love to have wild sex in a huge elegant bathroom as much as the next woman. But as far as my wedding night, I wanted to use every inch of the bed.

"We're going to do it here in the bathroom?" I asked.

"Shh!" Johnny covered my lips. "Trust me, baby."

We followed the path of scattered flowers that led us through the bathroom and in front of a door covered with a full-length mirror. I had noticed the door earlier but I assumed that it was for extra linen, or storage space, so I didn't look in it. Johnny placed his hands over my eyes and guided me through the door.

Johnny removed his hands from my eyes. "You like?"

"Dayum!"

I looked around the gigantic room. It, too, was covered with tulips and roses. I was captivated by the fact that the only wall was connected to the adjoining bathroom we had walked through. The other three walls were actually full-length, floor-to-ceiling windows. We couldn't have asked for a better view of the island; then again, the island couldn't ask for a better view of us. I suppose since our floor was so high, no one could see what was going on in there. Unless, of course, there was some fool with binoculars. And to be honest, that was kind of a turn-on.

Johnny cut on the switch next to us, illuminating the room with soft candlelight. The room was beautifully decorated. It had a unique style that had to be from Hawaiian heritage. He cut on another switch that started the sauna. He picked up a couple of wineglasses from the mini-bar and poured each of us a glass. We sipped as we took in the beautiful scenery of Maui.

The water from the sauna heated quickly and the steam instantly filled the room. Johnny took my hand and led me toward the sauna. He unpinned my hair and fluffed it out so that it could sway in his hands.

He turned me around and kissed me on my neck. He took his time slowly dragging my zipper from the top all the way to my lower back. Pulling my dress over my shoulders, he massaged them. Continuing to pull my dress past my waist and down to my ankles, he kneeled and kissed my back, my hips and then my ass.

I leaned forward and placed both of my hands on the long window. Johnny stuck his fingers in my panties and pulled them down. I stepped out of them one foot at a time.

He stood up and cuffed my breasts from behind. I put my head down and watched his large hands tug at my already stiffened nipples. I could feel his enormous penis bulging through his pants. I reached behind me and squeezed it tightly.

It took some pinpoint snatching and pulling, but I was able to unbuckle his pants. I started to pull them down little by little, one hip at a time. When they were at his knees, he kicked off his shoes, and slid his pants off. The man did all of this without releasing either one of my breasts.

He managed to get out of his shirt without interrupting the flow of the moment. When he was completely naked, he turned me toward him. He grabbed my face and stuck his tongue in my mouth. The kiss was long and unrushed.

The feel of his hard body against mine sent tremors up and

down my spine. I felt an overwhelming sense of anxiousness, knowing I was about to make love to my husband for the very first time. Not just have sex, make love. I felt new. I felt cleansed. I felt like a virgin.

I turned Johnny around and pushed him against the wall. I kneeled down in front of him on both knees. I grabbed his erect stick in my hand and kissed it. I turned it upward and then licked it from the base to the head. Johnny put his hand on top of my head and guided me to the rhythm he desired.

"Oh, baby." Johnny started to force his way into my mouth, making me gag.

I pushed his thighs backward to give myself room to breathe and stop his big stick from choking me to death.

"Agh!" I pulled my head back, leaving a long trail of saliva from my bottom lip to the head of his penis. "Whoa. Are you trying to kill me?"

"I'm sorry, baby. It just feels so good."

I put Johnny's stick in my mouth again, this time sucking much slower to prevent that uncomfortable choking. Gagging is okay. Choking is not!

"You like that, baby?"

"Oh shit, baby, I'm going to come like that if you don't stop." Johnny held the base of his stick in his hand and slowly slid his stick back and forth in my mouth.

"If you keep doing that, I'm going to come myself," I said, slurping loudly as saliva covered my lips.

"Come here, baby." Johnny laid me on the flat surface of the sauna and spread my legs.

He got on his knees, which put his waist even with the counter top. He leaned down and kissed my neck, laying his body on top of mine. He kissed me gently, sending tingling sensations to my toes. I wrapped my legs around him, feeling his stick press against my stomach.

"Kiss my neck like that," I said, "Yeah, baby, just like that."

Johnny kissed my shoulders and then my breasts. I tensed up when I felt his lips grip my nipples. He sucked them back and forth, and back and forth, sending me into a wild frenzy. I tried to watch, but the feeling was so good I kept closing my eyes.

He kissed down to my stomach, teasing my navel with his tongue. He gripped my hips and slapped them with his hand.

"Oh shit!" I yelled.

He kissed downward to my thighs, but not by using his tongue. He used only his lips to smack up and down the interior of my legs.

"Oh God, that's driving me crazy, Johnny!"

Johnny's kisses ended up on top of my clit and his tongue went to work.

"Oh! See! I can't take that, Johnny!"

The pleasurable pressure going on between my legs was unbearable. As many times, and as many different men I had enjoyed sex with, I had never felt the mounting anticipation of an orgasm that I felt on my wedding night. The sensation was so intense that it came without buildup. I came thunderously!

I pushed Johnny's head away from my vagina, and raised my hips. Oh my God, I opened my thighs and I shot a long wet stream in the air. Seeing that sent me into another powerful orgasm.

"SHIT! SHIT! SHIT!" I screamed.

For some reason, I always cursed when I had an orgasm.

"Help me! Help me!" I shouted. "Please, Johnny, it feels so good! Help me!"

I pulled Johnny on top of me and slid his hard stick inside.

"You got me like this you better give it to me right, gotdammit!"

"What?" Johnny said as he pounded me so hard, my pelvis was beginning to hurt. "You want me to give it to you, right?"

"Give it to me!" I shouted. "Damn, you all up in there, baby!"

"Uhn!" Johnny grunted as he lifted his penis out as far as he could, and then rammed it back inside of me.

"SHIT! Give it to me, baby! Rip me in half!"

Johnny turned around and sat on the steps. He snatched me like a piece of paper and put me on top of him. I slid down his long stick, one inch at a time. I wanted him to be rough, but I wasn't a damn fool. I wanted to have sex again.

I was facing Johnny with my legs wrapped around his waist. Once he was snug inside of me, I started to ride him back and forth. He had filled my vagina to its limit, but I wouldn't stop slamming into him.

"That's right, baby! Give it to me!" Johnny moaned. "Ride it, baby! Ride it like it's yours!"

"Oh shit, I can feel you, Johnny! I can feel you so deep!"

Johnny stood up and reached beneath my ass, bouncing me up and down on his pole.

"OH-MY-GOD!" I screamed. "I'm going to come again! Don't stop! Spank my ass, baby! Spank my ass!"

As Johnny held my ass with one hand, he spanked me with the other. The burning sensation from his hand trickled through to my soaking wet vagina, and I knew my next orgasm wasn't far away.

Johnny held me against the wall as he started to give me long, deep strokes. I dropped my legs to the back of his legs and used the wall to brace my thrusts. I put one hand above my head and pushed off of the wall, timing myself perfectly with Johnny's strokes.

"What's your name, baby?" Johnny mumbled as he kissed my neck.

"Alicia, baby," I said.

"No, I wanna hear you say your name!" Johnny moaned.

"Alicia Forrester!" I screamed, realizing what he wanted me to say.

"What?" Johnny grabbed my face and looked me in the eyes.

"Alicia Forrester!" I dug my fingernails into the top of Johnny's shoulders and dragged them down his spine to his ass.

"What's your name?" Johnny repeated.

"Alicia Forrester!"

Every time Johnny asked my name, he would pull his penis almost all of the way out, and slam it back in.

"What?"

"Alicia Forrester!"

"What?"

"Alicia Forrester!"

During the ruckus, one of my legs had fallen to the floor. I was balancing myself on the toes of one foot, while this gargantuan of a man rammed the shit out of me. And to think, my mother said all of those years of ballet would never amount to anything.

Johnny wrapped his hands around my neck, slightly cutting off my oxygen, but intensifying the sensation. I could feel my orgasm coming around that mountain! But his struck first.

"SHIT!" Johnny screamed. "I'M COMING, BABY! SHIT!"

In the midst of screaming my new name, and Johnny's slight choking of my neck, I came again. The orgasm shot from my vagina to my brain. That shit felt so damn good that I lost all mental and physical control. I opened my mouth as wide it could go, but no sound came out. I tried to breathe but couldn't catch my breath.

I lowered my head onto Johnny's shoulder and I bit the shit out of him. I don't know why, but I had to do something to start breathing again. He let out an agonizing moan, but kept stroking. When I was able to speak, I released a high-pitched, ear-screeching cry that I'm sure shattered mirrors and windows somewhere in that hotel.

"EEEEEEEEEEEEEEEEK!" I screamed into Johnny's ear.

We were bouncing from wall to wall, or window to window, I should say, as if we were fighting each other. Knocking over lamps and tables, oh my God, we crashed the room to bits. And if we had truly been fighting, that constant slamming against the wall may have really hurt. But pain is love, and love is pain when it comes to making love, right? We ended up pressed against one of the windows where when we looked down, we could see people and traffic below.

"Damn, I hope nobody saw us," Johnny said.

"I hope this window can hold your big ass." I laughed.

"If it has held me this long, I think we're good."

"Oh, my legs are sore," I said, lowering my legs to the floor.

"I think you broke my shit, Mrs. Forrester."

"You broke your own shit, acting like Tarzan."

"You okay?" Johnny held his flaccid penis in his hand. "Did Mommy hurt you?"

"You are crazy, boy!" I laughed.

We enjoyed the rest of our magical honeymoon and then it was time to return to our real lives back in Atlanta. We had to ship some of our items because we were returning with much more than we'd brought. We had a layover in Los Angeles and then it was nonstop to Atlanta.

CHAPTER EIGHT

A couple of weeks after we returned from our honeymoon, we received a call from Deirdra asking if Brittany could come live with us. She had become sick and was unable to take care of her properly. Johnny was happy to have Brittany come live with us, but not under those circumstances. He decided that he would commute back and forth from Atlanta to Orlando so that Brittany could spend as much time with Deirdra as possible.

Whatever happened between Deirdra and Johnny to cause their divorce didn't prevent them from loving each other. It wasn't the type of love that Johnny and I shared, at least I don't think it was, but there was mutual affection and respect between them.

As Deirdra weakened, Johnny spent more time out of town with her. It didn't bother me; I was actually proud of him for being so selfless. Not only that, as a woman, Deirdra understood how it may have affected me and she included me in everything. She called me and talked to me about girl things. Things she could no longer do, but yearned to do. I even got a chance to spend time with her and really got to know her before she died. I was overcome by her faith and her strength.

She was no longer in the hospital. They had sent her home to be comfortable and to enjoy the remainder of her time around family and friends. When I went to visit, I was nervous as I followed Johnny into her bedroom. I didn't know if I should act like there was nothing wrong with her and talk normal conversation, or extend my condolences and show compassion.

Johnny opened the door for me to go in. "Hey, Dee, you have a visitor."

"Hi, Dee," I said as I walked past Johnny.

"Hi, Alicia. I'm so glad you could come," Deirdra said. "Have a seat."

"Either one of you want anything to drink?"

"I'm fine," I said.

"I'll take a beer," Deirdra said.

"Yeah, right," Johnny said as he walked out.

"So, how are you feeling, Dee?"

"I'm feeling good today. God must have known I was going to have company."

"Good for you!"

As she was about to speak, her nurse walked in. She was a robust black woman. She looked like she could lift a truck. I guess she needed to be strong for all of the lifting that Deirdra required. I think she also needed a little sensitivity training. She was handling Deirdra awfully rough, especially when she started to comb out her hair.

"Alicia, this is my nurse, Janice," Deirdra said, "Janice, this is my friend, Alicia. Johnny's wife."

"Johnny's wife?" Janice asked as she momentarily stopped combing Deirdra's hair.

"Hey," I said.

"Hey," Janice said back as she resumed combing Deirdra's hair.

"Ouch," Deirdra said as Janice snatched her head wherever she wanted it to go.

"If you keep your head still, it won't hurt, Dee."

"My head is still and it hurts."

"I'm combing it as gently as I can now," Janice said. "Stop moving."

"Ouch!" Deirdra said again.

"Stop moving then."

"I can't move, Janice! I haven't been able to move in a long time!"

Deirdra really seemed to be in pain and Janice really seemed to not care.

"Look!" I said. "I'll comb her hair."

"You?" Janice asked.

"Yeah, me."

"Uh, that's okay, I got it."

"Nah, I don't think you do," I said. "You're combing her hair too hard."

"No, I'm not. She's just tender-headed."

"Tender-headed my ass, you're hurting my head," Deirdra said.

"Janice, I'll do it!" I reached out my hand for the comb.

"Is that okay with you, Dee?"

"Hmm, let me see," Deirdra said. "Getting my hair combed softly or getting my damn brains pulled out. What do you think?"

"Okay, I get the message." Janice handed me the comb and laughed as she walked out.

I climbed in the bed with Deirdra and slowly combed her hair.

"She looked like she was really hurting you, Dee."

"Oh my goodness, Alicia, she was killing me." Deirdra laughed. "But she's a good nurse."

"I couldn't tell."

"No, she's okay. These people do this so much that sometimes they become insensitive and don't even realize it. To them, the families are in mourning and so sympathetic for their loved ones that they hurt the sick by coddling us too much. As far as the care providers are concerned, it becomes a countdown to death and once that patient dies, then they're on to the next death sentence. Some are so efficient in recognizing the signs of death, they can tell you the day of death a whole week in advance."

"That's a trip," I said as I gingerly combed her hair.

"Yeah, but I don't want to make it seem like they're bad people, because they're actually angels. They have to separate themselves from the situation to do their jobs effectively. Sometimes they're going to be insensitive. Janice is a prime example. We both know that I'm dying. But she doesn't let me get away with anything. She forces me to keep fighting. I think that the main reason why I'm still hanging around is because she pisses me off to the point that I refuse to die, just to spite her." Deirdra laughed.

"May I ask a question, Dee?"

"Sure."

"How are you able to talk about death so freely? I don't know if I could do that."

"Because I know it's inevitable."

"Aren't you afraid?"

"Afraid of what?" Deirdra asked. "I have absolutely nothing to be afraid of. You have eliminated my only fear."

"Me? What did I do?"

"You promised to take care of my baby."

"Oh, girl, I thought you were talking about something."

"That's more than something to me, Alicia. That's everything."

"Well, we have to share that appreciation then. The fact that you asked me to be the mother of your child is everything to me. I have fallen in love with her. I couldn't have asked the Lord for a greater blessing."

"You're not just saying that because I'm sick, are you?"

"No! I'm saying that because it's the truth."

"Good. That makes me a happy woman."

"I really admire you, Dee."

"Now it's my turn to ask, what did I do to be admired?"

"Your strength! Your courage! Your ability to fight this dreadful disease! You're a role model for women who have suffered from this disease, and for those of us who haven't."

"Some of my friends encourage me to keep fighting and fighting. But I'm tired of fighting. I'm tired of the chemotherapy! I'm tired of being so sick that I can't feed myself! Clothe myself! Clean myself! I'm tired of all that! My battle hasn't been with cancer for a long time. I defeated my battle with cancer the first time I was given six months to live. I've been battling ever since to make sure my daughter would be taken care of when the Lord decided to take me home. I prayed to God to let me live long enough to win that battle. And He has blessed me with you. So now, I have won that battle, too. Like I told you before, I'm not giving up the fight because I have nothing more to fight for. I owe the Lord my soul, so I'm just giving up the ghost."

"Oh my God." I started to cry.

"Hey! Hey! There you go again with the tears, Alicia. I swear you are the most crying woman that I've ever seen."

"I'm fine, Dee."

"I didn't mean to upset you, Alicia."

"It's not your fault." I wiped my eyes. "I'm so glad I was able to meet you, Dee! Oh, I'm so glad!"

Listening to a dying woman's unselfish testimony of faith and courage put my life under an embarrassing microscope. Despite everything she had to face in her life, she had refused to die until she made sure her child was protected and loved. On the other hand, I was willing to take my life because I was humiliated to tell three men that I was unsure which one of them was the father of my child!

"Come here, girl," Deirdra said, barely able to lift her arms. "I'm sorry."

"I'm okay." I lay beside Deirdra and she hugged me as best as she could.

We laid our heads side by side and didn't speak. She patted my shoulders as I continued to cry. Johnny walked in with drinks, a glass for me, and a cup with a straw for Deirdra.

"Aw, what did you do Alicia?" Johnny joked.

"Nothing." I sat up and wiped my eyes. "Nothing!"

"Why are you crying?" Johnny asked.

"Nothing!" I repeated.

"I knew that when I came back in here one of you would be crying."

"Shut-up and give me my drink," Deirdra said.

Johnny walked to the side of Deirdra and put the straw to her mouth.

"Not so fast, girl!" Johnny said, stopping the water from flowing through the straw. "Slow down!"

"Boy, let me drink the way I want to drink."

"It's time to switch your gear anyway," Johnny said.

"You may want to leave for this, Alicia." Deirdra laughed. "It ain't pretty."

"What's going on?"

"Johnny calls changing my underwear, changing my gear."

"You need me to leave?"

"It doesn't matter to me," Deirdra said. "If you want to smell this funky smell, it's up to you."

"I'm good."

"Well, if you're going to stay in here, you can help. I don't feel like calling Janice anyway," Johnny said as he opened a bag of diapers.

"Okay, what do you need me to do?" I asked.

"When I pull this one off, make sure she stays on her side until I finish cleaning her."

"Okay."

Johnny turned Deirdra on her side and I held her in that position until he finished.

"Okay, slide that one on, while I throw this one away," Johnny said, walking into the bathroom.

"Okay," I said as I slid the diaper up Deirdra's bony legs. I noticed how she had lost so much weight since the last time I had seen her.

Deirdra didn't say a word while we were changing her underwear. She may have been embarrassed, or just so used to the process it didn't matter.

"Okay, you're good to go," Johnny said.

"Hey, Dee, it's time for your changing," Janice said as she burst through the door.

"Been there, done that," Deirdra said.

"Alicia and I knocked it out already."

"You and your current wife changed your ex-wife's underwear?" Janice said, pointing her finger at the three of us.

"Yup!" Johnny, Deirdra and I said in unison.

"I swear y'all are some weird people!" Janice said. She started to walk out of the door and then turned around and said to me, "Are you trying to come in here and take my job?"

"No." I laughed.

"In that case, can I make a bed for you to spend the night? I can use you to keep Ms. Thang over there in a good mood."

"Get out of here!" Deirdra laughed.

"Is there anything you need, sweetheart?" Janice asked Deirdra.

"No, I'm good," Deirdra said.

"Well, just buzz me if you need me."

Janice left the room and I understood what Deirdra meant about the care providers. She had appeared to be an ogre earlier; in reality, she saw Deirdra as a woman dying to live but I saw her as a woman living to die.

"I want some Chinese food."

"No, Deirdra," Johnny snapped.

"I want some Chinese food, Johnny!"

"You know you're not getting any Chinese food so stop asking."

"Can she digest Chinese food, Johnny?" I asked.

"Nope."

"Stop lying. Yes, I can!"

"You don't need to be eating that stuff, Deirdra."

"Can you eat Chinese food, Dee?"

"If it's chopped up real fine, I can."

"Then Chinese it is!" I said. "Do you have a favorite place?"

"Sure do. Wang's Chinese Buffet; look in the top drawer on my nightstand. There should be a menu in there somewhere."

I looked in her nightstand and found the menu. I asked her what she wanted and I was about to place our orders when Johnny called in Janice for reinforcement.

"JAAAAN-ICE!" Johnny shouted.

A second later Janice came through the door, completely out of breath.

"What's the matter?" Janice shouted.

"They're trying to feed Dee Chinese food!"

"Is that why you were yelling like that, Mr. Forrester?"

"Yeah," Johnny said.

"Don't do that! You almost gave me a heart attack!" Janice put her hand over her heart.

"Sorry about that. But tell them Dee's not eating Chinese food."

"Do I have to cut it up?" Janice asked.

"No, I'll do it," I said.

"Girl, please." Janice waved her hand at me. "Add some shrimp fried rice on that order for me."

"That's what I thought!" Deirdra laughed.

"Aha! Very funny! Gang up on the man!" Johnny said sarcastically.

"Do you need anything, Dee?" Janice asked.

"Nope, I'm good."

"If you need me, I'm going to be washing your clothes so you might have to ring that bell more than once before I hear it."

"Okay."

"Janice, can you give me directions to the Chinese place?" I asked. "I don't trust Johnny."

"Come on; I'll write them down for you."

I followed Janice into the kitchen and she gave me directions. When I arrived back from picking up the food, Johnny had moved Dee from her bed to the patio to get some fresh air. They were looking in a photo album when I walked up.

"I'm back," I said, setting the food on a table.

"Good, I am hungry," Deirdra said.

"I'll get a knife and cut up your food while you guys finish looking at your pictures."

"Thanks for the food, Alicia," Deirdra said. "I don't mean to rush you when you're doing me a favor, but you're holding up the reminiscence party. Hurry up and come sit down."

"You want me to look at the pictures, too?"

"Of course, that's why I pulled them out."

"Oh, okay, be back in a jiffy!"

Johnny followed me into the kitchen and held my hands in his.

"I want to thank you for being so understanding."

"It's no problem, baby."

"You don't have to be here. You don't have to do this."

"Actually, you don't have to be here either. We're both here for the same reason. Deirdra is a wonderful woman who deserves to die with dignity and love. Even if I didn't know you, honey, and God blessed me with an opportunity to meet a woman like her, I would be here, doing the same thing. I'm grateful to be able to spend this time with her."

"Thank you, baby." Johnny kissed me on the cheek and then joined Deirdra back on the patio.

I sliced the food up to its finest proportion and went back out to the patio. Johnny recorded Deirdra and I as I fed her and we looked through the photo album. We laughed and joked until Deirdra became exhausted and needed to take a nap. I intended on going back to my hotel room but I ended up spending the night. Deirdra insisted on returning the hospitality I had extended to her in Atlanta.

The next morning, we ate breakfast together and she told me that I had brought a sense of normalcy to her life. When I was leaving, it was like leaving a family member. We hugged and kissed as if we had known each other all of our lives. We made plans for me to come back in three weeks to spend an entire weekend with her. Two weeks later, Deirdra died.

Cynthia and Michael attended the funeral with us. Deirdra's mother convinced Johnny to give the eulogy. It was obvious that she really cared about Johnny. She praised him from the moment we arrived until we pulled off to leave. I found out where Deirdra got her sunny personality. Her mother was just as kind as her. She spent most of her time comforting others while she buried her only child.

ON OUR DRIVE BACK HOME, Cynthia and I discussed our plan to start our public relations firm. She convinced me that it was time to stop talking and to put the plan into action. Our husbands offered their support financially and creatively. We assured them that whatever they gave financially would be considered as a loan. Michael explained that an investment would be more advantageous to us than a loan. His interpretation of an investment meant to put money into a venture to make a profit; if the business profits, the investor profits. If the business fails, everybody fails. No one owes anybody anything but a, "*my bad*." A loan, on the other hand, is borrowed money to be paid back with interest. We quickly jumped on the investment concept.

The first point of action was to set up the business as an L.L.C. I really didn't know what the hell an L.L.C. was, to tell you the truth. Michael helped us with that, too. He was a professional football player turned attorney turned successful author. Did anybody say author? Guess who became our very first client? You're right. Michael!

Once the decision was made to make Michael our first client, it was also decided that he would be our only male. We were determined to build our clientele based on female talent. Our mission was to provide excellent media representation for women in various backgrounds in sports and entertainment. We called our company, Walk the Talk.

We picked up a few people, but nothing major. We were still missing an important element of our business. Cynthia was great at researching and soliciting clients. Once she pulled them in, I was pretty good at selling them on our commitment, but there were too many fish getting away. We needed a strong closer and we knew where to find her.

"I bet you're wondering why we invited you to lunch, huh?" I asked.

"Uh-huhn."

"We want you to become a partner in our company," Cynthia said.

"A partner in your company?"

"Yeah, what do you think?" I asked.

"I'm flattered, but I need one important question answered."

"What's up?" Cynthia asked.

"Why the hell took y'all so long to ask me?"

"Girl, I thought you were serious!" Cynthia laughed.

"I am serious! Shit, I'm hurt!" Pam said. "You heffas knew I didn't want to be up there at Upskon and didn't even ask me to join y'all little company. I should say no!"

"You were supervisor and everything. I thought you were happy!" I said.

"I'll never be happy working for anybody when I can be working for myself," Pam said.

"So are you a new partner with Walk the Talk Public Relations firm?" I asked.

"Hold up! Is that the name of y'all company?"

"Yeah, what's wrong with it?" Cynthia asked.

"You thought of that, didn't you, Cynt?" Pam asked.

"Shut up."

"If I'm going to be part of y'all company, the first thing we have to do is change that lame-ass name."

"What's wrong with our name?"

"Lame!" Pam said. "Are you serious? *Walk the Talk*? That's lame as hell and y'all know it."

"Our husbands think it's cute," I said.

"Those two nerd-ass niggahs?" Pam laughed. "Of course! What do you expect for them to say?"

"Forget you! I like it!" Cynthia said.

"What's this, Cynt?" Pam used her hand to make an "*L*" shape on her forehead. "Huh? What's that, Cynt? Loo-ser!"

I turned my head so Cynthia couldn't see me laughing.

"See, Alicia knows it's lame. Look at her! She's even laughing." Pam pointed at me. "Look at your girl."

"Do you think it's lame, Alicia?"

"I won't say lame, Cynt, but it's not like, powerful, or making a strong statement."

"Just come on out and say it. That shit is whack!" Pam said.

"Why didn't you say anything, Alicia?" Cynthia laughed. "I don't like it either!"

"For real?" I shouted.

"For real, for real!" Cynthia said.

"Who thought of that name?" Pam asked.

"None of your business!" Cynthia said.

"I knew it was your grandma ass, Cynt."

"Well, you come up with something better."

"I already got it," Pam said arrogantly.

"What is it?" I asked.

"It better be good!" Cynthia said.

"Here you go," Pam said, prolonging the moment, '*CAPs!*'"

"Caps?" I said.

"That sounds just as lame as Walk the Talk," Cynthia said. "What do you mean, caps? Baseball caps?"

"Naw, girl. '*CAPs.*' Our initials, C-A-P, Cynthia, Alicia and Pam."

"CAPs?" I said. "That's not bad."

"Yeah, CAPs Public Relations and Marketing Firm."

"I like it," I said.

"I don't like it," Cynthia said sarcastically. "I think it stinks."

"Stop hating, girl." Pam chuckled.

"Seriously though, I like it," Cynthia said. "But now we have to set up another company under another name."

"Who is that?" Pam pointed to the woman sitting at the table next to us.

"Oh my God!" I shouted. "That's Gizelle!"

"Who the hell is Gizelle?" Pam asked.

"She's like the biggest hip-hop artist out!" I said.

"Well, why are we sitting over here, when she's over there?" Pam said, walking over to Gizelle's table.

"Girl, don't go over there!" I said. "Somebody from her entourage might pull out a gun or something."

"That chick ain't nobody!" Pam said.

Pam was stopped by Gizelle's bodyguard. They were too far away for Cynthia and me to hear what they were saying. A minute later she was sitting back at our table.

"So what happened?" I asked.

"That big black niggah told me that Gizelle wasn't signing autographs. I don't want that bitch's autograph! I'm trying to get some business!"

"Stop talking so loud, Pam. They can hear you," I said.

"I don't give a damn if they can hear me! Watch!" Pam stood up and patted her butt. "All y'all can kiss my BIG BLACK ASS!"

"Pam, sit down," Cynthia whispered.

"Niggahs get a little bit of money and they always try to act brand-new!"

"Would you stop saying that word so much?" I asked.

"You say niggah, too, Alicia, don't trip."

"I say it sometimes but not every other word, Pam."

"Y'all heffas stuck up, too." Pam pointed back at Cynthia and me.

"Whatever!" Cynthia said.

"Alicia, girl, that chick looks just like you!" Pam pointed at me.

"That little girl doesn't look like me."

"Yup, you're right, Pam! That girl looks just like you." Cynthia laughed.

"She looks like your younger twin," Pam said.

"Yeah, it looks like y'all came from the same sperm, but only you could have been born a decade earlier."

"Now that you cracked your jokes, it's time to handle business. We need to sign Gizelle."

"If we can land her, we can attract the younger market."

"Forget that bitch!" Pam said.

"I see we're going to have to work on somebody's people skills," I said.

"Y'all ain't gotta work on shit."

"Oh yes, we do," Cynthia said. "If you plan on being a part of this company, you will."

"Y'all asked me to be a part of y'all company. I didn't ask y'all."

"I don't care who asked who. We didn't ask you to join the company for that tough ghetto crap. We want you to use your aggressive nature to show what we can offer our clients. Not scare them into thinking we're going to kick their asses if they don't sign with us."

Cynthia was always mild-mannered and reserved but when she was fed up with someone or something that little heffa became a Tasmanian devil. She didn't care how big, or how small you were. When she was pissed off, she bit into your ass hard! When she was like that, all of us listened, even Pam.

"Damn!" Pam said. "Get this little pitbull off of my ass, Alicia!"

"You know how she is." I laughed.

"Pam, take notes." Cynthia walked over to Gizelle's table and talked to her bodyguard.

The bodyguard walked over to Gizelle and whispered in her ear. They went back and forth whispering in each other's ears. Cynthia looked back at us and smiled. The bodyguard walked back to Cynthia and handed her a card. Cynthia walked back to our table and sat down.

"There you go, Pam." Cynthia placed a business card on the table.

"What is this?" Pam picked up the card. "Whose card is this?"

"That's Gizelle's business manager's card. I'm going to call her and set up an appointment to talk about Gizelle's future with Walk the Talk."

"You mean CAPs," Pam said.

"Do I?" Cynthia asked.

"Okay, I'd be willing to polish up my attitude slightly. But you heffas ain't changing me into no soccer mom like y'all. I'm going to change as much as it takes to make this paper and that's that!"

"That's fine with me," I said.

"Me, too," Cynthia said.

"I have a question, Cynt. What did you say to King Kong Bundy to get him to talk to Gizelle?" Pam asked.

"Oh," Cynthia said, "I apologized for my big-mouth friend and then I asked him if he would join my big-mouth friend for a romantic dinner."

"No you didn't!" Pam looked at the bodyguard and then he smiled and waved at her. "I'm going to kill you, Cynt!"

"Wave back at him, girl," Cynthia said.

"I'm not waving at that beast!" Pam covered her face with her purse.

"Stop talking about people, Pam."

"You shouldn't have set me up with that big black man, then!"

"Too late now. By the way, your date starts in about five minutes." Cynthia laughed.

Another huge man appeared at Gizelle's table to stand body-guard as Pam's date joined us at our table.

"I'm going to kick your ass for this, Cynt!"

The gigantic man towered over our table and introduced himself.

"Good afternoon ladies, I'm Big Walt."

"Good afternoon, Big Walt," I said.

"Well, we're about to leave so you two can have some privacy," Cynthia said.

"Hey, thanks a lot, shawty, for the hook-up," Big Walt said. "I'm gon' make sure you get that meeting."

"Thanks, Big Walt," Cynthia said.

"We'll talk to you later, Pam." I stood up to leave.

"I'm kicking both of y'all asses!" Pam snarled.

"Damn, I like 'em feisty!" Big Walt said.

"Shut the hell up, Big Walt, or whatever your name is!" Pam said as she crossed her legs and twirled her feet.

CHAPTER NINE

As we were getting started with CAPs, my husband decided to step out on faith as well, and opened his own practice. It was hard on our marriage, being that we were newlyweds. We were so busy that we barely saw each other. And when we did, it was in passing. Our professional endeavors, along with spending quality time with our child, were having a drastic effect on our sex life. I didn't want to be like a hot panty adolescent, but I was fiendish! I wanted more sex! I needed more sex! I realized sex was not a substitute for communication, but it beat the hell out of marriage counseling from my husband.

Johnny, being the psychologist, constantly analyzed our relationship and found different exercises to keep our marriage stimulated. I found them to be monotonously trite. I was beginning to feel as if I was one of his patients. I had to do something to get that man out of the therapy room and into the bedroom.

While I was coming up with a plan to seduce my husband, I received an unexpected telephone call. I was ripping and running downtown and I was just about to wrap up my errands. You know, life has a way of throwing shit on you when you're dressed in your clean white clothes!

"Hello."

"Alicia?"

"Yes, who's calling?"

"This is me."

"Me, who?"

"It has not been so long that you do not remember my voice."

Although I knew who it was, I didn't want to acknowledge him.

"Who's calling?" I asked again.

"It is the love of your life."

"What do you want?"

"I have missed you so very much."

"I'm kind of busy right now. Can we talk later?"

"No, I am here for only this afternoon. I need to see you. I need to apologize to you so that I can go on with my life."

"If you want to apologize," I said, "apologize."

"No, this is not right to do over the telephone. I must see your face."

"I'm sorry, I can't do that."

"Why not?"

"I just can't!"

"Is it because you are with another man?"

"No," I said. "That's not it."

I couldn't believe I was lying about my marriage. I knew that was the only reason keeping me from seeing him. The cheating, the lying, the down-low shit; I would have excused all of that just to see his face. But as horny as I was, I couldn't afford to take the chance on meeting with him.

"If it is not a man, why can you not see me?"

"I don't feel comfortable talking with you, after what has happened between us."

"Don't feel comfortable? That is American woman bullshit! You want to see me. Admit it!"

He was right. I did want to see him. Julian had a way of convincing me to do things I shouldn't do and he knew it. His persistence always persevered over my resistance.

"That's not a good idea."

"Why not, Alicia?"

"Because."

"I am at the Grand Hyatt on Peachtree Road. Meet me in the lobby."

"I can't."

"Why not?"

I opened my mouth to tell Julian the reason that I couldn't meet him was because I was married. But what I said was, "Okay, I'll meet you in the lobby but I'm not coming to your hotel room, Julian."

"Fine!" Julian said. "There's a nice restaurant in my hotel, we can meet there."

"Okay, I'll meet you there."

"How long will it take you to be here?"

"I'm not far. I should be there in a few minutes."

"I'll meet you downstairs."

"Okay."

"Good-bye."

"Bye."

A few minutes later, I pulled into the parking lot of the Grand Hyatt. It was an upscale hotel, one that celebrities frequently occupied. I was impressed. He'd gone from crashing with me in my house to one of the finest hotels in Atlanta.

I arrived before Julian and got us a table. I was very anxious to see him after so much time had passed. When he walked in, I found myself still mesmerized by his beauty. He was still as gorgeous as ever. His tailored suit fit him perfectly. I could see the shine from his shoes as soon as he stepped into my view. He kissed me on the cheek and sat down.

"I see that you have taken care of yourself, my sweet."

"You look nice yourself," I said.

"Nothing compared to you."

"Thank you."

"I have missed you very much, Alicia." Julian reached across the table and held my hands. "I am still in love with you."

"You're not in love with me, Julian, and you never were."

"Don't be ridiculous!" Julian said. "I may have been stupid and behaved like an immature child, but I have only loved one woman in my life. You!"

"Please, I don't need to be hearing this, Julian."

"Why not?" Julian said. "I tried to go on with my life but I cannot. I met a nice English woman and we were to be married next week. I cancelled it because I was still in love with you."

"You were engaged to be married?" I was stunned that after all the years we were together that fool had never once proposed to me. But in the short time since we'd broken up, he'd met and proposed to some other chick? I was pissed off. "Engaged to who, Julian?"

"Her name is Jayne."

"Jane?" I asked. "You're marrying a woman named, Jane?"

"Not Jane as in Dick and Jane," Julian said, "J-A-Y-N-E, as in British."

"What difference does it make?"

"You made her name sound like a limerick."

"Whatever! Why am I here?"

How pitiful was I? I was a married woman disappointed that my ex-boyfriend had found a woman that he wanted to marry.

"You are here because you love me."

"I don't love you anymore, Julian."

"Then let me ask you the same question you asked me," Julian said, "Why are you here?"

"Because you asked me."

"That is true. But you did not have to come."

"I can leave."

"You don't want to leave and you know it."

"Watch me!" I said as I stood up to leave.

Julian reached for my hand and pulled me to him. He stood up and held my face directly in front of his.

"I'm sorry, don't leave."

"I shouldn't be here."

"Why not?"

"What difference does it make?" I asked. "Stop asking me why I'm saying what I'm saying and just listen!"

Julian insisted that I explained why I couldn't spend time with him. It was frustrating because I felt pressured to tell him I was married and I didn't want to do that.

"I know you, Alicia," Julian said. "What are you hiding?"

"Nothing!" I said.

"Tell me the truth!"

"There's nothing to tell, Julian."

"I have traveled all the way to this country to profess my love for you and you refuse to be honest with me?"

"Oh my God!" I said.

"What is the matter with you?"

"My friend is here!" I said, pointing at Cynthia.

Cynthia was having lunch with Gizelle. I guess Pam's lunch with Big Walt had paid great dividends for CAPs. It was my bad luck that the meeting had to be in the same place where I was secretly having lunch with my ex-boyfriend.

"Where?" Julian looked in the direction that I was pointing.

"I gotta get outta here!" I was nervous as hell. "Damn! She's right by the exit, Julian! Even if I sneak past her, she can see me when I walk out of the hotel! Shit!"

"Why are you hiding from her?"

"Because I'm married to her husband's brother!" I shouted. "Is that what you wanted to hear?"

"Married?" Julian asked. "You are married?"

"Yes, I'm married."

"My heart, it is broken," Julian said, placing his hand over his heart.

"Stop overreacting, you overgrown drama queen! I have to go!"

I looked in Cynthia's direction and my paranoia convinced me that she was looking back at me.

"Come! Come with me!" Julian said.

He took my hand and led me through the kitchen. He spoke to the kitchen staff and they allowed us to use the kitchen elevator to the second floor. From there, Julian led me to the guest elevator and we quickly got on. Julian pushed the "up" button and I leaned against the back wall.

I knew what he was doing and I knew where we were going but I pretended that I didn't have a clue. The next thing I knew Julian was sliding his hotel key through the slot and I was crossing the threshold of infidelity.

"I can't stay long," I said. "I just need to give my friend time to leave."

Julian wasted no time coming after me. He knew that I was still very much attracted to him. He could also smell when I was sexually aroused. While I was talking, he pulled me to him and kissed me.

"I can't do this," I moaned.

"I love you, Alicia," Julian said.

"Please, don't do this to me, Julian."

"I can't help it! I'm addicted to you!"

Julian pulled up my skirt and stuck his hand in my panties, manipulating his fingers into my vagina while massaging my clit. My knees buckled and I had to hold on to him to keep from falling.

"Oh, shit, Julian," I moaned out loud.

"Make love to me." Julian led me to the bed and laid me down.

Everything was happening so quickly. I opened my legs and Julian fingered me with his middle finger. I managed to regain my composure enough to pull his hand out of my panties.

"Oh my God!" I said as my legs trembled uncontrollably. I got up and sat in the chair next to the bed. I couldn't help but rub my vagina in the spot where Julian's hand had just been, and moan. "Oh my God!"

Julian sat up and then walked over to me. He kneeled in front of me and held my hands.

"I want to make love to you. I want to talk to you and I want you to talk to me while I am inside of you. That is when we are most vulnerable. That is the moment when we tell nothing but the truth."

"I always believed that's the moment when people tell nothing but lies, Julian."

"It all depends upon your objective of the moment."

"What?"

"What I mean is; if your objective is to attain the moment of deceit, you will accomplish that objective. But if your objective is to accomplish the moment of truth, then the truth is what you will accomplish."

"When did you become such an expert on making love?"

"When I became successful at accomplishing both deceit and truth."

"Is that right?" I asked sarcastically.

"Absolutely."

"What if my objective is to deceive myself?"

"You can't deceive yourself of your truth. You may pretend to believe your self-deceit, only to better your performance to the world. But to thine self be true. Those are words to live by, but when denied, they are words to die by."

For the first time in Julian's life, I think he was finally telling the truth. His honesty led to my honesty.

"What if I want to make love to you physically, but nothing more? What if I convince myself that it's okay to make love to you for the moment, but never again? If I believe that it's only for a moment, and it is not deceit, am I wrong?"

"You know that if you make love to me once, twice or even three times, there is no moral righteousness to it. It's infidelity and it's wrong."

"But I want to make love to you without the guilt. How do I do that if I don't deceive myself?"

"Admit the truth."

"And what is the truth?"

"The truth is that you're a woman that has specific needs to be fulfilled. The truth is that I am the man to fulfill those needs. You desire my kiss, my touch and my attention. You want to feel my hands on your body, caressing your breasts and your thighs. You want to feel me deep inside of you. You want me to tell you how much I love you. You want to be my woman right now, and then you want to go home to your husband, and be his wife. That is your admission of the truth."

"And that doesn't bother you?"

"If this moment is all that I can get from you, then I'm more than happy to accept it."

Julian leaned forward and kissed me again. I no longer resisted his kiss, or his touch. We went back to the bed and I took off my skirt, careful not to wrinkle it more than it was already. Julian took off his shirt and pants and wore only his boxer shorts. I un-hooked my bra and tossed it on top of my skirt, leaving my panties as the only article of clothing on my body.

Julian reached for my panties and started to pull them down below my hips. The only thing standing between me and infidelity was my itsy-bitsy panties. But when I looked into Julian's face, all that I could see was the image of Johnny. As he pulled my panties down, I pulled them back up.

"What is the matter?"

"I can't do this, Julian."

"Of course you can," Julian said as he kissed my neck.

"No, please stop, Julian."

"I love you, Alicia."

"No, you don't!"

"Yes, I do, baby! I love you so much!" Julian slid between my thighs. "Come on, baby. You know you want me inside of you!"

"Get off of me, Julian!" I pushed Julian away and pulled my panties all the way up.

I jumped from the bed and put my skirt on.

"What is this?" Julian asked. "What are you doing?"

"I'm going home!"

"But I love you, Alicia."

"If you loved me, Julian, you would let me walk out of here and go home to my family."

I grabbed my shoes and sat in the chair to put them on. Julian put on his underwear and walked over to me. He took my shoes out of my hands and held them to his chest. I thought he was trying a last-ditch effort to convince me to stay. But he wasn't. He held my feet in his hands and put my shoes on one at a time. Julian put on his robe and walked me to the door. He kissed me on the cheek and rubbed my face.

"Like I told you, Alicia," Julian said, opening the door for me to leave, "I love you. Go home to your husband."

"Thank you."

"You are welcome. Good-bye, my love."

"Good-bye, Julian."

When I walked away from Julian that day, I knew two things. One, I was no longer in love with Julian. Two, I didn't want any other man but my husband.

As soon as I got in my car to leave, I called Cynthia to make sure she hadn't seen me. She was so excited about her meeting with Gizelle, she answered on the first ring.

"Hey, girl, guess what?" Cynthia shouted.

"What?" I asked, already knowing the answer.

"I had a meeting with Gizelle today and I think she's going to sign on with our firm!"

"Are you serious?"

I was sincerely surprised. Even though I knew she had met with Gizelle, but I didn't think she was going to reel her in that quickly.

"Yeah, we met today at the Grand Hyatt. She's excited about coming on board. I told her you would be giving her a call to set up another meeting."

"This is fantastic! Did you tell Gizelle when to expect my call?"

"No, I told her it would be soon, though."

"I'll give her a call when I get home."

"Okay."

"Well, I'll talk to you later."

"Don't hang up yet."

"Okay," I said.

"How's Julian?" Cynthia asked.

My heart almost jumped out of my chest. That chick saw me and she was waiting for me to confess.

"Why do you ask that?"

"I saw you two in the Grand Hyatt, Alicia."

"Damn!" I said.

"Was that lunch before or after?"

"I know how it looks but nothing happened, Cynt."

"Why did you run away?"

"To get away from you."

"What are we? Six years old?" Cynthia asked. "I can't believe you're cheating on Johnny."

"I'm not cheating! Nothing happened, Cynthia! I swear to God! Nothing happened!"

"Why were you even there, Alicia?"

"He said he wanted to talk and that's it, we talked."

"Is that all that you did?"

"Yes! We talked! That's it!"

Cynthia's my girl, but I wasn't going to tell her how close I had come to cheating on Johnny. The fact was that I didn't cheat. That's all that mattered.

"Alicia, don't mess up your marriage over something stupid like that, girl. Come on now, you have a good man. Don't blow it!"

"Cynt, I didn't do anything. I told Julian good-bye for the last time. That's it! I needed closure and I got it."

"Are you sure?"

"I'm positive."

"I hope so because that's *my* husband's brother and I don't want to get caught up in some mess."

"Don't worry, that's over with. I promise, Cynt."

"It better be."

"It is," I said. "I promise."

"Okay," Cynthia said, "Make that call to Gizelle while we have her interested. We don't want to let up."

"Okay, I'll call her as soon as I get home."

"Okay, I'll talk to you later."

"Bye."

"Bye," Cynt said.

Before I called Gizelle, I met with Pam to discuss our strategy. We met at my house, after I picked up Brittany from school. She gave me her opinion on how to initiate the conversation. It was a very productive meeting. I must admit, once Pam joined our company, things really took off. That extra person with fresh ideas was all we needed.

After talking business, we switched to our personal lives. I talked to Pam about my sexual deprivation issue and she informed me on what she considered to be a sexual fad. I was all ears as she talked about this new dance phenomenon sweeping the married and unmarried unlike.

"If I tell you this, don't be putting my business all in the streets, Alicia."

"My lips are sealed, Pam, what is it?"

"Well, my classes begin next week. It's not too late for you to join."

"Join what?"

"Pole-dancing class."

"What the hell is pole-dancing?"

"You know, like a stripper."

"Oh no, girl, I'm too embarrassed."

"Why are you embarrassed?" Pam asked. "There are all kinds of married women taking the class. Most of the women in the class are married."

"Like you said, I'm a soccer mom. That may be frowned upon in the soccer mom community."

"Girl, you better get your mind off of those checkered balls and focus on Johnny's balls."

"Shut up with your nasty self, Pam."

"So are you going to do it or what?"

"I guess it won't hurt."

"That's my niggah!"

"Pam, I thought we were cutting back on using that word."

"I'm trying."

"I think I'm going to ask Cynt to join the class with us."

"Girl, you know Cynthia ain't doing nothing like that."

"You don't know, she might."

"Yeah, I do."

"How do you know?"

"Because I already asked her."

"And what did she say?"

"Hell no!"

"Oh-oh! She really meant what she said if she cursed."

"We don't need her square ass anyway."

"Okay. Well, I'm in!"

"See you in class next week."

"A'ight! I'm there!"

THE NEXT WEEK PAM AND I HAD OUR FIRST CLASS. I was embarrassed, but Pam seemed to be at home. Once we got started and I saw how ridiculous the other women in the class danced, I was fine. The instructor, Kamille, came out highly motivated!

"Okay, ladies!" Kamille shouted. "Get ready to meet your new best friend!"

Kamille ran into the room jumping around, waving her hands in the air. Loud, strange music started to blare from the speakers in the ceilings. I mean very strange music.

"She's excited, isn't she?" I asked.

"She better calm her ass down!" Pam said. "I'm not going to be running around jumping up and down like that."

"Everybody out there readddddy?" Kamille shouted and clapped her hands. "Grab that pole!"

"Just like that?" I asked Pam. "We don't get to rehearse? Just grab the pole and dance?"

"I think this is motivational warm-up, Alicia."

There were about six poles from the floor to the ceiling and probably, twenty of us. We took turns spinning around the pole and falling on our asses. Kamille let us have fun for a while and then she showed us the technique of stripping.

Pam and I were the only two black women in the group. Let me tell you something, some of those white women danced like they were born in Harlem. They were so rhythmical it looked like they used to dance around the poles in their cribs when they were babies. I was a little intimidated at first. But after a few classes, they nicknamed me, "The Golden Lioness."

After the fifth class, Pam dropped out. I thought about it, but Pam wasn't married, I was. I started going to the class to spice up my marriage and I was going to see it through.

Once I received my Stripper's Certificate, I immediately had a pole installed in our bedroom. I had to have it installed and in working order in one afternoon. I moved the bed to the left side of the room to add more space to the area where I would be performing. I also had Johnny's favorite recliner—the comfy chair as he called it—moved upstairs.

When the carpenter was leaving, he asked if I could give him a complimentary performance on the house. He was sexy as hell, but of course I said no. I'm faithful! I'll admit that after he left, I enjoyed a hot fantasy about him in the shower.

I wasn't sure how Johnny would react to a stripper's pole in the center of our bedroom. But the look in his eyes was crystal clear. My conservative husband was drooling at the mouth. He couldn't wait for me to give my first performance. After Brittany went to bed that night, he got exactly what he wanted. Suffice it to say, we had animalistic sex that night. From that point forward, that area of the bedroom would be known as "the jolly ranch." That put a spark back into the sexual aspect of our marriage, and turned my frown downside up!

CHAPTER TEN

A couple of days later, I met with Gizelle at the Grand Hyatt, the same hotel where I had almost committed adultery. When I sat down and got a straight-on look at her, Pam and Cynthia were right; she could have been my twin. As I sat down, I noticed Big Walt at the table next to us. He gave me a subtle wave, and I waved back. I'm assuming that was his gratitude for Cynthia and me sacrificing Pam.

"Hi, Gizelle."

"Alicia?"

"Yes, hi," I said.

"You look familiar," Gizelle joked.

"And so do you." I laughed.

"It's a pleasure to meet you, Alicia."

"The pleasure is all mine."

"So, what can I do for you?"

"Ah, ask not what you can do for me; ask what I can do for your career."

"What can you do for my career that hasn't already been done?"

Her question kind of caught me off guard and I had to search my mind for a professional comeback.

"We can broaden your fan base."

"Why do I need to broaden my fan base?"

"You can never have too many fans," I said. "Think about it,

Gizelle. Every young artist that maintains longevity in the entertainment business goes through a maturation of style, music and
attitude because their fan base goes through the metamorphosis.
Of course you have to maintain that musical edge that your fans
have come to love about you. But you have to also develop a new
style to reflect what's happening in the now. CAPs can be your
marketing tool to make sure the world knows that no matter how
much music may change, Gizelle is here forever!"

"Hmm, that's good," Gizelle said. "I like that. I'm tired of the
company I'm with now anyway. I need something fresh! Something new to give my career a boost."

"Believe me! CAPs is what you need!"

"I'll tell you what, Alicia." Gizelle reached across the table and
shook my hand. "We have a deal!"

"Are you serious?" I said excitedly.

"I'm very serious!"

"Great! We'll be contacting you to go over the contract within
twenty-four hours and hopefully we'll have you signed, sealed
and delivered as the newest client of CAPs Public Relations and
Marketing Firm!"

"Sounds like a plan."

"This was a quick meeting; lunch hasn't even been served." I
laughed.

"I'm not hungry anyway, and I'm late for my session with my
psychologist."

"My husband is an excellent psychologist. Had I known you
were seeking the services of a psychologist, I could have given
you a coupon for a discount."

"Damn!" Gizelle snapped her fingers.

"It's been a pleasure."

Gizelle and Big Walt stood up to leave.

"I hope you don't mind eating alone, Alicia. I really have to go."

"I'm used to it."

"Order whatever you want; it's going to be put on my bill."

"That's okay; you shouldn't be buying my lunch."

"Believe me, Alicia, it's the least I can do." Gizelle smiled and walked off with Big Walt following right behind her.

Pam met with Gizelle's manager the next day and went over the contract. Gizelle agreed in principle and we arranged a dinner to formally sign the contract. The dinner was at Michael and Cynthia's since they had the biggest house.

We went all out to make the dinner as extravagant as possible. We reserved a limousine. We hired caterers and servers. I wanted to invite all of the office girls, but Pam and Cynthia out-voted me, saying that the dinner party should be professional, and not sociable.

Cynthia and I were running around like chickens with our heads cut off, making sure everything was perfect. Johnny and Michael were in the basement watching sports. Bless their hearts, they wanted to help but they would have only slowed us down.

Once the party was in order, we made them take showers and dress appropriately for the occasion. Pam finally showed up fashionably late as usual. Unlike our other occasions, Pam brought a date with her. I think we were all taken aback when we saw him for the first time.

Michael answered the door and led them into the dining room. He was making faces behind their backs. I tried to act as if it was no big deal, but I couldn't wait to get her alone to ask questions.

Cynthia nudged me as soon as they came into view. I nudged her back, hoping Pam didn't see us. The man was as white as a ghost! You have to understand Pam to understand how shocking it was. Pam is pro-black from the surface of her skin to the marrow in her bones. For a woman, she uses the word, *niggah* more than any man I know. It was just a huge question mark why she would flip the script and go jungle fever on us. I was going to find out one way or the other. My analytical husband took it upon himself to get his answers.

"So, where did you two meet?" Johnny asked.

"I met Christopher at a conference for young entrepreneurs," Pam answered.

It was a conference Cynthia and I had made her attend to help hone her professional skills.

"Okay, interesting," Johnny said. "So, where are you from, Chris?"

"I'm originally from Toronto, Canada," Chris said. "But I was raised in Texas."

"Oh, Canada!" Michael sarcastically sang Canada's national anthem. "Just kidding with you, man."

"Good rendition," Chris said back.

"How did you guys meet at the conference?" Johnny asked.

"I, uh, I sat next to Pam at the conference. We began a conversation and decided to stay in contact."

"Interesting."

"Okay, that's enough of that, Johnny," Pam said. "Don't pay any attention to him, Chris. He's a psychologist; it's just his nature."

"I understand."

"I talked to Gizelle on my way over and told her that the limo was on the way to pick her up," I said to Pam.

"Limousine?" Johnny asked. "You ladies are going all out, aren't you?"

"Yes, baby, we got a limousine! Gizelle is big! Really big! She's going to be our biggest client! I'm so excited!"

"I can see!" Johnny said. "Hope everything goes well tonight."

"Oh, this is a done deal!" Pam said. "By the end of the night, Gizelle will be CAPs' biggest client!"

"What about me?" Michael said.

"You'll always be number one to me, baby," Cynthia said.

"In that case, let's toast!" Michael lifted his glass.

As we were about to toast, the doorbell rang.

"I'll get it!" Cynthia ran to answer the door.

"Ooh, it's her!"

"Baby, calm down before you blow a gasket," Johnny said.

"I can't help it!" I was so excited I could barely contain myself.

"Alicia! Would you stop it?" Pam said. "We want her to think we're just as important to her, as she is to us. We can't be jumping around like we're her fans!"

It wasn't Gizelle; it was Tina and Curtis. Yeah, the same Curtis who tried to kill Tina at Upskon. The day he went nuts at the job apparently turned his life around. Ms. Virginia bailed him out of jail, got him off of drugs, took him to church, and the Lord took over from there.

At first the office girls were suspicious, present company included, but the guy was legit. He turned his life completely around and as devoted as he was to being a jerk, he became just as devoted, or more so, to being a Christian. He went to church almost every day of the week. Totally gave up chasing the three "A's": amphetamines, ass and alcohol.

Tina's name used to be scandalized for having a sorry-ass man. Now it's scandalized for thinking her man is better than everyone else's. Not that she is saying anything or acting a certain way; she's just happy and all of those sisters who don't have a man are hating on her. If I didn't have Johnny, I'd probably be one of them.

"Hey, y'all!" Tina waved her hands in the air. "I'm sorry, I'm late! Is Gizelle here yet?"

"No, but she's on her way," Alicia said.

"Good, we ain't too late!" Tina said.

"How's everybody doing this evening?" Curtis said.

"We're fine. How are you, Curtis?" I said.

"I'm feeling fine."

"Hey, Curtis, I forgot to drop off those clothes at the shelter, but I'll get to them this weekend, I promise," Michael said.

"That's okay," Curtis said. "We'll take 'em whenever we can get 'em."

As Curtis and Michael spoke so pleasantly to one another, I thought back to that day in the office when they had almost killed each other. God is something else.

"Curtis received approval for his loan to build for the church today!" Tina shouted. "God is blessing us, ain't He?"

"Curtis, you got the loan, man?" Michael asked excitedly.

"Yes! Praise the Lord!" Curtis said, balling his fists.

Pam, Cynthia and I were so excited for Tina and Curtis we hugged them repeatedly. It was good to know that our best friend was growing along with us.

"Oh my God, I'm so happy for you, Curtis!" Cynthia said as she hugged Curtis again. Curtis seemed slightly uncomfortable with the attention he was receiving. His modesty was charming.

"Thank you, Cynthia!" Curtis said. "May the glory be to God!"

"Toast to Curtis!" Michael shouted.

"Oh no, this is y'all night, not mine!"

"I don't care who we're toasting, I just need a glass!" Tina said.

"Tina," Curtis said, "Don't give in to temptation."

"Come on, baby, can I have just one drink?" Tina asked. "Come on, it's a celebration. Pleeeeeease?"

"Okay, sweetheart." Curtis kissed Tina on the cheek. "One drink!"

"Pass the sauce!" Tina lifted her glass.

"Curtis, what would you like to drink?" Cynthia asked.

"I'll take a soda," Curtis said. "But in a wineglass."

Cynthia gave Curtis his wineglass full of soda and again, as we lifted our glasses for a toast, the doorbell rang.

"Damn!" Pam said. "We're never going to finish this toast."

"Hold on, I'll be right back!" Cynthia ran to answer the door again.

I could hear Gizelle's voice when Cynthia answered the door. I was so excited that I grabbed Johnny by the arm. I had a reason to be excited. After that night, our company would no longer be an entity of obscurity. We would be on the map.

It was probably a matter of seconds before Cynthia and Gizelle walked into the dining room but it seemed like hours. As usual, walking right behind Gizelle was Big Walt. He looked pissed off when he saw Pam leaning against Christopher. I was hoping he wouldn't think we had used him to get to Gizelle and attempt to talk her out of signing with us. I was also hoping the big fella didn't go on a rampage and kick all of our asses.

"Hi, everybody!" Gizelle smiled.

"Hi, Gizelle!" I said.

"Hey, Alicia," Gizelle said.

"Okay, how was the ride over?" Pam asked.

"Nice, very nice," Gizelle said. "I'm going to get one of them."

Cynthia walked around the room, introducing Gizelle to everybody in the room. When she got to Johnny, I thought I heard something that I know I shouldn't have heard.

"This is my brother-in-law, Johnson Forrester," Cynthia said. "We call him, Johnny."

"Good evening, Dr. Forrester," Gizelle said.

I immediately thought to myself, how in the hell did she know that my husband was a doctor? But then I remembered that I told her at our lunch that he was a psychologist, so maybe I should have heard it.

"How did you know I was a doctor?" Johnny said. "Did the monogram on my jacket give me away?"

"Absolutely." Gizelle smiled.

Absolutely? She knew Johnny was a doctor because I told her. That heffa was flirting with my husband right in front of my face.

"Everybody sit down, so we can eat," Cynthia said.

Dinner went very well. We asked Gizelle plenty of questions and she asked us a lot questions. After dinner Pam pulled out the contract and we surrounded Gizelle as she formally signed with CAPs. While she was signing the contract, Cynthia, Pam and I posed behind her as Tina took a picture of us.

"Say cheese, y'all!" Tina shouted.

"CHEEEEEESE!" we said in unison.

We decided to celebrate by having a girls' night out on the town. We took a few bottles of champagne and climbed into the limousine. It was Tina, Gizelle, Pam, Cynthia and me. I wanted to sit next to Gizelle and feel her energy. She was magnetic. I could understand why she was so such a mega-star. I was star-struck.

"Damn! Y'all two look just alike!" Tina pointed at Gizelle and me.

"You think so?" I asked.

"Like twins!"

"We tried to tell Alicia," Pam said.

"Let me see." Gizelle held my face close to hers and looked in my eyes. "Naw, I don't see it."

We laughed and then Pam popped a bottle of wine.

"Everybody grab a bottle and drink the hell up!" Pam shouted.

"I'm not drinking no wine!" Cynthia said.

"Pass me a bottle!" Tina yelled.

"Come on, Cynthia, just for tonight," Gizelle said. "You don't have to get drunk, just drink!"

"Where's my bottle?" I said, bouncing up and down. I felt like I was back in college.

"Here!" Pam passed everybody their own personal bottle of champagne.

Tina rolled down the window and leaned out, pouring wine along the highway. "Now, this is for the sisters who ain't here!"

"Get your drunk ass back in this car, Tina!" Pam shouted.

"Girl, get back in the car!" I pulled Tina back and took the wine out of her hand. "Okay, that's enough for you."

Gizelle suggested that we go to a strip club. Cynthia wanted to have fun with us but that was going too far. While we were inside the strip club having fun, Cynthia was in the limo talking to Michael. Tina and I made her promise not to tell him where we were. We didn't want our husbands to find out.

I am not a lesbian or anything, but seeing those women rub their naked bodies in front of me was a turn-on. After we left the strip club, we had the limousine driver drop us off at our front doors. Gizelle said it was okay if we were dropped off first. Pam was first, Tina was second, Cynthia was third and I was last. When Cynthia got out, Gizelle knocked on the driver's window. The driver slowly let the window down.

"Excuse me, driver," Gizelle said.

"Yes, ma'am."

"Can you get back on I-285 and just drive until we tell you when to get off?"

"Sure thing."

"Thank you."

The driver slowly raised the window back up.

"I hope I don't get you in trouble with your husband, Alicia."

"He's probably asleep by now anyway."

"I bet you're curious to know why I asked the driver to keep going."

"Very much."

"Come sit next to me." Gizelle patted the spot next to her.

"Oh, okay." I moved closer to Gizelle and we were practically sitting on the same seat.

"Isn't that better?" Gizelle smiled at me and kissed me on the cheek.

I was so surprised by her kiss, I couldn't move. I thought to myself, did this girl just kiss me? I think she took my lack of response as a welcoming sign for her to kiss me again. She leaned forward and I backed away.

"What is this?" I asked. "What are you doing?"

"Nothing, I'm just showing you my appreciation."

"Appreciation for what?"

"For making me your client."

"I don't know what's going on here, Gizelle, but this is not me on so many levels."

"Are you sure?"

"Of course, I'm sure."

"I haven't heard you say that you wanted to go."

I knocked on the driver's window so hard that I bruised my knuckles.

"Ouch!" I shook my hand to try to shake the pain away. "Shit!"

"Yes, ma'am?"

"Can you take me to my house, please?" I asked.

"Where is that?"

I wrote down the address and handed it to the driver. "Here you go."

"You wanna go now?"

"Yes! Get me home as quickly as possible."

"Okay, on the way."

"Thank you."

"No problem."

The limo driver raised the window and I sat far away from Gizelle.

"Are you afraid of me, Alicia?"

"No."

"Then why are you sitting so far away from me? That kiss meant nothing. I was just trying to show my appreciation."

"That's a strange way of showing appreciation, Gizelle."

"I think you liked it."

"I think you're nuts!"

"Have you ever been with a woman before, Alicia?"

"No."

"Why not?"

"Because I'm not interested."

"Come on, you're not the slightest bit interested?"

"Not in the least."

"So the smoothness of a woman's body means nothing to you? The sexiness of her breasts and thighs doesn't excite you, Alicia? My legs? My thighs? You don't find them sexy?"

Gizelle lifted her skirt and raised her shirt and exposed herself to me.

"Please, Gizelle, stop."

"Come here, Alicia."

"This is making me very uncomfortable, Gizelle."

"You want me to stay on as your client, don't you? How would your partners feel if they knew you were rejecting me? Huh? Do you know what I could do for your company?"

"Are you blackmailing me?"

"Yes! If that's what you want to call it."

Gizelle slid over to me and opened her legs, placing one of them on my lap. She stuck her finger inside of her vagina and then cupped her breasts with the other hand.

"Gizelle, please!" I started to feel moisture between my legs and closed my thighs.

"Does this look good to you, Alicia?"

I didn't answer. I rubbed my thighs together and continued to feel the moisture develop. Gizelle started to finger herself very fast, knowing we were getting close to my house.

"I'm about to come, Alicia! Come with me!"

Gizelle took my hand and placed it on top of hers. I could feel the juices from her fingers seep onto mine as she started to come.

"Oh, shit, Alicia, rub it!" Gizelle said. "Rub my clit!"

I moved my hand away, and watched as Gizelle continued to enjoy herself. I rubbed my vagina against her thigh until I felt my own orgasm come. I tried not to let on that I was coming but she could tell by my involuntary body movements. She stretched out completely on the seat and opened her legs wide. I was extremely embarrassed. I could barely look at her.

"Aah, I'm coming, Alicia!"

Gizelle slammed her legs together and moaned loudly as she twisted on the seat. When she finished, she sat up and licked her fingers.

"You okay?" Gizelle asked.

The limousine slowed as we turned the corner of my block.

"No, I'm not okay! I'm a married, straight woman! This is wrong! Very wrong!"

"What's the big deal?" Gizelle said, adjusting her clothes.

"My husband is the big deal?"

"Dr. Forrester?" Gizelle laughed. "He can't complain."

"Don't bring my husband into this!"

"Your husband is already in this."

"Listen, little girl! You may be able to push people around with your superstar status, but you're barking up the wrong tree now."

"Am I?" Gizelle laughed. "I just made you watch me have sex with myself and you enjoyed it!"

"Shut the hell up!" I yelled. "What happened in this limousine tonight better die in this limousine tonight!"

"Don't threaten me, old lady!"

"Old lady?" I shouted. "Let me tell you…"

Gizelle snatched me by the collar, and pulled me close to her. I could have stopped her, but I didn't. She leaned forward as if she was going to kiss me and at the point where I was going to allow her to kiss me, she let me go and laughed.

Until that night I had never thought I would ever be willing to kiss another woman. The softness of her body when I squeezed her was so unfamiliarly pleasurable. The femininity I craved when I touched myself was being realized.

"Is this all a joke to you?" I asked.

"I just wanted to see how far you would go to make me happy."

"I would never go that far to satisfy anyone but my husband."

"You act as if your husband is so different from any other man. If he was in your position we'd be having sex by now."

"You don't know anything about my husband."

"Oh, is that right?" Gizelle said as she wiped my lipstick from her mouth. "Ask your husband about his patient named Anise."

"Who is Anise?"

"Ask your husband!"

"I'm asking you, Gizelle!" I shouted. "Who the hell is Anise?"

"The question is who the hell are you? You wanted to kiss me and if I hadn't stopped you, you would have. You and your husband are nothing but a couple of hypocrites!"

"What the hell do you mean by that?"

"Ask the good doctor." Gizelle laughed.

I remained calm; even though I wanted to strangle that bitch.

"See you tomorrow at the shoot, Alicia."

"This will never happen again, Gizelle."

"It will if I want it to happen."

"You spoiled little bitch!"

"If I'm a bitch, what does that make you? We are one and the same, Alicia. Oh, I almost forgot. Driver!"

The driver let down the window.

"Yes, ma'am?"

"Pass me that box, please."

The driver handed Gizelle the box and rolled the window back up.

"These are for you." Gizelle handed me the box.

"What is this?"

"Open it and see."

I opened the box and it was a dozen flowers, six tulips and six roses.

"Ask your husband."

The only way she could have known that my favorite flowers were roses and tulips was if Johnny or Julian told her. They were the only people privy to that information. My heart was broken.

The limousine stopped in front of my house and the driver stepped out and opened my door. Gizelle smiled and waved as the driver slammed the door behind me and then got back in the car. I stood in my driveway and watched as the limousine pulled away.

My anger at Johnny was surpassed by the disgust for myself. I walked into my house feeling repulsively filthy. I took a long hot shower and scrubbed my body from head to toe. As I was standing in the shower wondering if my husband had been with that malicious little vixen, I wanted to walk in that bedroom and cut his stick off at the balls! But how could I when I had practically kissed a woman?

Once my body was clean, my mind started to rewind the images of Gizelle and me in the limo. I went from Gizelle touching herself, to my husband and Gizelle, and I became wet. I tried to resist thinking about it but the thought of Johnny's big stick inside of her young hot body was stuck in my head. I was on fire and needed sex immediately.

I walked into my bedroom to see what kind of mood Johnny was in but he was knocked out cold. I couldn't wait until morning so I went back to the bathroom, locked the door and masturbated. I lit a few candles, put on some Luther Vandross and relaxed in my tub. I took my time making love to myself.

When I came, my body splashed around and I spilled half of the water in the tub onto the floor. After I collected myself, I cleaned myself again. I was still horny and in need of sex, so I made up an excuse to wake up Johnny.

I put on a brand-new negligee hoping that would entice Johnny from his slumber. I could have cut off the price tag myself, but I woke him up to do the honors.

"OH SHIT! Wait a minute!" Johnny must have been having a bad dream. He woke up screaming and cowering.

"What's wrong with you, boy?" I asked.

"What are you doing standing over me like that with those scissors?" Johnny asked. He sat up and clutched a pillow in his arms as if it were a woman.

"Here, can you cut the price tag off of this nightie for me?" I handed Johnny the scissors.

"Oh, sure, no problem."

"Were you having a bad dream?"

"Yeah," Johnny said, "something like that."

"Tonight was one of the most interesting nights of my life!"

"I'm happy for you, sweetheart!"

"I'm sorry for bailing out on you at the dinner party, but I thought this would make up for it." I slid the nightie down my body, twisting and turning as the silk touched my skin. "Come here."

I took Johnny by the hand and led him to the jolly ranch. I turned down the lights and closed my eyes as I started to dance with myself. I slid my body against Johnny's as he sat in the chair. I rubbed my ass against his stick and felt it rise. I turned around, putting my breasts in his face and teasing him with my nipples. Every time he tried to suck them, I would pull them back.

His stick had grown so hard it was sticking halfway out of his shorts. I helped release it by pulling it out of his underwear. I put my lips right at the head but didn't touch it. I stroked it up and down with my hand. I wanted to get him to the point where he was as horny as me. I didn't want routine sex. I wanted wild, un-rehearsed, uninhibited sex! When he started to moan and pump his hips, I knew he was almost there.

I slowly danced over to the "stripper pole." My body took over my mind and I started to exhibit dance moves I had learned on my back, and not in any class. I looked at Johnny with half-closed eyes, consumed by sensuality. I pulled my nightie above my head, allowing it to caress my body as it passed over my stomach, my breasts and my face. It fell from my hands to the floor. I used my toes to toss it to the side.

I grabbed the pole with one hand, switching from left to right. The passion growing inside of me made me more of a daredevil. I tried shit that I knew could break my damn neck, but I did it anyway. For example, I jumped in the air, feet first, and gripped the pole with my legs. I dropped my head to the floor, and slid my legs up and down. It had to be a turn-on for my husband because it was turning me on. I moved my vagina against the pole as if I were having simulated sex with it.

I held on to the pole with my legs and then braced myself by putting both of my hands on the floor. I slid down the slick pole until my knees were on the floor. I leaned backward with the pole between my legs and started to grind against it. I grabbed the pole with my hands and started to lick it with my tongue, humping it up and down.

I continued to grind up and down, and up and down, feeling that round pole between my legs, pressing against my clit. I could feel my orgasm coming rapidly. I sat up and wrapped my legs around the pole, humping faster and faster.

I slid my hand inside of my panties and rubbed my clit vigorously. Every now and then I would slide a finger inside of me to intensify the pleasure. I could feel my juices squirting from my vagina and landing on my pubic hair. I rested on my back, preparing to have the orgasm of my life.

I teased my clit as I ground my vagina against that long black pole. I lifted my hips to the pole, rubbed my clit hard on it, and then dropped back down to the floor. I moved my fingers faster and faster until they were cramping. I couldn't stop because my orgasm was right there. I pushed off of my toes and raised my hips in the air, trying to get there. I went from turned on to frustrated, because I could not come. I could feel it right there on the edge, but it wouldn't burst through. I was moaning loudly, grunting, everything, but I couldn't make it happen.

"Ah! Ah! Ah! Ah! Ah! Ah!" I was practically raping myself, trying to come.

Finally it hit, but it wasn't as powerful as I thought it would be. It felt great, but not GRRREAT! I turned on my side, exhausted from all of the energy I had spent. My body shook and shivered, obviously, that orgasm was much more powerful externally than internally.

The next thing I know, Johnny was sliding his shorts down and then lying behind me. I was so tired that I wanted to go straight to sleep. I didn't want any more sex! But since I woke him up, I figured it was the least I could do. I just wanted it to be quick and painless.

Johnny slid his stick in from behind. He lifted my leg in the air, grabbing my ankles and diving deep, deep inside of me. That woke me up quick! He was touching the same spot every time he went in. He was in so deep that I thought I was about to pee. I wondered if it felt the same way to Gizelle when he was inside of her.

He was going in slowly and precisely, deeper and deeper, hitting the same spot, over and over. It wasn't long before that sensation returned. I could feel another orgasm coming on. My feet flopped back and forth in the air as he plunged his stick inside of me.

I realized the one thing I was missing from my orgasm moments earlier was passion. Johnny was giving me passion. I turned to kiss him, but I was too consumed by lust to find his mouth. I was kissing him any and everywhere I could. Having Johnny inside of me made me know the difference between love and lust.

Johnny gave me one long, deep stroke and then shot his warm juice inside of me. That was all that I needed. That powerful evasive orgasm hit like a number seven earthquake on the Richter scale. Wow!

"Oh, baby," I moaned. "I love you so much."

"I love you, too, baby."

Johnny was no longer hard, but I could still feel him inside of me. I wanted to stay that way for as long as we could.

"Don't move," I said. "I want to just lay here with you inside of me."

"Alicia," Johnny said, "You know there's not even an adjective to describe how much I love you."

"Do you really love me that much, Johnny?" I turned on my back to look Johnny in the eyes. I wanted to see his sincerity.

"Until my daughter was born, I never knew that I could love anyone as much as I loved her. But then, that was my child, my baby, so that explained that special love between us. I never thought for a moment that I could fall in love with a woman and feel that special kind of love. I never felt that way until I met you and I've been head over heels ever since."

"Oh, that's so sweet." I caressed Johnny's face, and squeezed his penis inside of me.

"Get some sleep. You have a busy day tomorrow."

"Okay." I relaxed in Johnny's arms and kissed him on his chest. "Good night."

Johnny pulled the comforter from our bed and covered my body. "Good night."

I stayed awake most of the night, imagining Johnny and Gizelle. To prevent myself from going nuts, I had to either forget what Gizelle had said about Johnny, or confront him.

CHAPTER ELEVEN

The next morning I got up early to fix breakfast for Brittany. It was a bad morning for her. What I mean by bad is that she would wake up some mornings expecting to see Deirdra. As soon as she walked in the kitchen, I could tell something wasn't right.

"You okay, baby?"

"Yes."

I sat her in my lap and started to braid her hair.

"Are you thinking about Mommy?" I asked.

"Yes."

"Do you miss Mommy?"

"Yes." Brittany wiped her eyes.

"Aw, you wanna watch Mommy on television?"

"Yes!" Brittany shouted.

"Come on!" I picked her up and carried her into the den.

Before Deirdra died we had made a video for Brittany. We tried to make her look as healthy as possible. Deirdra was the leading actress and Johnny and I were costars. We had a ball. Whenever Brittany became sad, we played the video and she would feel much better.

"Feeling better, Brit?" I asked.

"Yes!" Brittany ran to me and I picked her up. "I want some pancakes!"

"Pancakes it is," I said.

I finished making breakfast and waited for Johnny to get up. I didn't know what I would say to him. How do you ask your husband if he's cheating when all that you have is the word of a conniving little bitch? I wanted to block out everything. Gizelle, Johnny, everything! I wanted my life to be like it was twenty-four hours earlier. While I was thinking, the telephone rang. I was expecting Pam and Cynthia to stop by so that we could ride together to the photo shoot. I thought the call was from one of them, but it wasn't.

"Hello."

"Hello," I said.

"Alicia?"

"Yes, who's calling?"

"Gizelle."

"Oh," I said. "Hi."

"Hey, I'm sorry about last night. We were drinking and I guess things got a little out of control."

"Okay," I said, but I was really thinking, *whatever, bitch!*

"I'm looking forward to the photo shoot today."

"Me, too."

"Good," Gizelle said. "I, uh, I just want to say that I wasn't quite sure about signing the contract until I dropped you off."

"Why not?"

"Well, your company is new, and you know, it takes time for a company to establish a reputation. Having a reputation is everything in this business. But you showed me last night that you are willing to do what's necessary for your company...and for me."

"I see."

"Now, if you keep me happy, I'll make sure your PR firm becomes one of the most-sought-after firms in the business. Isn't that what you want?"

"Of course."

"Then we're on the same page," Gizelle said. "We are on the same page, aren't we?"

"Yeah," I said.

I hung up the telephone and sat at the table. I remembering asking the question, *what the hell have I gotten myself into?*

Pam and Cynthia came over and we were eating breakfast by the time Johnny came downstairs. Michael stopped by to pick up Johnny for golf. He and Pam got into a big fight over black men and black women. I was preoccupied with my own problems to be concerned with something as trivial as that.

Michael stormed out and Cynthia checked Pam for disrespecting Michael. After a few apologies and a phone call to Michael, we managed to work everything out.

Later on, Gizelle arrived to the photo shoot unfashionably late. She cost us a lot of money, a lot of money that we planned on invoicing her ass for when the bill came out.

Gizelle flirted with me throughout the shoot. She was like an obnoxious man who wouldn't take no for an answer. I was convinced that she really didn't want to touch me; she just wanted to know that if she wanted to, she could.

THE NEXT SCHEDULED EVENT WE HAD was a magazine interview at Gizelle's hotel. I was running late, but as usual, Gizelle was running later. She asked me to meet her in her hotel room. I was apprehensive but figured she couldn't do anything to me that I didn't want her to do.

When I got to her room, Big Walt was standing outside of the door on the phone. He waved at me and walked away. I knocked on the door; it took Gizelle a while but she finally answered.

"Hi, Alicia," Gizelle said, opening the door.

"You ready to go?"

"Yeah, I just have to throw on some clothes and a wig right quick and I'm good to go."

"Can I use your bathroom?"

"Sure, go 'head."

Gizelle's bathroom was enormous! There was enough room to have a small party in there. I quickly handled my business and got the hell out. Gizelle was almost ready to go when I walked back into her bedroom. On our way out, something fell in her bathroom.

"What was that?" I asked.

"Some of my stuff probably fell, girl."

As I was turning to face the door, Gizelle pulled me to her and kissed me on the lips.

"Oh-kay," I said, wiping my lips. "I think we better go."

"I'm waiting on you."

Gizelle opened the door for me and as I passed her; she smacked me on the ass.

"Oh-kay!" I covered my ass and backed out, facing Gizelle.

"Your husband doesn't appreciate what he has, Alicia."

"Is that right?"

"Yeah, baby."

The interview went extremely well. Johnny showed up to offer a little support. He could only stay for a few minutes but I appreciated that. I wanted to see how he would respond in front of Gizelle and he acted as if he had never seen her before in his life. That caused me to be suspicious because I knew for a fact that he had met her at our dinner party. Gizelle smiled at me as Johnny and I talked. I stared at Johnny like, *will you be honest and tell me what is going on between you and that little girl?* On the other hand, as long as Johnny didn't admit he was cheating on me, I didn't have to accept it. My perfect man was still perfect.

THE NEXT WEEK, GIZELLE PLEADED AND PLEADED for me to go away with her for a private getaway. She told me she had made arrangements and the money would be lost if we didn't go. She emailed a brochure of the resort and it was beautiful. But not for me! I apologized and told her I was unable to make it.

She called me toward the end of the week as if to brag that she had found someone to take my place. I wished her luck and made sure our business relationship was still in good standards. She reminded me of the agreement we had made in the limo. As long as she was happy, our business relationship was happy.

The Friday before Gizelle's scheduled getaway, it just so happened that Johnny had to go out of town for the night. What a coincidence? I pretended that I was none the wiser and encouraged Johnny to go. I kissed him good-bye as usual and went to pick up Brittany so that I could drop her off over Cynthia's house to spend the night.

When I got to Brittany's school, they told me that her Aunt Cynthia had picked her up on an emergency request from her parents. We had placed Cynthia and Michael on Brittany's emergency list as contacts and pickups, but we had not made arrangements for them to pick her up. I called Cynthia to confirm that Brittany was with her.

"Hey, Cynt, did you pick up Brit?"

"No, I didn't know I was supposed to."

"You weren't," I said. "I'm at her school and they're telling me her Aunt Cynthia picked her up. But she's not with you, huh?"

"No, girl, is everything okay?"

"I'm about to find out what the hell is going on," I said. "Bye."

"Call me back when you find out something."

"Okay, bye."

"Bye."

I hung up the phone and headed back into the office. On my way, I spotted Gizelle walking with Brittany. She held her by the hand as they were getting out of a limousine.

I ran to the limousine and snatched Brittany from Gizelle. I tried to stay calm but my emotions got the best of me.

"Bitch! Have you lost your damn mind?" I screamed.

"Mommy!" Brittany shouted. She had never heard me use profanity before and I think that I scared her more than I scared Gizelle.

"Shh!" Gizelle said. "You shouldn't be using that language in front of the child."

"You stay away from her!"

"We had some fun; that's all!" Gizelle laughed. "Since people say we look so much alike, you think if I had a child, it would look like her?"

Apparently Gizelle thought Brittany was my biological child.

"I'm going to only tell you this one time. If you ever come near my child again, I'll kill you! Do you understand me?"

"Okay, then. I won't." Gizelle said. "I'll go near your husband."

"You crazy bitch!"

"You have a great weekend." Gizelle got in her limousine and drove away.

I kneeled in front of Brittany and checked her body to make sure she was okay. "You okay, baby?"

"Yes, I'm okay. Aunty Gizelle took me to have ice cream."

"She's not your aunty, baby!"

"She's not?"

"No! She's nothing to you! Okay? You understand?"

"Uh-huhn," Brittany said.

"Thank God, you're alright!" I hugged Brittany tightly. "Thank God!"

I dropped Brittany off at Cynthia's. I didn't tell her what had happened because I didn't want to upset her. Cynthia was very optimistic about marriage, and particularly, her marriage. Johnny and I had made a farce of our nuptials and I wanted to keep our business private from as many people as possible. That's why I only contacted one person: Pam.

"Hey, girl, what are you doing tonight?"

"I have a date with Chris," Pam said. "What's up?"

"I need you to cancel that date and ride somewhere with me."

"I ain't canceling my date. What's up?"

"I need you, man, for real." I started to cry and Pam could hear it through the sound of my voice.

"Hey, you okay?"

"Just ride with me, please."

"How long is it going to take?"

"I don't know," I said. "It could take all night."

"Is this something serious?"

"Pam, I wouldn't ask you to do this if it wasn't serious."

"Okay then," Pam said. "So are you coming to get me? You want me to get you? We meeting up? What?"

"I'm coming to get you," I said. "Pam?"

"Yeah."

"Put on some ninja clothes."

"For what?"

"Just put on some ninja clothes."

"I ain't got no damn ninja clothes, you ol' crazy-ass woman."

"Put on something black then, Pam."

"Whoa! What are we about to do?"

"Put on something black and I'll be over there in about an hour."

"This better be important, if I'm giving up my date."

"Just get ready. Bye!"

"Bye!"

An hour later, I picked up Pam and we hit the highway. As soon as Pam jumped in the car, she started drilling me.

"Okay, so what's up?"

"I'll let you know when we get there."

"Are you kidnapping me?"

"Just trust me, please."

"I trusted you this far. Now tell me what's up." Pam looked at the road and then at me. "You might wanna slow down, Alicia."

"I gotta catch them."

"Catch who?"

"I'll tell you when we get there."

"Well, if you're not going to tell me, Alicia, then don't say shit!"

"Okay, I won't say anything."

"Girl, you better tell me something."

"There they go! There they go!"

I slowed down and pulled behind Gizelle's limousine.

"Who? Who's in that limousine?"

"Gizelle and Johnny."

"What is Johnny doing in a limo with Gizelle?"

"I think they're having an affair."

"What the hell?" Pam stared at me.

"I think Johnny is in that limousine with Gizelle and they're having an affair."

"What? Why would you think that?"

"She told me."

"Gizelle told you?"

"Yeah."

"I knew it! I knew it! I told Cynthia that niggah was up to something, but she wouldn't believe me."

"When? Why would you think he was up to something?"

"Because the day we had that magazine shoot, Cynthia and I caught him on Gizelle's floor. I asked him what the hell he was doing up there and he said he was looking for you. I knew that was bullshit!"

"Why didn't you tell me, Pam?"

"Cynthia told me to stay out of your business."

"Aw, man!" I said. "Next time tell me!"

"I tried to tell y'all that bitch was crazy!" Pam said. "If Johnny is in that limo, you better kick her ass, or I'm going to kick your ass!"

"I have to catch them first."

"Oh, we're going to catch them. Stay close on their asses!"

"I don't believe this shit!" I shook my head and started to cry again.

We followed them all the way to Tybee Island. They checked in a bed and breakfast and we waited outside for them on the beach. When I saw them together, the reality of Johnny cheating on me hit me like a ton of bricks.

"Damn!" I sat down on the curb and cried.

"Get up, Alicia," Pam said. "Don't even give them the satisfaction of hurting you. Get up!"

I stood up and walked over to my car. I leaned on the hood and continued to cry. Pam patted me on my back and tried to ease my agony.

"If he's going to mess around with that bitch on you, that niggah ain't shit anyway, Alicia." Pam pulled me by the arm. "Let's go! Here they come!"

Johnny and Gizelle walked out of the inn together, laughing and holding hands. They drove to Savannah and we followed them. They went into a jazz club and we waited for them to come back out. They had to be the last ones to leave. By that time I had cried all of my tears. I didn't need any more evidence to prove he was cheating; I had seen enough. We took pictures of them making out and that was all the evidence I needed to convince the court to give me half of Johnny's shit when I divorced his ass.

We thought they were going in for the night, but they grabbed some romantic things like wine and a blanket. Romantic things Johnny and I had once shared at the beach.

We followed them down the beach to a remote area perfectly suited for inconspicuous sex. They lit some candles and talked for a minute. We were lying flat on top of the hill, not far from them but not close enough to hear what they were saying. It didn't take long for them to start speaking the language of sex. They started to grope and feel all over each other. I was crushed! I started to cry again.

"Stop crying and take pictures of them!" Pam said.

"I can't."

"I can. Give me that damn camera."

Pam snapped pictures left and right. If I hadn't known any better I would have thought she was a professional photographer.

"I can't stand any more of this shit, Alicia. Go whoop her ass!"

"I can't."

"What do you mean, you can't? Run your ass down there and start whoopin' her ass! It's as simple as that!"

Pam was very upset. She probably thought I was weak for not doing anything but I couldn't.

"I don't get it! You brought me all the way down here to bust their asses and you're not going to do nothing?"

"I don't want to make a fool out of myself."

"Hold up! You and your best friend are watching your man have sex with another woman and you're concerned about making a fool out of yourself? Tell me you're not that weak, Alicia? Please!"

"Being weak has nothing to with it, Pam!"

"If you won't say nothing, I will!"

Pam stood up to go down the hill and an old couple walked up.

"Shit!" Pam quickly flopped back down and hid. "What are their old asses doing up this time of the night?"

"I'm ready to go," I said. "I don't want to see any more."

"Say something to them, Alicia!" Pam whispered. "Don't let them get away with this."

"Let's go home, Pam," I said. "Please."

"Man, let's go," Pam said, pulling me up by the hand. "I swear you better divorce his ass tomorrow."

We left them having sex on the beach. Pam drove all the way back to Atlanta. She kept trying to get me to burn Johnny's clothes. Put sugar in his tank. Put his business with Gizelle on the internet. I wasn't feeling the hostility she was feeling so I didn't entertain those thoughts very long.

"I'm not going to do anything."

"You're crazy as hell!"

"All I want is the truth! He's going to tell me. One way or the other, he's going to tell me. And when he does, we'll settle it then."

"What about Gizelle?"

"She's probably going to blackmail me into shutting up, if we want to keep her as a client."

"I wish that bitch would!" Pam pointed her finger in the air with every single word. "We'll sue her ghetto ass for everything she got."

"I want to put all of this behind me."

"Am I missing something here?" Pam looked back and forth at the road and then at me. "Why are you acting so weak?"

"I'm not acting weak! I'm trying to remain calm but you're not helping me."

"Why are you acting calm, Alicia? Your husband is cheating on you! That's the type of shit you get upset about."

Pam fussed the entire four hours back to her front door. After I dropped her off, she called me and kept on fussing. When I got home, she still wouldn't let me off the phone. I pretended to go to sleep and then hung up the phone.

The next morning I picked up Brittany and we were back at home waiting for Johnny to arrive. I knew it wouldn't be too long before I received a call from Gizelle, and I did. She was back in Atlanta, so obviously, so was Johnny. Gizelle called to tell me that her attorney would be meeting with us on Monday to cancel the contract. I figured that was coming.

I went along with the program and acted like I was fine with it. I called Pam and we decided to make an impromptu visit to Ms. Gizelle later that day. I was fed up with being played and we were about to set some shit off.

I waited for Johnny to come and when he walked in, he hugged and kissed Brittany and me like he had really missed us. I didn't say a word. I went along with the game.

I told him about Gizelle canceling the contract and he gave me some pathetic speech about how sorry he was. Niggah, please! He received a supposedly emergency phone call from his secretary and had to leave. I had Pam call Big Walt to make sure he hadn't backtracked to Gizelle's bed. Johnny was telling the truth that time. Since Pam had Big Walt's attention we had him set up an impromptu meeting with Gizelle.

Pam picked me up and then we rode to the Grand Hyatt. We met Big Walt in the lobby and he took us to Gizelle's room. She was unpacking from her overnight trip with my husband when we got there. Big Walt had no idea that we were about to check Gizelle's ass. He really thought we were there for business. We walked in like straight hoodrats. It was hot as hell outside and we were wearing our black ninja gear. We dressed in black pants, black shirts, black baseball caps, and black shades.

"What's up, Gizelle?" I said as I walked into her bedroom.

"I'm not in the mood for you old-ass women right now."

"You better get in the mood, bitch!" Pam shouted. "You're not screwing us on our contract! You signed it! And you're either going to honor it, or buy your way out!"

"Get your man-lookin' ass outta my face!" Gizelle shouted back.

I wanted to join in the argument, but I wasn't expecting all of that so quickly. They looked like they were about to go to blows. I came for diplomacy, not fist-to-wrist action.

"I got your man, you fake-ass Mariah Carey-lookin' skank!" Pam shouted.

"You don't know who I am, do you? I can pay a crackhead fifty cents to take your broke ass out!"

"*You* take me out!" Pam screamed. "Don't pay nobody, bitch! *You* do it!"

I tried to hold Pam back, but she and Gizelle were in each other's faces. They were out of control. I tried to separate them, but that only made it worse. They really started tripping then. Pam pushed Gizelle in the forehead with her finger and then it was on. They started to swing at each other like men. I ran to the door to get Big Walt, but he was gone.

I heard furniture tipping over and I ran back into the bedroom to try to break them up again. They were in the bed, kicking and pulling each other's hair. I was surprised everybody in the hotel couldn't hear all the noise they were making.

"Stop it!" I shouted as I pulled on their legs to separate them. "Stop it!"

I ran into the hall, looking for someone to help me. I could have called the front desk but I didn't want to draw that much attention to us. I wasn't there to go to jail.

As soon as I opened the door to run into the hallway, I heard a loud noise. It sounded as if something was breaking, and then I heard nothing. I ran back into the bedroom and Pam was standing with her hands on her hips. Gizelle was lying motionless on the bed.

"What happened?"

"She hit her head on the bed!" Pam shouted.

"Is she okay?"

"I don't know! Let's go!"

"We can't leave her like this!"

"We can't stay here either!" Pam shouted. "Come on!"

On our way out of the door, a weird woman walked in. She looked like she was high or something.

"Hi. My name is Kimberly. Are you my friend?"

Pam pushed the lady out of the way and we ran down the stairway. We ran to the back of the hotel where my car was and Big Walt was waiting for us. He wanted to make sure he had another date with Pam.

"Y'all meeting go all right, Pam?"

"Yeah, everything went great."

"Hey, let me holla at ya?" Big Walt grabbed Pam's arm.

"I can't right now!" Pam snatched away from Big Walt.

"You ain't say that when we got busy!" Big Walt asked.

"Niggah, ain't nobody get busy with you!"

"What y'all do up there?" Big Walt grabbed Pam's arm again. "Why you trippin'?"

"Would you please let me go?"

"Hell naw! Somethin' ain't right!" Big Walt pulled out his cell phone and called Gizelle. "She ain't answerin'! What ya'll do up there?"

Pam freed herself from Big Walt's grip while he was waiting for Gizelle to answer. I ran to the passenger door and jumped in the car, locking the door behind me. Pam was trying to get in the driver's side but Big Walt caught her. He bent her arm behind her and told me to get out before he broke it.

Pam screamed at the top of her lungs but no one came to our rescue. I got out and ran on their side of the car and hit Big Walt with everything that I had. Of course, he didn't feel it. I started to scratch at his eyes. I remembered that from a self-defense class. He let Pam go and we jumped back in the car.

When we pulled off, he smashed his big arm through Pam's window, shattering glass all over us. We screamed and Pam let go of the steering wheel. Big Walt stuck a gun in the window, yelling for us to get out of the car. Pam backed up and hit a car. The impact knocked the gun out of Big Walt's hand and onto the passenger side, right between my legs.

"Grab the gun, Alicia!" Pam yelled.

I was in shock! I reached for the gun, but I was too afraid to pick it up. I could hear the engine being revved up, but we weren't moving. When I finally got the nerve, Big Walt was snatching my door open.

"Get yo' ass out that car!" Big Walt yelled.

"Grab the damn gun, Alicia!" Pam screamed.

I saw Big Walt's eyes make contact with the gun as I was reaching for it. He reached for it, but I snatched it quickly and then he reached for me. I started to kick him away as I scooted onto Pam's seat with her. Big Walt started to crawl through my passenger door on top of me. I pointed the gun at him to scare him, but he wouldn't stop coming.

"Get back!" I shouted.

"Shoot him, Alicia!" Pam screamed.

"Gimme that damn gun!" Big Walt grabbed the barrel of the gun with his big paws. "Gimme my gun, bitch!"

"Shoot his ass, Alicia! Shoot him!"

"I can't!" I screamed.

Big Walt tried to pull the gun forward as I was pulling it backward and it went off like a cannon. There was a bright flash and a small cloud of smoke. My hands were on fire. I dropped the gun instantly as Big Walt's giant body shot backward out of the car. The blood splattered over me onto Pam.

"Oh shit!" Pam shouted.

"OH MY GOD!" I screamed. "Oh my God, Pam!"

"Damn! I got blood all over me!"

"We got to call the police!"

"It was an accident! Stay calm! Just stay calm!"

Pam slowly turned the key in the ignition and drove off. On our way out of the parking lot, we smashed into the side of a car. The car slid sideways into a tree and the driver's head went forward and then backward.

"Stop the car!" I shouted.

"Are you crazy?" Pam shouted back. "We gotta get outta here!"

"She may be hurt, Pam!"

"So!" Pam spun the car to the right and sped down the street.

"Oh my God! What are we going to do?"

"Calm down, Alicia!"

"We're going to jail!"

"Alicia! It was an accident!"

"Oh my God!" I said. "What are we going to do?"

"I got to get home to get this blood off of me!"

"Take me home! Please! Take me home!"

"I have to get this blood off of me first, Alicia!" Pam shouted.

"Okay! Okay!" I shouted.

Pam zoomed through traffic to her house and ran to her bedroom. She jumped in the shower and I paced back and forth in her living room. Pam came out, fresh and calm.

"Okay," Pam said, "Let's try to get control of the situation."

"Okay." I sighed. "How do we do that?"

"We're going to have to go to the police and explain what happened."

"What are we going to say about leaving the scene of the crime?"

"Shit! We're going to tell them the truth!" Pam said. "We panicked!"

"What if somebody died, Pam?"

"Stop thinking negatively! Everything is going to be alright."

"Oh my God!"

"Alicia, you're going to have to stop being so weak, man. I can't do this by myself."

"I'm not weak, Pam! Do you realize what we just did?"

"I know what we just did. That's why I need you to be strong. We have to be smart and think this through."

"I don't want to go to jail, Pam."

"We're not going to jail. If somebody saw us, the police would be here by now. It doesn't take that long to run a license tag."

"What about the video tape? I know the hotel had to have cameras! What if they caught us on camera, Pam?"

"If they got us on camera, we're caught."

"We have to do something!"

"Okay, let's think."

"Alright." I said nervously. "Okay."

"So let's come up with a plan."

"Okay," I said. "The only question is if they're dead or not. If they're dead and nobody saw us, we're good to go. But if they're alive and they tell the police their stories, we're in a lot of trouble. So, here are our options. We assume they're dead and forget about what happened today, or we turn ourselves in and confess to our part in what happened."

"I'm not turning in shit!" Pam said. "They dead! If they weren't dead they would have called the police."

"But we don't know that for sure."

"I'm not turning myself in, Alicia. That's not an option."

"I guess that answers that."

"Call Cynthia and Tina and invite them over tonight."

"We're not going to tell them what happened, are we?"

"Hell no! But just in case we need an alibi, we'll have a couple of witnesses."

CHAPTER TWELVE

I invited Tina and Cynthia over to spend an office girls' evening at my house. When I got home, Johnny was still out visiting with some of his patients. That gave me time to focus on getting my mind back to normal.

My telephone rang and I nearly jumped out of my skin. My first reaction was that the police had found out what had happened at the hotel and they were calling to ask questions. But if it were the police, they wouldn't call; they'd be coming to pick my ass up.

"Alicia?"

"Pam?"

"I just talked to Cynthia."

"Okay."

"Gizelle called Mike this morning to have him write her biography."

"Are you serious?"

"Yeah, Mike is on his way to her hotel room to sign a contract."

"Wait a minute!" I said. "Why is Mike writing her biography?"

"She asked him to," Pam said.

"Damn!" I snapped. "This is going from bad to worse."

"Does Johnny know?"

"Hold on." Johnny called as Pam and I were talking. "Speak of the devil. Let me take this call."

"Alicia, be cool. Act normal, man."

"I'm cool. I got it."

"Okay, girl, bye!"

"Bye!"

I clicked over to Johnny's call and took a deep breath before talking. Before I could speak, Johnny started the conversation.

"Hey you!"

"How did it go today, sweetheart?"

"Not good. Not good at all," Johnny said. "Veronica is battling for her life."

Veronica is one of Johnny's patients who's losing her battle with anorexia.

"That's a bummer!"

"Yeah, I probably don't need to be discussing this."

"You're not telling me her intimate secrets or anything like that so what's the big deal?"

"I don't know. I guess I just need to deal with this myself before I discuss it with anyone else."

"You sound really upset, sweetheart," I said. "Are you going to be okay?"

"I'll be okay." Johnny switched the subject. "How did things go with Anise, I mean Gizelle, today?"

"I have to go, honey." I became nervous and quickly hung up the phone.

Later on, Pam and I told Cynthia about Gizelle's decision to opt out of the contract and she was very disappointed. She asked a million questions. Most importantly, why wasn't she included in the dialogue?

We explained that the decision was made without any dialogue from us as well. We discussed our next move as a company. Pam and I used our business issues to try to block out our personal issues. We were successful until Johnny came home with some devastating news.

Michael had been taken to the police station for questioning in the murder of Gizelle. Pam and I looked at each other but didn't say a word. Cynthia was in shock. The realization of Gizelle being dead was so upsetting that I went to the bathroom and vomited.

Tina stayed with the kids while Pam and I went to the police station with Cynthia and Johnny. We tried to console Cynthia as much as we could. We eventually called the office girls and they came down to give their support as well. It was a rough night. Johnny called one of his attorney friends, who just happened to be one of his patients, and she arranged for Michael's release.

A FEW DAYS LATER, JOHNNY AND I WERE GETTING READY FOR BED. It had been a while since we made love and I was horny. I wore something sexy, something like my birthday suit, and waited for Johnny to come to bed. He climbed in the bed and turned his back to me.

"Come on, baby." I massaged Johnny's back up and down. "I want some."

Johnny turned around and faced me. He started to kiss my neck, making me squirm from pleasure. It felt so good to feel his body against mine again.

"Oh, keep doing that, Johnny," I said.

Johnny squeezed me in his arms, pulling me close to him. I could feel his stick poking against my thighs. I grabbed his ass and tried to guide his stick inside of me. I rolled over on my back and opened my thighs to encourage Johnny to give it to me. He continued to kiss my neck so I reached between his legs and grabbed a handful of penis. It was as soft as a marshmallow.

"What's wrong?" I squeezed Johnny's penis in my hand to let him know that there was nothing going on down there.

"What do you mean?"

"You're not ready."

"Okay, give me a minute!"

He kept grinding on me like his stick would eventually get hard. It was actually annoying to me.

"Can I help?"

"Okay," Johnny said.

I turned Johnny on his back and slowly licked and kissed his chest. I licked down to his flat stomach to his navel where I played there for a while. I moved downward to his inner thigh, and he jumped when I kissed him really hard. He clutched his fists and stiffened his feet.

"You like that, baby?"

"Oh yeah," Johnny moaned. Finally, I could feel some jubilation growing in that big stick of his.

I lowered my mouth onto his stick and sucked him gently. My mind started to wonder if Gizelle gave my husband fellatio as well I did. Did she make his eyes and toes curl? Did she make him moan as loudly as I did? The more I fantasized about Gizelle, the wetter my vagina got. At one point, I was bobbing my head up and down and then from side to side like a lion ravaging the carcass of a gazelle. No pun intended and of course I used no teeth.

Johnny was so deep in my throat that there was no room for air to pass. I tried to breathe through my nose, but I couldn't get air to come through there either. I had to take a mini-break to recuperate.

"Seems like you're ready now!" I said as I massaged his stick up and down.

"Oh yeah," Johnny said. "Lay down, baby."

Johnny turned me on my back and I opened my legs again. I reached between Johnny's legs and grabbed his stick. It was as hard as ever! I gave him a big smile of approval and then slid the head in. I moved my hips into the bed and then raised them to try pull him inside of me with one long stroke.

I opened my mouth and let out a long sigh, half was for pleasure, and the other half for relief. I grabbed Johnny by the back of his head and pulled it on top of mine, sliding my tongue into his mouth. He rubbed my face as we kissed passionately.

As Johnny stroked me, I felt his thickness decrease more and more. I thought to myself, *I know this niggah is not going flaccid on me again.* He kept on stroking like I couldn't feel the difference. I couldn't do anything with that. I was like, *would this fool get off of me?* I was pissed off. Gizelle was in his head. She was in mine, too, but she wasn't stopping me from making love.

"What's the matter, Johnny?" I asked. "Are you stressed out or something?"

"No! I'm not stressed out!"

"Then why can't you make love to me?"

"I can! I just need time!" Johnny shouted in frustration.

"Time for what?" I shouted back. "I'm here, naked, in all of my glory! What do you need time for?"

"I don't know! But I know screaming at me is not the answer!"

"Well, what's the matter?"

"I don't know, Alicia, I want to do this very much. But something is going on here that I can't explain."

I wanted to scream, "you can explain it if you open your damn mouth." I just wanted him to bring it up and I would take it from there. But if I said a word about Gizelle it would have opened a can of worms that may have incriminated Pam and me. If Johnny found out that we let Michael get accused of our crime, he would go berserk.

"Johnny, what's going on?" I asked. "I'm horny as hell!"

"I want to make love to you, too, baby," Johnny said. "But there's something going on in my head that I can't explain."

"Can't explain to who?" He was trying to use one of his psychological lines on me but I wasn't having it. "You? Or me?"

"Right now," Johnny said, "both!"

Damn! The truth! Good comeback. I wasn't expecting that. Johnny pulled me to him and caressed my body. I longed for his touch, but to satisfy my sexual urges, not as my husband. His hands felt wonderful against my skin. But my mind wouldn't allow me to enjoy it. I was fed up with waiting. I wanted to get the truth out.

"Are you having an affair, Johnny?"

"Are you serious?"

"Well, what am I supposed to think when I don't seem to be able to turn my husband on? There are normally two things that are going on when that happens." I was trying to give him an avenue to discuss his affair. "An affair, or loss of interest. Which one of those is the case here, Johnny?"

"Neither," Johnny responded quickly. "Perhaps it's just stress, like you said. I've had a lot of emotional incidents in the past couple of days. Maybe I need to relax and relieve my mind of some of those issues."

"Are you sure?"

"Absolutely!"

"Okay, this better not happen again!" I said. "You hear me?"

"Of course it won't."

My frustration was growing stronger and stronger. I wanted to put my two hands around Johnny's throat and choke his ass until he confessed his affair. I turned my back to Johnny, fluffed my pillow and then slammed my head on it. Johnny reached his arm around my waist and I grabbed one of his fingers and tried to break that sucker.

"Ouch!" Johnny said as he shook his hand.

"Good night, Johnny."

"Damn!" Johnny turned his back to me. "Good night."

You would think it couldn't get any worse than that, right? Wrong! A few days later Cynthia came to our house pounding on the door. As soon as the door was cracked, Cynthia walked past me in a hurry.

"Where's Johnny?" Cynthia shouted.

"What's the matter, Cynthia?" I could tell something was very wrong. "What's wrong with you?"

"Mike was arrested for murdering Gizelle!"

"What?" I shouted. "Johnny!!!"

Johnny peeked around the corner, wearing a housecoat.

"What's going on?"

"They took Mike to jail, Johnny!" Cynthia said, stomping her feet.

"Why?" Johnny asked. "Why would they take Mike to jail now?"

"They said they found evidence against him!" Cynthia said. "Oh my God!"

"Sit down, girl!" I said.

"I can't! I have to get Mike out of jail!"

"Do something, Johnny!" Cynthia screamed.

"Okay!" Johnny shouted back. "Everybody just calm down so we can think this through!"

"Think what through?" Cynthia yelled. "My husband is in jail and I want him out!"

I was wrong, but I also felt Johnny was responsible. If he hadn't cheated, none of this would have happened. I wanted to make him suffer the same guilt that was eating at me. I wanted him to face his responsibility and make everything right.

"Johnny!" I shouted. "What are we going to do?"

"We're not going to do anything," Johnny said. "I'm going to get my brother out of jail."

Johnny changed clothes while I consoled Cynthia. Cynthia was too impatient to sit still so she walked back and forth, in and out of the house, until Johnny came downstairs.

"Let's go!" Johnny grabbed his keys from the rack and walked past us. We followed him out of the door.

JOHNNY, CYNTHIA AND I WERE AT THE JAIL waiting to see Michael. Johnny called his attorney friend, Stacey Hemphill, to the station for Michael's legal counsel. They told me only immediate family could see him. So while Johnny and Cynthia were in the visiting room, I was sneaking calls to Pam to get her to come down to the station and confess with me.

Questioning was one thing, but being under arrest was another. I told Pam that we needed to come forth and tell the police what had really happened. Michael was innocent and it was unconscionable for us to let him go to prison for our crimes.

"They arrested Michael," I said nervously.

"For questioning?" Pam asked.

"No, for murder! They think Michael did it."

"Damn!"

"We can't let this happen to Michael, Pam."

"What can we do?"

"Tell the truth!"

"We know Mike didn't do it. The police will find out the same thing."

"But what if they don't?"

"But they will, Alicia."

"I'm not going to let Michael go to jail. I can't do that to him or Cynthia."

"Okay, let's be cool for right now and see what happens. If we try to be good Samaritans and turn ourselves in, we know we're going to jail. Mike is going to get off, I'm telling you."

"Michael better get out of this, Pam."

"He will. You act normal and continue to be Johnny's supportive wife. Don't let him know that you know anything about him and Gizelle."

"Shit! What have we done, Pam?"

"Just act normal, Alicia. Okay?"

"Okay."

"You're okay," Pam said. "Keep me posted."

"I will."

"Bye."

"Bye."

Michael spent the night in jail and Johnny stayed with him. Pam and I decided that we wouldn't talk anymore that evening since Cynthia and the baby were spending the night with me. Cynthia and I stayed up late talking about Michael. Having to lie to her was unbearable. When I went to bed I couldn't sleep at all. As many times that I had slept alone, that night, my bed seemed much larger than normal.

In the middle of the night I went to Brittany's room and slid in bed with her. I played with her hair as I stared at her precious little face. I wanted to absorb some of her innocence, some of the angelic purity that makes a child God's favorite. I wanted to be ignorant to the temptations of hatred, lust and greed. I kissed her forehead lightly, and my kiss momentarily woke her up.

She smiled briefly and said, "I love you, Mommy."

Brittany went back to sleep and soon after, I feel asleep as well. In a quiet ordinary moment I came to an extraordinary realization. I had unsuccessfully sought love, strength and adoration my entire life. But through three simple words from the mouth of a child I found what I should have been seeking all the time...peace. Peace with myself and peace with the world. Lying next to my child I felt like a parent! A provider! A protector! I felt like the woman I'd been trying to find inside of me.

THE NEXT DAY, MICHAEL WAS FREED ON BAIL. Johnny stayed at the jail the whole time. Despite my resentment toward him, I was proud to see him so devoted to his brother.

Johnny came in tattered and torn from his overnight stay in jail. He showered, dressed and was off to see another patient. I was quite certain he wasn't sneaking off to see Gizelle that time. Wink! Wink! You can never be too sure so I went to the office to make sure there weren't any other Gizelles lurking in the shadows.

His strange secretary, Rosemary, was sitting comfortably at her desk. I peeked my head in first, and then walked in. I smiled and waved at Rosemary as I walked through the waiting room heading for Johnny's office.

"Dr. Forrester is not here."

"I thought he had sessions today."

"He does, but they're outcalls."

"Outcalls?"

"Some of his patients are not capable of coming to the office so he has to make outcalls."

"Are you sure?" I wasn't trying to question Rosemary, but that seemed a little odd.

"I'm positive." Rosemary looked to have an attitude. "Is there some kind of an emergency?"

"No, I'm just curious to know why Johnny has to make outcalls."

"Well," Rosemary said. "Not that it's any of your business, but one of his patients was in an automobile accident in front of the Grand Hyatt last week and she was injured. I would think that you would be proud of him for showing such concern, instead of questioning his judgment."

"Last week?" I remembered that Pam and I rammed into a car in front of the hotel. But it couldn't have been the same car. "I'm sorry; I'm way out of line. But with everything going on with his brother, I guess I'm just a little overprotective."

"I understand," Rosemary said. "Mrs. Forrester, I don't know exactly what transpired between Ms. Lawrence and Dr. Forrester, and frankly I don't care to know. But one thing I do know is that he loves you dearly."

"Ms. Lawrence?" I asked. "Who's Ms. Lawrence?"

I remembered Gizelle mentioning an Anise Lawrence when we were in the limousine. Was this woman one of Johnny's patients?

"Oh, I'm sorry, ma'am, perhaps I was out of line."

"No, who is Ms. Lawrence?"

"You may know Ms. Lawrence as Gizelle. She was the young woman murdered recently in the Grand Hyatt."

"Gizelle was Johnny's patient?"

"I'm sorry, Mrs. Forrester, I thought with your brother-in-law being arrested you were aware of the information."

"Uh, no, no, I wasn't."

Rosemary's information answered a lot of questions. It explained Johnny and Gizelle's relationship.

"Despite what may have happened, Mrs. Forrester, Dr. Forrester is a good man."

"Then you marry him!"

I walked out of Johnny's office and went home to put on my counterfeit smile for my counterfeit marriage.

WHEN JOHNNY CAME HOME THAT EVENING I had his special meal waiting for him. After dinner, I gave Brittany a bath and put her to bed. Johnny and I went to bed early and talked, and caressed, and talked and caressed. We continued to talk and caress until we were ready to rip each other apart.

"Oh God, I want you so bad, Johnny."

I was so horny I was grinding on Johnny's stick before he put it in.

"I want you, too, baby!" Johnny said.

"I want you to give it to me!" I said. "Give it to me, hard! I don't want you to make love to me, baby. I want you to sex the shit out of me!"

I slid Johnny's stick inside of me. I was already well-lubricated. He sighed heavily and then shoved his hard penis into me as deep as it would go. I held my ankles and spread my legs far apart. He folded my legs backward, putting his body weight on them. They kept going backward until my toes were touching the bed.

Johnny began to stroke me deep and hard for about ten strokes. Do you hear me? Ten strokes! And then he went flaccid. Soft as cotton! There was no steady decline. He went from rock hard to cotton soft in a matter of seconds. Although he had to know I wasn't feeling that shit, he kept on stroking.

"What's wrong?" I asked.

"What?" Johnny said. "What's the matter?"

"You're not hard," I said, very frustrated.

Johnny started to pump slowly like that was going to make a difference.

"It's not going to go in like that," I said.

"Give me a minute!" Johnny tried pumping faster. I was embarrassed for him. He was breathing hard, pumping fast and was getting no results.

"Just stop!" I said, pushing him away. "Get off of me."

"Just hold on!" Johnny grabbed his soft penis and tried to aim it at my vagina.

I was fed up. I wanted him to admit that he cheated. I wanted to know the truth; not figure it out based on circumstantial evidence. I wanted to know why he would find another woman so attractive that he would jeopardize our marriage. I wanted to know if that dead woman was still affecting his mind.

"Something's not right!" I shouted. I snatched the comforter and wrapped it around my body because I no longer felt Johnny was worthy of looking or touching it.

"What do you mean, something's not right?"

"I mean what I said! Something is not right and I'm tired of asking what it is! You either tell me what's going on, or I'm going to assume you're having an affair."

"Okay," Johnny said nervously, "Shit!"

"What?" I asked.

"It's bad," Johnny said.

Of course it was bad. He had an affair with one of his patients. I was a part of her murder and his brother was being charged for it.

"What?"

"I guess there's no easy way to say it."

"Okay." I cut on the lamp because I wanted to see the sincerity on his face when he finally admitted the truth. "Say it?"

"First of all, I want you to know that I love you," Johnny said. "I love you more than life itself."

"Look, this is killing me!" I was anxious and I wanted to hear the truth. "Would you just come out with it?"

"Okay!" Johnny said.

"Well?" I said folding my arms. "Go 'head."

"This is so hard for me." Johnny was still trying to buy time. "I had an affair, baby, but it meant nothing to me!"

"You had an affair?" I asked calmly.

I sat patiently, relieved by hearing the truth.

"Yes." Johnny hugged me and then apologized. "I'm so sorry."

"With who?" I asked, pushing Johnny away.

"Does it matter?"

"It does to me." I had an admission, but I needed a confession. He admitted that it happened, but I needed to know how, why and with whom.

"Okay," Johnny said, "Since you have to know, it was with Anise Lawrence."

"Gizelle?" I was still very calm, very tranquil. "That girl? That little girl?"

I tried to remain calm but I felt myself beginning to cry. I didn't want to cry and I especially didn't want him to see me cry. I had to get out of that room and fast before I lost complete control. I got out of the bed to leave.

"Let me explain!" Johnny blocked the door to keep me from leaving.

"Explain what?" I shouted. "That you cheated with a little girl?"

"That's not how it was!"

"Move out of my way!" I screamed.

"Would you please stop yelling before you wake Brittany?"

"I don't even know who you are!" I shouted. "Move! Get out of my way!"

"Alicia, please! Don't do this!" Johnny said. "I need you!"

"You don't need me!"

"Baby, I'm in trouble! I don't know what I'll do without you! I need you!"

"Get out my way, Johnny!" I stopped trying to get around him. That niggah was just too damn big.

"So you're going to throw our family away, just like that?" Johnny asked.

"Did you care about our family when you were out whoring around?"

"That's not fair, Alicia!"

"You'll get sleepy before I will!" I pulled my suitcase out of the closet and started to pack my clothes.

Johnny kept talking about staying together and I wasn't trying to hear that shit but then he hit me where he knew it would hurt.

"So what about Brittany?" Johnny asked. "You're going to walk out on her, too?"

I didn't stop packing my suitcase, but I slowed down tremendously. I thought about my commitment to Deirdra and Brittany. I wasn't going to turn my back on my promise to them because of my anger toward Johnny.

"So you're going to punish Brittany for my mistake?" Johnny repeated.

"Okay." I closed my suitcase and put it in the closet, but I didn't unpack it. "I won't leave tonight, for Brittany's sake. But you better not say anything to me! Until I decide to speak to you, don't even look my way! You understand me?"

"Yes, ma'am!"

I snatched a pillow from my bed and started to walk out again.

"Where are you going?" Johnny asked.

"I'm going to sleep with my baby!" I slammed the door behind me so hard that I broke a fingernail. "Ouch! Shit!"

My anger began to subside, lying next to Brittany. That peaceful feeling started to take over again. I felt confident. I felt strong. I loved my husband, but I also knew that I couldn't be with him any longer. One of us had to go.

CHAPTER THIRTEEN

The next morning Johnny was up and gone unusually early. I fixed Brittany's breakfast and, while she was eating, I called the office girls and asked them to meet me over Pam's house. I dressed Brittany, packed her suitcase and we left. On my way to Pam's house, Johnny called my cell phone.

"Hi."

"Hi," Johnny said. "I was just calling to check on you, to see how you were doing."

"Oh, I'm fine."

"You sure?"

"Yeah, I'm sure."

"You don't want to talk about it?"

"I'd rather not discuss it right now."

"Okay," Johnny said. "We'll discuss it when I get home then."

"Okay," I answered as normal as possible.

"I love you," Johnny said. "Bye."

"Bye," I responded. I wasn't about to say "I love you" back.

CYNTHIA WAS THE ONLY OFFICE GIRL AT PAM'S HOUSE when I arrived. I expected as much since the three of us didn't live far from one another. I pulled into Pam's driveway and she walked outside to greet me. She made me pull into her garage alongside Cynthia's car while she parked on the street, in case she had to leave before us. Pam met me in the garage to talk before we entered the house with Cynthia.

"What's up?" Pam asked.

"That niggah finally admitted that he cheated with Gizelle last night," I said.

"But you already knew that. Why are you leaving now?"

"Because."

"Because, why?"

"I don't know, I guess it's just now really hitting me."

"You mean after Gizelle is dead?"

I looked at Pam but didn't respond.

"Hi, Ms. Pam." Brittany waved from the backseat.

"Hey, babygirl!" Pam said. "Come here!"

Pam helped Brittany out of her seatbelt.

"Johnny let you leave with Brit?" Pam whispered.

"He doesn't know."

"Girl," Pam said, "You know how that niggah feels about this girl. Don't have him coming over here pulling my house out the ground."

"Y'all hurry up!" Cynthia yelled from the doorway.

"Here we come!" I yelled back.

"You know Cynthia don't believe in divorce and separation, right?" Pam asked.

"I'm not Cynthia."

"You're about to get a sermon, girl."

"I can use one."

We went inside and I was about to tell Cynthia what had happened, but then Val and Wanda arrived together. I decided to wait until Darsha and Lisa showed up so I wouldn't have to keep repeating myself.

When everybody was there, they gathered around me and I

told them what had happened. They were very supportive. Well, most of them were anyway. Cynthia and Wanda thought that I was rushing to a conclusion.

"Look, all I can say is that don't sound like the Johnny I know," Wanda said.

When Johnny opened his office, Wanda had helped him organize, and in return he offered free sessions. She was one of his biggest supporters.

"Well, it's the Johnny you know because I saw him with my own two eyes," Pam snapped.

"If you want to leave, Alicia, you're a grown woman," Cynthia said. "Leave. But you can't stop Johnny from seeing his daughter."

"You're right, Cynt. I can't keep Brittany away from him, but I can't be with him either."

"Hold on." Cynthia looked at her cell phone and put it back down. "My husband is blowing me up. Johnny probably knows you're gone by now and he thinks I know where you are. Now he has Mike tracking me down."

"I need some time to think."

"We got your back in whatever you want to do," Val said.

"Thanks, Val. I don't want to go home tonight. I need a place to stay."

"Sorry, can't help you!" Val said. "Got a date."

"I don't want to spend the night with you, girl." I laughed. "I'm staying here, or over Cynthia's house."

"Oh no, you're not. You're not staying with me until you talk to your husband," Cynthia said.

"You can stay here, Alicia," Pam said.

"Oh-oh!" Cynthia looked at her cell phone. "I got a text message from Mike. I think they're on their way over here."

"I got to get out of here!"

"Let's go to my house!" Val shouted.

"Hell nawl!" Wanda laughed. "Val get us up in there, she might try to Jeffrey Dahmer our ass!"

"Don't nobody want your ol' fat ass, Wanda." Val laughed.

"Y'all always playin'! Let's go before your husband gets here, Alicia!" Darsha said.

As were getting into our cars we saw Johnny's SUV heading toward us.

"Here they come!" Wanda shouted.

"Alicia! Go back in the house!" Pam yelled. "We got this!"

I started to run back into the house with Brittany when Pam screamed for me to get her house keys.

"Hey, girl!" Pam shouted. "You forgot the damn keys!"

I raised my hand in the air and waited for Pam to throw the keys. She tossed them back to me and, without breaking stride, I ran to her front door. I unlocked it quickly and ran in the house before Johnny could see me. I peeked out the window and couldn't believe what I was seeing.

The office girls had surrounded Johnny's SUV and had them trapped. They were talking back and forth but I couldn't hear what they were saying. He and Michael were sitting there until Johnny crawled out of the passenger window. He was mad as hell. As the saying goes, "all hell broke loose."

Pam left her car on the street and ran back into the house. The other office girls dispersed and got the hell out of there. Pam was breathing hard as she peeked out of her window from one side and I peeked out from the other. Johnny was pounding on the door, demanding that Pam open it. Eventually he gave up and sat on the steps with Michael and cried. I felt bad for him, but not bad enough to open the door. Eventually, they left.

"That niggah was mad!" Pam said.

"I know," I said.

"And he should be," Cynthia said as she was walking behind us.

"OH SHIT!" I screamed. I had forgotten that Cynthia was still in the house. "Don't do that, Cynthia!"

"I can't believe y'all."

"What?" I said.

"Y'all are acting like a bunch of immature teenagers," Cynthia said.

"How are we acting like teenagers? He cheated on her," Pam said. "If you would have seen Mike having sex with another woman, Cynt, you would be acting the same way."

"If I would have seen Mike having sex with somebody, I would have said something then."

"Well, she didn't. And?"

"And why are you tripping, Pam?" Cynthia yelled. "It's not even your man! Alicia is a grown woman! She needs to be talking to her husband, instead of running around trying to get her girls to feel sorry for her. This office girls' shit is getting old! Y'all act like y'all can't do nothing individually. Grow the hell up!"

"You grow up!" Pam shouted.

"Look at you, Alicia," Cynthia said. "You got Pam defending you like you can't defend yourself."

"I don't need anybody to defend me."

"Obviously you do!" Cynthia had her baby on one hip and her hand on the other.

"I don't see why you're getting so mad at me," I said. "Johnny is the one who cheated."

"Because you're my friend and you got me caught up in the middle of this foul shit. You got all of us caught up in it! That was my brother-in-law sitting out there on those steps crying! That's a problem, Alicia!"

"I'm sorry; I didn't mean to drag you into this."

"You don't have to apologize to her, Alicia," Pam shouted. "If she was your friend, she wouldn't be so concerned about her husband. She'd care about you, too. You're the one that's hurting."

"That's just stupid, Pam," Cynthia said. "Even for you! That's a stupid thing to say. I see why you don't have a man."

"I got a man!"

"Who? The white dude? The white dude who only sees you at your house, or at night? The white dude who never allows you to visit his home? Get real, Pam. You're fooling yourself."

"I wasn't fooling myself when I had your man!" Pam slammed herself down on her couch and twirled her feet, waiting for Cynthia to respond.

I thought Pam's comment was a low blow and very unnecessary. When Cynthia and I disagreed, no matter how intense the conversation, I never went there. And after Cynthia finished with Pam, she wished she hadn't gone there either.

"What did you say?" Cynthia asked, putting her baby on the floor.

"You heard me. I didn't stutter."

"Pam, you were nothing but a piss-on piece of ass for Mike. If I thought for one second that he cared about a weak-ass, bitter, man-bashing slut like you, I wouldn't have given him the time of day. I think of Mike having sex with you like I think of Mike jacking off on a towel. Just like that towel, Pam, you were a place for Mike to dispose of his useless sperm. And just like I did with that towel, Pam, I cleaned up behind your nasty ass, too!"

Cynthia was mad and she was tearing into Pam's ass. Pam was not the type to let things go so I intervened. "Okay, y'all, let's not say anything we're going to regret."

"No, I'm tired of this shit!" Cynthia shouted. "I'm tired of tiptoeing around this psycho because she wants to go off on everybody's man because she's not happy. Those were our husbands sitting out there on her steps! She don't want any of us to have a man so we can suffer in misery like her!"

"Kiss my ass, Cynthia!"

"Wait a minute," I said. "This is my problem. You two shouldn't be fighting over my problem."

"That ain't why we're fighting," Pam said. "We're fighting because Cynthia thinks she's so much better than us."

"I don't think I'm better than either one of you. I keep telling y'all, I'm an office girl until it comes to my family. If it comes down to choosing between my family and the office girls, my family comes first. You think we're so cool because of what happened in that office? That was a damn job! We're friends! Not family! Y'all don't get that!"

"We do get that, but for me, when my family was not there, the office girls were. The office girls were, and always will be, my family."

"Me, too," Pam agreed. "It's like you're obsessed with Mike and his kids. It's like you put them on such a pedestal."

"I'm supposed to," Cynthia said. "That's my husband and those are my children."

"Those are not your kids, Cynthia. Those are Mike's kids!" Pam said.

I was offended by that comment. I knew how Cynthia felt about Brimone and Alexiah, and so did Pam. She felt the same way that I did about Brittany.

"Wait a minute," I said, raising my hand in the air. "How are you going to tell her those are not her kids, Pam?"

"'Cause they're not."

"Damn, you trippin'!" I shook my head.

"Whatever!" Pam rolled her eyes and twirled her feet simultaneously.

"What happened to you to make you so rotten, Pam?" Cynthia asked.

"Ain't nothing wrong with me. I'm just tired of you thinking you got the best man in the world and he ain't nothing but another niggah like any other black man."

"Okay." Cynthia picked up the phone and handed it to Pam. "If you think my husband is like any other niggah, why don't you call him and find out."

"Girl, please, get that phone out my face." Pam pushed the phone away.

"I want you to call my husband and tell him whatever you want to tell him. Go ahead." Cynthia put the phone in Pam's hand. "I want you to prove that my husband ain't shit like you claim, or shut the hell up!"

"I ain't got time for this childish shit." Pam knocked the phone out of Cynthia's hand.

"You have time to run your mouth about everybody else's man; here's an opportunity to prove it. Call Mike and tell him whatever you want to tell him about you, about me, about anything or anybody. I bet before you can get it out of your mouth, he'll be calling me to tell me what your stupid ass said."

I was surprised, to say the least, by Cynthia's challenge. She really had faith in Michael, to put herself out there like that. Pam must have really had faith in Michael, too, because she refused to call him.

"You call him; he's your husband," Pam said sarcastically.

"Okay," Cynthia said, dialing Michael's number. When Michael answered she stood directly in front of Pam and talked. "Hey, baby, I'm sorry about everything but I was trying to be a friend to

Alicia. I'll be home soon. Can you fix lunch for me? Thanks, baby. Bye."

Cynthia slowly closed her cell phone, still staring at Pam.

"My man is fixing my lunch. Call your man and see what he's doing." Cynthia held out her cell phone for Pam to use. "What's the matter?"

"You act like you're such a Christian and you just as trifling as everybody else." Pam got up and walked out of the room.

I walked Cynthia to the door so we could say our good-byes.

"I love Pam like a sister, but her bitter views on men, especially black men, are cancerous, Alicia," Cynthia said.

"I know."

"Johnny messed up, and if you can't deal with it, that's cool. But talk to him about it. Not Pam; not me; him."

"I will," I said, "But I just can't today."

"Okay." Cynthia hugged me. "Take care, girl, and tell that old thang in there that I still love her."

"I will." I laughed.

"Bye."

"Bye."

I stayed at Pam's for the next couple of days. Johnny called or text messaged me almost every hour on the hour. I responded only to questions referring to Brittany. I made arrangements for him to visit her at Cynthia's when I wasn't around. I cut my cell phone off the night before so that I wouldn't be tempted to call him, or accept any of his calls.

The day he was supposed to visit with Brittany, I was blind-sided by more unimaginable information. I was dropping Brittany off and had no plans on staying, but Cynthia hit me with another bombshell.

"How are you holding up?" Cynthia asked.

"Okay, I guess." I smiled to be more convincing. "Those first couple of days were pure hell. But I'm doing better."

"What do you mean the first couple of days? It just happened last night."

"What just happened last night?" I braced myself for more bad news.

"Johnny was arrested last night for Gizelle's murder."

Hearing the news made me dizzy and I thought I was going to faint. I gripped Brittany's shoulder to keep myself balanced. I leaned against the door and I started to slide downward. I could hear Cynthia talking but I couldn't respond.

"Michael!" Cynthia screamed.

The next thing I knew, Michael was picking me up and carrying me to the couch. I wasn't out; I was just dazed and everything was fuzzy.

"Hey, you alright?" Michael asked.

"What?" I tried to regain my wits.

"Alicia! Alicia!" Cynthia shouted. "Do you want us to call an ambulance?"

"No," I said.

I felt Brittany holding my hand and I imagined that my situation reminded her of Deirdra's being sick. I told myself at that point, dizzy or not, Brittany was not going to see me like that. I sat up and tickled her tummy.

"I fooled you." I was dizzy as hell, but Brittany didn't know.

"You scared me, Mommy." Brittany wiped her eyes.

"Oh, don't be scared. Mommy was only playing." I hugged Brittany and kissed her forehead. "You okay?"

"Yes."

"Give Mommy another hug." I embraced Brittany again.

"Is there anything you need?" Cynthia asked.

"Tylenol!" I said. "Quick!"

Cynthia laughed and got me some Tylenol to take for my sudden headache. I sat up and talked as if nothing was wrong, trying to put Brittany at ease. She was clingy and didn't want to leave my side. I let her sit on my lap and she held on to my neck for dear life.

I was still stunned about the news about Johnny. Cynthia talked about his arrest in a roundabout way so that Brittany would not understand.

"Yeah, Johnny was there last night and this morning. We don't know the details but we are on our way there now to find out everything."

"I don't believe this," I said. "Why him?"

"I have no idea and if Mike knows anything he's not talking."

"Wow!" I said. "Unbelievable."

"He needs you, Alicia."

"I know, but I feel so uncomfortable talking to him right now, Cynt."

"You better get over it."

"Why didn't anyone call me last night?"

"I did call you. But I kept getting your funky voicemail so I left you a message."

"Damn! I had my phone off."

"I talked to Pam and I told her to give you the message."

"That mean heffa didn't give me the message."

"Well, we're on our way to see him now, if you want to come with us."

"No, I have other things to do right now."

"Other things?" Cynthia said. "Like what?"

"Like get my things out of Pam's house and put them back where they belong."

"That's what I'm talking about!" Cynthia smiled and gave me a high-five.

"Come on, baby, let's go." I removed Brittany's hands from around my neck and sat her down so that she could walk. She clung to my leg and tried to help me walk. "Mommy's okay, let's go."

"That is remarkable." Cynthia pointed at Brittany.

"What?" I asked.

"The way that girl clings to you."

"Yeah, she's something else." I smiled and rubbed her head.

"Go do what you gotta do," Cynthia said. "We'll try to get your husband back to you as soon as possible. I know exactly how you feel."

It was impossible for her to know exactly how I felt. Although it was true that both of our husbands had been accused of murdering the same woman, unlike me, she didn't have to bear the burden of knowing that she was actually the murderer.

The only upside to that very bad situation was that Johnny was not being charged for Big Walt's death. They had no evidence at all that tied him to the scene of the crime in the parking lot. There was no video, no witnesses, no weapon, nothing! There was so much media coverage about Gizelle's murder, the police acted as if they didn't give a damn what happened to Big Walt anyway.

BY THE TIME WE GOT TO PAM'S HOUSE, Brittany had fallen asleep. I laid her on the couch and started to pack our suitcases. As I was packing, Pam came in and tried to convince me to stay a little while longer. I had zero tolerance for her girl power "let's stick together" movement. I was already pissed off at her for not giving me the message Cynthia had left about Johnny.

"You sure you want to do this?" Pam asked.

"Positive," I said as I continued to pack my suitcase.

"That niggah cheated on you and you're just going to go back to him, just like that?"

"Pam, what is wrong with your brain?" I stopped packing my suitcase and stared at her. "Johnny is in jail for a murder we committed. You don't feel the slightest bit guilty?"

"For what?" Pam asked.

"For killing somebody and allowing the man I love to take the blame."

"You don't love Johnny." Pam laughed.

"I don't love Johnny?"

"You heard me; I didn't stutter. You don't love Johnny."

That was the last straw.

"Why would you say something so mean and cold, Pam?" I sat on the bed, waiting for an apology, waiting for some kind of humanity.

"Because it's true."

"Cynthia was right. You are a very bitter woman and you don't want any other woman to be happy. You want every woman to be miserable, mean and bitter, just like you."

"I'm just telling the truth."

"I feel sorry for you, Pam," I said as I returned to packing my suitcase. "I really do."

"Don't feel sorry for me." Pam chuckled. "I got a man."

"No, you don't," I said. "You don't have a man, Pam. A man spends time with his woman. Shares intimate moments with his woman. Day or night, it doesn't matter. He wants to be with you. Not just come over to your place for an hour to tap that ass and then he's gone. That's not your man."

"Oh, but I guess if he was cheating on me with his patient, then he would be my man? Or if I was chasing him and another woman down the highway, then he would be my man? Or if I was hiding on a damn sand dune watching him have sex with another woman, then he would be my man?"

"No," I said calmly, trying to take a page out of Cynthia's cool textbook. "That just means that your man cheated on you."

"That's what I thought."

"I'm about to go home and greet my man when he gets out of jail. You try getting in touch with yours."

"That shit is old," Pam said. "I can find him when I want him."

"You think about this, Pam." I laughed as I closed and locked my suitcase. "While I'm making love to my man tonight, some woman is going to be making love to yours."

I WAS HAPPY TO BE BACK HOME. I couldn't believe Johnny had kept the house so clean. I unpacked our suitcases and waited for Johnny to come home. When they pulled into the driveway I wanted to run out and kiss him so badly, but I didn't.

Cynthia, Michael and Stacey stayed near the car as Brittany and I greeted Johnny in the doorway. He picked us up and spun us around.

"Oh my God, I'm so happy to see you two!" Johnny kissed us several times all over our faces.

"I missed you, Daddy!" Brittany laughed. She was finally letting me go.

"Did you miss me, too?" Johnny asked.

"Let's not talk about that right now," I said as I walked into the house.

"Well, we'll give you two time to relax and I'll check in with you later, Dr. Forrester, okay?" Stacey said.

"Thanks, Stacey," Johnny responded. "Thanks for everything."

"No problem. Bye!"

Stacey left and a few minutes later Michael and Cynthia said their good-byes. Johnny told me that he had been indicted for first-degree murder and if he was found guilty, the district attorney would most likely seek the death penalty. Looking into Johnny's eyes, I became consumed with guilt. That guilt was forcing me to face the truth. The truth was that I was using Johnny's infidelity as an excuse to punish him for my crime.

I couldn't be nice. I couldn't be affectionate. I couldn't show any form of consolation because if I did, I would not be able to control my heart from confessing the truth about Gizelle.

Johnny attempted small talk at first and then he apologized for his infidelity. I didn't want an apology. I didn't want him to feel sorry. I wanted him to be heartless and inculpable so that I could have a reason to hate him.

I called Tina and talked to her about how I was feeling. She suggested that Johnny and I talk to Curtis, who had traveled all walks of life. He would be nonjudgmental and serve as the mediator between us.

Of course I didn't tell Johnny that they were coming over for Curtis to counsel us because it would have affected his ego. His position would have probably been, *'why would a scientific psychologist allow an uneducated religious fanatic to counsel him on anything?'*

I surprised him at the last minute and only told him we were having them over for dinner. It didn't take Johnny long to figure out he had been bamboozled, but he wasn't as condescending as I thought he would be. As a matter of fact, he was very receptive to it.

We shared a very meaningful conversation and learned a lot about one another. He found out that I'd had a mini-affair with Julian that devastated him, and I found out he'd once suffered from some sexually addictive disease called erotomania. What the hell? I ended up running out of the room. I couldn't handle the emotional pressure that had built.

CHAPTER FOURTEEN

A couple of days later Cynthia and I were talking and she told me that Johnny's parents were coming to town. Neither one of us knew our in-laws very well. I decided to do what I do best; throw a dinner party. Johnny seemed to love them. I invited his legal team over so that I could hear more about the case.

Johnny and Michael drove to the airport to pick up their parents while Cynthia and I prepared dinner. She asked me how Johnny and I were coming along and I told her that we were trying. We were making efforts to reconcile, but only time would tell.

When Johnny arrived from the airport, he came back alone. I was expecting my in-laws to stay at our house since they were coming to support Johnny. However, they had decided to stay with Michael instead.

Dinner went very well and since it was still relatively early, our guests hung around for casual conversation. In case you didn't know, that's the sign of a very successful dinner party! Eventually they got around to discussing Johnny's case. Mr. and Mrs. Forrester didn't look comfortable when the attorneys started talking.

"It's going to be a fight, but a fight we can definitely win," Ms. Hattley said. "Their whole case is pretty much circumstantial."

Ms. Hattley and Ms. Carroll were two additional attorneys assigned to Johnny's case.

"We're pretty confident that there's no way a jury will convict you based on the evidence the state has," Ms. Carroll said.

"We may not even go to trial. If your blood comes back positive, Dr. Forrester, we have a legitimate reason to explain why."

Johnny's dad looked at Ms. Carroll, and then Johnny. It was obvious that he was still under the impression that Michael was being charged for Gizelle's murder. His pleasant attitude turned on the dime when he found out it was Johnny. He may have been pissed off because no one had told him, or it could have been that liquor in the bottle that he kept turning up to his mouth.

"If Johnny's blood comes back positive?" Mr. Forrester asked. "What you mean, if Johnny's blood comes back positive?"

"Do you think we should be discussing this in front of your parents?" Stacey asked. "There's going to be very sensitive information involved."

"Hold on, white girl!" Mr. Forrester shouted. "Don't talk like I ain't in the room! I'm right here! If you got something to say, say it to me!"

"Pop!" Michael said. "Stop it!"

"I ain't stoppin' shit!" Mr. Forrester yelled. "What does Johnny's blood got to do with anything?"

"Do you really want to know, Pop?" Johnny asked.

"I wouldna asked if I didn't wanna know!"

"Okay," Johnny said. "I was the one who found the girl's body in that hotel. Not Mike."

"Aw, hell, Johnny!" Michael said.

Apparently, Michael felt it was best that Johnny said nothing in front of their parents.

"You?" Mrs. Forrester asked.

"Wait a minute!" Mr. Forrester said to Johnny. "Are you trying to tell me you killed somebody and your brother is taking the rap for you?"

"I didn't kill anyone!" Johnny was becoming upset, something very unusual for him.

"Somebody did!" Mr. Forrester yelled. "'Cause somebody's dead!"

"Buddy, please," Mrs. Forrester said, patting his hand.

Buddy was the name Mrs. Forrester affectionately called Mr. Forrester.

"Pop! Cut it out, man!" Michael said.

"You still ain't man enough to stand up for yourself, huh?"

Mr. Forrester looked at Johnny as if he hated him. His face was twisted. His eyes were bloodshot red and his fists were clenched so tightly you could see his veins.

"Leave him alone, Buddy!" Mrs. Forrester said.

"Are you gon' have your brother fight your battles for the rest of your life?" Mr. Forrester stood up and walked toward Johnny. "Huh, Johnny?"

"Buddy!" Mrs. Forrester yelled again. "Leave him alone!"

"This weasel been runnin' with his tail between his legs ever since he been alive! Look at him! He's a goddam' giant! And scared of his goddam' shadow!"

"Okay, Pop!" Michael said. "That's enough!"

Johnny lowered his head like a five-year-old boy while his father terrorized him. I had never seen a grown man treated that way before in my life. Mr. Forrester bent down and yelled directly into Johnny's ear. Johnny didn't budge. He sat right there and took it.

"You make me sick!" Mr. Forrester screamed. "You're a yellow-belly spineless coward whose balls are smaller than the ones you was born with! You ain't no man! You ain't nothin'!"

Johnny's attorneys were just as shocked as I was. They had a ghastly look of horror in their eyes. Whatever the problem between Johnny and his father that night, it was not just about Gizelle's murder. It was something deeply rooted. I don't have to be a psychologist to know that what we witnessed was manifested frustration and anger.

Michael and Mrs. Forrester tried to calm Mr. Forrester down, but he was too far gone. As he yelled and screamed, Johnny sat still with his head down. I became irate. I couldn't stand to see my husband being emasculated by a mind-controlling miserable old man. If anyone was going to emasculate the man I loved, it was going to be me. But at that moment, he needed protection, not emasculation.

"Why are you yelling at him like that?" I slammed my plate on the table and started walking toward Johnny. "Johnny, why are you letting that man talk to you like that?"

Johnny sat still. He wouldn't even raise his head to look at me. Mr. Forrester's abusive control over him was mind-blowing. He put one hand on the back of Johnny's chair, and balled the other into a fist and placed it between the tiny space between Johnny's face and the table.

"Johnny!" I shouted. "Say something to him!"

"He bet' not say a mumbling word!" Mr. Forrester said. "If he so much as blinks a eye, I'll slap the piss out of him!"

Johnny kept his head down and his mouth shut. Enough was enough! Johnny couldn't help himself if he wanted.

I pushed Mr. Forrester away from him. "Leave him alone!"

"This my son!" Mr. Forrester shouted and then pushed me backward.

The attorneys must have felt that it was getting "*too hot in the kitchen*" because they jumped from the table and got the hell out of the way. Cynthia ran around the table and hugged me. Mrs. Forrester walked over to me as well.

"Pop, what the hell is wrong with you, man?" Michael shouted.

Johnny snapped out of his shell and went off on his father.

"Don't you ever put your hands on her again!" Johnny grabbed Mr. Forrester by the collar and slammed him into the wall. "Do you understand me?"

"Niggah, I'll kill you!" Mr. Forrester shouted back.

Mr. Forrester was trying to break Johnny's grip but Johnny was like a madman. Michael pulled Johnny away and separated them. Mr. Forrester fumbled around in his pants pocket and then pulled out a small pistol. I thought it was a play gun at first. Mr. Forrester took a few steps backward to allow some space and then aimed the gun at Johnny.

"You think you a man, niggah?" Mr. Forrester shouted.

"Buddy Forrester! You put that gun down now!" Mrs. Forrester shouted. "That's yo' son!"

"He ain't no son of mine!"

"Okay, everybody out!" Michael screamed as he pushed all the women out of the dining room. "Ma, you too!"

We stepped out of the room and then turned around and headed back.

"Pop," Michael said. "Put that gun down, man."

"You would shoot your own son?" Johnny asked. "What kind of a man are you?"

I thought Johnny was very courageous. He would not back down. I didn't want to see him hurt, but I wanted to see him be a man.

"Give me the gun, Pop!" Michael reached for the gun.

I was holding Mrs. Forrester's hand as we waited to see what Mr. Forrester would do with that gun. She let go of my hand and started to walk back into the dining room.

"Mrs. Forrester, let them handle it," I said.

"Let them handle it?" Mrs. Forrester asked.

"Yeah, the men can handle it." I reached for her hand.

"That's your husband in there and you're willing to stand out here and watch him die?"

"No, ma'am." I was caught off guard by her straightforwardness. "That's not what I meant."

"Alicia, let her go if she wants to go!" Cynthia shouted.

"Let go of my hand!" Mrs. Forrester looked at me like she was about to smack me. I let her hand go quickly.

I followed Mrs. Forrester to the doorway where I could hear and see clearly.

"You think I'm a coward, Pop?" Johnny asked. "Huh? Shoot me, then! I'm right here! Shoot me!"

Mrs. Forrester calmly walked between Johnny and Mr. Forrester.

"Put that gun down now!" Mrs. Forrester said.

"Move!" Mr. Forrester shouted.

"I ain't moving nowhere!"

"Move, Ma!" Johnny moved her to the side.

"If you hurt one hair on my baby's head, I swear to God in Heaven the next time you sleep, will be the last time you sleep!"

"You stubborn, mean, old hateful man!" Johnny cried. "What kind of a man would shoot his own son?"

Michael snuck up behind Mr. Forrester while Johnny was talking and snatched the gun out of his hand. Mr. Forrester fell against the wall and then onto the floor. Knocked out cold! I mean, his mouth was wide open and his arms were stretched out as far as they could go. Mrs. Forrester ran to Mr. Forrester and tried to wake him up.

"Buddy!" Mrs. Forrester said nervously. "Buddy!"

"Let him sleep it off, Ma," Michael said.

"You alright?" I ran to Johnny to make sure he was okay. "Oh my God! What is wrong with your father?"

"I don't know." Johnny sat down in the chair next to his father lying on the floor, but didn't say another word.

Stacey stepped in the doorway with Ms. Hattley and Ms. Carroll standing behind her. I'm sure they saw one hell of a show.

"Is everything okay in here?" Stacey asked.

"Yeah," Michael said. "We sincerely apologize, ladies. Our father had a little too much to drink."

"We probably should be going." Ms. Carroll waved.

"I'm sorry you all had to witness this," Johnny said.

"We understand." Ms. Hattley walked over and shook Johnny's hand. "We'll see you tomorrow in the office. Have a good night."

"Good night." Johnny shook Ms. Hattley's hand and took a long, deep sigh of relief as she walked away.

Michael and Johnny carried Mr. Forrester to the car and tossed him in the backseat. Mrs. Forrester apologized once again and that was that. Mr. Forrester went back to Michigan the next day and the rest of the Forresters went on as if nothing had happened.

JOHNNY'S EVIDENTIARY HEARING DIDN'T GO AS WELL as we expected. They found the DNA evidence, which was all that they had really, to be enough to move forward with a trial. His attorneys were still very optimistic that he would be acquitted of the murder charge.

My confidence that Johnny would be found not guilty alleviated a lot of the guilt that I harbored for Gizelle's murder. I thought once he was freed of the charge we could move forward with our lives as normal. I wasn't a suspect. No one had a clue that I was involved, so what good would it do to ruffle those feathers?

The stress of the trial and having to keep the murder a secret took its toll on my relationship with Pam. To be honest, we never fully recovered from the argument we had when I stayed with her those couple of days. She and Cynthia didn't speak at all.

The office girls didn't quite pick up on the feud because we were not gathered as a group as much. They kept in touch and offered help in any way they could, but they allowed us our privacy to deal with the situation. Contact from Pam was far and few between.

Johnny's trial didn't take long to begin. We were as confident with the acquittal as we were with the evidentiary hearing. Our confidence was met with the same disappointment. Guilty!

"Mr. Foreman," the judge said, "would you please read the verdict?"

"Yes, sir," the juror said. "We, the jury, find the defendant, guilty of first-degree murder, as charged in the indictment."

"Oh Lord, no!" Mrs. Forrester said as she rocked back and forth. "No! No! No!"

I was stunned! Mrs. Forrester turned to me and cried out loud. I felt her body shake as she cried on my shoulder. I wanted to be strong for her and Johnny, but I couldn't. I started to cry so severely that I totally lost coherency.

Michael and Cynthia came over to comfort us. I remember Cynthia asking me questions. If I answered them, I'm sure I didn't answer them correctly. It felt as if everything was moving in slow motion. What seemed like days to me was only a matter of minutes.

The judge was merciful and allowed us time to gather ourselves. But once we did and it was time for him to announce Johnny's sentence, he had no mercy whatsoever.

"Mr. Johnson Forrester," the judge said, "you have been found guilty by this jury of murder in the first degree. I am allowed by law to sentence you to life with the possibility of parole with a minimum of twenty-five years, *or*, life without parole, *or*, death by lethal injection. Although I would like nothing more to give you the maximum sentence for this hideous crime, the laws of the state of Georgia prohibit me from administering that sentence if evidence does not support the premeditation of the crime."

I held Mrs. Forrester's hand in mine. We were still reeling from the verdict when the judge stunned us even more.

"Mr. Forrester," the judge said, "you will be sentenced to spend the remainder of your life in a state penitentiary without the possibility of parole! You are now turned over to the sheriff's department."

Johnny showed no outwardly emotion. To some people, he may have appeared as cold and heartless. To me, he was the strongest of men. He did not commit that murder, and when his unjustified sentence was announced, he stood as a justified man. He showed no guilt! He showed no sorrow! He showed no fear! He knew that he was not a murderer, and so did I.

After the sentence was read, Johnny and his attorneys briefly talked amongst themselves. The spectators started to trickle out once the deputies placed Johnny in handcuffs and took him away. Mrs. Forrester and I sat in the courtroom, in the same spot, speechless. I think we both felt that as long as we stayed in that courtroom there was still a chance that Johnny would walk back through those wooden doors. But once we walked out that dream would become a nightmare.

Michael eventually convinced us to leave. We walked out of the courtroom where the office girls were waiting for us. They hugged us, one by one. Pam looked at me. I saw the guilt in her eyes and then I heard it with my ears.

"I'm so sorry, Alicia," Pam whispered in my ear.

The other office girls that heard Pam probably thought she was just offering her condolences. They had no idea she was apologizing for helping me send my husband to prison.

Mrs. Forrester decided to spend her remaining stay in Atlanta with me. I was overwhelmed by her kindness. She knew what I was going through, and she reached out to comfort me. My own mother hadn't even called to see how I was doing. That's a story of its own right there.

The following Sunday was Mother's Day. I managed to pull off a miracle to surprise Mrs. Forrester. It was nothing short of a miracle. Three generations of Forresters and former Forresters. The group consisted of Mrs. Forrester; Cynthia, Michael's current wife; Tonita, Michael's first wife; Cecelia, Michael's second wife; Brimone, Tonita's daughter and Cynthia's stepdaughter; Alexiah, Cecelia's daughter and also Cynthia's stepdaughter; Brittany, and last, but not least, me.

"You all have put a big smile in my heart." Mrs. Forrester smiled.

"How much longer are you going to be in town, Mrs. Forrester?" Cecelia asked.

"Two more days."

"I was thinking that maybe I could come pick you up and we could go shopping or something."

I looked at Cynthia and Tonita, who were looking at each other. We were astonished that she was offering to take Mrs. Forrester to lunch. People called me snooty, but Cecelia was something totally different. She only socialized with the elitists of Atlanta.

Apparently, Mrs. Forrester had the same effect on her that she had on the rest of us. Through her, we realized that day that we all had something in common. We were missing that bond between mother and daughter. None of our mothers were constant figures in our lives. Mrs. Forrester, though in our lives for short stints of time, had a motherly effect on us.

"I would love to, Cecelia," Mrs. Forrester said. "I remember the last time I came here, you took me to that place downtown with all them little shops."

"The Underground?" I asked.

"Yeah, that's it!" Mrs. Forrester pointed at me excitedly.

"You went to the Underground, Cecelia?" Tonita laughed sarcastically.

Tonita and Cecelia did not get along at all. From what I knew, they had stopped their daughters from seeing each other because they were tripping with each other. That's why Michael got them both at the same time to make sure they stay in contact. Cecelia says it's Tonita and Tonita says it's Cecelia. I thought Tonita's comment would fuel a cat spat, but Cecelia rolled it off of her back and laughed along with it.

"I go to the Underground." Cecelia laughed back.

"When?" Tonita looked at Cecelia jokingly.

"None of your business!" Cecelia stuck out her tongue.

"I ain't mad at ya'!" Tonita chuckled.

"Okay, girls," I said. "I want everybody to say why Mother's Day is special to them."

"That's a good idea," Cynthia said. "Who's first?"

"Let's go left to right, beginning with our guest of honor, Mrs. Forrester."

I was sitting to the right of Mrs. Forrester, which meant that would put me last. I needed the time to think up a lie because my relationship with my mother was anything but motherly.

"As a mother, the good Lord blessed me with two sons. I loved them. Fed them. Raised them and turn them loose to you. I am proud of those boys. They made something out of nothing with their lives. The good Lord has also blessed me with four beautiful grandchildren and four beautiful daughters. I don't believe in that in-law, or stepfamily, mess. If I love you, I love you. It doesn't matter if it's in-law, step, half, ex, whatever. Mother's Day to me is enjoying the lives that have come from my tree."

"That's so sweet." Tonita smiled.

"Is it my turn now?" Brimone asked.

"Yeah, baby," I said.

"Mother's Day is important to me because I have been blessed to have four mothers. Mommy, my stepmother, Ms. Cynthia, Grandma Wintry, and you, Grandma." Brimone kissed Mrs. Forrester on the cheek. She was sitting next to Cecelia and remembered that she had forgotten her. "Oh, and you too, Ms. 'Celia."

"Aw, thank you, baby," Cecelia said. "Well, Mother's Day to me is a day that men have to bow down and admit that if it wasn't for us, there would be no them!" Cecelia laughed. "Seriously, it is a day when a woman is truly appreciated. She's made to feel special, needed, wanted and loved. That's it for me."

"Okay, I like! I like!" I said. "Your turn, Alexiah."

"Um, it's a day to be kind, sweet and love my Mommy!" Alexiah said. "And I'll also do everything she asks me to!"

"You supposed to do everything she asks you to do anyway, Alex," Brimone said.

"I wasn't talking to you, Bri!" Alexiah snapped.

"Are they like this all the time?" Cecelia asked.

"*All* of the time." Cynthia laughed.

"I just let 'em go at it," Tonita said. "I sit back and laugh. I wish I had a sister so that we could act that way."

"I hear you." I gave Tonita a high-five.

"That doesn't bother you at all?" Cecelia asked. "What if they start fighting, Tonita?"

"Oh girl, please. They'll take on the world before they do any harm to each other, 'Celia. I don't know how they are over your house, Cynt, but they are inseparable at mine. When it's time for Alex to leave, they act like they're never going to see each other again."

"Yeah, and when they see each other, they act as if they've never seen each other before," Cynthia said. "I'm like, calm down, it's only been two weeks."

"Really?" Cecelia smiled. "They're that close?"

"Oh man, they get on my nerves sometime," Cynthia said. "My sister this and my sister that. I'm like, I know that's your sister."

"Wow! I didn't know that." Cecelia looked down at Alexiah. "Would you like for your sister to visit more often?"

"Can she, Mommy?" Alexiah's eyes grew big with excitement.

"Of course, baby." Cecelia looked at Tonita. "I see what you mean. Wow! My sister and I grew up in the same household and we don't get along as well as you two. We'll be going to Disneyland in a few weeks, Bri, if it's okay with your mom, you're certainly welcome to come with us."

"Can I, Mommy?" Brimone shouted to Tonita.

"It's fine with me. I want to get you out of the house anyway."

"I'm going to Disneyland with you, Alex!" Brimone shouted.

"Now I can have some fun!" Alexiah said.

"So you weren't going to have fun with me and Brent?" Cecelia laughed.

Brent is Cecelia's rich white husband.

"You're too old, Mommy."

"Okay! Okay! Okay! Not funny, Alex," Cecelia said. "Your turn, Cynthia."

"Mother's Day to me is the day we celebrate the glory of God for allowing women to have children," Cynthia said.

"That's good," I said. I looked down at Brittany and I asked her what Mother's Day meant to her. "Brittany, baby. Do you know what Mother's Day is?"

"Yes."

"What does Mother's Day mean to you, baby?"

Everybody was silent. We were all aware that this would be the first Mother's Day for Brittany without Deirdra. I took a deep breath to prepare myself because I didn't want to cry.

"Um, Mother's Day is love."

It was simple, not complicated. It was happiness, not sadness. It was inspirational, not melancholy. Then why could I not just leave it the hell alone?

"Mother's Day is love to you, baby?" I twisted her long pony-tails.

"Yes, because my mother made me pray that God bring another mommy to love me after she was gone to Heaven. I wanted a bike, but my mommy told me not to pray for a bike. She told me not to pray for toys and stuff. She told me to pray for you to be my new mommy, and now you are my new mommy. So my mommy was right. Mommy said she loves me. And you say you love me; that is why Mother's Day is love."

By the time she finished, there were waterworks falling all over the place. I was the first one to leave the table. I didn't want the girls to see me cry.

"I'll be back in one second." I held up a finger and wiped my eyes with a napkin.

"Me, too," Cynthia said, getting up from the table as well.

"Wait for me." Cecelia excused herself, too.

"We'll be right back, Mrs. Forrester," Tonita said.

The four of us walked to the other side of the restaurant where the kids couldn't see us and cried our eyes out.

"That was so sad," Cecelia said as she wiped her eyes.

"Didn't you know her mother well, Alicia?" Tonita asked.

"Yes, we became really close. She was the nicest person in the world. She was strong. Beautiful. She was just a nice, nice, person."

"We look crazy standing over here crying like this." Tonita laughed.

"Okay, are y'all ready to go back?" Cynthia asked.

"Come on," I said.

"Hold it," Cecelia said. "I want to let you all know that this is the best Mother's Day I've ever spent. My mother and I are not close. My sister and I are not close and this is the closest I'm probably going to get to family. I appreciate my husband and we will have our own celebration later, but this has been a time for me to remember. I guess I just wanna thank you all for inviting me."

"Hey, girl, we thank you for accepting." Tonita smiled.

We wiped our eyes one last time and started to walk back to our table, but Cecelia stopped us.

"One more thing," Cecelia said. "Tonita, I know we haven't always gotten along, and I know most of it was my fault. But looking at those two girls so happy to be around each other makes me feel so silly for not doing enough to make sure they see each other more. How about we work together to make that happen?"

"I've been waiting a long time to hear those words from you." Tonita grabbed Cecelia by the arm. "Come on; let's celebrate over a glass of wine."

"Sounds good to me."

We walked back to our table and everything was wonderful until Tonita reminded everyone that I hadn't said what Mother's Day meant to me.

"Hey, we haven't heard you yet, Alicia," Tonita said.

"That's right!" Cynthia added. "You came up with this, you better say something."

"Okay, let me see." I thought momentarily. "Mother's Day to me is having the blessing from God to be a mother, even when you're not blessed to give birth."

"I like that," Mrs. Forrester said. "I really like that."

"Thank you," I said.

"No, thank you for making an old woman feel wanted," Mrs. Forrester said.

"It was my pleasure."

Finally, I was one of the daughters. We enjoyed the rest of our afternoon and then went home to our respective families. For me, my family was Brittany and Mrs. Forrester. We enjoyed ourselves the remainder of the evening, watching Disney movies and eating ice cream.

CHAPTER FIFTEEN

My mother-in-law went home to Michigan a couple of days later and I fell into a deep state of depression. I was fine as long Mrs. Forrester was in the house, but as soon as she left, my guilt consumed me.

I started to have those old suicidal tendencies. I couldn't shake the irrepressible feeling that my life was useless. I didn't really want to die; I was just so tired of living.

CAPs was floundering and we were about to go under. Even though she was dead, Gizelle still managed to ruin it. We never recovered from all of the time and money we had spent luring her. Cynthia was determined to keep it going, but then she had a best-selling author to support her financially. Pam was set for life by her ex-professional basketball baby's daddy. My husband was in prison. I had no money, and a child depending on me.

Two weeks after Johnny was locked up, we went to visit him. We visited him a few more times but each time it took a little more out of me. Months started to pass and reality started to settle in. With each passing day, I was facing the fact that Johnny was not going to get out of prison. I would have to raise Brittany alone.

I couldn't handle it. I couldn't handle the pressure. I couldn't handle the responsibility. I couldn't handle being a mother and I wanted out. I wanted out of the situation but there was nowhere for me to go.

I decided to take the easy way out. The easy way out for me was death. People think that suicide is a sign of weakness. I didn't see it that way. Suicide to me was not a decision about death. It was a decision about life, a life that was serving no good purpose to anyone. If my life was doing no one any good, why stay?

When I woke in the morning all that I had to do was dress Brittany. After that, I had the remainder of the day to think about what was happening with Johnny in prison. He shouldn't have been there; I should have.

Pam and I weren't talking so I couldn't turn to her. That was probably for the best. Talking to Pam about the murders only made them more real. I often wondered if her soul was suffering as much as mine.

One Friday night, Brittany spent the night at Cynthia's with Brimone and Alexiah. That night, I was lying on my bed tossing and turning. I couldn't sleep without Brittany. My rational thoughts became irrational and the peaceful idea of death took over. It was the perfect time. I was alone and didn't have to worry about Brittany finding my body.

I cut on my CD player and stuck my girl in. You already know who she is—Phyllis Hyman. I pressed play, and then forwarded to "Somewhere in my Lifetime." I stared at myself in the mirror before I opened the medicine cabinet and took out a bottle of pills. I didn't even look like myself. I didn't know who I was looking at in my mirror but it wasn't me.

I swallowed as many pills as quickly as I could and walked over to the tub. I cut on the water in my huge garden tub and lit some candles. I tested the temperature by placing my toes in first. Hot, steamy, perfect!

I relaxed in the tub and closed my eyes. I reached for my razor that I shaved my legs with and took the blade out. I turned my arms upward and with my left hand, sliced across my right wrist. It was painful, mostly a burning sensation. Next, I took my right hand and sliced across my left wrist. Once I saw blood come to the surface I stretched my arms across the sides of the tub and closed my eyes.

WHEN I WOKE UP, I WAS IN THE HOSPITAL. Cynthia was asleep in one chair and Pam was asleep in the other. Damn! I couldn't even commit suicide without making an ass of myself. I was so embarrassed I wanted to stay asleep, forever!

"Stop acting like you sleep; I saw you open your eyes, girl," Pam said.

"What happened?" I moaned.

"You know what happened!" Cynthia said. "What is going on with you, Alicia?"

"I don't know," I said. "It's like I can't help myself."

"Why are you doing this?" Cynthia asked. "Why are you trying to hurt so many people?"

"I'm not."

"Do you know how many people you will hurt if you kill yourself?"

"It's not like that."

"It is like that." Cynthia said. "How do you think Johnny will feel, hearing that you killed yourself while he's in prison?"

"I'm sorry."

"No, Alicia, sorry is not good enough this time!" Cynthia looked at me and started to cry. "You have to stop doing this to yourself! We can't watch you twenty-four hours a day!"

"Have you told anybody?"

"Why?" Cynthia stopped crying and folded her arms angrily.

"I don't want anybody to know."

"Oh, I get it! You can kill yourself and to hell with everybody who loves you, but if you survive, you want everybody to care about how embarrassed you are. How can you be so selfish?"

"I'm sorry, Cynthia. I don't want to hurt you or anybody else."

"Stop lying, Alicia! You don't care who you hurt!"

"Cynthia, maybe we need to let Alicia rest for a while." Pam held my hand. "I know you're hurt, but this is not helping Alicia. She shouldn't be talking at all."

"Fine!" Cynthia walked out of the room without saying good-bye.

"I think she's mad at me." I tried to laugh but couldn't.

"I'm going to get your nurse right now, but as soon as she says it's alright, I'm going to get knee deep in your ass, girl."

"Okay." I was so groggy that I would have agreed to anything.

Pam left and, a few minutes later, my nurse, Betty, entered. She was very excited to see that I was alert. She wanted friends and family around me when I woke up to stimulate my memory.

"Good morning," Betty said. "How are you?"

"I'm fine."

"Seems like somebody had a little accident."

"Yes, it seems that way."

"We're going to get you on your feet and get you back out there in the world. You hear me?"

"I hear you."

"Is your name Alicia Forrester?"

"Yes."

"Are you in any way related to Dr. Johnson Forrester?"

I was hesitant to answer because I didn't know why she was asking me about my husband, but I answered anyway. "Yes. He's my husband."

"I just think what they did to him was dead wrong!"

"Thank you."

"I know him and he would never kill anybody. He cared too much about people to ever harm another human being. I just don't believe it."

"You know my husband?"

"Yes, ma'am, he was my psychologist."

"Johnny?"

"Yes," Betty said. "What a coincidence, huh?"

"I'll say."

"I was unjustly accused just like he was, and Dr. Forrester helped me to deal with it. I was accused of trying to hurt my child. That's ridiculous! I love my child more than anything! I had to divorce my husband and let him have custody, in order for us to keep our child. I became frustrated. Angry! I was mad at the world, girl. But that husband of yours helped me in my mind and in the courtroom."

Most of the men in my life had been mentioned as assholes. I was so proud to hear someone speak so highly of my man that I didn't want it to stop.

"How did he help you in the courtroom?" I asked.

"He went before the judge and told him that I would never intentionally harm my child. The judge tried to take his testimony and get him off of the stand, but Dr. Forrester asked for more time to make sure he understood his statement with undeniable clarity. He was so convincing, the judge gave me full visitation rights the same day."

"Johnny did that?"

"Yes, he did," Betty said as she tucked in my sheets. "And what he did for Veronica goes beyond generosity."

"Who's Veronica?" I asked.

"She's another one of his patients. She was blindsided one day by a car in front of the Grand Hyatt. It happened to be the same day that singer, Gizelle, was killed."

"She was blindsided?" I knew it had to be the woman Pam and I had hit on our way out of the hotel.

"Yeah, somebody knocked the shit out of the side of her car. Oh, excuse my French." Betty laughed. "Somebody rammed her car and the poor girl was so frail that she couldn't even call for help. She suffered from an eating disorder and it picked that particular day to finally consume her. The accident may have bruised her a little, but the disease shut her body down."

"Oh, wow, that's not good." I was relieved to hear that the accident Pam and I had caused did not cause anyone harm.

"Veronica had practically given up on life. She was ready to die. There was nothing her family or friends could say or do; she was ready for death. Somehow, your husband got inside of her head and gave her a reason to live. She became dependent upon his faith. Knowing he was the key to her recovery, Dr. Forrester came to this hospital every single day to see her until she was up and walking!"

"My husband did that?" I smiled from ear to ear.

"Yes, he did." Betty nodded her head. "You know, I was wondering."

"Wondering what?" I asked.

"I was wondering why a woman who could have such a fantastic husband like Dr. Forrester would not want to spend every minute of her life with him."

"I don't know what you mean by that, Betty."

"Yes, you do. Death ain't going nowhere. It's going to always be waiting for you. Life is too short to spend it on death. Enjoy your life! Enjoy your family! You only have one shot at this thing. But God gives you plenty of opportunities to get it right."

"Do you always talk this much to your patients?" I laughed.

"Only to the ones I like."

"Thank you for liking me."

"You probably won't be thanking me by the time you leave here."

"What does that mean?"

"That means that by time you leave here, I will have preached so much on the joy of life you're never going to want to hear my voice again."

"I want a new nurse!" I joked.

"Oh no, girl, you're in trouble. This is the least I can do for Dr. Forrester."

"Thank you."

"I think there are some people outside who want to see you."

"Is one of them about three feet tall with ponytails?"

"She can't wait to get in here."

"Please send her in!" I couldn't wait to see my baby.

"Ready or not," Betty said as she was leaving the room.

The door slowly opened, but Brittany was so small I couldn't see her. I saw Cynthia standing in the doorway, holding the door for her. As Brittany walked in, Cynthia balled her fist and pointed it at me. She closed the door and then Brittany finally came into view.

"Hi, baby!" I opened my arms for Brittany to climb on the bed with me, but she wouldn't come. "What's the matter, baby?"

"Are you going to die, Mommy?"

"Am I going to die? No, baby! I'm not going to die."

"I'm scared, Mommy."

"Why are you scared, Brittany?" I asked in my baby voice.

"I don't want you to die."

"I'm not going to die, baby; come here." I reached my arms out for Brittany again.

"I'm scared that if I come over there, you might die like my other mommy."

"I'm fine, baby. I was sick, but now I'm fine."

"That's what my other mommy said and then she died."

"Baby, I'm fine! Come here, please!"

Brittany took one step and then stopped.

"Promise?" Brittany said.

"Promise what, sweetie?"

"Promise you won't die."

"I promise!" I started to cry as I reached out my arms for the third time. "Oh, I promise! I promise! I promise!"

Brittany took one small step and then sprinted to me. She climbed on top of the bed and lay beside me. I stared at her face as I always did, and couldn't imagine my life without her. And then I thought how she must have felt about spending her life without me. I was her last and only link to parenthood. I held her tight and we fell asleep.

Betty stayed on my ass like she promised, morning, noon and night. I asked her if she had a schedule because it seemed like she never took her ass home. We played cards together, had Bible study, everything. She snuck me in a little drink here and there and we talked about the troubles in our lives. She wasn't one of the office girls but she was damn near close to it!

I stayed in the hospital for a week. I was given psychological examinations and I was diagnosed as suffering from manic depression. You think? I could have told them that when I slit my wrists. How in the hell could I deal with it was what I wanted to know. They gave me a prescription that made me too lively. You can believe the last thing I felt was depressed.

Cynthia and Pam didn't trust me being alone when I got out of the hospital, so I received an unexpected visit from my mother-in-law. I gave Mrs. Forrester our master bedroom and I moved in with Brittany. I didn't want her to know I had attempted suicide but Cynthia couldn't keep her mouth shut. She promised Cynthia that she would watch me every second of the day.

I felt guilty about her coming because she wasn't feeling very well. Being ill didn't stop her from fulfilling her promise. If I stayed in the bathroom too long, she knocked on the door to see if I was okay. If I left the house for an extended period of time, she called me to make sure I was okay. The only time she didn't check on me was when I was alone with Brittany. She knew I wouldn't do anything stupid with her around. I wasn't that crazy.

Mrs. Forrester also got an opportunity to visit Johnny while she was there. He was only allowed so many visitors at once so Brittany and I stayed home so that she could go. When she came back from Johnny's prison, she was so full of life. She had an extra pep in her step, so to speak.

We started to do more things outside of the house. We had plenty of mother-daughter conversations. We discussed the nature of a man and Mrs. Forrester schooled me royally. Some of the things she was saying completely blew my mind.

"You young ladies nowadays, you too bent on trying to find a perfect man. You build up this fantasy and then you try to find a man to fulfill your dream."

"I agree," I said as we dipped into our ice cream at the same time.

I was lying on one couch and she was lying on another. Brittany was going back and forth. It depended on who was giving her the ice cream the quickest.

"For example," Mrs. Forrester said as she took another bite of her ice cream. "As you saw, my husband got all kinds of issues. Now, somebody your age might say, leave him. Go! Y'all are so quick to give up when things get rough. If me and my husband would have broke up every time we got mad at each other, we would have never got married."

"I know, but marriage is so hard."

"Of course, it's hard. The Lord never said that it would be easy." Mrs. Forrester handed her ice cream to Brittany. If she was giving up her ice cream, something deep was about to follow. "I'm going to tell you something and I swear it better not leave this room."

"Okay." I sat up straight; I didn't want to miss a word.

"You promise?" Mrs. Forrester asked.

"I promise."

"Well, a long time ago, right after Buddy and I got married, he went off to the Vietnam War. It was hard on me, trying to survive on my own. I was a young woman at the time and I got lonely. Buddy's best friend and I started going to the movies and doing stuff we shouldn't have been doing.

"When Buddy came home from the war, I stopped seeing the best friend and went back to my wifely duties. Buddy was home for about three months when we found out I was pregnant. I wasn't that big and I wasn't sick or anything. I thought I had just got pregnant when Buddy got home. It turned out that I was actually five months along.

"It didn't take a math genius to figure out the baby wasn't his. Buddy went crazy. He went out looking for the man, but I told him he wasn't going to find him because the man was from down south. Buddy packed his bags and moved out. I was so hurt that I didn't know what to do. I wanted to tell him the truth about his best friend, but I knew that would only hurt him more.

"He had every right to divorce me and never say another word to me again in his life. But he didn't. He started coming around and we started to talk. Back then, men kept things inside of 'em a lot more than they do nowadays. He didn't want me to see his pain."

"What happened to the baby?"

"He's your brother-in-law."

"Michael?" I covered my mouth with my hands. "Michael is not Mr. Forrester's son?"

"Why sure he is." Mrs. Forrester pointed to Brittany. "Just like she's your daughter. That's why I don't like all of that half, and step, and all that kind of mess. If you love somebody as a mother and treat her as your mother, she is your mother! The same thing goes for your child. Biology ain't bigger than God's love."

"Amen!"

"But my point is that, when you saw me wiping my husband's head after he had pulled a gun on my son, I wasn't rewarding him for acting like a fool. I was showing him love when he needed love. Just like he loved me when I needed love. We all make mistakes, but we have to try to understand them instead of just condemning them.

"I understand my husband. 'Cause before he found out I was pregnant by another man, he was never angry. He was always smiling and laughing. He never took one drink of liquor. But once he found out, he hasn't taken that bottle from his mouth. I did that to him."

"Does Michael know any of this?"

"No, nobody knows but me and Buddy. I'm quite sure his best friend figured it out because he stopped coming around."

"Did you love his best friend?"

"No. I needed attention from a man and he was the closest to me."

"Mrs. Forrester?"

"Yeah, baby."

"Can I tell you something that you may end up hating me for, but I pray to God you don't?"

"What's the matter?"

I didn't want to beat around the bush, or stall, so I came right out with the truth.

"I killed the lady in the hotel, not Johnny."

"What?" Mrs. Forrester looked at me with total confusion.

"I am responsible for the murder Johnny is in prison for. He is serving my time."

"Why would you say that?"

"Because it's true."

"Wait a minute. What are you saying, Alicia?"

"I'm saying that I have been keeping this locked up inside of me ever since it happened and if I don't tell somebody, it's going to kill me, Mrs. Forrester! I swear it's going to kill me!"

I began to hyperventilate and Mrs. Forrester went to get a cold wet towel to place on my forehead. She stretched out my legs and placed a pillow beneath my head. I saw Brittany crying, and I sat up instantly.

"Come here, baby," I said.

Brittany was afraid to come to me.

"I'm fine; I'm just hot. Granny got mommy a cold towel because I'm hot. I'm not sick, baby! I'm fine!"

Mrs. Forrester held Brittany's hand and brought her over to me, "See. Mommy's not sick."

"I'm fine." I hugged Brittany tightly. "I'm hot. Aren't you hot?"

"Yes."

Brittany sat on my lap, and Mrs. Forrester and I talked about other things until she fell asleep. I carried her to bed and then Mrs. Forrester and I continued our conversation.

"Mrs. Forrester, I want so badly to go to the police and tell them everything but I'm afraid."

"Are you telling me you let my son go to prison for something you did?"

"Yes, ma'am."

"How?" Mrs. Forrester pleaded. "How could you do that to somebody you love?"

"I am so sorry, Mrs. Forrester," I said. "I've wanted to tell somebody for so long."

"I'm confused, Alicia. If you wanted to tell somebody, you could have told the police when they charged my son with first-degree murder! You could have told the district attorney when they tried my son for first-degree murder! You could have told the jury when they convicted my son of first-degree murder! And you could have told the judge when he sentenced my son to prison without the possibility of parole! But you didn't."

"I'm sorry, Mrs. Forrester." I wanted her to believe me but she wasn't having it.

"I think I need to take a nap." Mrs. Forrester slowly stood up. "While I'm asleep, I think you need to come up with a reason why I shouldn't call the police."

Mrs. Forrester went upstairs and closed the bedroom door. I called Pam as soon as I heard the door shut.

"Hello."

"Pam?"

"Hey, what's up, Alicia?"

"I told Mrs. Forrester."

"You told Mrs. Forrester what?"

"I told her about Gizelle and the bodyguard."

"WHAT?" Pam screamed. "Why?"

"I had to tell somebody, Pam, or I was going to burst!"

"What if she tells the police?"

"I can live with that."

"I can't! I don't want to go to jail!" Pam shouted.

"And I don't want my husband in jail!" I shouted back.

We held the telephones silently for a few minutes, waiting for the other to speak.

"I better go," I said.

"What are you going to do, Alicia?"

"I don't know. But, for the record, I didn't mention your name. And I won't mention your name."

"I don't want you to go to jail either."

"But it's okay if my innocent husband goes to jail?"

"He's a man!"

That pissed me off! Pam was always comparing women to men, particularly, black women to black men. And believe me; the comparisons never, ever favored black men.

"Don't give me that, 'he's a man' bullshit! You claim to be so strong! So independent! You're always trying to be a damn man but when the shit gets thick you want to be a defenseless woman! You can't have it both ways!"

"Whatever!" Pam said.

"No, Pam! This is my husband we're talking about. I love him! I can't come up with any more selfish excuses for him being in prison for our crime. I'm sorry, but that, 'he's a man' shit doesn't cut it anymore."

"Your man should want to do time for you, Alicia!"

"Not for murder!" I snapped. "And he's not going to. And he's not going to do time for you, either."

"Please don't do this, Alicia," Pam begged me. "We can't make it in prison."

"We're going to have to."

"Not me. If I go in there, I'll never make it out."

"Look, I have to go."

"But..."

I hung up the phone as Pam was in mid-sentence. I didn't feel like arguing about the situation. My mind was made up. I was at peace with myself. I just wanted to enjoy my dinner with my family.

I prepared dinner and waited for Mrs. Forrester to come downstairs to eat. She was a diabetic so she had to eat around seven o' clock every night. Either she, or myself, had dinner ready at seven on the dot each night she was there. It was like clockwork. She must have really been upset about me letting Johnny sit in jail; she refused to come downstairs. I was ready to turn myself into the police, but I needed her support to do it.

I waited, and waited, and waited. I sent Brittany upstairs to convince her to eat since she was apparently very pissed off with me and understandably so.

While I was standing at the bottom of the staircase waiting for Brittany, the doorbell rang. I peeked through the peephole and it was Pam. Damn! I didn't want to deal with her in front of my mother-in-law. At first, I wasn't going to answer but she wasn't going to go anywhere; she knew I was home.

"What are you doing here?" I asked with the chain still on the door.

"Open the door."

"This is not a good time. My mother-in-law is on her way downstairs."

"So! Open the door or I'll knock it down."

"Shit! I'll let you in but you better not say a damn word." I opened the door and walked back to the bottom of the stairs and called Brittany. "Brit! Is everything okay up there, baby?"

Brittany walked out of the guest bedroom and stood at the top of the stairs. "Grandma won't wake up."

"What do you mean, she won't wake up?"

"I shook her really hard but she won't wake up."

"Okay, let her sleep. Come back downstairs for dinner."

"Okay!" Brittany ran downstairs and into the kitchen.

"Say your grace before you eat!" I yelled as I walked upstairs.

"Where you going?" Pam asked.

"Something's wrong."

"With what?" Pam followed me upstairs to the guest room.

"Something's wrong! Mrs. Forrester is diabetic; she takes her shot and has dinner every night at seven like clockwork."

I knocked on the door but there was no answer. I called her name as I pushed the door open. "Mrs. Forrester?"

She was lying peacefully on her side. I tiptoed to the bed and gently touched her. She didn't respond. I pushed her a little harder and she still didn't respond. I turned her onto her back and she rolled over with no bodily control.

"I think something's wrong!" I grabbed her wrist to check for a pulse. "She doesn't have a pulse, Pam! Call an ambulance!"

Pam ran to the phone and picked up the receiver. I waited to hear her dial the number and request an ambulance, but she didn't. I looked back at her and she was holding the phone in her hand.

"What are you doing?" I shouted. "Call an ambulance!"

"Hold on; she's the only other person who knows the truth."

"Are you crazy?" I ran to Pam and snatched the phone out of her hand. "Give me that damn phone!"

I called an ambulance and waited for them to arrive.

"Look! I need you to get Brittany out of here before the ambulance gets here! Go! Go! Now!"

"And take her where, Alicia?" Pam asked.

"Anywhere! Just away from here!"

While Pam was getting Brittany ready, I was putting the car seat in Pam's car. I didn't want Brittany to see another person in her life in that way. I called Michael and Cynthia and told them to come to the house.

I ran downstairs and opened the front door, waiting for the ambulance to arrive. It didn't take long at all. They were there in a matter of minutes. I waved them in and they followed me upstairs. The medics went to work immediately and I stood back and watched. While they were attempting emergency CPR, Michael ran into the bedroom.

"Mama?" Michael tried to get to Mrs. Forrester but two of the medics helped Cynthia and me to hold him back. "What's wrong with my mama?"

"She's suffered a major heart attack, sir," the medic said. "We've managed to revive her but we have to get her to the hospital as soon as possible!"

"Thank God!" Michael took a deep sigh of relief. "Whoo! Thank God!"

Cynthia, Michael and I followed the medics as they quickly pushed Mrs. Forrester's gurney to the ambulance. Michael jumped in the back with his mother while Cynthia and I rode in their car.

I called Pam and asked her to keep Brittany until we returned from the hospital. She asked how Mrs. Forrester was doing and I told her they had revived her. She seemed sincere when she wished her to have a healthy recovery. She also apologized for her momentary lapse in judgment.

When we got to the hospital everything was chaotic. Doctors and nurses were moving fast and using terminology that I couldn't understand. They worked on her the rest of the evening, into the wee hours of the morning.

We called Tonita and Cecelia to tell them of Mrs. Forrester's condition. They rushed to the hospital as well. The four of us stood in the waiting room, holding hands and praying out loud.

We asked the Lord to allow us to have Mrs. Forrester a little while longer. And about three o'clock in the morning, our prayers were answered. Michael came from the Intensive Care Unit with an update. God had answered our prayers, and His answer was, no.

"She's gone," Michael said as he walked toward us.

"I'm sorry, Michael," I said.

Cynthia hugged Michael as he cried on her shoulder. We patted his back and offered our condolences. I couldn't help but feel responsible. The woman was doing fine until I had placed my heavy burden on her weak heart. I was forced to keep another menacing secret inside of my miserable soul.

I couldn't go back to that big house all by myself that night. Brittany and I spent the night with Michael and Cynthia. Brittany kept asking about Mrs. Forrester and I lied and told her she had to go back to Michigan. She was sad that she didn't get a chance to say good-bye, but she got over it quickly when Brimone and Alexiah came over.

Michael and Cynthia had a full house: Tonita and Rob, Cecelia and Brent. It was Cecelia's first visit since her and Michael's divorce. Tina and Curtis were there along with their three girls. Brimone, Alexiah, Brittany, Pam and me.

Everybody in our immediate family was there, except for my husband. I thought about how I would break the news to Johnny as everybody started to leave around daybreak. Michael and I decided we would go to the prison the next day to tell him. Cynthia said, from the very beginning, that she would not go. She couldn't stand to see him behind bars under regular visiting circumstances. There was no way she could stand to see him being told his mother had died.

CHAPTER SIXTEEN

The ride to the prison was long. We didn't say very much; neither one of us could pretend to be in a talkative mood. Brittany was ecstatic since she had become familiar with the route. She recognized certain landmarks and knew we were going to see Johnny.

"We're going to Daddy's house!" Brittany jumped up and down in her seat.

"Yes, baby, we're going to Daddy's house." I smiled as I looked at her in the backseat.

There was an unusually dark overcast that day that didn't help the mood at all. The rain started to fall as we entered the prison gates. The prison walls even seemed taller. Inescapable! Not just for those in the physical realm, but also for those existing in the spiritual. I felt that what was about to happen from our conversation with Johnny would always remain with me. Contrarily, it would also snatch a piece of my soul to stay behind those tall prison walls.

When we walked into the visiting room, Johnny was already waiting. He was smiling and in an upbeat mood. Brittany ran to the window and did her and Johnny's hand-playing game.

"Hi, Daddy!" Brittany said.

"How's my baby?" Johnny was acting like a kid himself.

"I'm fine!"

Brittany chased Johnny's hand as he moved it around on the window. I watched them talk and play for a while, until Johnny asked me to pick up the telephone. I picked it up and I looked into Johnny's eyes. I couldn't tell him. I couldn't tell him that his mother had died.

I blew him a kiss and I whispered, "I love you with all of my heart."

He whispered it back to me, and I took Brittany's hand so that she couldn't see Johnny's reaction when Michael gave him the news. He was not going to accept it well. Michael picked up the phone and I yearned to high-tail it out of there. Unfortunately, I couldn't. I had to wait on Michael.

I stood to the side where Johnny couldn't see us, and Brittany couldn't see Johnny. I tried to distract her by playing games with her. I could hear every word Michael and Johnny were saying; I was still in the vicinity of that phone. I was hoping that Brittany couldn't.

"What's going on?" Johnny asked. "It can't be good; Alicia can't even talk to me."

"Johnny…" Michael paused momentarily. "I have some bad news."

"Hey, man." Johnny sounded as if he were laughing. There was no way he could have prepared himself for what Michael was about to tell him. "It's alright; come on out and say it. We can start over from square one and try again."

I think Johnny thought we had bad news about his appeal. If only it were that simple…

"Johnny…" Michael paused again. "Ma died this morning."

There was a deafening silence and then Johnny spoke.

"What?"

"Ma's dead."

"Don't play with me, Mike!"

"Johnny," Michael said, trying to convince Johnny as gently as possible. "She's gone!"

"No, I just saw Ma last week and she was doing fine," Johnny said. "You must be mistaken. Go call her!"

"I can't, Johnny."

Johnny started to laugh. Either he thought Michael was joking or he was losing his mind.

"Go call her right now, Mike! I'm telling you, she's alright!"

"I'm sorry, Johnny."

Johnny became angry and started yelling. I wanted to step around the corner to let him know that I was with him, but I had to prevent Brittany from seeing him like that.

"Mike! Please, go call her, man!" Johnny shouted. "Just go call her and bring her down here to see me! I need to see her one more time, man!"

I heard a loud crashing sound and it made Brittany and me jump. Johnny really started to scream and it sounded like he was ripping the place apart. I realized that he would not take the news well, but I didn't expect for him to go off like that.

I held Brittany behind me and peeked around the corner to see what was going on. Johnny was smashing the phone to bits. He was screaming incoherently.

"Who is that, Mommy?" Brittany asked.

"Nobody, baby," I said, keeping her behind me. "They're playing around."

"Where's my daddy?"

"He had to go back inside of his house." I turned to Brittany and kissed her on the cheek. "But he told me to give you that."

I pushed her behind me again, and then glanced around the corner at Johnny.

"Okay, that's it!" the guard said.

Another guard came over to help him restrain Johnny. I wanted to take my shoes off and start hitting them over the head but they were on the other side of the glass. They were handling him way too rough.

"Johnny! Johnny!" Michael screamed. "Calm down!"

"Let me go!" Johnny continued to resist them. "Mike, go get Ma! Please! Go get Ma!"

I could do nothing but watch as the guards dragged my husband away. He fought them tooth and nail until he was out of our sight. I stared at Michael and he stared at me.

"I have to get him out of here!" Michael said.

"How?"

"I don't know, but I am." Michael walked past Brittany and me, and I knew somehow, some way, he was going to do it.

MICHAEL, ALONG WITH JOHNNY'S ATTORNEYS, tried to get him out of prison for his mother's funeral, but the warden denied their request. He only had one more chance, an impossible chance.

In order for Johnny to get out of prison, his attorneys would have to find the missing witness: a woman named Kimberly, who came up missing after Gizelle was murdered. Johnny's attorneys felt that Kimberly could supply an alibi to set Johnny free.

They had somehow connected Kimberly and Gizelle, Anise, or whatever the hell her name was, as relatives. That is why she was at the hotel the day Pam and I were there. She had not been seen since that day and they believed that if they found her, they would find the witness to exonerate Johnny. Unfortunately for Pam and me, Johnny's exoneration would mean our incrimination.

While Michael and the defense team worked to find that witness, I was assigned the role of traveling to Michigan to make the funeral arrangements for Mrs. Forrester. It would just be me in the house with that mean old man. I have to tell you, I wasn't happy about that at all. But what could I do?

My first responsibility was to get Mrs. Forrester's body home to the state of Michigan. We had to have a local mortician in Atlanta embalm the body to preserve it until we could get her to the funeral home in Buena Vista. I had to fly with the body to release her to the funeral home once we arrived in Detroit.

Brittany and I flew into Detroit's Metro airport. I signed the body over to the funeral home and then I had to rent a car and drive to Buena Vista. I had been to Detroit before, but nowhere further north than that. It was a straight shot once I got on I-75. It took maybe an hour and a half to get there. On the way, Brittany asked me plenty of questions.

"Where are we going, Mommy?" Brittany asked.

"We're going to see Grandpa."

"Goodie! And Grandma, too?"

"Grandma has gone to Heaven, remember? She's going to be with God and Deirdra in Heaven, remember?"

"Yes," Brittany said. "My other mommy is not sick anymore in Heaven, right?"

"Right, baby."

"She feels better and she can walk, and run, and have fun, right?"

"Yes, baby."

"Mommy?" Brittany asked.

"Yes, dear."

"I don't want my other mommy to be sick, but I miss her so much."

"That's okay, baby! It's okay to miss your mommy. I miss her, too."

"Me, too!"

"Mommy?"

"Yes, baby."

"Why do I have two mommies?"

"Because we both love you so much! And we both want to take care of you and make sure you're okay."

"But how can my other mommy take care of me from Heaven?"

"Sometimes when I'm not around and you need someone to take care of you, Deirdra is always watching over you. She can watch over you all the time from Heaven."

"She can?" Brittany asked excitedly.

"Yes, she can."

"For real?"

"For real!" I responded enthusiastically.

It was almost dark by the time we arrived in Buena Vista. The houses looked old. I thought I had gone back into a time warp. Cincinnati, my hometown, has old neighborhoods, too, but these houses were really old. I looked at all the abandoned buildings and houses and wondered how they had played a part in Johnny's life growing up there.

I pulled into Mr. Forrester's driveway and looked down at my directions to make sure that I had the proper address. I took a deep breath and stepped out of the car. I knocked on the screen door twice, and then I saw the curtain move in the window. It took a minute, but Mr. Forrester finally opened the door.

"Hey there." Mr. Forrester opened the door to let us onto the screened porch.

"Hi, how are you?" I asked.

"I guess I'll do."

"Hey, Grandpa!" Brittany said as she gave Mr. Forrester a big hug.

"Hey, who are you?"

"I'm Brittany."

"Who is Brittany?"

"Your granddaughter."

"OHHH, that Brittany." Mr. Forrester laughed. "Then come give me another hug!"

We walked up the three squeaky wooden steps and onto an enclosed porch. The porch was paneled like the houses of the seventies. It had a couple of chairs aimed toward the three windows; I assumed to watch the activities of the neighborhood.

We walked into the house and the walls inside were also paneled. They had different arrangements. The den had the darker brown wood like the inner circles of a tree. The living room's paneling was white with flowery decorations. The kitchen was paneled white with pots and pans.

Mr. and Mrs. Forrester slept on the bottom level, but the remaining four bedrooms were on the upstairs level. I slept in Johnny's old bedroom, just to be close to him. I unpacked a few things and we made ourselves comfortable.

I went to the kitchen and it was so cluttered that I could barely walk around. There were cards, flowers, cakes, hams; all of the bereavement gifts. I tidied up the kitchen and put everything in its proper place.

Brittany helped as much as she could until she disappeared. I went to check on her, and she and Mr. Forrester had fallen asleep together in his recliner. They looked so cute. Both of them had their mouths wide open and an arm each hanging from either side of the chair. She was sitting on his lap, and I wasn't sure if he was holding her, or if she was keeping him from sliding on the floor.

I took Brittany out of his arms so that neither one of them were injured. It was late in the evening so I decided to get her ready for bed. She had endured a very active day. When I picked her up, it woke Mr. Forrester. He was still reaching for her as I carried her away. He couldn't go back to sleep so we watched television together until I went to bed. I left him sleeping in his recliner.

When I got up the following day, Mr. Forrester and Brittany were sitting on the porch counting the cars as they passed. Brittany was already washed and dressed.

"What are you two early birds doing out here?" I asked.

"Counting cars," Brittany said.

"Are you ready for a bath?"

"Grandpa already took me a bath."

"Thank you, Mr. Forrester," I said. "Anybody hungry?"

"We already ate, Mommy."

"You already ate?"

"Yes."

"Did you leave anything for me to do, Mr. Forrester?" I joked.

"I sure did," Mr. Forrester said. "Eat! Your plate is warming in the stove."

"Are you serious?"

"Two things I don't play with, my family and my food."

"Well, while you two are having fun counting cars, I'm going to have myself some breakfast."

"Help yourself."

After they finished counting cars, Mr. Forrester played some animated movies for Brittany. If I ever needed a baby-sitter I knew where to look. Brittany sat in the same spot glued to the television.

I did a mini-tour of the house and I could feel the sense of family Mrs. Forrester had created over the years. In the den, she had an entire wall of pictures filled with Johnny and Michael from birth to the present. She had report cards; academic degrees, newspaper clippings and all of them were in mint condition. It was amazing.

On another wall, Mr. Forrester had different kinds of memorabilia. His was a sports shrine to his sons. He must have had every single sports achievement they had ever accomplished on that wall. There were so many trophies and awards; there was barely any wall left. Mr. Forrester sat silently in his recliner as I stood in front of Mrs. Forrester's wall. Once he saw me looking at his wall, he got out of his chair to explain each and every one.

"Yeah, that one right there was when Michael was the offensive player of the year. That's almost impossible for a tight end." Mr. Forrester glanced over the wall to find something else important to show me; he didn't have the time to explain every single one. "Right there is when Johnny won Rookie of the Year in the NFL."

"Johnny was Rookie of the Year?"

"Yeah, that boy made me the proudest man on earth," Mr. Forrester said. "Well, not really. He made me the proudest man on earth when he did this. Come here."

Mr. Forrester held my hand and we turned around to Mrs. Forrester's wall. He pointed to Johnny's degrees on the wall. He lifted my hand with his, as he pointed to several of the degrees.

"Outside of my sons being born, these are the proudest moments of my life." Mr. Forrester took two of Johnny's and Michael's degrees from the wall and held them in his hands. "You always want your kids to do a little better than you. But my boys have done that and much, much more."

"You're proud of your sons, aren't you?"

"*Proud* ain't the word for it."

"Have you ever told them that, Mr. Forrester?"

Mr. Forrester hesitated before answering.

"I want to."

"I think they would love to hear you say that."

"You think so?"

"I know so. Would you like a cup of coffee?"

"I would love a cup of coffee," Mr. Forrester said.

"Follow me, young man."

We went into the kitchen and I fixed a pot of coffee. We discussed a lot of different topics but I noticed Mr. Forrester had not mentioned Mrs. Forrester at all. Perhaps he was in denial. Whatever the case, he would not discuss her.

"I made the funeral arrangements for the day after tomorrow," I said. "Is that okay with you, Mr. Forrester?"

"That's okay."

"How are you holding up?"

"I'm okay."

"You sure?" I tried to get him to open up and discuss his feelings. The man had been with the woman for almost fifty years; he had to be devastated, but if he was, he didn't show it.

"I'm sure."

"If you need to talk, I'm here. Just let me know, okay?"

"Okay."

"Can I ask you a question, Mr. Forrester?"

"Go 'head," Mr. Forrester said.

"What happened between you and Johnny?"

I thought he would clam up and try to avoid the conversation, but he didn't. He talked. Openly and honestly, he talked.

"Well," Mr. Forrester said, "for the most part, we couldn't understand each other. He thought I hated him, and I thought he hated me. Whenever we talked, that's all that came out of us. Hate! But I guess since I'm the father, I shoulda been the one to put my pride to the side and tell my son how much I loved him."

"It's never too late."

"You must have been drinkin' that night, too." Mr. Forrester laughed, sarcastically. His sarcasm turned serious very quickly. "I pulled a gun on my own son! My own child!"

"But you were drunk."

"That ain't no excuse, baby. I coulda killed him!" Mr. Forrester stared into space. "I coulda hurt my boy that night!"

I wanted to reach out to Mr. Forrester but I wasn't sure if he would be receptive to my compassion. I sat quietly, thinking that I could not for the life of me understand the nature of a man. His wife of fifty years was dead, and he showed no emotion, but he was on the verge of crying over the threat of hurting his son. I understood his regret for possibly harming his son, but his wife, on the other hand, was dead!

"Talk to Johnny, Mr. Forrester."

"He don't want to hear from me." Mr. Forrester wiped his eyes.

"How do you know, if you don't reach out to him?"

"He sent his mama letters all the time, but he never sent me a single one."

The man I was talking to was not the mean old ogre that had pulled a gun on his son in my dining room. Perhaps Mrs. Forrester was right. He was so traumatized about her affair and pregnancy that he could only find solace in the bottom of a liquor bottle. Maybe being drunk was his way of suppressing all of the anger and frustrations he had pent up. I was certain that the sober man I was talking to that day had a soft, gentle soul.

"Mr. Forrester?"

"Yeah, baby."

"I know about Michael."

"You know what about Michael?"

"Mrs. Forrester told me about what happened when you were in the war and what happened when you came back."

"That big-mouth woman!" Mr. Forrester looked up and put his hands together. "Oh, I forgot, Lord! God bless her soul."

"Why didn't you ever tell Michael?"

"Telling him woulda made no sense. 'Cause it didn't matter how he got here. Once he got here, he was mine."

I pulled out a chair and sat next to Mr. Forrester. Our conversation was becoming more and more interesting.

"If I'm getting too personal, just let me know," I said. "Do you really love both of them as your own sons?"

"Of course," Mr. Forrester said proudly. "I may have not been perfect in my life. But as far as Mike and Johnny are concerned, I showed no difference because of what happened. Mike is so much like me I could have spit him out. Johnny, now that's a different story. We had problems because we were as different as night and day. But I love them both! I may get along with one better than the other, but I don't love either one of them more than the other. You can take that to the bank, sign it, and cash it."

I didn't know what the hell Mr. Forrester was talking about with the bank analogy, but I knew he meant it.

"You don't plan on telling my boys none of this, do you?"

"Oh no, sir. I promised Mrs. Forrester I wouldn't tell anybody."

"A woman tell you to keep a secret on her deathbed and no sooner than she dead you tellin' it!" Mr. Forrester laughed. "I know better than to tell you any secrets."

"That's not fair. You already knew."

"I'm just jokin' with you."

"You wanna another cup of coffee?"

"That'll be wonderful."

I stood over Mr. Forrester and poured the coffee into his cup. I wasn't paying attention, but my wrists were exposed and he saw my suicidal scars.

"What happened to you?" Mr. Forrester asked.

"Oh..." I used my sleeve to cover the scars. "Oh, I had a little accident."

"A little accident?" Mr. Forrester asked. "Let me see that."

I put the pot back on the warmer and sat next to Mr. Forrester. "You don't want to see them," I said. "They look nasty."

"Yes, I do. Let me see." Mr. Forrester reached for my wrists and held them out so that he could see. "What happened to you?"

"It was an accident."

"You said that already, what kind of accident was it?" Mr. Forrester turned my wrists in different directions to get a better look.

"I, uh," I said. "Okay, now if I tell you, you have to promise to keep this between us. Deal?"

"Deal."

"Well, a few weeks back, I wasn't feeling good about myself. I was depressed because Johnny was in prison. My business had folded and I was having a hard time trying to take care of Brittany. I felt responsible for everything that was happening around me. I didn't love myself and I didn't think anybody loved me either."

I was waiting for Mr. Forrester to call me crazy, selfish, stupid or some derogatory name, but he sat quietly and listened. No negative reaction at all. I felt comfortable so I kept talking.

"I was depressed in the worst way. I couldn't find any answers on earth or from Heaven. I needed love from somebody or something, but I wasn't getting it." I paused to look at my scars momentarily and then I kept talking. "After a person takes their life, people always say that if they would have known what they were going through, they could have done something. Some of the time, people know. They have to know. But they sit back and they do as little as they can until it's too late. I don't mean to sound as if I'm blaming anyone for my decisions. I'm just saying that after I tried to take my life, I was called selfish. I realize that maybe I was selfish, but people don't realize that they are, too.

Where was their love when I needed it? You probably think I'm crazy, too, don't you?"

"Let me show you something." Mr. Forrester rolled up his sleeves and held out his arms to me. His wrists had scars similar to mine. "People do strange things when they're hurt and lonely."

"What happened to you?"

"I made it through the war thinking that I had to get home to my wife. I thought about how much she needed me and how much I needed her. She was my life. When I found out my wife had cheated with someone close to me, I didn't have a reason to live anymore."

"So you knew who it was?"

"Yeah, my best friend. Don't tell me she told you that, too?"

"I'm sorry, yes, she did."

"Y'all got real close down there in a short time, didn't you?" Mr. Forrester asked.

"We had some good conversations. Just like I'm having with you," I replied with a smile.

"She thought I didn't know. I could tell by the look on her face every time he came around. I asked her who it was, but she wouldn't tell me. She lied and said it was some ol' niggah from down south, but I knew who it was. And several times I had made up my mind to kill that son of a bitch! At first, I thought she was trying to protect him. But then I realized she was only trying to protect me. I wanted to walk away and leave her alone, but I loved her too much. And then I tried to stay and act like it had never happened, but I was hurtin' too much. I was trapped between joy and pain, and pain was kickin' joy's ass. So, if it hurt too much for me to leave and it hurt too much for me to stay, I felt like the only thing else for me to do was die. I didn't want to die necessarily. But I couldn't live like that anymore. Between life and death, I thought death had to be a little bit more peaceful."

Mr. Forrester had summed up my life. That was exactly how I felt. He had explained the unexplainable to me. I was trapped between misery and happiness, and I had always chosen to be miserable.

"So how did you feel afterwards?" I asked.

"I felt shame and I was embarrassed."

"I know the feeling," I said.

"I put all of that behind me and went on with my life. Well, at least I thought that I had gone on with my life until I pulled that gun on my son. I realized that I was still suffering, but instead of taking it out on me, I was taking it out on the world. I found a lot of false happiness in a lot of liquor bottles. All of my false happiness was causing everybody else real pain." Mr. Forrester held my hands and then rubbed the scars on his wrists against the scars on my wrists. "What I'm trying to say is this; don't waste your life letting your pain get the best of you. Deal with the pain. Deal with the shame. Deal with it and then move on."

"That's easier said than done."

"The Lord never said the road would be easy, baby. But you have to understand one thang. There's some good in the worst of us, and there's some bad in the best of us. I used to think I was the worst of us with a little good inside of me because that's how the world saw me, but not no more. I have the rest of my life to be the best of us, with a little bad inside of me. And so do you."

"Thank you so much, Mr. Forrester!" I held his hands and then reached over and hugged him tightly. "Thank you so much!"

"I don't know why you thanking me, but you're welcome," Mr. Forrester said into my ear.

"Your telephone is ringing, Mommy." Brittany handed my cell phone to me.

"Thanks, baby." I took the phone out of her hand and answered. "Hello."

"You probably want to get on a plane and get your butt down here right now!"

"Who is this?" I asked.

"Cynthia."

"What's up, Cynt?"

"Johnny is getting out of prison tomorrow!" Cynthia screamed into the phone.

I didn't, or should I say, I couldn't respond.

"Alicia!" Cynthia shouted. "Alicia! You there?"

"Yeah, yeah, I'm here."

"Johnny's getting out tomorrow! So get your ass back down here now!"

"Are you sure, Cynt?"

"I'm positive! Mike wouldn't let me call you until we were absolutely sure."

"How? How is he getting out?"

"They found the witness! They found the witness yesterday and she told them that Johnny was not in the room when she saw the body and ran! And she was there before Johnny ever arrived!"

"How did they find the witness?"

"Who cares?" Cynthia shouted. "Johnny is getting out! Now get your ass on the next plane and get back down here!"

"What about the funeral?"

Mr. Forrester stared at me curiously as I talked to Cynthia. He couldn't hear what she saying; all that he had to go on was my response. That had to be killing him.

"We're all flying up tomorrow evening. Everybody!"

"Is Johnny really getting out?"

"Girl, yeah!" Cynthia screamed.

"AAAAAAAAAAAAAAAAAAH!" I screamed. "Thank you, Jesus!"

"Girl, what the hell is goin' on?" Mr. Forrester shouted.

"Bye! I have to go!" I shouted to Cynthia.

"Bye!"

I hung up the phone and swung Brittany around.

"Daddy's coming home tomorrow!" I shouted.

"Daddy's coming home?" Brittany said.

I swung her around again.

"Yes! Daddy's coming home tomorrow!"

"Johnny's coming home?" Mr. Forrester asked humbly as he stood up.

"Yes, sir." I put Brittany down and opened my arms for Mr. Forrester. "Johnny's coming home."

"Thank, God!" Mr. Forrester slowly walked into my arms and we rocked back and forth in each other's arms.

CHAPTER SEVENTEEN

I didn't bother packing our suitcases. Brittany and I drove to the airport in Flint instead of Detroit and waited for the next flight to Atlanta. The minutes seemed like hours as we waited and waited. We finally boarded the airplane and I took a deep sigh of relief. I counted every single second of the hour and forty-five-minute flight.

When we landed, Michael and Cynthia picked us up from the airport. I asked a million questions, and Michael patiently answered as many as he could. I asked one question, at least a thousand times: "Are you absolutely sure he's getting out?" Michael reassured me that there would be no disappointment.

The only issue was that while Johnny's attorneys were working to get him released, the district attorney's office was working to keep him in prison. His temporary release was imminent, but his permanent release hinged on a future hearing.

I couldn't sleep at all that night. As soon as the sun rose, I got up, showered, and put on my clothes. I wanted to go with them to the prison to make sure everything went according to plan. Johnny's attorneys made me wait for them in their office. I was a nervous wreck.

Brittany and I sat alone and I heard voices coming closer. The voices got even closer and then I heard a male voice say, "Are they in this room?"

It was Johnny. I jumped to my feet, anxiously waiting for him to open the door. I saw the doorknob twist in one direction and then back in the other in what seemed like slow motion. The door finally opened and Johnny walked in. I ran to him and jumped in his arms.

"Oh my God, baby! I missed you so much!" I started to cry hysterically.

"Daddy!" Brittany ran to Johnny as well, and he held both of us tightly.

"Oh my God, look at you two!" Johnny said.

We kissed and hugged as if there were no other people in the room. Stacey had to interrupt our reunion to keep things moving along.

"I hate to interrupt, Dr. Forrester," Stacey said, "but we need to go over a few things before you go to Michigan."

"Okay." Johnny released Brittany and me. "I'm sorry, Stacey."

"I understand," Stacey said.

"So what are our chances of having the case dismissed?" Johnny asked.

Stacey opened her mouth to answer, but her phone rang.

"Excuse me." Stacey held up a finger and then started to leave. "Excuse me; I really have to take this call!"

I was nervous when Stacey walked out. I wanted to make sure Johnny's freedom wasn't temporary.

"What's going on?" I asked Johnny's other attorneys.

"I don't know," Ms. Hattley said.

Ms. Carroll smiled. "Stacey is always on the move."

Stacey rushed back into the room as Ms. Hattley was answering Johnny's question.

"Anyway," Ms. Hattley said, "I think our chances are pretty good."

"Dr. Forrester!" Stacey said. "I think your chances just improved drastically!"

"Why? What happened?" Johnny asked.

"Well, let's just say if you've been praying for a miracle, you just got it!"

"What do you mean?"

"It just so happens that my mentor is in town for a conference. I asked him to advise on this case and not only did he say yes, he's on his way up to my office!"

"Who is it?" I asked.

"He's the best attorney in the United States of America!" Stacey said. "And you have him on your team!"

"Who?" Johnny asked. "Who do I have?"

"Yeah, I would like to know, too," Ms. Hattley said. She didn't seem very happy about the new addition to their team. "Who?"

Before Stacey could answer, Michael and a tall, older gentleman walked in. It was obvious he was someone important because all of their mouths dropped to the floor. I have to be honest; I didn't know who the hell he was.

"Good evening, Stacey."

"Thank you for coming, sir." Stacey led the man to us. "These are the Forresters."

"Good evening," the man said.

"Oh my God." Ms. Hattley acted like an excited little girl at the circus. "I am honored to meet you."

"Good evening, young lady. My name is Solomon Chambers."

Solomon Chambers was one of the most prestigious attorneys in the United States of America. He had won some of the most high-profile civil and criminal cases in the past forty years.

"Yes!" Ms. Carroll stepped in front of Ms. Hattley to shake the man's hand. "Oh my God!"

"Yes, but I still don't know who you are," Mr. Chambers said.

I felt stupid. Everybody in the room was treating Mr. Chambers like he was the president and I had never heard of the man in my entire life.

"I'm sorry. I'm Tori Carroll, Stacey's partner."

Mr. Chambers shook Ms. Carroll's hand and then turned to Ms. Hattley.

"And you are?"

"I'm Wendy Hattley." Ms. Hattley shook Mr. Chambers hand very zealously. "I'm Stacey's partner as well."

Mr. Chambers bent down to shake Brittany's hand.

"Pleasure to meet you," Mr. Chambers said. "And you must be daddy's little girl?"

"Yes, sir!" Brittany said.

"You look like you can use a bite to eat, young lady," Mr. Chambers said. "Are you hungry?"

"Yes."

Mr. Chambers looked at me. "Why don't you take this pretty little girl out and put some food in her belly?"

"I can't eat," I said. Mr. Chambers gave me a look as if he were saying, *Niggah, if you don't get your ass out of here.* "On second thought, a little snack might be what we need."

While they discussed Johnny's case, I went home and packed Johnny's suitcase for our flight back to Michigan later that evening. The funeral was the next day so everybody from Atlanta flew on the same flight. There was Tonita, Cecelia, the four grandchildren, Cynthia, Michael, Johnny and me. We were scattered all over the cabin, but at least we managed to get everybody on the same flight.

Michael, Cynthia and the grandchildren stayed with Mr. Forrester. Johnny insisted that we get a hotel room. I tried to encourage

Mr. Forrester to talk to Johnny to get their differences out in the open, and he may have tried, but Johnny wasn't very receptive. I think he wanted to focus on one thing at a time. At that time, the one thing he wanted to focus on was his mother's death.

After the funeral we flew back to Atlanta. Although Johnny and I were together almost every second, we hadn't had plenty of alone time. Meaning, we hadn't touched each other sexually. I was waiting for him to initiate the romance and he was probably waiting on me. Regardless of who was waiting on whom, I hadn't had sex in almost a year, and I was horny as hell.

Days passed and Johnny still hadn't touched me. I understood the pressure he was under, not knowing if he was going to remain out of prison or not, but he never gave me a second look. My mind started to wonder if he was being faithful to somebody back on the cellblock! I would wear seductive clothes to bed, but still nothing.

Johnny came to me one evening and told me he had something very important to tell me. He wanted to take me to dinner and discuss it. He suggested we drive to dinner separately, and that really piqued my curiosity. I prepared myself for the worst possible news, which was that he had finally decided to be faithful, but not to me, to a big rugged man in prison.

Johnny was there when I arrived at the restaurant. As I walked near his table, I saw a woman sitting with him. My heart started to beat fast. Whatever he had to discuss was going to be involving that woman.

"Hey, baby." I kissed Johnny on the cheek to establish my position as being his wife. I sat down and reached across the table to shake the woman's hand. The chick was young, very young. She had to be even younger than Gizelle. I wasn't a spring chicken, but I still turned men's heads, young and old. "How are you?"

"I'm fine. How are you, ma'am?"

I wanted to reach and slap that little heffa for calling me ma'am.

"Alicia, this is Shante," Johnny said. "Shante, this is my wife, Alicia."

"I'm so glad to meet you, Mrs. Forrester."

At least she was a respectful little home wrecker.

"You know me?" I looked at Johnny. "Hmm, I don't seem to know you."

"Alicia." Johnny smiled. "Shante is my ex-cellmate's daughter. I've told you about her. She couldn't wait to meet you."

"Your ex-cellmate's daughter?" I was embarrassed for being suspicious, but can you blame me?

We started chatting and I fell in love with the girl. The fact that she threw compliment after compliment my way could have something to do with it, but I'd rather think it had something to do with my compassion. She told me about her life growing up in foster care. I felt sorry for her, but she sure didn't. She was so bright and charismatic.

After dinner, Johnny explained why he wanted me to meet Shante. He told me that he had made a promise to his cellmate that he would take care of her once he was released. There were a lot of invariables in our final decision. Johnny told me that his cellmate had protected him in prison and he was also responsible for his freedom. The man pulled strings from behind bars to find the missing witness to free my man; what else could I do?

Johnny was also contacted by Gizelle's attorney and informed that he was the executor of her estate. Now why in the hell would Gizelle choose Johnny as the executor of her estate? Johnny tried to explain that there must have been a mistake, but after several legal conversations between Gizelle's attorney and Stacey, Johnny was legally upheld as her executor. It was obvious the bitch was trying to haunt us from the grave.

ON THE DAY OF JOHNNY'S EVIDENTIARY HEARING I planned a surprise dinner party for him. It was going to be a celebration or a memorial. If he went back to prison he would never be free again.

I called everybody we knew and made sure they got off their lazy asses and went down to that courthouse. It was packed with friends and family. I sat behind Johnny so that I could see and hear everything that was said and done between him and his lawyers. Pam sat next to me to offer support.

I kept looking at the door, waiting for Michael to come in. He was the key to my surprise. Just before the bailiff was about to call the court to order, Michael walked in with my surprise, Mr. Forrester.

I had been calling Mr. Forrester ever since I'd left Michigan. We talked every day, and those conversations had paid off. I finally convinced him to come to Atlanta to be by Johnny's side. I think he wanted to come in the beginning but he felt Johnny didn't want him to be there.

I tapped Johnny on the shoulder and he turned around and saw Michael walking in with his dad. Mr. Forrester surprised more than Johnny. He surprised me when he walked in front of Johnny and started to talk to him. I was proud of both of my men!

"I don't know what to say, except I love you, son," Mr. Forrester said. "And no matter what done happened between us, I always loved you. And I always will love you. I pray to God that He gets you out of this mess so we can start over."

I almost cried when I heard Mr. Forrester speak so openly. You know I cry over almost anything; shit, I can't help it. I had totally blocked out everything else in the courtroom.

"Pop..." Johnny smiled and said, "You just don't know how much that means to me!"

"You a good boy!" Mr. Forrester said. "No matter what happen in here today, I'm proud of you. You hear me?"

"Yes, sir," Johnny said.

Mr. Forrester kissed Johnny on the top of his head. He walked away and I gestured toward him. I pushed Pam's ass down a few spots and allowed my father-in-law to sit next to me.

"How did I do?" Mr. Forrester asked.

"You did fantastic!" I kissed him on his cheek. "Fantastic!"

I held his hand and the judge called the court to order. Mr. Chambers called a lot of character witnesses, including Johnny's patient. Some well-known lady, again, someone I had never heard of, had the courtroom in awe. Her name was Mrs. Dewitt, and she was an international recluse that no one had seen or spoken to in over forty years. The judge even thanked her for coming!

They also brought out Johnny's other patients who celebrated him as a psychologist and a human being. I could see Mr. Forrester's chest swell with pride as person after person doted over his second-born son. I couldn't blame him. I had always been a fan of my husband, but I, too, was impressed by the reverence his patients felt toward him.

Both sides presented their evidence to the judge why the case should, or should not be brought to trial. Johnny's defense was well-represented. I felt confident that the nightmare would be over, for once and for all. The only thing standing between Johnny and freedom was the judge's decision.

"Is there any further evidence on either side?" Judge Robinson asked.

"Well, we feel that Mr. Forrester's DNA found on the victim's body is sufficient evidence to proceed with a trial, sir," the district attorney said.

"I'm sorry, but I don't see it," Judge Robinson said. "All that you have with that DNA is evidence that there was sexual intercourse between the accused and the deceased. And the accused has already admitted that there was an affair between him and the deceased. Now as far as I know, you can't try a man for having an affair. This sounds too much like a witch hunt and I want no parts of it! At this point, you do not have sufficient evidence to proceed with trying this man for murder. If you can present additional evidence that will hold up in a court of law, you are certainly welcome to do so at that time. But for now, this case is dismissed!"

BAM!

And just like that, Johnny was free! Mr. Forrester hugged me, and then I turned and hugged Pam. After Johnny was released I ran to him and we spun around as he picked me up and hugged me tightly. When we were on the outside of the courtroom, there were reporters pushing microphones in front of Johnny's face.

"How does it feel to be exonerated, Dr. Forrester?"

"It feels wonderful!" Johnny said. "I've always maintained my faith in God, and my attorneys, that I would be acquitted. My family and friends have stood by me and supported me throughout this entire ordeal. I never once doubted that the truth would be revealed."

"You've been acquitted, but the truth has not been revealed, Dr. Forrester," another reporter said. "Gizelle's murderer is still at large."

"I was talking about *my* truth, ma'am." Johnny smiled.

Johnny held my arm tightly and we walked through the crowd. The media followed us until they saw Mr. Chambers leaving the building with a police escort. They ran away from us and swarmed to him. We snuck away, avoiding more questions.

As soon as we stepped inside of our house, I grabbed Johnny and pulled him to me. We laughed like teenagers and kept hugging and kissing. We put our heads together and sighed. After everything we had been through, we were still together. We were still married. And we were still in love.

I held Johnny's hand and led him upstairs. I gently pushed him down on the bed. I pulled his suit coat off and loosened his tie. I pulled it around his neck and tossed it to the side. I unbuttoned his shirt from top to bottom. I pulled off his shirt and kissed his chest, nipple to nipple. I was on fire. My vagina was drenched. I pushed Johnny all the way on his back and pulled his shoes off.

I tossed his shoes to the side and then pulled off his socks. I unbuckled his pants and pulled them down his legs. He kicked his feet so that I could snatch them off. His massive body glistened from perspiration. I gripped his underwear and pulled them down, exposing a bouncing black log of a penis.

I reached out for Johnny's hands and I pulled him off of the bed. He stood up and kissed me as if it was for the first time. We stood in the middle of our bedroom and kissed as we spun in a circle. It was so romantic.

We stopped kissing long enough for Johnny to undress me. He raised my arms above my head and rolled my dress upward until it was above my breasts. He reached behind me and unsnapped my bra. He kissed each one of my nipples, sucking them gently.

Johnny sat me on the bed and lifted my left foot in the air. He unbuckled my leather strap and slid my shoe off. Then he grabbed my right foot and unbuckled the strap on that foot. He folded my legs back and held my feet in front of his face. He kissed my toes and sent shivers up my spine.

He placed my legs straight in the air and stuck his fingers inside my panties. He slowly pulled them over my hips, down my thighs and over my feet. The sight of our bodies naked together was more than I could stand. I was ready to attack that man, you hear me?

Since Johnny's release, I had worn long-sleeved shirts, or kept the scars on my wrists hidden from his view. But I no longer cared if he saw the scars. I no longer cared what the scars represented. All that I cared about was making love to my husband.

I climbed out of the bed, and gave Johnny another long, wet kiss. I held his hand and led him to the bathroom. I had arranged the bathroom before I left with roses and tulips. I was hoping that he remembered it was an assimilation of our honeymoon in Hawaii. I had oils and creams placed in strategic positions for my man's pleasure. I lit scented aromas, filling the room with a mystical mist. Johnny stood in the doorway with his stick swaying like a baseball bat.

"Wow!" Johnny said. "This is amazing. Wow!"

I grabbed Johnny by the penis and led him to the garden tub. I cut on the water and turned it as hot as it could go. Johnny stepped in the tub first, and then reached out for me. I dipped one toe in the water and it was steaming hot. I walked in and pressed my body against Johnny's.

We started to sweat profusely. Our bodies clung together from our sticky perspiration. Johnny grabbed me and pulled me closer to him. He pushed me against the edge of the tub and placed his stick between my legs. I didn't need any more foreplay. I wanted him inside of me.

He must have felt my vagina pulsating because he opened my legs with his legs, and slid his stick between my thighs. I closed my legs and ground my vagina on top of his thickness. It felt like I was grinding on a wet pole covered with black skin. I moved back and forth, making the water splash about.

I reached behind me and grabbed the head of Johnny's stick. I squeezed it as he slid it between my thighs. Every time the head slid through, I squeezed it and Johnny would jump. I massaged the split of his head and it made his legs buckle.

Johnny grabbed the side of the tub behind me and leaned his head backwards as I stroked his penis. For a moment, I thought he was going to come. I cut that shit out quickly! There was no way he was going to come before I got rid of all the yearlong sexual tension I had built up.

I pulled Johnny's head down and pushed his face on top of my breasts. He began by sucking them gently, left to right and back and forth. He started to bite my nipples and I wanted him to suck them harder. Much harder!

"Oh my God," I said. I moved Johnny's head back and forth. I shoved his mouth on my nipples. "Suck 'em, baby."

I snatched Johnny's head from my breasts and I kissed him long and passionately. Enough was enough! I grabbed Johnny's stick and plunged it into my vagina. My legs shook from the intense pleasure and then I lifted them in the water and wrapped them around his waist. Every time he rammed me, his stick went deeper inside of me.

"Oh God!" I screamed out loud. I could feel the love from Johnny filling me up inside, but I needed to hear it. "Do you love me?"

"Oh, Alicia," Johnny said, "I love you so much."

"You do?" I asked as I slid up and down Johnny's long stick. "You love me?"

"Baby, I love you so much!" Johnny said. "Look at me! Open your eyes, Alicia! Look at me!"

I could barely separate my eyelids. They were clenched so tightly; the pleasure was too intense.

"Okay, baby!" I moaned.

I felt my orgasm coming and I started to pound Johnny's stick as hard as I could. I was pounding so hard I caught a cramp in my left thigh. Cramp or not, I wasn't going to stop until I came all over Johnny. I bounced up and down, grunting loudly every time I slammed into him.

"OH-YEAH! OH-YEAH! OH-YEAH!" I screamed with the rhythmical smacking of our bodies.

Johnny snatched my head backward by pulling my hair. I screamed so loud I'm sure the neighbors heard for miles around.

"AAAAH! Oh God!" I yelled, "Pull my hair!"

I wrapped my legs around Johnny's waist a little tighter to give me a better grip. I clamped my feet together, interlocking my toes. I locked my hands around the back of Johnny's neck and I prepared myself for the biggest orgasm of my life.

I bucked my hips as fast as they could go as I rode up and down on Johnny's shaft. The water splashed all over the floor as we moved faster and faster in the tub. I lost all sense of rhythm with him as my feet kicked wildly in and out of the water.

"Shit!" I screamed as my body started to shake. "I don't wanna come, baby, but I can't help it!"

"Come for me, baby!" Johnny shouted.

Johnny pushed the top of my body away from him to get a little space between us. He needed to take his time and jab me with long, deep strokes in the water. I wanted to delay my orgasm as long as possible but when he started to hit it like that, it was a wrap. I was out!

"Oh shit!" I shouted. "Give it to me! Give to me!"

"You love me?" Johnny frowned with each long deep thrust. "Huh? You love me?"

"Oh shit! I love you, baby!" I screamed.

I felt my orgasm right there so I leaned backward to use the tub to brace myself. I let go of Johnny and put my arms behind me.

As I leaned backward, Johnny followed me. The weight of his body made me slide out of the tub and onto the slippery floor.

He folded my legs back so far my feet were beside my head. He placed his hands under my knees and slid his stick inside of me. Over and over he slammed inside of me.

"I'm almost there, baby!" I shouted. "Right there! Right there! Right there! Don't stop!"

Johnny let out an unbelievable loud groan that sent me over the top.

"Oh God, I'm coming, baby!" Johnny shouted.

I felt his juice shoot out of his stick and into my vagina. He kept pounding and I kept bucking. Our bodies were sliding up the slippery floor every time he stroked me. We went as far as we could and I was still in the middle of my orgasm. I was having convulsions.

"Oh! Oh! Oh!" I whispered.

I dug my fingernails into Johnny's back, hoping that would alleviate some of the agonizingly pleasurable sensations shooting through my body. I lost my sense of sight. I lost my sense of hearing. I lost my sense of speech. But my sense of touch was magnified to the tenth power. I could feel everything on a much greater scale.

When I thought my orgasm had subsided, I tried to speak. As I began to speak, I had tremors flowing through my body, making me shake and lose my ability to think. I grabbed Johnny and pulled him to me as I moaned loudly in his ear.

The tremors kept coming over and over. Each time I thought I was finished another one would come. My body jerked and quivered so much I became dizzy. I kept trying to talk, but my words were coming out incoherently. I could feel saliva running down the outside of my mouth and my juices running down the inside of my thighs.

After a while, the tremors stopped. I kept hugging Johnny until I was certain there were no more left.

"Oh my goodness!" I said as I fanned myself. "My God! That was fantastic!"

"You like?" Johnny joked.

"Oh my God!" I said. "That was amazing!"

We showered together and prepared for Johnny's party. Johnny hugged me and then I wrapped my arms around him. As my arms were wrapping around his neck, I saw the scars on my wrists. Throughout our amazing lovemaking session, he never even noticed.

CHAPTER EIGHTEEN

There were people starting to show up for the party before we were finished dressing. Of course all of my office girls were in attendance. We took refuge in Johnny's lair, the basement. We wanted to get caught up with each other and talk amongst ourselves before we mingled with the rest of the dinner party.

Our main topic as always was about men. We had the usual questions with the usual suspects. Who was dating whom? Who had a good man versus who had a sorry man? Who was breaking up? Who was making up? Who was getting laid? Who wasn't getting laid? Most of the time I would have been smack dab in the middle of the conversation. But when you're happy with your man, and more importantly, with yourself, that type of conversation seems inconsequential.

Darsha was the focus at hand. She was telling us that she liked a guy named Jensen, but she still had a relationship with her ex, Morgan. She said her relationship with her ex was platonic but she still spent holidays and special occasions with him. The guy that she liked, Jensen, didn't really care too much about her relationship with Morgan.

"I like Jensen a lot and would like to get to know him and see what could happen between us, but he says if I'm trying to get to know him, I don't need to try to get to know anyone else."

"You're single, right?" Val asked.

"Yeah, I'm single."

"That niggah can't be telling you what to do then."

"I know, right?" Darsha laughed. "He says that if I want to date other guys, he and I can have a fling but that's it."

"What do you expect for him to say?" Cynthia asked.

"I'm single; I can do whatever I want."

"He's single too, right?" I asked.

"Yeah, he's single."

"Then why do you expect for him to wait on you while you the play the field?" I asked.

"That ain't what I'm saying."

"Then what are you saying?" Cynthia asked.

"You don't have to explain yourself to them, Darsha," Pam said.

"I see what's going on here." Wanda laughed. "You got the married sisters against the single sisters goin' on up in here."

"No, it's not." Tazzy laughed. "I'm not getting in that mess."

"Neither am I," Susan said.

"I just think that it ain't nothing wrong with me waiting to commit to somebody until I find out if I like them or not," Darsha said.

"It's not," I said. "But you can't make all the rules. If you want to play the game, you have to expect to be played as well."

"As a single woman, I can date whoever I want."

"Stop using being single as an excuse to be promiscuous. If you want to date more than one guy, then date more than one guy. But stop trying to make it seem as if it's a right-or-wrong situation. If you're going to date multiple guys, and you don't think it's anything wrong with it, stop trying to justify it and just do it. But don't portray yourself as a player, if you want to be treated like you're not."

"Look at ol' Alicia talking like a grown woman." Wanda hugged me around my shoulders.

"That's my girl!" Lisa shouted. "She's married and mature now!"

"Girl, I'm so glad you got your husband back," Tina said.

"Yeah, we have things we need to work out, but I really love that man."

I knew some of my girls had negative opinions about me and Johnny but I wanted them to know that I was serious about my marriage and I wanted them to respect it.

"Just keep the faith, Alicia, and you'll be alright," Tina said.

"I don't know him as well as the rest of the girls, but he seems like a really nice guy," Tazzy said.

Tazzy was the type of woman that if you haven't done anything to her, she doesn't hold it against you. I knew she would be in my corner.

"Thank you! I'm so glad you could make it!" I hugged Tazzy and held her hand.

"No problem," Tazzy said, "I'm glad to be here."

"And I thank you for coming, too, sweetie." I stepped past Tazzy and hugged Susan.

"I'm just sorry I can't be here more for you, Alicia!" Susan said. "The good thing is that you have your husband home with you again. And that's all that matters."

"Susan's right, just be happy you got a man!" Lisa said.

"What?" Pam said. "Why should she just be happy to have a man?"

"I'm not even going there with you, Pam." Lisa waved her hand at Pam and poured a martini.

Lisa walked away from the bar and sat on the couch, trying to end the conversation. Pam followed her, instigating it even further.

"I'm just asking…" Pam held a drink in her hand as she talked.

I think she was a little tipsy by then. That was her third drink. "Why should Alicia *just* be happy to have a man?"

"That's not what I'm saying, Pam, and you know it." Lisa got up from the couch and walked back to the bar, making another attempt to end the conversation.

Wanda took the glass out of Pam's hand. "Pam, you done had one too many of them drinks."

"I'm saying, Johnny cheated on Alicia, went to prison for killing the woman he cheated with, and you're saying she should be happy to have a man like that. He should be thanking God every minute of the day that Alicia is even talking to him!"

Okay, Pam was officially drunk. She knew Johnny didn't kill Gizelle. She killed her! I think her inebriated state had either made her delusional or caused severe hallucinations.

I was about to put her ass in check but Johnny and Michael walked down the stairs. Johnny heard what Pam had said and he was pissed off! I didn't have to say a word; the man went the hell off.

"Not that it's any of your business, but I do thank God every minute of the day for my wife, Pam," Johnny said. "I know what I've done. I know how much I have shamed and hurt my wife. I know I was wrong. But I still love her and she still loves me. I've admitted my mistakes to her. I've apologized for my stupid, selfish acts, but what about you?"

"What about me?" Pam shouted.

"What is your reason for trying to make her feel stupid for forgiving me?" he asked. "Does it make you feel good about yourself to make Alicia feel bad about herself? Huh? Is that what this is about?"

"Don't even come at me like that!" Pam said.

"No," Johnny said, "Answer my question. You are a classic

example of the old adage that misery loves company. Since you can't find a man to make you happy, you don't want any other woman to have a man to make her happy."

"If being cheated on means being happy, then you're right. I don't want to be happy," Pam said.

"Alright, you two, this is supposed to be a happy occasion," Val said.

"We all family! Let them say what they have to say," Wanda said.

Pam looked like she was about to explode. I didn't want her to get so mad that she chose that moment to tell Johnny about the murders.

"I don't feel like hearing it." I sighed.

"Yeah, stop starting a fight, Pam!" Darsha said.

"I'm not starting anything!" Pam said. "I was talking to y'all, and Johnny butted in. If he says something to me, I'm going to say something back."

"Do you have to do this right now, Pam?" Tazzy said.

"Why are all of y'all talking to me?" Pam shouted. "Say something to him, too. I'm just saying what every last one of y'all are thinking!"

"You have no right to speak for me, Pam," Tazzy said. "That's not what I'm thinking."

"You don't represent me neither!" Wanda said. "I gotta couple of more free sessions left; I'm staying on Johnny's good side!"

"All I'm saying is this," Pam said. "You got to be your own woman, Alicia. Don't let nobody make a fool out of you!"

"Make a fool out of her? Are you serious? Pam..." Johnny paused and calmed himself. "You wanna talk foolish? Do you realize the quixotic gentleman you've been parading around as your white knight-in-shining-armor has a wife?"

"Oh snap!" Wanda covered her mouth and ran around the room.

"Day-um!" Darsha said.

"Please, Johnny," Pam said.

"Your Christopher is my attorney's husband, Pam!" Johnny said. "I guess white guys cheat, too, huh?"

"You're just saying that because I'm trying to keep my girl's head straight."

"No," Johnny said. "I'm saying it because it's the truth! You're sleeping with a married man! You try so hard to make it seem as if it's the man's fault you're always getting hurt, but it's not! It's you! At some point you have to take responsibility for the men that you attract, Pam! By now, you should know the signs and the routines. You ignore them because you keep getting caught up in the fantasy of having a perfect man! There is no perfect man! Once you realize that, you'll be better off. The whole world around you will be better off!"

"The dead has arisen!" Michael, who had been standing silently enjoying Johnny rip into Pam, folded his arms and laughed.

"You're right," Johnny said to Pam. "I was wrong. I made poor decisions and I hurt my wife. But I don't blame anyone but me. I made those decisions and I have to deal with the consequences. And until you stop blaming black men for the pain you've suffered and take responsibility for the choices you've made in selecting bad men, you're going to always be bitter and angry. And you're going to try to make the people around you bitter and angry. And why? There are plenty of good men out there. But you have to stop eliminating half of them because they're not lawyers, or doctors, or professional athletes. You keep setting yourself up for failure.

"You can forget that fantasy man. He only exists in your mind. And where you may judge Alicia and me because of our situation, we're going to get past this, and we're going to be happy. And you'll still be bitter and angry. You're going to remain miserable because you're going to always be looking for your perfect man."

"Wow!" Darsha said.

"See!" Wanda said. "That's why that niggah is my shrink!"

"Wanda." Val pointed at Susan.

"Sorry, Susan." Wanda hugged Susan.

"Whatever, girl!" Susan nudged Wanda with her hip.

"So, did you know that Chris was married, Alicia?" Pam asked me.

"You know if I had known I would have told you, girl," I said.

Honestly, I didn't know anything about the guy. I barely even knew Stacey. All that I knew about her was that she was Johnny's attorney.

"Did you know, Mike?" Pam asked.

"Yup!" Michael chuckled.

"Well, why didn't you tell me?"

"Pam. Pam. Pam," Michael said sarcastically. "You practically spat on black men and said you didn't give a damn! But I'm supposed to give a damn when you're being spat on by a white man? I'm sorry, but to be honest, I think you got what you deserved."

"So, I guess I'm the butt of everybody's joke now, huh?"

"I'm not joking with you, Pam." Johnny was very serious. "I care about you. But what good is it for you to use all of your energy on anger? Stop judging men so harshly, and men will stop judging you so harshly. Believe me, when you become understanding of men and other people's situations, men will be more understanding to you and your situation. And treat you the way you want to be treated. But if you want love, you have to give love."

"Pam," Wanda said, "Every last one of us has been hurt by a

man. And every last one of us done hurt a man! You just got too much damn pride! Let that shit go! You hurt and you get hurt! That's life! Now move the hell on!"

"I miss this!" Tazzy joked.

"I don't!" I joked back.

"Wanda, did you see your girl up there?" Darsha asked, changing the subject.

"What girl?" Wanda asked.

"The crazy chick from Johnny's office."

I assumed that Wanda had run into Kimberly at Johnny's office. Darsha and Val would sometimes go to Wanda's session with her for moral support, and to also see the so-called circus folk. My concern was that Kimberly may remember Pam and me from the hotel. I had to stay away from her.

"Stop calling her crazy!" Wanda said. "Yeah, I know she here! I brought her. And?"

"I mean," Darsha said, "I was just saying."

"Kimberly's here?" Johnny asked.

"Yeah, she's here. Speaking of which, I need to go check on her." Wanda walked toward the stairs.

"Me too," Johnny started to follow Wanda to the stairs. "Alicia, you coming? Our guests are probably wondering where we are."

I was paralyzed with fear. I couldn't go upstairs. If Kimberly recognized who I was, I'd be on my way to prison after going through so much to put the murder behind me.

"I'll be up there in a minute, Johnny." I stood in the same place and couldn't move. "There's no telling when my girls and I will be together again."

"Come on, Cynt, let's go," Michael said sarcastically. "You don't need to be around all of this masochistic women's movement."

"Masochistic women's movement?" Val said. "What the hell?"

"You ain't got to worry about that comment, Val!" Wanda said. "You ain't no damn woman!"

"Keep on, Wanda!" Val said. "You gon' make me whoop yo' ass yet."

"Come on, Wanda." Johnny pushed Wanda up the stairs to keep her from talking.

We talked for a minute and the office girls insisted that we join the party. On our way upstairs, I pulled Pam to the side so that we could have a private conversation.

"Come here," I whispered.

Pam stood to the side as the office girls joined the party, leaving us alone in the basement.

"What's up?" Pam asked.

"We can't go up there, Pam," I said nervously.

"Why not?"

"You remember when we were running out of Gizelle's hotel room?"

"Yeah, why?"

"You remember there was this crazy looking woman standing in the doorway on our way out? She's in my house!"

"Oh my God!" Pam started to pace the floor back and forth. "Oh my God, she's going to remember us!"

"We can't go up there!"

"We can't stay down here either! We look guilty standing down here like a couple of fools!"

"We have to stay away from her."

"I don't even remember what the chick looks like, Alicia."

"She looks crazy," I said. "It's been so long, maybe she won't remember us."

"I can't take that chance. I'm going home, girl."

"You can't just leave, Pam."

"Watch me!" Pam stomped her way up the stairs and I went running behind her.

"Pam! Pam!" I shouted.

Pam burst through the door and by the time I opened it up, she was heading for the kitchen. I walked past the study and I saw Johnny and Wanda sitting in there with the strange woman from the hotel. My feet froze momentarily. I got a good look at her face and she got a great look at mine. She pointed at me and I ran into the kitchen to mingle with the crowd.

The kitchen was off limits to everyone but those close to us. We had it barricaded so that we could keep the stragglers out. Unfortunately, Christopher was the first person we saw when Pam and I finally squeezed our way through. When Christopher saw us he tried to casually walk away, but it was too late.

"Pam, don't say anything," I said.

"Hell naw! I'm about to go off on this bitch!"

Pam walked in front of Christopher and put one hand on her hip and the other hand in Christopher's face. The kitchen was crowded with most of the office girls, Tazzy, Tina, Susan, Lisa, Valerie and Darsha. But that's not all. Our close friends, Curtis, Tonita and Rob, Cecelia and Brent, Mr. Forrester, oh, and did I mention Christopher's wife, Stacey.

"Good evening, Christopher," Pam said sarcastically. "Aren't you going to introduce me to your wife?"

At first, nobody paid attention to Pam and Christopher's conversation. I was hoping it stayed that way. But then Pam became Pam, and elevated her voice after Christopher tried to downplay the situation.

"Pamela, can we discuss this later?" Christopher asked nervously.

"Hell nawl!" Pam said. "Let's discuss this right now!"

"I'm not going to do this here, Pamela."

Stacey, along with everybody else, noticed something very wrong was going on between Pam and Christopher. They just didn't know what it was. Stacey walked between the two of them to defuse the situation.

"Hey, what's going on, guys?" Stacey asked.

"Nothing, dear." Christopher held Stacey's hand and started to walk off. "Just a minor misunderstanding; that's all."

I crossed my fingers and prayed that Pam would let the situation go, but then, if she did, she wouldn't have been Pam.

"A minor misunderstanding?" Pam yelled. "Who in the hell do you think you are?"

"Pam! Shh!" I stepped in front of her and tried to cover her mouth.

"Move!" Pam pushed my hand to the side and kept yelling. "It wasn't a misunderstanding when we had sex!"

"Let's go, dear," Christopher said.

"Wait a minute." Stacey pulled away from Christopher. "What is this lady talking about?"

"Don't pay any attention to her, sweetheart. I think it's time for us to go."

"No!" Stacey said. "What is this lady talking about?"

"What I'm talking about is your husband and I have been having an affair. He told me that he was divorced! But apparently he's not."

"You've been having an affair, Christopher?" Stacey asked.

"I can explain, sweetheart."

"I'm listening! Please explain."

"Let's wait until we get home, Stacey."

"All that I want to know is did you have an affair with this woman?" Stacey pointed at Pam.

"I think you better get your damn finger out of my face!" Pam snapped.

"Lady," Stacey said. "I don't have a problem with you and I'm not trying to have a problem with you. I'm trying to ask my husband a question, so please keep your mouth shut until I'm finished."

"Bitch! I will whoop your ass up in here!" Pam yelled.

"Lady, that is harassment! If you so much as raise your voice to me one more time, I'm going to take your ass to court and, by the time you get through paying for all of the charges I'll slap on you, you won't be able to file for social security!"

"Pam," Tina said. "I think you need to be quiet."

"Whatever!" Pam folded her arms and patted her feet.

"Did you have an affair with this woman?" Stacey asked again.

"I'm sorry, sweetheart," Christopher said. "We were having problems and I needed someone to talk to. Pam was there for me."

"I didn't ask for an explanation, Christopher. I asked for confirmation. I'll take that as confirmation."

"Please, can we talk about this at home, Stacey?"

"You have no home, Christopher," Stacey said. "I'll have your things packed and sent where you want me to send them in the morning."

"Stacey, let's discuss this in private."

"Discussion over!" Stacey turned to Pam and winced.

Then Stacey stormed out of the room.

"Wow!" Cecelia laughed. "Are your parties always this exciting, Alicia?"

"No!" I replied. "This is supposed to be a celebration but all I'm getting is aggravation!"

I walked out of the kitchen and found Johnny walking in the living room. I wanted to make sure that I steered clear of that Kimberly lady. Since he was alone I wanted to do our co-hosting and get it out of the way before Kimberly came back around.

"Hey, you," I said. "Ready to escort this beautiful maiden around the castle?"

I wanted to make an appearance and then disappear.

"It would be my pleasure," Johnny said. "Then what are we waiting for?"

I grabbed Johnny's arm and we walked around the house. I wanted to stay with Johnny to keep him away from that nut.

"There's something strange about tonight," Johnny said.

"Strange?" I asked. "Strange how?"

"Kimberly told Wanda and me, the woman she saw hurting Anise in the hotel was in this house. But I could never get her and the woman in the same room for her to point her out. And she doesn't seem to be able to describe her."

I was scared to death. "Oh, really?"

"As a matter of fact, I need to speak to her anyway before she leaves. I have to make sure she has some type of understanding of her inheritance of Anise's will. Come with me."

"Uh, you go ahead, baby. Go handle your business."

"Alright," Johnny said.

I tried to get the hell away from there as fast as I could, but then Johnny grabbed my arm and pulled me to him.

"Alicia?" Johnny asked. "Is there something you want to tell me?"

"Uh," I said, "no, no, baby."

"What's going on?"

"I...I..."

CHAPTER NINEEEN

I was about to come clean and just tell Johnny the truth. The stress was overwhelming. Before I could speak a woman walked up and interrupted me.

"Are you Dr. Johnson Forrester?"

"Yes, I am," Johnny said.

"My name is Seneca Rogers."

"Have we met?"

"No, we haven't," Seneca said. "I don't know if you killed that bitch or not, but if you did, wives all across this country owe you a huge thanks. And instead of putting you in jail they should have been throwing you a party."

"Excuse me?" Johnny looked very confused. "I don't understand, ma'am."

"You would if she was sleeping with your husband," Seneca said. "That bitch used my husband to start her career. She took his career, his money, and then she took his mind! So as far as I'm concerned, she's better off where she is. Dead!"

"I don't know what to say." Johnny hunched his shoulders.

"You don't have to say a word," Seneca said. "The look on your wife's face says it all."

Seneca turned around and walked away.

"What was that all about?" Johnny asked.

"I don't know," I answered.

"Scary!" Johnny said. "Let's find Kimberly."

"No, you go, honey," I said. "That's your patient and she'll probably feel comfortable talking to you alone."

"Okay." Johnny held my hand and said, "But don't go far."

"I won't."

I walked around the party nervous as hell and trying to steer clear of Kimberly. Pam was drunk, mad, and didn't give a damn. I pulled Pam to the side to douse her overzealous spirit of vindication.

"Pam, you might want to stop making a spectacle of yourself," I whispered.

"I'm just having fun."

"But what if Kimberly sees you?"

"I'm tired of running and hiding, Alicia."

"What are you saying?"

"I'm saying that I'm tired of running; that's all."

"You're drunk, Pam."

"You're right! I am drunk!" Pam said as she slurred her words. "But I'm not so drunk that I can't make the decision of ending all of this tonight."

"Ending what?"

"The lies, the deceit, the hiding." Pam took a drink out of the glass she was holding.

"You need to lie down, Pam."

"Where Johnny at?" Pam held her glass in the air and started to walk through the crowded room. "I'm going to talk to Johnny."

"No!" I said.

"Hi!" Shante was standing in front of me with two suitcases in her hands. "I made it."

"Yes, you did, dear!"

It had totally slipped my mind that Shante was coming to live with us that night.

"How did you get here?"

"I took a taxi."

"Oh, okay. Let's put your stuff in your room."

I had to forfeit my interception of Pam's confession to Johnny. Hopefully she was only talking nonsense.

Shante followed me upstairs and we put her in the guestroom next to Brittany's room. We didn't talk long because I had to get back to the party and stop that crazy-ass Pam from running her big mouth. When Shante and I got to the bottom of the steps, Wanda and Kimberly were standing right there.

"Hey, girl!" Wanda shouted.

I couldn't speak. I stared Kimberly straight in the eyes with my mouth wide open and couldn't speak. I was hoping and praying that she did not recognize me from the hotel. I wanted to run back upstairs, but it was too late. The moment of truth had come.

"I know you." Kimberly pointed at me.

"No," I said nervously. "I don't think you know me."

"Yes, I do." Kimberly pulled her hair. "Gizelle!"

Although Kimberly suffered from schizophrenia, it didn't mean that she wouldn't recognize me from the hotel, the night Gizelle was murdered.

"Don't pay no attention to her, Alicia, she needs to have her medicine." Wanda laughed. "Right now, she probably thinks you're a Martian."

"Are you my friend?" Kimberly asked.

"Uh…" I looked at Wanda for an answer.

"It will probably go a lot quicker if you just say yes," Wanda said.

"Yes, I'm your friend."

"You're pretty."

"Thank you." I smiled. "You're pretty, too."

"Some people say I'm not so pretty on the outside, but I'm very pretty on the inside and that's what counts."

"They're right, Kimberly."

"I just got through talking to your husband, and girl, he just dropped a bomb on me!" Wanda said.

"What did he say?" I asked curiously.

"I can't tell you right now but can you say," Wanda moved her hands as if she was playing a slot machine. "CHA-CHING!"

"Good for you," I said nervously. "Have you seen Pam?"

"Yeah, she's in y'all basement."

"Oh shit!" I shouted.

"What's the matter?"

"Nothing! I just have to go!"

I RAN TO THE BASEMENT AS PAM WAS OPENING THE DOOR. I stood behind her as she walked in first. My objective was to start talking before Pam to keep the subject off of Gizelle. But before I could speak, our little secret was revealed.

"I'm sorry," Pam said.

"Oh my God!" Johnny said. "It was *you?* You were the one who texted me?"

"Yeah, it was me."

I walked in and stood beside Pam.

"Alicia?" Johnny quickly stood up looking bewildered. "Will somebody please tell me what's going on?"

"We're responsible for Gizelle's death," I said.

"What is this all about?" Johnny looked back and forth at Pam and then me.

"You wouldn't hurt a fly, Alicia."

"Not intentionally."

"She didn't kill her." Pam clutched my hand in hers. "I did."

"I want to tell you everything, Johnny, for once and for all."

Pam and I sat down and explained what happened on the day we killed Gizelle.

"Pam and I followed you and Gizelle to Tybee Island the night before she was killed. We saw you two making love on the beach."

"You were there?" Johnny was stunned. "Where were you?"

"That's not important. The next day when you returned to Atlanta, Pam and I went to her hotel to discuss her reneging on our contract. She was belligerent and things got out of control."

"The truth is," Pam explained. "Gizelle and I started fighting and as we were tussling on the bed, I pushed her against the headboard. She stopped fighting and grabbed her head. She sat on the bed and then keeled over. There was no blood. I didn't see a bruise on her head or anything. I knew she was hurt but I didn't think she was hurt that bad. But Alicia wasn't even there. She had run out of the room for help."

Johnny didn't say a word. He had his hands folded on his desk and looked at Pam and me as we talked back and forth.

"And then there's the matter of Big Walt." I fumbled nervously with my hands.

"Who?" Johnny asked. "Who the hell is Big Walt?"

"The bodyguard who was killed. We knew him as Big Walt."

"Okay, what about the bodyguard?"

"I shot him!" I was very demonstrative in my explanation. "I tried to stop him from taking the gun out of my hand and it went off! I saw him fall to the ground!"

"Okay, let me think." Johnny rubbed his chin over and over. "Look, the police don't know anything about you two, and they're not going to. We're going to have to keep this to ourselves and never mention it again. And I mean never!"

"I don't even know what you're talking about," Pam said quickly.

"Sweetheart?" Johnny asked. "How do you feel?"

"I don't know how to feel right now," I said.

"So…" Pam sighed heavily. "What happens next?"

"You walk out of that door and forget about everything that happened that day."

Pam hesitated and then stood up. She walked up the steps to the door and put her hand on the doorknob. She turned around and looked down at us.

"Thank you, Johnny."

"For what?" Johnny asked.

"For giving me back my life."

Pam walked out and Johnny reached across the desk and held my hand. He pulled me around the table and I sat on his lap.

"Do you love me?" Johnny asked.

"Absolutely!"

"Do you trust me?"

"Of course."

"Then forget this ever happened and let's move forward with our lives."

"I want to, but before I do, there's something else I think you should know."

"What, baby?"

"Well…" I started to speak and then Johnny interrupted me.

"Hold on to that thought, baby. I think it's time to shut the party down. That way we can have all the privacy we need."

Johnny led me out of the basement by the hand. We started our evacuation process and cleared everyone out. After Shante and my father-in-law went to bed, Johnny and I sat in our den to reacquaint ourselves. He stretched his long body along the couch and I lay beside him.

"Baby?" I said as I rubbed Johnny's chest.

"Yeah, baby."

"There's, uh, there's something I have to tell you."

"Oh, shit." Johnny sat up and folded his hands. "Do I need to lie back down?"

"I don't know, you might."

"Wow! Okay, I'm ready."

"While you were away I had trouble maintaining our finances."

"How much trouble?"

"Big, big trouble!"

"Let me put this another way," Johnny said. "How much money do we have in our savings?"

"None." I stood up and walked away. "Nothing! I tried to keep everything in order while you were gone, Johnny, but things spun out of control."

"I don't understand, Alicia, what happened?"

"The bills kept coming in, but there was no income coming in with it."

"What about the income from your firm?"

"CAPs went under, baby," I said. "We're trying to revive it but we just don't have the capital or the clients."

"Damn!" Johnny lowered his head and then raised it again. "So do we have any money at all?"

"Your dad has paid the mortgage for the next six months, so we're good there. But I don't know how we're going to survive with our other expenses."

"What happened, baby? What happened to all of our money?"

"I'm sorry, Johnny! I'm irresponsible! I messed up! What do you want me to say?"

I stormed out of the room and started to head outside. Johnny hurried from the couch and stopped me as I was opening the door.

"Whoa! Whoa! Whoa!" Johnny grabbed my arm and pulled me back into the house. "What is this? What's happening?"

"I can't handle this, Johnny!"

"What the hell is going on with you?"

"This!" I pulled up my sleeves and showed Johnny the suicide scars on my wrists.

Johnny reached for my hands and examined them. "What happened to you?"

"This is who I am!" I snatched my hands from Johnny and held them in the air. "This is who I really am!"

"Come here!" Johnny tried to grab me and I ran upstairs.

"Alicia!"

I could hear Johnny's footsteps running quickly behind me.

"Alicia! Alicia! What is the matter with you?"

I ran into the bedroom and slammed the door behind me. I went into the bathroom and cut on the water and sat on the floor of the shower and let the water run on top of me. I extended my arms and let the water cascade down on my scarred wrists as if it was holy water that would miraculously cleanse them from my horrid past. Finally, after years of feeling as if I was going to lose my mind, I had. I had completely lost my damn mind.

"Alicia?" Johnny asked. "Baby, you okay? Come on, get up."

Johnny cut the shower off and picked me up. He wrapped a towel around me and laid me on the bed. He removed my clothes and dried me from head to feet. My body shivered and my teeth chattered.

He lay in the bed next to me and held me tightly. I could feel my body start to warm and my sanity return. I had no explanation for my mini-breakdown other than I simply couldn't take it anymore. I couldn't deal with another disappointment. But as I gathered my senses, I realized that even though I had a meltdown,

I never even contemplated taking my own life. Although a sad revelation, it was a joyous one as well.

"Please," Johnny said, "what happened to you?"

"Well, when you were away, things started to unravel around me and I felt my world crashing in on me. I had so much pressure on me to take care of a family and financial responsibilities that I just couldn't maintain. I felt like my existence on earth meant nothing. I felt like I was hurting the people I love more, by being alive, than dead."

"Are you crazy?"

"I don't know. Sometimes I think I am."

"Listen to me, Alicia! After everything we've been through you think money is going to separate us? Money can be replaced. You cannot! I can't even believe we're having this conversation."

"I'm tired, baby," I said.

"No, no, you're not. I'm home. I'm home now, baby, everything is going to be all right." Johnny held my hands and then kissed my wrists. "I'm never going to leave you again, baby."

"You promise?"

"I promise with my life," Johnny spoke passionately, "let our past die, baby. All of it! Let it go. Let's start tomorrow with a new life, a new way of thinking. Our lives can, and will, be happy. Do you believe that?"

I stared into Johnny's eyes and I believed him. I opened my mouth and with the sound of nothing more than a whisper, I said, "Yes."

Johnny's words made me feel secure. I relaxed into his arms and then I closed my eyes. Looking back in retrospect, I'm forced to assume that sometimes one has to lose his or her mind in order to find it.

THE NEXT MORNING I WOKE TO SHANTE NUDGING MY SHOULDER. I was exhausted and refreshed at the same time, tired from stress, renewed by a fresh vigor for life.

"Ms. Alicia?" Shante asked.

"Huh?" I was drowsy and couldn't understand why I was being awakened.

"You have company."

"Huh? What?"

"There are two ladies downstairs who say they're your sisters."

I sat up and rubbed my eyes. "What did you say?"

"There are two ladies downstairs who want to talk to you. They say they're your sisters."

"My sisters?" I jumped up and ran to the mirror. "Okay! Tell them I'll be down there in a minute."

"Oh, okay."

Shante walked out of the room and then downstairs. I could hear them talking but I couldn't understand what they were saying.

"Damn! It's just like those heffas to barge in here without calling!"

I took a quick shower and pinned up my hair. I threw on my fake ponytail and walked downstairs. My two older sisters, Rita and Bobbie, were standing in the den when I walked in with smiles and kisses.

"Hi, what a wonderful surprise," I lied.

"How's my baby sister?" Rita asked.

"I'm wonderful, just wonderful."

The number one clue that everything is not wonderful is when a person claims that everything is wonderful.

"Looks like you're doing well for yourself." Bobbie glanced around the room.

"We're blessed."

"Well, baby sister, we're here to bring bad news." Bobbie sighed.

"Is Mama okay?" I asked nervously.

"Mama is fine." Rita answered. "It's Daddy."

"I don't have a daddy."

"We know how you feel about Daddy, Alicia." Bobbie placed her arm around my shoulder. "But he's sick. I mean, very sick."

"I'm sorry that that man is sick, but there's nothing I can do."

"He wants to see you."

"Well, I don't want to see him, Rita!" I snapped.

"The man is dying, Alicia, have some compassion," Rita pleaded.

"Why should I? All that he's shown me my entire life was that I was nothing to him! Nothing!"

"Well," Rita said, "we know how you feel and we felt that we owed it to Daddy to fly all the way down here to get you to come back with us."

"I'm not going to no St. Louis."

"Daddy's not in St. Louis. He's back in Cincinnati with Mama."

"Mama took that man back, Bobbie?"

"No, dear, he took Mama back."

"I appreciate it, I really do, but I'm sorry. I can't go."

"It's been years since you've seen Mama. Can you at least go for her?"

I walked around my den trying to force myself to go, but I couldn't. "No."

"We tried." Rita said as she shook her head.

"So how long are you in town?" I asked.

"We leave tomorrow morning. We want to get back to help take care of Daddy."

"In that case, you have to stay for dinner."

"You sure it won't be an imposition?" Bobbie asked.

"Don't be ridiculous." I giggled. "You're my family and I haven't seen you n years. Besides, you haven't met my wonderful husband."

"You sure are using that word, wonderful, a lot." Bobbie chuckled.

"I know!

"Ain't nobody that damn happy," Rita added.

My sisters stayed for dinner and met my husband and the rest of my family. I actually enjoyed them as they told stories about our childhood that I had completely forgotten. We talked and laughed well into the night. It reminded me of when I was a child and I thought the greatest thing in the world was just to be around them.

The next day was extremely saddening. I felt as if I was being abandoned once again by my family. I drove them to the airport and walked them through security as far as I was allowed. I waved good-bye and watched them disappear within the crowd of passengers. If asked, I would never admit to it, but I cried on the way home. Good or bad, bad or good, the truth was, I loved and I missed my family.

When I arrived home Mr. Forrester was waiting for me in the kitchen with a fresh pot of coffee. As soon as I entered the kitchen he led me to the table and sat me down.

"Let's have a cup of coffee," Mr. Forrester said.

"Thank you, sir, but I think I can make it today without the caffeine."

"Girl, you know when somebody ask you to have a cup of coffee what they really mean is, let's talk." Mr. Forrester smiled and then poured me a cup of coffee.

"Am I in trouble?"

"That depends."

"Depends on what?"

"Depends on if you willing to take my advice or not."

"What's the advice?"

"Go see your daddy before it's too late."

"Oh, okay, I see. You overheard me talking to my sisters."

"I didn't overhear nothin'. I just snuck and listened."

"Mr. Forrester, I know you mean well, and I may sound hypocritical by asking you to patch your broken relationship with Johnny when it appears that I'm not willing to do the same with my father."

"You're right. You do sound hypocritical."

"Our situation is different though."

"How so?"

"Well…" I tried desperately to think of something quickly but nothing would come to my mind. "You see, it's like this."

"I'm listening."

"See, here's the thing, Mr. Forrester…" I stopped in mid-sentence and smiled. "Okay, maybe it's not that different but I wouldn't even know where to begin with the man."

"You begin by calling him Daddy."

"He's not my father, Mr. Forrester."

"Then go tell him that."

I stared at Mr. Forrester and I decided that maybe he was right. "You know what? That's exactly what I'm going to do!"

"That's my girl," Mr. Forrester said.

I booked a flight to Cincinnati to leave the first thing in the morning. Johnny and I spent a romantic evening out and he encouraged me to have a positive attitude toward my father. Despite his persistence, I was steadfast in my resentment.

CHAPTER TWENTY

My flight into Cincinnati's International Airport was smooth and quick. It seemed as if I barely had time to close my eyes and we were already landing. I rented a car and I headed to Regency Hospital.

As I parked my car in the garage of the hospital, I remained seated to compose myself. Memories of my childhood flooded my mind as I stepped out of the car and approached the entrance. I walked through the hospital doors and the smell of medicine and death consumed me.

I approached his room, and prepared myself one last time before I opened the door. I took a deep breath and pushed the door as gently as I could. As the door opened, I could see the images in the room revolving in a circle from left to right.

My two sisters, Rita and Bobbie, and brother, Glenn, were already there, along with my two other sisters, from his second marriage. The youngest of our siblings, from yet another one of our father's relationships, was en route. None of us had met her and had just recently found out she even existed.

When the door opened wide enough for me to capture the first glimpse of my father, my eyes instantly filled with tears. He had wires running from his body to several machines. He looked weak and vulnerable. His eyes were closed and his arms were resting peacefully at his side. I confessed to myself that deep down

I really did want to see him again, but definitely not in that condition.

I hugged my siblings and then walked to my father's bedside. They informed me that he had been floating in and out of consciousness and that he may not remember or recognize me.

As I stood over him, I stared and wondered what my life would have been like if he would have only been there, if he would have only taken the time to love me. Slowly, he opened his eyes and looked up at me as I looked down on him.

"Alicia?"

"Yes," I said, trying desperately to hold back tears. "I'm here."

It took him a while, but he slowly raised his hand so that I could hold it. I looked at his hand and then I looked over my shoulder at my siblings, seeking guidance. Glenn nodded and smiled. I held his hand and placed it in mine.

"Alicia?" my father repeated.

"Yes, yes, I'm here."

His eyes were barely opened and they were yellowish. He was small and frail; nothing like the big strong man that I had last seen as a child. I almost felt sorry for him.

"Where you been?"

"Where have 'I' been?" I asked sarcastically.

I realized the man was sick but the mere fact that he would ask me where I'd been, after abandoning me twenty-five years earlier, nearly pissed me off.

"Alicia?"

"Yes, I'm here."

"You know who I am?"

"Yes, you're my father."

"Alicia?" my father asked faintly.

"Yes?"

"Alicia?"

"Yes!" I said firmly.

"Alicia?

"I'm right here."

He gripped my hand very tightly and whispered, "I love you, Alicia."

After he spoke those words he released his grip of my hand and took one last, long, deep breath. I squeezed his hand with both of mine as if I was never going to let it go and I placed my head on his chest, and cried! Oh my God, I mean I cried.

"DAAA-DDDY!"

WE BURIED MY FATHER THREE DAYS LATER and a lifetime of anger and resentment was buried with him. The day after the funeral, I helped my mother pack some of my father's things and we had a very enlightening conversation in the process.

It was the first time we had talked in years. Our relationship turned distant after I became pregnant at sixteen and against my mother's wishes. I chose to have an abortion. My mother was a devout Christian who'd rather suffer embarrassment than risk the wrath of God.

Eventually I moved in with my older brother, Glenn, and he became like a father figure to me until I attended Spelman College. Mama always held the title of mama, but since the age of sixteen, she had not been my mother. I sent cards, visited on certain holidays, but we never rekindled that special bond between mother and daughter like most women.

My mother never remarried after my father left us. The church and her children were her everything. I was the last one to leave the coop, and when I left it took a lot out of her. But almost twenty years later, we were all back where we started, in the same city, on the same block, in the same old squeaky house. We'd gone a complete three-hundred-sixty degrees.

"Ma?"

"Yeah, baby."

"I'm sorry for not staying in touch like I should have."

"I know you were busy, 'Licia."

"No, Ma, I wasn't that busy. I was selfish and stupid and I was only concerned about myself. When Daddy left, I thought it was all my fault, and I felt sorry for myself. And I've been feeling sorry for myself ever since."

"Everybody makes mistakes, baby."

"I know, and I want to ask your forgiveness."

"Sweetheart, we've all made mistakes. I have. You have. Your father has, but if we judge each other only by the mistakes that we've made, we will have no room for forgiveness."

"I know, Mama."

"Then let's forget about the past."

"I'd love that. I want us to be like a mother and daughter should be."

"That would make me so happy, baby; come here."

I hugged my mother and her arms felt just as secure as they did when I was a child.

"Mama, after all of these years, why did you take Daddy back?"

"I didn't take him back, baby, he took me back."

"How can he take you back when he was the one who left you?"

"Hold on." Mama moved a few items around and then reached into an old chest and pulled out a small wooden box. "This was your father's most prized possession."

She handed me the box and on top of the box, my name was written.

"What is this?" I asked.

"Open it and see."

"Um, you don't mind if I do this on the porch do you, Mama?"

"Go 'head, baby."

I walked outside to be alone and sat on the steps. I opened the box and found my original birth certificate. I kept digging through the box and ran across photographs from early childhood with my father and me.

I continued to carefully cipher through each item in the box. I'd pull it out, stare at it, and then kiss it. The more items I pulled out of the box, the more my tears flowed.

At the bottom of the box was a Bible. It was the same bible I had tossed aside the day my father left. I opened the Bible and while I was handling it a letter fell on the ground. It was titled "A Letter from Daddy," and this is how it read:

"A Letter from Daddy"

I put this letter in this Bible because I figured it was the only place your mother wouldn't look to keep me from you. Although I still love your mother dearly, she no longer loves me. She has asked me to move out and for her sake; I think it is best that I do so. I have said some mean things to you that were not meant for you; sometimes pain will make you do foolish things.

You are the love of my life. The day you were born was the happiest day of my life. I held you in my arms and I named you Alicia. That seemed like the perfect name for you. Your mother fought and fought with me because she wanted to name you Francis. For the life of me I couldn't figure out why. Why Francis?

On the second day of your life, I visited your mother at the hospital. She was asleep when I walked in, so I sat beside her. She didn't even hear me walk in. Dangling from the fingers on her left hand was a letter. I gently removed the letter from her hands, careful not to wake her. As I was placing it on her nightstand I noticed the name, Francis, at the bottom.

I read it once, and then I read it twice. In the letter, a man named Francis was professing his love for your mother, and also for you, his first child. I was destroyed and I felt like dying. For the first time in my adult life, I cried.

I never mentioned the letter to your mother. Over the past ten years I've pretended that Francis, whoever he was, did not exist. I assume for the sake of you children, your mother tried to make our marriage work until she couldn't stand it anymore. I don't blame her though, sometimes people just grow apart.

I want you to know that no matter where I am, or where you are, I love you and I will always love you for the remainder of my life. I left my forwarding address with your mother so that you can contact me whenever you feel like it, and I will write you as soon as I get settled in St. Louis.

I hope this letter will stay with you throughout your life because my love will remain with you always. When it seems no one else loves you, I will love you. On your darkest day, in your darkest hour, I will love you!

Love Always,
Daddy

After I finished reading the letter I went back into the house to confront my mother. Holding the letter in my hand, I asked, "Is this true?"

"Is what true?" Mama asked.

"Daddy said in this letter that he wasn't my father; is it true?"

"Sit down, child."

"No, Mama, please," I said. "Just answer the question, was that Francis man my father?"

"You just buried your father!"

"But this letter says…"

"I don't care what that letter said; you just buried your father."

"How do we start over if we don't start with the truth, Mama?"

"I JUST TOLD YOU THE TRUTH!" Mama shouted. "Baby, it seems like you're not happy unless you're hurting. The man that you knew as your daddy; was your daddy! That letter was written twenty-five years ago and it means nothing."

"But…"

"That's it! I'm not discussing it anymore! Let it go!"

I was about to open my mouth to ask my mother one final time to tell me the truth, but before I could, the doorbell rang.

"Go get the door!" Mama said.

I walked to the front door and Mama followed. I peeked out of the window and Johnny was standing on the porch. "Oh my God!"

I quickly opened the door and jumped in Johnny's arms. Mama followed me outside.

"Oh my God, baby, what are you doing here?"

"I'm here to see you," Johnny said. "How are you ma'am?"

"I'm fine, how are you?"

"I'm wonderful, ma'am."

"That's good. You wanna come in and make yourself comfortable?"

"Uh, I will, but first I have a little surprise for Alicia."

"A surprise? What surprise?"

"I have someone I'd like you to meet."

"Who?" I could see someone sitting in the car but whoever it was, was way too big to be Brittany.

"It's your younger sister."

"I'll let you all have your privacy," Mama said.

"No, Mama, don't leave."

"I'm not going anywhere, baby. If you need me I'll be in the house."

Mama smiled and walked back in the house.

"Well," I said. "Where is she?"

Johnny gestured for her to get out of the car. The door opened and I anxiously waited for my newest sibling to step out. When she did, my mouth dropped and my hands clenched Johnny's arm as I held on to him for dear life.

"Sweetheart, I want to formally introduce you to your youngest sister, Kimberly Mathis."

DAMN! It was the fruitcake who saw Pam and me in the Grand Hyatt the day Gizelle was killed. The gig was up! She was about to blow my cover wide open! How in the hell was *she* my sister?

Kimberly walked up the porch steps and shook my hand. Somehow, she looked different. She looked normal. She smiled and extended her hand as if all of her faculties were in order.

"Hi," I said.

"Hi, Alicia, I'm your sister, Kimberly."

I looked at Johnny and Kimberly and said, "I'm confused. How are you and I sisters?"

"You want me to tell her?" Kimberly asked.

"Be my guest," Johnny said.

"It seems that you, Anise and I shared the same dad."

"What?" I was shocked by what I was hearing.

"Yes, she was our sister."

"I'm sorry, Kimberly, but I can't believe that."

"Believe me, it's true."

"How? How?"

"I met Anise in Atlanta when we were living on the street. After getting to know one another we realized that we knew some of the same people in St. Louis. The more we talked the more people we knew in common. When we mentioned our father's name it happened to be the same. Turned out we had the same father. I never knew my biological father and all that my mother ever said was that he lived far away. God bless her soul.

"When Dr. Forrester was searching for Anise's nearest next of kin, they found me. It wasn't hard being that Anise had broadcast it all over the city and I was right there in Atlanta with her."

"If you and Anise were sisters, where were you when we were signing her as our client?"

"I was living in a shelter, that's where I was!"

"You have to forgive me but I'm still trying to swallow all of this." I walked over to Johnny and sat down next to him and held his hand.

"Take your time."

"How, uh, when did you, uh, you know?"

"When did I become sane?" Kimberly chuckled.

"Yes."

"I was never insane. I did what I had to do to survive."

"When did acting insane become a means of survival?"

"I wasn't totally acting. I had some emotional issues, but there wasn't one day when I didn't know I was Kimberly Mathis."

"Wow!" I paced back and forth on the porch. "Agh! This is too much for me right now."

"Uh-oh," Kimberly said.

"Uh-oh, what?" I stopped pacing and put my hands on my head. "Now what's wrong?

"I don't know how you're going to handle this then." Kimberly handed me an envelope.

"What's this?" I sat down and opened up the envelope.

"It's your half."

"OH DAMN!" I shouted as I jumped from seat. "What is this?"

Johnny wrapped his arms around me and said, "That's a check for seven million dollars."

"What?" I shouted. "Is this real? Is this a real check? Johnny, is this real?"

"Yeah, baby." Johnny laughed. "It's real."

"I have never seen this many zeros on a check before, baby. Is it mine?"

"Yup, it's yours, baby!"

"Where did it come from?"

"It was half of my estate from Anise."

Johnny reached out for Kimberly and brought her closer to us, "Well, not all of it, but Kimberly had to pay taxes, and legal fees, and she divided some of it with your other siblings, well, you know what I'm saying."

"You gave me half?" I asked. "Why? You don't even know me."

"I know that I have wanted a family ever since I was little girl, and now I have one, a good one, and anything that I have, my family has."

"I still don't get it, why do I get seven million dollars?"

"Because I know how much Anise hurt you. And I sat back and did nothing to stop her."

"But why? Why would she want to hurt us?"

"She felt that our father loved you more than her and she was trying to punish you. Despite all of her faults she loved me. And I loved her, too, but I had to stop her from hurting you."

"She's gone now, so let's just put that behind us." Johnny pulled us closer to him and we hugged in a tight circle.

"Okay, but I still have a question for Kimberly," I said.

"What's your question?"

"You looked us straight in the eyes when Pam and I were running out Anise's room, why didn't you go straight to the police then?"

"I knew you didn't kill her."

"How did you know?"

"Because I killed her!"

THE NEXT MORNING I WOKE UP BEFORE EVERYONE ELSE. I decided to get some fresh air so I went for a walk. For the first time that I could remember, I walked outside with no makeup on my face. I didn't comb my hair. I didn't put on my best clothes. I put on a T-shirt, sneakers and jeans and walked through my old neighborhood.

I ended up at the park where I used to play when I was a child. It was rundown, the swings were gone, and a few of the monkey bars were missing. I sat on an old wooden bench and pulled my father's letter out of my pocket and I read it again and again.

Throughout my life, I've always tried to understand the nature of a man through the eyes of a woman. I've tried to rationalize the male psyche and react to it from a female's perspective. I've tried to find that biological denominator that makes men and women the same. The reality is; we are not the same! We are two contrasting thinking creatures. I am a woman! And the only way for a woman to understand the nature of a man, and contrarily, for a man to understand the nature of a woman is for us to communicate by listening to understand and not just speaking to be understood. Through my discovery of the nature of a man, I discovered the nature of a woman. And through my discovery of the nature of a woman, I discovered Alicia Murray Forrester.

I looked around and saw a broken pencil on the ground and picked it up. I turned my father's letter over and started to write on the back.

The nature of a woman is an extraordinary enigma. It is undefined, unpredictable and undeniable. From a mother to her child, it's irreplaceable. From a woman to her man, it's irresistible. And from a sister to her sister, it's irrepressible. My self-empowerment is not to be deter-

mined by the opinions or standards of anyone other than myself. My existence is not to be predicated on love from without, but love from within. Because it is up to me, to love me!

Behold, for Beautiful and Bold I stand,
Defined by who "I" say I am.
To love my wide or narrow hips,
My thin, thick or smoke-covered lips.
My brown, blue or grayish eyes,
My slender or my bulging thighs.
My breasts, be they large or small,
My height, be it short or tall.
My hair, be it nappy and black,
Or straight, blonde, and down my back.
For it is up to me, to love me!
My love exists internally!
My love exists externally!
My love exists eternally!
And men can love me if they wish
But you just remember this.
I am your wife, mother and lover, so please,
Respect me for the breath you breathe.
Respect me as a woman should be,
As if your ass was born from me.
I birthed you! Nursed you!
Fed you! Bed you!
Bathed you! Raised you!
Cried for you! Dammit, I have died for you!
From the day you were born to the day that you die!
Your life is my life and this, do not deny!
Now respect me as a woman should be

As if your ass was born from me.
I am not your bitch, your whore, or your slave,
Your life is my life from my womb to your grave!
But even in death, my love keeps comin'
BEHOLD…THE NATURE OF A WOMAN!
Love Always,
Alicia!

ABOUT THE AUTHOR

Born in Saginaw, Michigan as the seventeenth of eighteen children to Henry and Orabell Stephens, Sylvester Stephens was introduced to the arts by his elder siblings. His desire for writing was developed not by the literature of Shakespeare, or the poetry of Robert Frost, but by the ever melodic, soulful voices of the sound of Motown. The lyrics that emanated from the phonograph, or record player, as it was called, created images of stories in his mind.

Sylvester later attended Jackson State University in Jackson, Mississippi where he honed his craft for literature. While attending college, Sylvester became a member of the largest international fraternity in the world, the Free and Accepted Masons, Prince Hall Affiliated.

Sylvester has taught creative writing courses for the Young Voices United Youth Program and has raised literacy awareness with poetry contests and book fairs in inner city schools.

Sylvester's first novel, *Our Time Has Come* was released in October, 2004. *The Office Girls*, published by Strebor Books in January, 2008, was his second novel. He followed those in 2009 with the publication of *The Nature of a Woman*.

Sylvester has also written the screenplays to *The Office Girls*, *The Road to Redemption* and *Our Time Has Come!*

Sylvester's sensational stage plays include *Our Time Has Come*, *The Nature of a Woman*, *Max*, *The Office Girls*, *My Little Secret*, and *Every Knee Shall Bow*.

WANT TO KNOW WHAT REALLY HAPPENED IN THAT HOTEL
ROOM? FOLLOW JOHNNY IN THIS EXCERPT FROM

THE NATURE of A WOMAN

THROUGH THE EYES OF A MAN...

BY SYLVESTER STEPHENS

AVAILABLE NOW FROM STREBOR BOOKS

CHAPTER 3

As I pulled into the parking lot of the hotel, I considered turning around, but only for a moment. I realized what I was about to do was a serious setback in the stability of my recovery, but my mind was made up and I was going to go through with it. I stepped out of my car and walked into the lobby. I wasn't totally sure of what was about to happen, but whatever it was, it was going to have to happen quickly. My next appointment was within two hours and I had to be back in my office.

There she was, sitting in a short dress that showed off her legs. Her open-toed shoes exposed her perfectly manicured toenails. I walked slowly to her, admiring her beauty until I stood directly in front of her face.

"Hi," Anise said with that seductive smile.

"Hi." I stood there amazed by the sensuality of Anise's presence.

It was apparent that Anise and I shared an uncontrollable sexual attraction, which bordered on being animalistic wild, but there also existed a powerful enigmatic romance that had linked us together in such a short period of time. We did not ask for it, it was forced upon us through the interaction of the other's company. What began as a doctor-patient relationship had unpredictably blossomed into an indomitable relationship of spontaneous passion and lust.

I picked up Anise's little duffel bag that was sitting beside her feet and then clasped her hand in mine. We walked silently through the lobby of the hotel and onto the elevator. Once the door was closed, she leaned toward me and rested her head on my shoulder. We stood in that position until the elevator door opened and we walked out.

Once we arrived at her room, she scanned the key and we walked in. I dropped her bag on the floor and we sat side by side at the foot of the bed. I reached for her hand and we sat in silence intertwining our fingers. We leaned backward together on the bed and faced each other. I caressed her face and stared beyond her eyes. We wrapped our bodies together and became one. Without even realizing it, we unclothed ourselves and moved to the center of the bed.

We lay totally unclothed and unconcerned about anything other than the moment we were sharing. Her eyes were looking directly into mine. Her lips and her tongue were passionately and slowly kissing my lips and sucking my tongue. Her breasts clung to my chest. Her navel pressed against my stomach. Her thighs rubbed against mine as they intertwined. Her toes gently slid up and down the top of my feet, but with everything that we were sharing in that moment, we did not share a single word.

I could feel my hands caress the spine of Anise's back. The indention in the rear of her body felt so feminine, so naturally created for my hands to fit. I pulled her closer to me and all that stood between our bodies was my firm manhood.

I turned Anise on her back and she slowly opened her thighs. I placed my manhood at the entrance of her vagina as she moved her hips and raised them slightly to meet me. I lowered my face and began to kiss her on the neck. She turned her head to the side to give me full access. As I kissed and sucked on her succulent neck, Anise moved her hips more rapidly. I could feel the juices from her vagina seep onto the head of my manhood.

She began to moan loudly and then grabbed me by my hips. She tried to adjust our bodies so that my manhood could slide into her soaking wet hole. I pulled away, teasing her, making her legs shiver from anticipation. My kisses moved further south as I sucked gently on her left nipple. Then I moved over to the right breast and engulfed as much as I could into my mouth. Back and forth I went until she was moaning uncontrollably.

I continued to kiss her, moving down to her stomach and licking her navel with long, wet licks. Up and down her stomach. I turned my head to the side and began to lick up her right leg, and then all the way down to the toes on her right foot, sucking them, one by one. I clutched her big toe in my mouth with the suction of my tongue.

Next, I licked her left leg, from her inner thigh down to her toes. On my way up, I stopped at her womanhood and licked the outer region of her vaginal lips. She arched her back and raised her hips. I continued to lick up and down, and then side to side, brushing my tongue against her erect clitoris. She spread her legs far apart and placed her hands at the back of my head.

She pushed my face into her womanhood and began to grind

rhythmically against it. I buried my face so deep into her thighs I could barely breathe. Her lustful reaction made me so willing to please her that I continued to lick and suck her relentlessly, not caring if it rendered me unconscious.

From the wild bucking of her hips and the loud moaning of her voice I knew her orgasm was approaching. This made me all the more eager to make sure her orgasm was strong and powerful. I licked even faster and harder, and then side to side with the tip of my tongue. Finally, Anise pushed my face into her again and raised her ass completely off of the bed. She screamed and kept my head in one position until she dropped back down on the bed, gasping for air.

I quickly slid up to her and held her in my arms as her body jerked and moved uncontrollably beneath me. Once her orgasm subsided we looked each other in the eyes, but still, no words were spoken.

After a few moments of recuperation, Anise turned me on my back and straddled me. She lowered herself on top of me and, inch by inch, slid down my manhood. Once I was inside of her, she placed her hands on my massive chest and began to grind back and forth. Her eyes were closed and her mouth was wide open. Her knees were on the bed beside my hips, and her feet were behind her. She continued to rock back and forth on my manhood, faster and faster. The faster she moved, the louder she moaned. Her hips began to move so fast that I had to grab them and guide her to prevent her from causing me permanent injury.

Her breathing became so heavy she had to pause to catch her breath. I turned Anise on her back so that I could take over the reins. I grabbed her by the ankles and spread her legs as far apart as possible. I grabbed the head of my manhood and slid it inside of her. She gasped as I went as deep as I could possibly go.

Once I was inside of her, I began to slide in and out, feeling Anise's moist wetness. She reached behind me and grabbed me by my ass, pushing me deeper inside. We continued to make love as I slammed between her thighs. Our bodies clung together from the stickiness of our perspiration.

After a while, I raised Anise to her knees and positioned her on all fours and then I stood behind her. She grabbed her ass cheeks and separated them to allow me access to her pulsating womanhood.

I slid my manhood inside and pulled her back into me by her waist. I watched, again, as she rocked back and forth, crashing backward into me harder and harder. I began to smack her ass every time she slammed backward. Every time my hand hit her ass, her legs would quiver and she would scream loudly.

She lowered her head and arched her back. She pulled the sheets from the corners of the bed and bit the pillow. I continued to slap her ass and ram her until I felt a huge orgasm approaching.

I pushed her onto the bed and closed her legs tightly. As my orgasm erupted, I rammed my manhood inside of her over and over and over. My muscular body completely covered hers as she lay on her stomach. She wrapped her feet around my ankles and lifted herself as much as she could against my weight and matched me stroke for stroke, slamming backward into me. I turned her head to the side and kissed her wildly.

I poured so much juice into her it started to overflow. After my orgasm, we lay together in the same position. She lay on her stomach, with me on her back, and my manhood still inside of her. We eventually fell asleep in that same position.

When we woke, I hurriedly got up, grabbed my clothes and ran into the bathroom. I took a quick shower and then she followed. Once we were dressed, we stood face to face in the middle of the room. I took her face in my hands and slowly kissed her forehead. *My God*, I thought, staring into Anise's eyes, *she looked just like Alicia*. Then I put my hand in hers and led her out of the room.

We walked back to the elevator, still not uttering a word. Once the elevator door opened, we stepped inside patiently and watched it close. Anise leaned toward me and rested her head on my shoulder. We stood in that position until the elevator door opened and we walked out. We walked silently through the lobby and back to her car.

"Bye," Anise said with that seductive smile.

"Bye." I was still amazed by the sensuality of Anise's presence.